Reviews of

"*Feeding the Demons* is a psychological thriller with a New-Age bent. Information about police technique and alternative therapies sit side by side, and the plot fulfilment is both a confirmation of spiritual and psychic life, and the solving of several murders. This combination of soft and hard edge is part of Lord's unique appeal... *Feeding the Demons* is certainly a page-turner and an absorbing read. Lord is very good at menace."

Margaret Simons, *Australian's Review of Books*

"Lord deserves a wide, discerning audience."

Peter Pierce, *Bulletin*

"*Feeding the Demons* is a nasty, nasty story, and one of the most effective, harrowing and intense Australian crime fiction novels of the past decade.

"Anyone who's read Lord's previous novels such as *Whipping Boy* and *The Sharp End* will be aware of the praise inherent in the statement that this is the Sydney-based writer's finest novel... Lord weaves a complex, masterfully paced story peppered with memorable characters and superb dialogue... astonishingly powerful and crafted."

Stuart Coupe, *Sydney Morning Herald*

"Lord is unputdownable."

Graeme Blundell, *Weekend Australian*

"She writes with compulsive power."

Penny Hueston, *The Age*

"Adroitness distinguishes Gabrielle Lord's ninth novel, *Feeding the Demons*, a racy page-turner exploring the nastier side of human nature. Intricate plot, ratcheting tension and intrepid heroines plus psychopaths, psychotherapy and police profiling equal an engrossing read."

Murray Waldren, *Australian*

"The many strands of her plot are neatly woven into a coherent and suspenseful whole, complete with the double climax beloved of crime writers."

Katherine England, *Adelaide Advertiser*

"The narrative is rivetting...Apart from powerfully conveying high and low life in a beautifully evoked Sydney, Lord writes with authority and elegance about troubled and threatened lives. Her novel never misses a beat."

Veronica Sen, *Canberra Times*

"*Feeding the Demons* is trim, taut and terrifying and involves the reader until the last page...Lord is a skillful writer who avoids cliches and cheap thrills without diverting attention from the action."

Jan Dwyer, *Burnie Advocate*

DEATH DELIGHTS

GABRIELLE LORD

HODDER

A Hodder Book

First published in Australia and New Zealand in 2001
by Hodder Headline Australia Pty Limited
(A member of the Hodder Headline Group)
Level 22/201 Kent Street, Sydney NSW 2000
Website: www.hha.com.au

Copyright © Gabrielle Lord 2001

This book is copyright. Apart from any fair dealing for
the purposes of private study, research, criticism or
review as permitted under the *Copyright Act 1968*, no part
may be stored or reproduced by any process without prior
written permission. Enquiries should be made to the publisher.

**National Library of Australia
Cataloguing-in-Publication data**

Lord, Gabrielle, 1946- .
    Death delights.
    ISBN 0 7336 1313 6.
    1. Suspense fiction. 2. Psychological fiction. I. Title.

A823.3

Text design and typesetting by Bookhouse, Sydney
Printed in Australia by Griffin Press, Adelaide

To Greg, the original Reginald
and to all friends of Bill W.

Let conversation cease. Let laughter flee.
This is the place where death delights to help the living.

Inscription from the Office of the
Chief Medical Examiner, New York city

ONE

I was sorting through the second victim's clothing when my mobile rang, sounding very out of place in this rented room reeking of old food and stale sex, the grubby chenille bedspread over an iron bedstead, the dun-coloured walls, veneer and plastic wardrobe with matching chest of drawers and the fraying holland blind knocking against the window. I didn't answer the phone, leaving it to voice mail. I can do that these days without feeling too guilty now that I've paid my dues and am no longer tied to the lab. I've taken leave from the Division of Forensic Services while I sort out the end of the marriage and decide what to do next. It's taking a lot of time and energy. Certainly as much as the beginning of the relationship. But without the younger hopes and dreams.

At one end of the dead man's room was a sad little eating area, jars, bottles, a cheap radio and a mouldering sliced white loaf on a checked plastic tablecloth. As my young brother Charlie, the clinical psychologist, says 'you can get a lot of information about how a person is on the inside by noticing what they create around them on the outside,' so I stood there, letting the surroundings speak to me of the desolate individual who had lived there. Nesbitt's room was like an extension of the crime scene. Every little thing an investigator can learn about the victim is helpful. If I hadn't already known why they'd locked Ernest Leslie Nesbitt up, I might've been thinking, 'poor bastard, and only just out of gaol'. But I knew that the pile of *Bambino* magazines beside the bed and the KMart catalogue with its photographs of pubescent kids in their knickers wasn't because of his interest in fashion. I'd already pulled on my gloves, lifted his suitcase onto the bed and started sorting through his belongings before the phone rang. The investigating police had been through all his stuff already and it was now up to his next of kin to claim it. Or the landlord to dump it. But my partner in the old days, Bob Edwards in Homicide, hoped I might notice something everyone else had missed. I thought it was unlikely.

A couple of T-shirts, one white shirt, some trousers, shorts, underpants and singlets in a greyish pile, socks, a book on the Northern Territory, a Bible, a framed and tinted 1950s photographic portrait of a woman I guessed to be his mother, some very basic toiletries, some references—Nesbitt had both front-end loader and 'C' class licences—claim forms for Special Benefits papers from the Department of Social Security, a pack of playing cards. There wasn't a birth certificate; no doubt the investigating police still had that. A man doesn't have much when he comes out of gaol after many years and there's nobody waiting for him.

I crossed the room in three and a half strides, which made it about the same size as the cell at Goulburn Gaol where he'd lived the last six years, to look out the window. On the way, I caught sight of myself in a spotted wall mirror. Genevieve used to say she was first attracted to me because I looked like Harrison Ford. I've never been able to see the resemblance myself and it's been a long time since my wife found me attractive. For a second, I felt the awful clutch of angry grief, but I stopped that in its tracks by refocusing myself into the present, unpleasant as it was. To break the mood, I switched on the tinny radio, interrupting a talk-back program.

'My nephew,' a woman was saying, 'works as a police officer and he says that there's a huge cover-up going on. The police know what it is that's doing these killings, but they're forbidden to talk about it.'

'Madam,' the DJ interrupted, his professional politeness edged with contempt, 'the police are not permitted to talk about active investigations at any time.'

'But this is different,' said the woman. 'Pete says he's seen the report from the scientific people. And it's written in black and white and it says that whoever or whatever did these murders definitely isn't human.'

'Does Pete say what it is?' asked the DJ.

The woman's voice dropped, as if she was concerned that

500,000 listeners might hear her. 'Yes,' she said, 'but I can't say over the air. And anyway, you wouldn't believe it.'

'Anyone out there able to say it?' the DJ asked. 'I'm sure we'd love to hear. Please ring the station.' The mocking tone of his voice was unmistakable. 'We'd all love to know. Especially the men of this town.' His voice shifted up a gear and he started advertising a hardware chain. I thought of the woman's certainty about the information she was broadcasting. It's amazing what myths can arise in the public mind when a journalist gets something half-right.

From the lane below, the smells of old cooking oil, overflowing rubbish bags and cats' piss drifted up. From the plane tree across the road, an Indian mynah screamed, *'Cheaper cheaper cheaper!'* and from somewhere behind me in the boarding house came the sound of chronic coughing. I turned away from the backside of Kings Cross and leaned against the window ledge. Despite the grime, there was something reminiscent of my own bachelor digs, the same monastic bed, chair and table in a small room.

I opened the door and peered out. Over a century ago, this house would have been the proud residence of a professional man of Empire. Now, it was one of the few dwellings still licensed to operate as a rooming house in an area dominated by high and low rise apartments. I knew that number 31 next door, the mirror image of the house I was in now, operated as a brothel. Or had done so, years ago when I was in the job in Sydney.

On the landing outside the murdered man's room was a tiny kitchenette, old gas stove and sink, both badly in need of a clean up. Down the hall were three more rental rooms and I caught a whiff of the bathroom—the smell of men who don't care very much—a smell that reminds me of the zoo. But one man never came back to his rented room in number 33; Ernest Lesley Nesbitt, and I looked again at the photograph Bob had given me.

There's something about mug shots that's unique, that mixed expression of sullen defiance and submission to an overpowering force. I'd seen it in my own daughter's face eighteen months ago before she ran away. My daughter, Jacinta. It's one of the reasons my colleagues know not to call me to a PM on any young female until she's been identified. The last images I have of my daughter and her mother are bad enough.

I brought my attention back to Nesbitt's picture. Late forties, a tight, closed-up face. Thin-lipped, close-shaven, unattractive, and something smeared and distorted about the entire lower face, reminding me of a photo I'd seen of Sir Anthony Blunt, cold war communist spy and art adviser to the English queen. Nesbitt's form was long and ugly, the usual pattern I've come to expect for killers like him, and he'd finally been put away for the rape and attempted murder of a thirteen-year-old girl. It's the sort of crime that makes any father think of his own daughter. Or an older brother of his little sister. And I don't permit myself those sorts of thoughts.

After a long time in this game, it's almost impossible not to see the world divided into the goodies and the baddies. My brother, Charlie, says it's not rational to look at things this way and intellectually I have to agree with him. He tells me it's an attitude fostered by the work I've been in all my life, and the events of my past—a past he doesn't share because he was only a baby and too young to remember that summer. So I looked again at the pathetic items spread out on the bed in front of me and forced my mind back to the job at hand.

Ernest Nesbitt stared out at me from his mug shot and I tried to find some compassion for the dead man. I found none. Just a sense that he'd walked straight into something dreadful and inevitable, set on track with breathtaking precision like the *Titanic* and the iceberg. Two weeks ago, someone had encountered him near the stone seawall at Birchgrove and hacked off his penis and scrotum. Another deep wound had severed his right femoral artery. Both injuries had combined to kill him quite quickly. The young psych nurse who'd responded to his screams from a house across the road could only hold Nesbitt's hand while his boyfriend rang the ambulance. It was almost all over by then and Nesbitt was dead by the time the ambulance arrived. Because of the nature of his crime and manner of his death, police had re-interviewed certain angry relatives of the young girl he'd murdered years ago. They'd drawn a complete blank.

Nor was he the first man to have died of such horrific injuries. Only a few weeks before Nesbitt's death Cecil Warren Gumley had died in the same savage way. Gumley had been dead for some hours before he was found. There'd been no kind stranger to hold his hand while his body emptied of blood. Naturally, Bob and the other Homicide fellows considered the likelihood of the same killer. Some of the old dinosaurs were reminded of Macdonald, dubbed 'The Mutilator' by the Sydney newspapers, a murderer active around East Sydney in the early 1960s who neatly removed the working tackle of his unfortunate victims. Now, nearly forty years later, the newspapers had started a story that refused to go away. 'NON-HUMAN DNA!' the first headlines announced in connection with the Gumley murder, 'POLICE PUZZLED BY LAB RESULTS'. Despite our assurances that we weren't puzzled in the slightest, the story seemed to be gaining ground all over town that some sort of beast, accredited with almost supernatural powers, was on the loose in Sydney, depriving men of their virile member.

'Would you take a look?' Bob had asked me after the second death. 'We've just had our budget cut by one third. The boss is a total dickhead and you owe me a couple.' Then he looked me straight in the eye. 'I need your expertise,' he added. Bob is one of those friends who gets through to me, even though I like to keep people at arms' length. I made some joke of it, but of course I agreed.

It was true that I owed him and we go back a long way, Bob and me, to the time we both joined the Service—the Force as it was then called—as keen young probationary constables. On the second day of my appointment, the sergeant called us all into his office. 'Right, he said, 'you might have noticed that as well as me, there are four blokes with the name of John in this station. So from now on *I'm* John,'—he swung round on me—'you're Jack, and the rest of you, use your second names.' And that's how I became Jack, and why my workmates of the first year or two in the job were named Melvaine, Herbert and Cleever.

After serving nearly twenty years in various divisions and sections, but mostly Physical Evidence, and with my recently completed Masters in particle examination, I applied for a job as a scientist with the Federal Police in Canberra. Genevieve was scathing. 'If you get that job, you'll be completely impossible,' she said. 'Not only will you *know* everything like you already do now, you'll be able to prove it.' I remember that I laughed then. I got the job, much to the contempt of some of my colleagues—the 'plastic cops' they call us Federal police. Maybe one day they'll hear what we say about them. And as Genevieve well knew, I wasn't laughing these days.

I picked up the framed sepia portrait of the woman, tinted in the pastels of the 50s. *Esme Nesbitt, Ramsgate, New South Wales, 1954* I read, when I turned it over. You'd be in your late seventies now, at least, I thought as I picked at the little metal tabs that pressed the backing of the frame against the picture. The whole thing came apart easily. I lifted the backing carefully away from the photo and I was hardly surprised to find what I was looking for. I took them out and lined the six pictures up on the greasy tablecloth. It's such an obvious place to check, and any experienced investigator does it as a matter of course. Obviously nobody had and I started to see why Bob might feel the need for my assistance.

I put the pictures in a labelled and dated plastic bag and then refitted the portrait, wondering what his mother would have thought of the images her own photograph had been hiding for her son. 'Perfect,' I could imagine Charlie saying.

Alerted now, I took a closer look at his book on the Northern Territory and the Bible. The Northern Territory was clean but it didn't take me long to find the extra leaves of Bible-quality paper with Nesbitt's own crude illustrations depicting a tiny girl and a grotesque penis distributed among Jeremiah. *Behold*, I read, when I lifted the drawings up and read Jeramiah's words directly underneath, *a whirlwind of the Lord is gone forth in fury, even a grievous whirlwind: it shall fall grievously upon the head of the wicked.* And not only his head, I thought.

I was replacing the ugly sketches where I found them when an envelope addressed to Nesbitt in gaol fell out of the Bible. I picked it off the floor and peered inside. There was nothing in it. I flicked through the Bible again, finally turning it upside-down and shaking it. But nothing further was revealed. Nesbitt's name and the address of Goulburn Gaol were handwritten on it, with no return address on the back. It was postmarked Kings Cross and the date was obscured. Why, I wondered, does a man keep an empty envelope? I looked more closely, then saw some pencilled writing on it: *Long blonde hair, red jacket.* I threw the envelope down in disgust. One of Nesbitt's 'sightings', no doubt. From my time in Child Sexual Offences, I knew enough about pedophile behaviours and how many of them kept lists of children who 'appealed' to them.

I repacked the photograph and the clothes from the bed and closed the suitcase, putting the pornographic photographs to one side. One glance alone told me they were prohibited imports. I couldn't imagine anyone demanding their return.

I left the premises, pleased to be out of there. On another day, I'd have rejoiced in the cloudless summer sky and the warm breeze, the beautiful Sydney girls in their pretty dresses, but not today. Where other men my age might be contemplating the end of kids' schooling in a few years and a future of relaxation and leisure, I had been thrust into the pain and confusion of the end of my marriage. The end of the known way. Old habits die hard and the human heart hates change. The month of November is always pain-ridden for me and I had to admit to myself that investigating the murders of these two repulsive men, coming as they did in this month, was something of a godsend.

I have heard that smell is the most primitive of our senses. It's certainly the most evocative. The painful mess of my collapsing marriage seemed to have stirred up the two great losses of my life; the scent of privet and gardenias reminds me of the grief that's never far beneath the surface. In the lingering light after sunset, when jacarandas glow like soft lamps, something happens to my vision. Sometimes it feels like twenty-five years ago and I see things that aren't there. If I had my way, I'd re-write the calendar, and go straight from October to December.

•

Bob was waiting for me in the foyer at the Institute of Forensic Medicine on Parramatta Road, his rangy body leaning against the wall, a newspaper tucked under his arm. Dr Bradley Strachan had done the autopsy on the first murder victim, Gumley, and then again on the second one, Nesbitt, whose room and possessions I'd just inspected. Bob and I walked through surroundings that could've been the reception area of any successful corporation on our way to speak with Dr Strachan. I'd always presumed the word 'morgue' came from the Latin *mors*, death, but it comes from the French, *morgeur*, 'to peer', from the days when the bodies dragged from the Seine were displayed in the basement of the Petit Châtelet

Prison in Paris and relatives of the missing peered at the corpses through grilles. So much of the work people like myself, Bob and Bradley Strachan spend our time doing was pioneered by the great European scientists of the nineteenth century, working closely with police and the judiciary. That is still how it goes today, although the tests are becoming more and more refined, with results that our scientific forebears could only dream about.

Bradley Strachan filled out the doorway as we followed him into his office and I remembered the time some years ago when he and I had found ourselves swept up in a pub brawl while we were having a drink and discussing a case. His powerful presence at my side as we made our way through the violence towards the exit was something I'll never forget.

'In my opinion,' Bradley said from across his desk, 'both men were killed by the same individual. There were five deep cuts on Gumley, four on Nesbitt, grouped in a very similar way. The knife used in each assault was identical.'

He pulled out his photographs and spread them on the desk. I could see the similarity in the knife work in both cases. Nothing fancy, just yawning wounds around the groin. And a meaty gap between the thighs on each corpse. It was very determined, very consistent work. The whole game, set and match had been removed, and again in both cases, the gashes on the right groin revealed the muscles and bone deep to the severed femoral artery. Bradley Strachan placed a large piece of drawing paper on the desk next to the photographs.

'This is the sort of knife used in both attacks,' he said as I studied his drawing of the knife. 'Double-bladed,' the doctor continued. 'No wound was deeper than fifteen centimetres, nor wider than two and a half.' He indicated the calculations he'd drawn beside the knife's blade. 'From the bruising around the stabbing injuries, I calculate a hilt of some sort, a little under seven centimetres in width and sloping away from the blade.' In my mind's eye, I was getting a picture of the winged dagger of the assassin, the one that appears on the patches of the Special Air Services.

'What do you think?' Bob was asking Dr Strachan. Bradley spread out the photos as he spoke. 'It's the sort of design that's basic to many knives,' he said. 'My eldest son has a diving knife that could have made injuries of the same dimensions.'

'Anything else?' I asked, knowing how valuable an off-the-record opinion can be from someone who's spent over thirty years examining every possible sort of injury to human flesh. Dr Strachan paused and then looked up from the sketch of the knife. 'It's the sort of thing,' he said finally, 'that I've come to associate with homosexual homicide. Simply because of the nature of the injuries.' He paused. 'But that's only a personal observation.' I knew what he meant. There's a sixth sense developed by experienced investigators and it's very subtle. It's something like a shadow, or a non-physical scent, more like a feeling that permeates a crime scene and its victim. Like the mood that a painting or a piece of music can evoke, and as ephemeral. But somehow, it just didn't feel right to me. The mood I was sensing in these murders so far didn't match up to the mood my medical friend was suggesting. But then I hadn't attended the autopsies, let alone either crime scene, so I nodded to Bradley, because his expertise was legendary and any investigator who doesn't take advantage of that sort of thing and keep an open mind is not only a fool, but will never write up the paperwork on a successful case.

'I wonder,' said Bradley, 'what the killer does with the bits and pieces.'

Bob and I had discussed this very point a day or so earlier. 'We don't know,' said Bob. 'It's possible he just chucks them down a drain somewhere. He could have thrown them into the Harbour at Birchgrove.'

'It's also quite possible he souvenirs them,' I said to Bradley.

The doctor nodded. Compared with the number of items American mass murderer Jeffrey Dahmer souvenired and stored in his apartment—torsos, frozen heads, dissected shoulder muscles in vats and bins—our killer's possible matching set of male genitals seemed almost modest. But I couldn't help imagining how the wet specimens might look, bottled and suspended in formaldehyde like some unclassified marine coelenterate. Bradley Strachan's face lifted in his guarded smile. 'I'd introduce you to the deceased and emasculated Mr Nesbitt in person,' he said, putting the photographs down, 'except that when the coroner released him, he was finally claimed for burial. His mother read about him in the newspapers.' Esme Nesbitt's soft-edged and tinted image smiled faintly in my memory and I wondered briefly at how she would react, seeing the body of her son, knowing what he had come to all these years later. 'She hadn't heard from him,' Bradley was saying, 'in over twenty years.'

There's something about morgues that always makes me hungry so Bob and I went across to the University for lunch. I used to be very familiar with the Science Department here when I was studying. Now, years later, the two of us sat under the trees with the students laughing and chatting around us, reminiscing about our time in the 1980s when we had to mingle with demonstrators and take photos for Special Branch. Among the jeans and flowing locks, our short back and sides, neat attire and professional photographic equipment stuck out like balls on a canary. The students confronted us and took photo after photo of us taking photos of them. We'd been pissed off then. Now, we smiled and shook our heads, thinking how young and naïve we'd been. Even more naïve, perhaps, than the kids we'd been delegated to check out.

'How's everything?' Bob asked, after devouring his steak sandwich and stirring his tea bag around. I shrugged.

'So-so. You know.'

'I know you've moved out,' he said to me. 'Genevieve told me. When I rang about Nesbitt's gear. She sounded pretty upset.'

Bob didn't know my reasons for leaving the marriage and I didn't feel like telling him now. I didn't respond to the slight accusatory tone I felt in his voice. 'It seemed the best thing to do,' I finally said.

'What about Greg?'

I didn't answer him for a moment. My seventeen-year-old son had come round to my house four nights ago, very distressed and saying he wanted to come and live with me. I'd put him up for the night and rung his mother. It had only created more fuel for Genevieve's fire.

'I don't know what to do about him,' I admitted. 'He goes into Year 12 next year. I thought that him staying put at home would be less upheaval than moving in with me. But I just don't know.'

Bob must have seen something in my face because he stopped the interrogation. 'Doing any painting?' he asked. I'd been doing watercolours all my life, on and off. I also like working with acrylics in a more abstract way and Bob owns one or two of my wilder works. Genevieve never liked those. She wanted paintings to look like photographs.

'Not lately. Maybe once I get settled.' I took out the six photographs I'd found behind Nesbitt's tinted mother and passed them under the table to Bob—old police habits die hard. He took my cue and reached under to take them, shielding them with his hands while he examined them. 'I found them behind a framed portrait,' I answered his enquiring glance, 'among Nesbitt's gear.'

Bob pulled the sealable fastening open and, holding them by the corners, frowned as he looked through them. Black and white stills from what looked like hotel rooms, perhaps in Bangkok. Overweight Caucasian men, doing ugly things to slight-bodied Asian girls with dead faces. They were shocking to see, even for me. Men like Nesbitt are constantly committing crimes even by purchasing or looking at such stuff because every piece of child pornography is a crime scene.

'Looks like it was processed overseas,' Bob said, examining them front and back. He resealed the pictures and passed them back.

'I'll take them down to Canberra and put them through the wringer,' I said. Even though I hadn't undertaken any new jobs in the lab for some time now, there were still a number of outstanding items that awaited my final report and I'd have to go back to complete those and any others that might have come back for my attention. We search our own items unlike some other labs where work is delegated out to skilled technicians.

Back in the lab, I could check for fingerprints, body traces, particles, fibres, anything in fact that might tell me its story. Every piece of information that I discover is like one tile of a mosaic. Get enough of them in different colours and a picture slowly starts to build. The profile I was getting of Nesbitt was of a preferential pedophile, a man whose only sexual interest lay in children.

'What sort of pornography did you find at Gumley's place?' I asked, after a pause. As yet, I had no picture of Gumley, the first victim. Bob considered my question. 'The usual stuff. Bondage, sadism.'

'Featuring children?' I waited while Bob recalled. 'No,' he said slowly. 'It was adult stuff as I remember. Nasty but grown up.'

This presented a different picture from the sort of man who

collected images of children. I had no doubt that the only reason I hadn't found a lot more child pornography at Nesbitt's place was that he was broke at the moment and couldn't afford it. As well as their 'conquests', dedicated pedophiles create collections of child pornography. Sex involving children is the only interest they have. For men like this, every spare moment is taken up with their obsession with children as sex objects, and the recording of their encounters. Instead of seeing the sweet, rounded bodies so precious to parents and those adults who really love them, these men can see nothing but their own sexualised reflections. When they go on holidays, they don't bring back videos of resorts, scenic tours and tropical idylls, but images of children. Their diary entries are all about children. They can only talk of their interests to others of like taste and so their friendships are also only about children. They reduce them to objects, referring to them as 'she's' or 'queens'. The only thing they fear is exposure. The law they treat with complete comtempt. I remember going through the files of a man who suicided shortly after we charged him. Many of them do this. I found boxes and boxes of exercise books crammed full of figures, but this was no ordinary accounting. He had recorded every detail of every child who had ever crossed his path. Each encounter was colour-coded: green indicated the sighting of a desirable child with masturbation following, mauve meant masturbation with the child watching, blue stood for masturbation with the child touching his penis, and red meant he'd been able to touch the child as well. Gold meant penetration or its attempt. The amount of energy that had gone into the recording, grading and colour-coding in these books was the work of a lifetime. Many, many children had been involved with this man. And there were a lot of red and gold stickers. We've come to learn that although investigators may only get enough evidence to charge these predators with one or two cases of abuse, as a general rule, their victims number in the thousands.

Knowing things like this meant I never took my eyes off my own kids on the rare occasions I took them to parks or other public places. And because of my training, it wasn't only my kids that I kept under close scrutiny. I constantly scanned the people who sat around, reading or chatting. It was a rare day that I didn't spot one of them, the men who sit alone, watching children. Maybe I overdid it. Sometimes, when the four of us were together on a rare family outing, I'd point out someone I knew from police records, or had simply noticed. 'Just watch him,' I'd say, 'that nondescript man in the grey pullover and dark blue jacket. Let's just wait here a moment and you just watch him.' Genevieve would start arguing, saying I was turning what was supposed to be a family outing into a police lecture, and I suppose she had a point. But the two kids would watch. Pretty soon they'd see that the objects of the man's interest were young kids. He might pretend to be reading the paper, but over the top of it, he was watching the little boys climbing the slippery-dip the wrong way, or the little girls as they squealed on the swings opposite him.

Genevieve said that I frightened our children, particularly Jacinta, with this sort of thing. My response was that I was protecting her in the only way a parent can—training her in the vigilance and prudence that replaces the presence of a parent and keeps a child safe in their absence. I was insistent that we always know where the kids were. Every minute of the day and night. Especially Jacinta. Without anyone knowing, I checked out the families of the girls she sometimes 'stayed over' with. Police records made that easy and although these days it's becoming increasingly difficult to do things like that, it's still not impossible. Genevieve always said I made too much of it. But she had never been called out in the early hours of the morning to a crime scene and the corpse of a small, naked body. Now Genevieve says I drove Jacinta away with my fear. That I drove her towards the very thing I feared the most. But then she would.

'Maybe Gumley was more a situational pedophile rather than a total devotee like Nesbitt seems to have been,' I said, bringing my painful thoughts back to the discussion and using the psychiatrists' labels. Bob shrugged. Either way, we still had two dead men who'd committed horrible crimes against youngsters.

'What did you think of Dr Strachan's feelings about the killings?' I asked my friend.

'That they're homosexual?'

I nodded.

Bob shrugged. 'Could be. Or could be some sort of revenge. We'd have to know a lot more about Nesbitt and Gumley's past. They're hardly the sorts of murder victims who arouse much sympathy. No one's going to be breathing down our necks to find their killer, if you know what I mean.'

I did. There is a hierarchy to murder investigations. The more public emotions are stirred, the more manpower we get. And the only exception to that is a cop killing. Bob turned round at a roar of student laughter behind him.

'In my fantasies,' said Bob, tapping the face of one of the kids in the photographs, 'someone like this little fellow grows up to be a millionaire kung-fu expert who dedicates his life to tracking down bastards like this and getting rid of them.'

I grunted at Bob's dream and continued my own line of reasoning. Revenge was certainly not to be discounted. 'If Nesbitt was abusing kids in Asia,' I said, 'you can be sure he was doing it right here at home, too.' Less than a year ago I'd spent a lot of time at work with a stained piece of fabric full of jagged holes, the shirt of a man stabbed to death by a youth who had been a past recipient of the 'fatherly love' this man had bestowed on him and several hundred others over a decade ago. But that type of revenge murder was still a rarity. And just as well, I was thinking, because if all the kids in the world grew up to seek homicidal vengeance on all the men who'd ever stuck their cocks in or at them, the male population of this planet would be decimated. Looking around, I saw that Bob's grey eyes were on a gorgeous young woman in a filmy top and no bra. I couldn't help looking, either. We didn't say anything for a while as she bounced past, laughing up at a pimply youth who wouldn't know what to do with it.

'Nesbitt only went after little girls,' Bob reminded me. 'And as far as we know, Gumley went after older girls. But somehow, I can't see a woman growing up to do this.'

I remembered the man stabbed to death by two lesbians, and the fifteen centimetre nail driven through his ballbag. 'If it was a woman,' I said, 'she may not have worked alone.'

But Bob was already reconsidering. 'However,' he added, 'it's possible.'

'And,' I went on, 'young girls have brothers.' The words were out before I realised what I was saying.

But, in a minute or two, I had everything under control again.

'So what else have you got so far on these two murders?' I asked him.

'Almost nothing,' said Bob, as he put down his plastic fork. 'That's why I want you to have a look.' He picked out a burnt chip and put it to one side of his plate. 'Some loony from the Greens rang this morning, saying they had proof that the Federal Government has been carrying out illegal experiments with DNA. And that's what killed Gumley and Nesbitt.' For a moment, I wondered what on earth he meant, then I remembered the woman on talkback radio.

'What?' I asked. 'A genetically modified murderer?'

I finished the rest of my lunch and later we walked back through the grounds of the University, crossing the pleasant lawns with their European trees. 'Maybe,' I said, 'there was some kid that they both knew. Someone who grew up and never forgot or forgave.' Bob nodded in agreement. We were at that stage of an investigation where anything was possible. Slowly, painstakingly, my job would be to keep peeling away these possibilities until there was only one left. Indian mynahs picked around the rubbish bins and I was aware of the monotonous whooping call of a koel. Bob walked on but I stood, looking around until I eventually spotted it. They are usually almost impossible to see, but this one flew to a higher branch and I was able to spot the movement. I know the koel drives a lot of people crazy, especially in the night with its fever-bird call, but I've always felt a kindred feeling for them, perched high and solitary, cursed with insomnia and their monotonous, rising whoop.

I said goodbye to Bob and as I watched him walking towards his car, I switched to the message on my mobile: Genevieve.

TWO

I drove across the Harbour Bridge back to what used to be my home, passing places that hold vivid memories for me of my working days in this part of the city. Almost every street and corner, particularly around East Sydney, is filled with the ghosts of people I bailed up in my early days, or squatted or knelt beside later in my Crime Scene years, pulling my rubber gloves on, opening my murder bag. Even after all this time, I still can't drive through Oxford Street without recalling the pretty young woman who jumped from a tenth floor building, catching her legs in an awning on the way down. The resulting neat amputations of both legs made an odd corpse. When I knelt beside her with my little suitcase, one leg was lying crossways over her head and the other several metres away. Her upper body lay with the back of her head flattened, and her once pretty blue eyes half-closed, the whites discoloured with blood, the result of *contrecoup* damage to the front of the brain. You never forget something like that. Not, as some people mistakenly assume, simply because it's horrific. After years in the job, what might strike an outsider as shocking is simply what we come to expect; people fall or jump, their bodies get injured, bits come off or disintegrate and it's not remarkable. It was what would have been her beauty if it hadn't been broken and bloody and her wasted life that haunted me. I recently did a painting of her, putting her all together again, lying on a bed of fallen jacaranda blossoms. As I worked on her, my eyes filled with tears, and I knew it was a memorial to two little girls—my daughter, Jacinta, and for what happened to our family in the summer of 1975.

In more recent years, at Forensic Services, I analysed specimens and samples as part of a team of chemists, physicists, biologists, ballistic experts and document examiners. Our laboratory in Canberra has an excellent international reputation. The great French criminologist, Edmond Locard, taught that whenever two objects collide, particles are transferred from one locus to another. Traces I've examined and analysed—paint from cars, glass from headlights, fibres and skin cells found under fingernails, hairs, timber, seeds, vegetation, fabrics, carpets, poisons, drugs, carbon residues, bomb fragments, whatever they may be—connect me to the very origins of a crime. Even though much of my work over the last few years has been concerned with examining interstate and overseas evidence, I'm bound to this city by blood and memories in a weird, funny, painful mutuality. And stuck above the screen where I write up my findings, is a quotation from the famous nineteenth-century medico-legalist, Dr P.C.H. Brouardel: *If the law has made you a witness, remain a man of science. You have no victim to avenge, no guilty or innocent person to convict or save—you must bear testimony within the limits of science.*

I wish I had a wise pronouncement regarding the ending of a marriage that I could stick up over my desk. It is so much harder to remain a man of science in such a situation. Old angers and resentments get in the way of clear-sightedness. But I knew I had to be free of Genevieve. She always blamed Jacinta's problems on the last few years because I was a weekend father, away in Canberra from Monday to Friday. Whenever I pointed out that it was she who insisted that I take the job, and that it was also she who decided she didn't want to live in Canberra after all, she'd become completely enraged, demanding to know if she was supposed to do my job as well as her own, or did I expect her to live in two places at once. Then she'd rush straight on to blame me for coming *back* to Sydney as she'd wanted. Because, according to her version of events, my return interrupted a paradisiacal state of mother–child bliss, as she would have it, existing between Jacinta and herself. It's true I wasn't there Mondays to Fridays. But I didn't see much sign of mother–daughter bliss in the two days a week that I *was* home, and Greg occasionally makes comments about some of his mother's behaviour towards both him and Jacinta that I can't discount either. It's too painful to revisit these memories and I don't feel so much rage any more since Jacinta ran out of our lives. Sometimes I wonder if it is all still there, deep down in me just like a volcano waiting to erupt.

I was thinking of all this as I backed the car up towards the house in Lane Cove that, apart from the last few months, had been my home for many years. Always reverse in, someone had told me years ago. You never know when you might need to get out fast. The place was already looking neglected as if my departure had made an impact on the building, the garden, the lawn and rockery at the front. Two noisy miners hopped about in the grevillea bush outside Jacinta's bedroom. She'd painted her room completely black the summer she ran away, with weird figures lurking on the walls and dark red lights in cobwebby shades. It was like going into a witch's cave. Charlie told us it was all part of the adolescent need to make an impact on her world and suggested we enjoy it. But I was uneasy and Genevieve went hysterical the first time she saw it, although I must say, the pink and mauve she'd chosen a few years before for her daughter's room would've made any red-blooded human being take a stand.

My thoughts were interrupted when Genevieve herself ran out to greet me, looking youthful in a soft-fitting long singlet with her dark hair falling over her shoulders. She still has the slim figure she had when we married eighteen years ago and I can't deny that my estranged wife is a good-looking woman.

'Jack,' she said, 'it's so nice to see you.' She came up and kissed me, pressing herself against my chest, letting me smell her perfume, trying as hard as she could to play down our recent fight about Greg. 'Have you eaten?'

She looked a little disappointed when I told her I'd already had lunch with Bob. But she stood back sweetly enough while I stepped into the house. Since I left, I noticed the new stuff cluttering surfaces. Genevieve loves to collect things. I didn't mind even though I couldn't share her enthusiasm. She can spend hours in those shops in country towns, full of over-priced rubbish, picking up and turning over little cups and saucers, egg cups, plates, teapots, ornaments, little china people. Now I saw that the mantelpiece over the gas fire in the lounge room had a row of plates, each featuring the same bamboo pattern in different pastel colours, seven of them, all standing the same distance from each other, like a line-up. The several little tables that drove me mad—

she was always picking them up and putting them in different places—now had new little china people on them with frilly pantaloons and dresses.

'I rang,' she said, 'because I've got some big news.' I looked at her. Genevieve has always been almost impossible to read. So often her face is a mask and I have no idea what's going on behind the smile.

I stood waiting, shaking my head at her offer of a chair. I didn't want to settle in this room ever again. She frowned, but it wasn't only at my rejection of the chair. She was having great difficulty in saying the next words.

'John has heard...' she began, looking at my face, wondering at my reaction to the name. In spite of all the business that's gone on between us, the misery of our mismatched marriage, the staleness and resentment, the downright hatred that's exploded between us from time to time, I still felt the cold shiver of jealousy at the sound of that name. I'd disliked and distrusted Kapit since I'd worked with him years ago, but I kept my face impassive as I'd learned to do in the job and waited till she continued. 'He's heard something. Something about Jacinta.'

The shiver went from my chest to my legs and it suddenly didn't matter about John fucking Kapit, ex-cop, now private investigator. 'What?' I asked. 'What's he heard?'

'Kings Cross police had an anonymous call. A woman. A tip-off. Said she knew where Jacinta was.'

'And?'

'John felt it was a very genuine piece of information. He's following it up and he'll let me know if anything comes of it.'

I didn't say out loud I already knew what came of John Kapit's following up—dropping in on my wife too often. Then shafting her during the week for good measure. I still don't know when it started. I've never asked. I know it was well before the time I developed what I jokingly called a 'convenient association' of my own in the nation's capital.

In the first six months of my daughter's absence, alleged sightings of her came thick and fast, anonymous or otherwise. Our sad story made page three of the *Sydney Morning Herald* and her photo accompanied it. A beautiful picture from the end of Year Eight, Jacinta smiling at the thought of the summer holidays spreading ahead of her. And every now and then, one of the newspapers would do an update on Sydney's missing teenagers and the phone would ring for a day or two. Eighteen months ago, I ran myself ragged chasing up every little tip. I met kids in squats, I talked to crims, I flew to Perth and also to Nimbin. I even went to Christchurch because someone reckoned they'd seen her auditioning for a dance chorus. I handed out bribes, paid for dozens, perhaps hundreds of beers and coffees, while people told me about how they'd seen her, or spoken with her. But everything fizzled out. Now I knew better than to get too interested. These days, I was more selective, better defended against the inevitable disappointment. Now I concentrated on what Genevieve was saying rather than dwelling on my own messy thoughts about my failed marriage.

'Do you have the name of the officer who spoke to Mr John Kapit?' I said the name without expression. Genevieve shook her head.

'Please get that name for me and I'll follow it up,' I told her. There was no way I was going to contact that little shit. 'No,' I added, 'don't bother. I'll get it myself.'

'Jack...' she started.

I stared at her. I could feel her wanting me back, so as to punish me. It filled the room like the atmosphere of a crime scene and I couldn't wait to get out of that house.

'Jack, why are you getting yourself mixed up in those two killings? They're nothing to do with you.'

'What I do now is nothing to do with you either,' I said.

I saw anger fill her eyes. I wondered at the same time how she knew about my newest investigation and guessed that Kapit had passed it on.

'Why won't you see someone?' she said. 'Talk to someone? You are impossible! You know yourself you need to...I don't know...do something about what happened in your bloody family.' She looked as if she was about to cry, but it didn't touch me. Her distress was not about me, but the nuisance my absence created in her life. 'You've always been so superior. As if you know everything,' she was saying. 'It's not just Jacinta and what happened with us.'

I wasn't going to let her get away with that. 'True,' I said. 'A certain John Kapit does have some bearing on the matter.'

'Jack, please,' she said. 'That's not what I meant. You need help. I hardly recognise you any more.'

Genevieve's solicitude always made me nervous. It was true I'd changed. I'd started taking responsibility for my behaviour and feelings. Genevieve was light years away from this: blame was her favourite word, essential to her constant air of injured innocence. For years she'd wanted me to get help because in her eyes, every problem in our marriage was my doing. It was as if the past fifteen years of sobriety, hard work and making up for my sins had never happened. But I'd had enough of always being the bad guy.

'Why don't *you* get help, Genevieve? Find out what lies under your hostility towards your own daughter?'

I thought she was literally going to explode at that one. Her lips and eyes narrowed into hard lines.

'What do you mean?' she asked between gritted teeth.

'You drove her away,' I said. 'I gotta go.'

That did it. The explosion erupted. 'You blame me?' she screamed. 'You blame me for Jacinta's decision to leave?'

I reined in my anger and turned to face her again. 'Jacinta didn't make a "decision to leave" for chrissake! She just bolted.' I can't forget what happened that night. 'You know you were screaming at her,' I said. 'She was only a kid, Genevieve. She was only *thirteen*.' I had to harden my voice to stop it wobbling on that last word. I could see all her defensiveness rear up like a copperhead, snaky old Genevieve attacking anything that might challenge her unqualified belief in her own perfection.

She started shouting. 'So now I'm to blame for trying to raise my children in a decent—'

'Stop it!' I roared. 'I don't want to hear it,' and I raised my hand like a traffic cop, glad that Greg wasn't around to witness more of this endless awfulness.

'Don't you dare raise your hand to me!' she screamed, her eyes blazing with triumph that I might be going to do something as stupid as that. But she had to call it out after me because I was slamming the door behind me and gunning the motor before she knew it.

I could hear the two noisy miners' *'Quick quick quick!'* alarm call even over the sound of the car and the New Holland honeyeater who'd been flicking around the bottlebrush I'd planted a few years ago shot out of the bush, collided with my windscreen like a tiny missile, then vanished. I drove straight out, taking the corner at the bottom of the driveway too fast, so that the back of the car swung wildly around.

As suddenly as it had risen, the anger left me and I settled down to drive with more care. I'd talk to anyone, I was thinking, even shit-for-brains John Kapit, if this recent sighting had any substance. I'd talk to the police concerned and I'd chase up whoever passed on the information. I'd do anything to get my daughter home.

I pulled up outside my place and got out of the car. A tiny bundle of black, yellow and white feathers slid from somewhere off the bonnet and the honeyeater lay dead at my feet. It felt like a bad omen.

•

I'm renting a house in La Perouse, the Sydney suburb named after the French explorer who anchored in nearby Botany Bay for six weeks before disappearing forever with his two ships sometime in the late eighteenth century. Until Genevieve and I try to sort out the financial end of things, I'm not in a position to buy anything. Lapa, as the locals call it, was never regarded very highly as a desirable address. But prices have started to surge ahead now like any coastal area close to the city. I can leave the central business area of Sydney and be sitting on an almost deserted beach in half an hour. The hoists of the huge power station form the backdrop against which aircraft land just across the bay, but all that industry is far enough away to be romantic rather than a nuisance. At twilight, the calm bays become molten gold and by night the power station is decked with fairy lights.

My new home is an old weatherboard cottage that's been partly renovated by the owner and then abandoned in favour of the new brick two-storey house he's built at the front of the large block. Between the new building and the old is a jungle of palms that creak and rustle in any light breeze and the remains of a neglected rose garden. On my right is another humble cottage, hidden from sight by a wall of tall dark cypresses, stark against the local coastal scrub, while on my left is a glamorous batch of four town houses, no doubt replacing a house similar to the one I'm renting.

This house has been partly renovated over the years, the floorboards polished and sealed and a good-sized skylight of opaque polycarbonate allows daylight to fall directly over the table at which I work these days. There are a few areas of incomplete renovation such as my bedroom, where the job's only been half done and some of the new floorboards barely tacked into position, still unsealed and unpolished.

The hallway and living areas are stacked to the ceiling with folders and cartons, the result of a huge and overdue cleanup. Old briefs and case notes that I shouldn't have, my reference library, piles of science magazines, the personal albums that I always make up about any particularly interesting case, the books that I never have time to read, and shelves of compact discs and crime scene tapes. It's hard to keep orderly, but over the last few days I've started sorting it out and I was filing it away in chests in the tiny third bedroom I'm using as a sort of office cum storage area, but if Greg's going to be coming to stay with me from time to time, I want to make a reasonable area for him. I can give him the second bedroom, currently filled with more of my boxes and files and move my work back into the living-kitchen area.

I've tried to make the place a bit homely with the few odds and ends I hold dear: a painting Jass did of me when she was three, all glasses and hair, one of Greg's Fathers' Day cards, depicting me in a lab coat with a giant lab rat on my lap, and on the sideboard where there's a little clear space, the fierce bronze figure of Kuan Ti, Chinese god of detectives, prostitutes and triads, robes flaring, wields his pole-knife. Bob had given him to me years ago.

I made myself a coffee as soon as I arrived home again, and the ugly case I was now working on took a back seat while I sat in the shade outside my front entrance, and listened to the birds around me. La Perouse is a good place for birds; there's still plenty of coastal heathland for them to hide away from predators. And through the sonic pipings of honeyeaters and the rattle and clacks of wattlebirds, I could hear something else. I stood and walked closer to the brush at the back of the overgrown yard and beyond the derelict paling fence. Four clear, plaintive notes, repeated. I listened again. Sometimes three, sometimes five, but almost always four clear piped notes. It was a song without words from the sacred kingfisher and my heart lifted to hear it. It is my favourite bird, with its azure blues and soft golden buff colours, sharp flat forehead and keen fishing bill. I stood listening to its call, then I walked down the backyard and looked over the neighbouring fence on the right. They had a small pool where goldfish hung in the dappled water and the odd frog called during rain. I stood still, trying to spot the kingfisher. He'd be motionless, watching the water, waiting for a careless flash of gold too near the surface. I couldn't see him so after some minutes I walked back to my door. Knowing that he was around went a long way to redeeming the death of the honeyeater.

The backyard didn't have much to recommend it, except for its northern aspect, being mostly neglected lawn and weeds. It was only small but very private, the high bushes and shrubs of both adjacent gardens forming a dark green enclosure for my small patch. A previous resident had started making a brick patio that petered out halfway, swallowed up by unmown grass and the thicket of brush near the back fence. I'd already put two large tubs of tomatoes at the edge of the brickwork and marked out an area for a vegetable garden. I'd also bought several good-sized native shrubs and trees still in their pots that I planned to put in with the other natives after I'd cleared the overgrowth at the back. It's good to plant trees, even in rented accommodation, putting something back into the earth. To my right, several limbs of next door's huge camphor laurel hung over into my yard and the scent of it filled the night air. Over the back fence that formed my northern boundary was a bank of thick grevilleas and bottlebrushes and behind that, when I peered through the bushes, was a small park with a bubbler, two swings, a slippery-dip and a couple of rustic seats that no one ever seemed to use. I was transported to those summer night games we played when I was growing up in Springbrook. We'd had a huge backyard in those days and baby Charlie, imprisoned in his little playpen, used to stand on tiptoe to watch us playing. Sometimes when we played hide and seek, I'd drive Rosie crazy by climbing up a tree when it was my turn to hide. I didn't do it very often, so that she'd spend ages looking for me in all the usual places before turning her attention to the trees. The memory had popped up unbidden. To keep the thoughts away, I walked to the front of the house to check my mail. The mailbox yielded three bills and a letter addressed to me. It was very brief and quite anonymous, printed on a laserjet printer.

You don't know anything about me, but I know everything about you, I read. *People like you just don't care. But don't worry, you'll be made to. And soon.*

I was startled at the shock it gave me. In the past, I'd investigated letters like this, but I'd never been on the receiving end. Its anonymous malice hit my stomach and I instinctively turned round. Someone out there didn't like me. My immediate thought was Genevieve but in the years I lived with her, I'd never seen anything to indicate she'd turn to anonymous threats and abuse. God knows she did them well enough face to face. I turned the letter over and placed it and the envelope that housed it in a plastic bag. Neither the paper nor the envelope gave anything away: name and address printed on a label, the postmark illegible. I knew there'd been a lot of recent work done using plasma-mass spectrometry to isolate trace elements in computer paper, so as to determine its place of origin. But without the ream of paper owned by the suspect to match it against, even the most sophisticated physical evidence is just something with a certificate in a labelled bag. I carefully put the letter away in a drawer in the sideboard, then poured myself a blackcurrent drink with ice, surprised to find how hard my heart was beating.

I went outside and walked around on the half-built paved area. Just doing this made me feel less targeted. It's an unpleasant feeling, to know that someone holds such animosity towards you, and wants you to know it without letting you know who they are. Oddly enough, I also felt a little ashamed, that I should be the target of something so childish and spiteful. I didn't like to think I knew someone like that. Even if I didn't know anything about them, as they claimed. I wanted to talk to someone, to hear someone say, 'It's nothing. Just some silly ratbag. Don't worry about it.' I tried ringing Alix, my 'convenient association' in Canberra, but couldn't raise her on either her work or home number. Charlie, when I tried him, wasn't answering either.

Next morning I was still restless; the anonymous letter had agitated me more than I cared to admit so I drove to Kings Cross and walked into the police station. At the counter, I showed my

ID and if the young constable recognised my name and raised an eyebrow, I didn't notice. In a few minutes, I had the information I wanted. The bloke I needed to see was out crewing a patrol car and it didn't take me long to track him down. We met just as he was about to knock off his shift.

'You can listen to the caller,' said Chris Hayden, the keen young senior constable with cropped ginger hair and a good-humoured face who'd happened to pick up the phone. 'I remembered your name and the case very well. I ran off a tape of it for you.'

All incoming calls to police stations are monitored by logging tapes that mostly just go round and round with nobody taking much notice of them, except when something like this happens. Alix often enjoyed making fairly explicit remarks about what she wanted to do to me when she rang me at work just for the tapes. I quite enjoyed it, too.

I went with Chris into the meal room where he set up a radio tape deck. There was a moment's tape hiss and then a woman's melodic voice, low and shaky, as if she were stressed, sick or hungover. Maybe all three. I'd heard those strains in my own voice over the years. And there was something else, a deep and rich underlay to the voice. For a second I even wondered if she might be a he.

'I want to talk to someone in charge of the investigation dealing with those two...'—then she paused and her voice changed—'I want to talk to someone in charge about the fact that under-age girls are working at the House of Bondage. Someone should check it out.' Then came the click as she rang off. I waited, but that was it.

'I don't understand,' I said. 'I was told that my daughter's name had been mentioned. Jacinta McCain.'

Chris took the tape out. 'It was. But not on this one,' he said, indicating the tape as he rehoused it. 'Your daughter's name came up on the second call.'

'There were two calls?'

He nodded. 'The first one four days ago.' He looked at his screen. 'November 14th at 5.07 am, to be precise.'

November 14th. My heart stilled. The older you get, the more tombstones there are on certain dates of the year. 'She's an early bird,' I said as casually as I could, 'ringing at that time.'

The young man pulled another tape out of his drawer. 'This is the second one. It came yesterday.' He slipped the second tape into the cassette player. 'I want to tell you,' the voice said, 'that missing schoolgirl Jacinta McCain is working in a brothel. The House of Bondage.' Again, the click as she rang off.

'Public phone,' said Chris. He leaned back in his chair. 'That's it.' He saw my face, so continued. 'We made inquiries in the right places, but there's nothing happening with under-age girls in that place. We watched who came and went last night. The woman who runs it invited us in and we had a good look around. She doesn't want any trouble, she says. It's bad for business. Everything seemed in order. We didn't see anyone who remotely resembled your daughter. I'm sorry.'

My mind was racing. Girls come and go in those places. They don't turn up for a shift. They ring a friend who goes instead. It would take months of very close scrutiny to discover the identity of everyone who worked there. And even then you could still miss the girl you wanted if she was in Detox or had moved on. Or was recovering somewhere from an overdose. Or in gaol. Or dead. I couldn't even begin thinking about how my daughter might be working like that, in those places. She was fifteen in May. I indicated the tapes. 'Can I have these copies?'

'Be my guest,' said Chris.

•

My next engagement was a drink with Staro. He'd earned his nickname by starring in an advertisement years ago for a decongestant. Staro had always been associated with drugs one way or another, mostly of the illegal variety. Our meeting was at a bar miles away from where either of us lived. As I drove, I tried to remember his real name, but it escaped me for the moment. Staro was one of my gigs from years back and we still keep in touch. I'd contacted him when I first came back to Sydney, just to pick up where we'd left off and for him to give me the feel of the place and any changes I should know about now that I was possibly going to be living here again. My thoughts still wandered to the anonymous letter back home, but the power of the first impression was fading. Surely it was just some idiot out to punish me. Some minor crim from the past who wouldn't have it out with me in a straightforward way. Really, I should have just chucked it.

Staro was on methadone and trying to go straight but it was an uphill battle. The money in dealing is just so good that if you're an addict you've got to have a very good reason not to do it. But if he could live past thirty-five and wean himself from one drug to another, 'switching the witch for the bitch' as the Alcoholics Anonymous program terms it, he'd make it as an alcoholic rather than a heroin addict, and that way at least, the supply is reasonably cheap, plentiful and freely available. And he'd most likely live longer.

Sydney crime is very different now from how it was over twenty years ago when I joined the wallopers and the crims mostly had Anglo-Celtic names, apart from a light sprinkling of Italian and Greek. Now the Lebanese and Vietnamese battle it out with the old hands, cutting out their slices of the crime pie. And Staro, too, was no longer the handsome surfer boy he'd been when I coerced him with an inducement because he had information we needed and he was facing seven to ten years and was understandably shit scared. After a short period of reflection, Staro had given me several names, the Drug Squad cleaned up a couple of middle-sized baddies and Staro walked. Since then, he's lived the narrow, anxious life of an addict informer, looking over his shoulder, never knowing whether it would be the cops, the crims or the gear that'd finally do for him.

'Have you heard anything about under-age girls around the traps?' I asked him after we'd exchanged the usual pleasantries.

Staro shrugged over his double vodka while I watched him through my raised soda and bitters. 'You can get anything you want,' he said, 'if you've got the dough. And you don't even have to have much of that round here. There are plenty of under-age addicts who'll do anything for what they need.'

'We had a tip-off. The House of Bondage. My daughter's name was mentioned in connection with that place.'

He shook his head. 'Nah. I haven't heard anything about that. I'll keep an ear out for you.' Staro tossed back his vodka and ordered another. 'How come you never drink?' he asked, poking his head forward between his hunched shoulders, looking puzzled.

I picked up my glass. 'What do you mean?' I was teasing him a bit. 'This is a drink,' I said, swishing the fluid around in the glass.

'You know what I mean,' he said. 'A proper drink.' His blond hair was almost gone from the top of his head, his face an unhealthy tan that must have come out of a bottle because it was very rare that he was awake, let alone out, during the hours of sunshine.

'It's a very long story, Staro,' I said.

'You could tell me,' he said. 'Maybe I'd understand.'

'Maybe you would,' I said.

'But I'm on the 'done now,' he reminded me, 'to replace what I used to use. What do you use instead?'

I considered. It was a good question, better than Staro realised. 'Clean hands and a clean heart,' I said. 'And a job I enjoy. If you hear anything,' I added, 'about under-age girls...'

Staro picked up his new double and actually touched the back of my hand. He must have seen my look of amazement at this familiarity, because he pulled his hand back fast. 'You know,' he said quickly, 'if I heard anything, I'd let you know asap.'

I felt bad that I'd been so transparently startled by Staro's breach of protocol and, looking away, I noticed a fellow nearby reading a paper with "NEW MUTILATOR MURDERER FEARS" heading the page. Staro followed my line of sight and also saw what I was reading. 'What about this character who removes the three piece suite?' I asked, changing the subject. 'Is there anything going around about that?'

Staro's eyes widened. 'There's a lot of talk,' he said 'about the DNA result.' He shook his head. 'You know, it's not right to go tampering with nature. It starts off with soya beans and then you get something like this happening.'

I knew Staro had done himself a lot of brain damage over the years, but I was getting more irritated by the minute. 'Staro,' I said sternly, 'what are you talking about?'

'The DNA result on those two murders you just asked me about. You're a scientist. You should know. What killed them?'

I leaned back in my chair. 'A human being killed them,' I said. 'I'm working with that investigation.'

'Jeez, are you? I'd be careful if I were you.'

'Let me put you straight, Staro,' I said. 'I presume you're referring to the report about non-human DNA in connection with the first of the killings?' Staro nodded, reddened eyes wide.

'It was a dog,' I said.

Staro paled. 'My God. That's horrible. Some sort of human and dog mix?' He was looking at me in an accusatory sort of way, reminding me of how these sorts of conversations often go with Staro. When Staro fastens onto something, getting him to unfasten was a bit like turning the *Queen Mary* around. It could take a nautical mile or two.

'Just plain dog,' I said. 'Not human. Before Gumley's body was found, it seems a dog had licked the body'—Staro's face was a picture—'and left traces of saliva. This resulted in a DNA profile that was non-human. We sent it to the relevant experts. Because it *was* a dog. That's all. There's no mystery. There's no genetic modification. Just some dickhead journalist failing to check out a story properly. So can we please drop the wolf-man theory?'

Now Staro looked hurt and drew lines in the condensation on the side of his glass. 'Have you heard anything else about the killings?' I asked. I wasn't very hopeful. Even without all the complications of an urban myth I knew this question was a long shot. The sort of crime we were dealing with in this case was very different from armed holdups or drug deals. Or even more run-of-the-mill murders which usually turn out to be family or business affairs and where someone's usually heard something or, in the case of the more professional killings, someone wants to do a deal. But the sort of killer who'd dealt with Ernest Nesbitt and Cecil Gumley was invariably a loner, despite the conjectures Bob and I had tossed around, someone who preyed on random victims when and where the opportunity presented itself. We'd come to understand that killers like this operated outside of a relationship with anyone. Over the last twenty years, there's been an exponential growth in psychological understanding about murderers, murders and victims. But this doesn't reduce the need for the age-old basics of good investigation: diligence, tenacity and experience. My mobile rang and I took it into a corner. It was Bob wanting me to come into town.

'Okay,' I told him. 'And I've got something for you, too, Bob. I want you to listen to something.' I'd decided to play him the tapes about Jacinta. Bob and I made a time for the next day and I rang off.

Staro could see that the drinks were drying up. 'You know who you should talk to?' he began, but I was already standing up. Reluctantly, Staro tossed back the ice at the bottom of his drink. A split second before he said the name, I'd remembered, too. 'Ask Marty Cash,' said Staro. 'Old Pigrooter knows everything. Knows where the bodies are buried.' It was true. Because Marty Cash, who used to be Marty Kaczsinsky, had buried a couple of them himself.

Staro and I gathered up our keys and phones and walked past the poker machines to the back entrance of the pub.

'That bloody queen must have been bullshitting me,' he said out of nowhere.

'What queen?'

'The one who told me about the sub-human DNA profile. She...he...said his aunt worked in the lab and had seen the result. Talk about lying.' He sniffed. 'Typical. She's always playing for drama, that one.'

I was going to remind Staro that years ago, I'd heard he wasn't averse to a frock and false eyelashes as well as other things, but now wasn't the time to mention it. 'Not sub-human,' I said, '*non-human.*' I started walking away. 'Did your draggie mate say his aunt's name was Florence?'

'What?' Staro looked bewildered.

I kept going, then turned to see him walking away across the carpark to his battered old Renault. In that moment, his real name came to me. There was something about Robin Anthony Dowzer's lonely life, his isolation, the weird worlds he moved between, that was familiar and for a second, I felt we had something in common.

•

The next day when I walked into the House of Bondage's beige and white entrance showing my ID card and asking for the manager, the platinum blonde receptionist didn't look at it and rolled her eyes.

'You people have already been here,' she grizzled. 'It's bad for business. You scare clients away.' She stood up and walked to the stairs.

'Jules?' she called, 'can you come down here a sec?'

The proprietor, Miss Juliana, descended, looking like a prim headmistress in her navy dress with white earrings. She must have retired from the more active work here, I thought, and now manages it. One look and she knew what I was. I wondered if she'd remember me from the old days, simply because I was one of the few she hadn't serviced. She gave no hint of that, however, and took me into a room to the right of the entrance area where there was a bar and a lot of pink and gilt furniture. Bad paintings of naked women hung in ornate frames. Miss Juliana positioned herself near the bar and poured herself a lemonade. She didn't offer anything to me. 'Our licence is in order,' she said, indicating the certificate on the wall behind the bar. 'We've had fire doors installed. What's the problem now?' I looked at the frowning woman in front of me, her pencilled eyes, the red lipstick painted over the lip line on a narrow top lip, the sun-coarsened skin under too much make-up. A tiny tatt on her temple had smeared into an indecipherable bluish stain, and the smell of cigarettes staled her breath.

'It's about a missing juvenile,' I said, finding some detachment in the jargon. 'Jacinta McCain. We're acting on information received that she was working here.'

Miss Juliana swung round behind the bar and found a packet of cigarettes, pulling the cellophane off, getting one out, putting it between her lips.

'Look,' she said, 'I've heard all that and it's not on. I've got kids of my own. I've got a daughter. Just because I run an establishment doesn't mean that I'm some sort of pervert. Hell, I told all this to the baby-faced kids who came round yesterday. I want a quiet life. I'm not interested in that sort of thing. I've had kids come here wanting to work and *I've* rung up Missionbeat or the Wayside Chapel for godsake.' She swung round to face me. 'I even talked one girl into using my phone to ring her dad and she waited here till he came and picked her up. No drugs, no underage. House rules.'

'Why do you think someone would make such an allegation?' I asked.

Miss Juliana started walking with me towards the door. 'Use your head. Why wouldn't they?' she asked. 'It's a competitive business I'm in. There are illegal joints everywhere. If I wanted to put someone out of business, I'd start a rumour like that. Or say the place was used as a distribution centre for drugs. Say something like that, have the place crawling with bloody cops. Our gentlemen don't like that sort of thing. They'd start going elsewhere.' She paused on her way to the front door. One of their 'gentlemen' was going upstairs with the platinum receptionist. Miss Juliana took in the situation, flashed him a fabulous false smile, then hurried to the front door, opening it slightly, standing there till I joined her.

'Can you tell me where I'll find Marty Cash these days?' I asked her.

'Why should I?'

'For old times' sake,' I tried. Miss Juliana peered at me. 'I remember you. You used to work round here. And I also remember there *were* no old times.'

'What about just for the hell of it?'

'He used to have an office in Victoria Street, down near St Vincent's,' she said, frowning. 'But he lost his licence. And I don't know where he is.' Satisfied, she opened the front door wide. 'Now,' she said, 'I don't want to see you lot again. It's harassment. I do the right thing and it's been nothing but trouble.'

I stepped outside into the real world again, but the woman was still grizzling behind me. 'I wish we could go back to the old days when we just paid the cops. Things were simpler then.'

I walked away, and the door slammed behind me.

•

I drove home, all the while considering my impressions of Miss Juliana. The experts on counterfeit notes in the Fraud Squad spend a very long time going over and over the real thing, note after note, poring over each portrait and number, every little flourish and curl, every detailed area of cross-hatching, the different gradations of colour and density, the feel, the size, the texture of every denomination of paper and metal currency. All they study for months is the genuine article. After that sort of intensity, a faked note practically jumps up at them and screams, 'I'm a dud!' Likewise, when you've spent as much time as I have with people who lie to you, you discover that when people tell the truth, it shines out. Even though I was pretty sure Miss Juliana was telling the truth, I decided to keep an eye on the place anyhow. I'd get

Staro to ask around as well and keep me informed on street talk and I'd certainly chase up Pigrooter. If anyone knew what was going on in this town, ex-cop, ex-private investigator Marty Cash certainly did.

While the coffee was perking, I cleared a spot on the dining table and made room for my cassette player. Then I sat down with a strong brew and listened to the tapes Chris Heyden had given me, playing them, rewinding and playing again. I kept listening over and over to the way the caller's full voice spoke the words: 'I want to talk to someone in charge of the investigation dealing with those two—' and the way she repeated the first eight words in her second statement although the information after that was quite different. I was intrigued by the way the tone and the energy in the woman's voice changed so much during that first tape. I was sure there was something important about those changes and I wanted Bob's opinion.

I did some more sorting of my boxes and then realised it was a very long time since lunch. I looked in the fridge. There was exactly the same pathetic line-up as there'd been when I last looked, so I went up the street and bought some Italian take-away from the waterside café, bringing it home and eating ravioli in my disorganised kitchen, realising it was about time I rang Alix in Canberra and told her about my new single status and address. Clear-eyed and sharp, with an excellent memory, she was the opposite of my wife. She had a lovely, long, golden body with a boyish figure. Once, she'd covered herself with some glittering oil, from top to toe, so that every move she made caused her body to scintillate and flash. It was, as I told her, like making love to a sparkler. For days afterwards, I'd see tiny flashes on my skin and smile, remembering how they'd got there. She was a producer of educational videos for the corporate world and I knew she was often in Sydney for her work. She laughed at my jokes, and she loved sex; she said she especially loved sex with me. I had no idea if she meant that or not, but she was always keen to get in the cot.

I finished my meal and looked around my new domain. The good thing about starting over again was that there was almost nothing of Genevieve and absolutely nothing of Jacinta here. At the marital home, Genevieve kept her bedroom like a shrine with linen changes and fresh flowers every few days. There was something funereal about that, and I couldn't be part of it. I had once made the mistake of voicing my feelings, that if Genevieve had been as attentive to the girl as she had been to the room, things might have been different. It was a harsh thing to say and I've always regretted it. I can't know what it's like to be a mother.

My memories were taking a gloomy turn so I deliberately changed my thoughts. Apart from the nasty letter, my life was greatly simplified. I had a fresh start and a new investigation to keep my mind occupied. And a lot of boxes to unpack.

I was repacking the Rosie box when I found a package I'd forgotten and opened it. On top was a folded pair of shorts and T-shirt together with Rosie's favourite book, *The Sword in the Stone*, one that she'd read over and over. We'd used it years ago to get her prints on record in case we ever found a suspect and a place to search for her presence, but so far, we'd never had occasion to use them. Right at the bottom of the box in a plastic bag was her old bear, Mrs Gumby, an almost bald teddy she'd had since kindergarten. Rosie had slept every night with that bear, chewing on its ears like a puppy. I'd taken it and hidden it when all my sister's things were rounded up and removed because my mother couldn't bear anything around to remind her of her vanished daughter. Now, I looked at the bear through the plastic. One eye was missing, the other hung on a thread. I pushed the bag down into the box again and picked up the book. I turned it over in my hands then opened it and read: *To dear Rosie, Christmas 1973, from Mother and Dad with love*, in my mother's stiff handwriting.

The T-shirt and shorts had been used on a mannequin with Rosie's colouring, placed in the Mall some days after she'd disappeared. Accompanying it was a brief outline of the incident and the question: 'Have you seen this girl?' together with the Springbrook police phone number. I repacked the book and the clothes. My sister had been driven away to some vanishing point, and neither she, nor the car used in her abduction, had ever been seen again.

I took the rubbish out to the wheelie bins at the front of the place. All was very quiet and still and I could hear the sound of the sea, soft and distant, like a shell held up to the ear. Beyond that was the drone of aircraft approaching the airport. There was an odd salty haze around the streetlights, pollution rather than condensation, reminding me that somewhere in this city was a killer who operated in darkness, slashing and killing lone men. The thoughts made me quicken my steps, and I hastily walked past next door's cypresses and around to my back door. I was just stepping inside when an odd sound made me stop. It was an eerie metallic squeal. I stood there, straining to pick up every sound. All I could hear was the distant sound of traffic and the occasional car driving past. Then I heard it again. This time, I wondered if it might be an injured bird or animal. My imagination played tricks, and for a second created a crouching, bestial figure in the darkness near the fence, Staro's murderous wolf-man. I looked again and saw it was the shadow from a mock-orange bush. The sound teased me and I racked my brains trying to work out what it was. I hurried inside and made sure the place was securely locked before I went to bed.

I dreamed about a beautiful blue monkey swinging from a tree that grew just below me, sprouting out of the side of the cliff I was standing on. As I watched in horror, some monstrous dark predator swept past me, swooped on the monkey and bit his fingers off so that he fell, shrieking, into the abyss below. I woke up and looked at the time. It was two fifty-one.

THREE

Next morning, outside the Sydney Police Centre in Surry Hills I boldly parked in an Authorised Police Parking zone and, after being given my visitor's badge and walking through the scanner, I made my way up to Bob's office. His printer was humming away when I knocked on his office door and he turned to welcome me.

'Take a look at this,' he said, passing me the print-out records of Ernest Nesbitt. 'And here's Mr Gumley for you. Want a coffee?'

I nodded and he went to make it while I busied myself reading Nesbitt's record. His sheet started with offences against minors.

The man who'd died last month, Gumley, had been charged with three violent rapes and on three occasions he'd walked. Finally, they'd got him on rape and manslaughter. I went through the folder put together by the investigating police, the little packets that had gone off to the experts for analysis and returned with their accompanying certificates for the courts, the original records of interviews made by the fellow who'd found the body and some other witness statements.

Bob returned with another envelope and I opened it. 'That's the young girl he killed,' Bob said. Tiffany Jo Bentley had died of asphyxiation from the attentions of Cecil Gumley.

I flicked through the crime scene photographs, then turned to Gumley's folder again. I read the date of his conviction and sentence, noting with satisfaction that he'd gone to Goulburn Gaol, the hardest prison in the State. I did some mental arithmetic and frowned.

'He should still be inside,' I said to Bob. 'Did he get early release?'

Bob looked over at me. 'I checked with Corrective Services,' he said. 'Gumley only served five years of a nine year sentence. He was released on November 10th after the parole board recommended it.'

I met Bob's eyes and wondered if he was thinking like I was. I've never been able to understand why it is that if a homicidal criminal is a good boy in gaol and gives the right answers to the parole board's questions, this in some way proves that locking a person up for years in a brutal institution brings about some deep character transformation. Ten years of good behaviour in a narrow prison cell doesn't tell me anything about how this person is going to be in the real world. In fact, we already know all too well how he is in the real world. It's why he ended up doing ten years in the first place. And yet the passage of time is somehow thought to produce change. It's like a modern scientist still believing that graveyard air causes disease. Or that mice spontaneously generate in rag heaps.

'That's only a few weeks ago,' I said to Bob. 'When was he killed?'

Bob checked his notes. 'The fourteenth of November.' The rush of adrenalin again as that date came up. A man is murdered on a day of the year that has special significance for me. Big deal. Other things can happen on the fourteenth of November, I heard some inner voice say. Relax.

'And when was Nesbitt released?' I asked quickly.

Again, Bob consulted his notes. 'He was released the day after Gumley's death. Then he's killed a week later,' We looked at each other for a second and then Bob shuffled through his notes. I knew what he was thinking. You get a feel about this sort of thing.

'It's looking more and more like someone was waiting for them, Bob,' I said.

My friend considered. 'Could they have offended someone very powerful inside?' Bob suggested.

I shook my head. 'If that had been the case, they'd have been dealt with inside. Much easier to arrange.' Only a few years ago, a man was murdered in the yard at Goulburn in broad daylight with dozens of witnesses who weren't saying anything. Why complicate things by letting the person you want dead get away out into the big world when you can do it with ease and simplicity in a controlled environment? Something else occurred to me and I picked up the Nesbitt folder again. I looked through it more carefully. He'd been sentenced to twelve years for the brutal bashing and rape of a thirteen-year-old girl he'd left for dead. I read her statement and the hot rage boiled inside me. He had subjected her to things no living creature should be forced to endure, let alone a young girl. My hackles rose and in that minute I hated him and was glad that he'd died so horribly.

'But this was only six years ago,' I said, noticing the date of the trial. 'He's got out early, too.' Two violent rapists, one also a killer, and both murdered only days out of gaol. My instinct was buzzing. 'Men like this are being released all the time,' I said. 'Not droves of them, but several a year. Why *these* two?' Profiling the victims is as important as profiling the killers.

Bob shrugged as he replied. 'Could be someone was waiting for them. Or it's also possible that these two nasty bits of work fit the *profile* this particular killer targets. Lonely men, wandering round late at night looking for whatever it is they look for. High risk victims.' He paused then added, 'Remember Dr Strachan said it felt homosexual to him.'

I'm a scientist, not a psychologist, but some time ago, Charlie had given a very interesting paper to the Forensic Society about several cases of what is termed 'homosexual homicide'. The gist of it was that in some cases, a certain sort of homophobic man, homosexual himself but not aware of it, and drawn to flirt with other men in his unconscious way, acts outraged and disgusted when they respond to him. And on some occasions, the situation can turn homicidal. It's still used as a defence on occasions, although as social attitudes about homosexuality relax, juries are less inclined to think that it's legitimate for a man to be murdered for merely making a pass. However, it was possible that Gumley and Nesbitt had both fallen foul of someone like that. But there was nothing in the case notes of either man to indicate that the two sex offenders were homosexual, conscious or otherwise. 'Surely a killer with that sort of profile would go to gay bars,' I said, 'and not just wander around late at night in dark and deserted places hoping that he'd bump into a flirting partner who also might just happen to be there.'

But then I remembered some of the beats I'd sat off, and recalled that it was like a highway in those dark places, when honest citizens are tucked up in their beds. Bob and I sat looking at each other unseeingly, each focused on our own thoughts. Our discussion was mere conjecture, but after many years of working with Bob, I knew that it was conversations like these as much as the leads that might develop elsewhere that often shaped an investigation. And because of how things were with me, the awful business with Genevieve, the enigmatic tip-off about our missing daughter and the spite in the mailbox, it seemed essential that I keep myself as busy as possible. I didn't want any spare moments, no spaces in my mind, no gaps in my time through which a little ghost from twenty-five years ago could slip.

'I'm going to check Goulburn,' I said. 'See if there's something in common there.' I felt suddenly more alive. A big new job loomed before me. These two murders and the constant alertness about anything concerning Jacinta would fill my days and nights. And I would definitely take a sleeping pill tonight to crush REM sleep. I didn't want any more dreams like last night's.

I remembered the tapes Chris Hayden had made for me. 'There's something I want you to listen to,' I said to Bob. 'I'll need a cassette player.' I pulled the tapes out of my pocket and Bob produced a small stereo radio and cassette player.

'Tell me what you think of this,' I said, shoving the first tape in and starting the player. Again, that strained, husky voice. 'I want to talk to someone in charge of the investigation,' the voice said, 'dealing with those two...I want to talk to someone in charge about the fact that...' I stopped it and just played that section several times. Bob leaned over, rewound and played it one more time himself.

'It's a very distinctive voice,' he said.

I nodded, feeling oddly irritated that her voice had touched him, too. Maybe it was all a reaction to the messiness of my life right at this minute, but for some reason, I found the voice of the unknown informer almost irresistible. So many women of my acquaintance have sharp-edged voices, honed over years of disappointment and resentment. To hear a voice like this caller's, soft even under strain, went straight to what was left of my heart. The anonymity was exciting as well. I couldn't help building a woman around that rich, trembling voice. Dark hair, thick, longish, pale skin, a medieval look. Dark red jacket. A black skirt, high heels.

A cream silk blouse. Deep red lips. A full-bodied pinot noir woman. Somewhere, I'd seen a painting like her. A Renoir, I wondered. No, a Goya. In my mind's eye, I mixed the colour on my palette, crimson lake, rose madder, a hint of vermillion and black.

'What do you think about her voice?' I asked, getting myself back on track. 'Particularly that first message.'

Bob rewound and played the few sentences one more time then leaned back in his chair, came forward again and put his elbows on the desk. He was thoughtful a moment. 'I reckon she changes tack,' he said finally. 'Halfway through, she seems to change her mind.'

'That's what I thought, too. It's like she's going to say one thing and then she swerves away from it and says something else instead.'

'What did she go on to say?'

'She said that my daughter was working at the House of Bondage.'

'Jesus!' said Bob.

'It's been checked out,' I said. 'And I went round there in person yesterday. It seems to be a false alarm. The woman who runs it appeared to be telling the truth.'

'Glad to hear it,' said Bob. Then he stood up, seeing that I was ready to leave. 'Here,' he said, turning to pick up two sealed packages. 'I've retrieved the clothing belonging to the two dead men,' he said, handing them to me. They were both bagged and sealed with the blue and white tape of Forensic Services Division as well as the red serrated security tape. 'What they were wearing the nights they died. Bradley wondered if you might want to go over them again.'

I looked at the signature on the tape: F.E. Horsefall. I shook my head and handed back the bag. 'Lidcombe must've sent the samples to Florence for double-checking,' I said, 'and Florence is the best. She would have found everything and anything.' Dr Florence Horsefall had been with Forensic Services longer than anyone else, yet seemed arrested forever aged about forty. She drank carrot juice and practised tai chi. I remembered once catching her smoking behind a tree and her massive embarrassment had seemed out of all proportion to the infringement of her self-imposed health regime. It was an odd incident and that's why I'd never forgotten.

It was as if I'd caught her with her hand in the till, or up someone's dress.

Bob was indicating a couple of envelopes. 'I've also given you copies of the analysts' reports to read. You might find something helpful there.' I took the reports from him, thinking I'd read Florence's reports later.

'Marty Cash,' I said, changing the subject. 'Where does he hang out these days?'

Bob raised an eyebrow. 'What would you want with old Pig-rooter?'

'Information,' I said, picking up my things. Bob made a face and frowned with his increasingly bushy eyebrows. Over the years, Bob's got more and more eyebrows above his grey eyes and less and less hair on top. 'He drinks at the Collins Club,' he said. 'Or used to.' The Collins Club is a gentlemens' club, stuffy with leather and dark colours, that pretends to gentility, yet has walls of poker machines and carpet that looks like a tapestry based on the pattern of the technicoloured yawn.

•

I went home with Dr Florence Horsefall's reports. I made coffee and glanced through the results my colleague had written up regarding her examination of the clothing of the two dead men. My work is mostly in and around the various chemistry labs, wet labs, analysis rooms or search room. Anything biological is transferred through a double hatch into the Biological Division. We don't usually examine the blood stains of the victim: there's no need to. We know who he or she is and we know how they died. What we don't know is who did it and that's where trace and particle analysis can be helpful. In both cases, Florence had taken further samples from the upper arm area of the shirt each man had been wearing, because if there'd been a struggle and some grappling enough DNA material from the killer might have transferred itself from his hands onto the clothing of his victim. In Gumley's case, there were several foreign hairs and these had been stored—it was possible that our investigation would turn up a person whose hair matched. The follicle needs to be still attached to the hair for DNA processing. In Nesbitt's case, there was even less. I put the reports aside. They were disappointing but not unexpected. It's only in the movies that the lab gets a result that matches some old warb on the database, let out for weekend release. And our database is only just getting up now.

I glanced through the local newspaper and noticed that the council was running an art competition, and today was the last day for entries. I went to the big carton marked with my initials and opened it, pulling out the large folder. Underneath this were several paintings that I'd liked enough to have framed and over the years, I'd collected half a dozen. My favourite was a misty view of several cottages on the ridge at Blackheath, called *Morning Mist*— my tribute to Turner in acrylics. I looked at it again, still pleased by the way I'd captured the bluish mist that settled around the lower reaches of the ridge and the way the eastern light edged trees, buildings and rocks. There was one murky corner on the lower left-hand side that I'd abandoned because it was already overpainted, but taken altogether, I thought the whole thing worked passably. And I'd never exhibited this one before. I put the other paintings away and shoved the box back in a corner. I clipped and filled out the entry coupon, noting the address to deliver my work.

Later in the afternoon, I was on the road, having delivered *Morning Mist* to the council only hours before the competition closed, and at Goulburn Gaol by four o'clock. Just for a moment, when I'd handed over my painting and glanced at the other entries stacked along the wall, sniffing the odour of fresh oil paint, I'd felt a surge of something I hadn't felt in a long time. Life, enthusiasm, reality. Even coming back to life after all the drinking years hadn't had this quality to it. And it was something completely different from the mechanical misery of the last few years. Whatever it was that had made me want to paint in the first place. The loss of Rosie, although it had caused immense grief, hadn't dulled me. After the initial shock, there was a terrible realness about everything, a starkness that pierced and stabbed. I'd done a painting then, not long after she went, of her room and her belongings thrown on the floor, the book she'd been reading still open, face-down on the bed next to Mrs Gumby, her chewed bear, the little silk bag that had housed the blue and yellow enamel necklet lying empty beside the bed, the view to the trees outside her window. It had been some sort of comfort to sit in her room and paint. By that time, my father was almost never in the house, and my mother stayed in her room. Charlie and I had a few months of feral living until our mother's sister came to see how things were in the house and installed a live-in housekeeper, Mrs Moss.

In those days, and in the early days of my marriage, I'd turned out a few paintings a year. But it seemed that over time, my responses to life had become smaller and flatter. It was years since I'd finished my last painting, yet the smell of oils and acrylics, the canvases and pieces of masonite stacked modestly with their faces to the wall in the council warehouse where *Morning Mist* now joined them, ignited a long-dormant urge to paint again.

•

Goulburn Gaol is a terrible place, not so bad as it was in the old days when the Corrective Services vans had to be hosed out after the prisoners got out because men had soiled themselves in fear, knowing the reception beating that awaited them at the worst gaol in the state. Maybe that doesn't happen any more, but Goulburn is still the hardest, and it takes prisoners no other gaol will house.

I walked past the rose garden with its magnificent display of pinks, golds, whites and mauves, thinking of the hundreds of men who were about to be locked up at four thirty until next morning in a small stone room with a solid iron door and a narrow, barred window way up near the high ceiling with just the walls for company. I announced myself on the intercom, was identified and permitted to climb through the little padlocked door in the great fortress double doors. On the other side of the gates is a large caged-off area containing the scanning section, the receptacle for bags and other items and, above it, the grey security video screens, keeping every section under electronic surveillance. This steel cage needs to be unlocked by another officer with a different set of keys before anyone can get into the next stage of the prison, the sterile area, a wide 'corridor' which, as its name indicates, is completely empty apart from the digital cameras and microwave movement detectors running along each side of it.

In an interview room, I talked to two of the Corrective Services officers who'd known the murdered men. They took me to see Ron Herring, the ex-army assistant superintendent with whom I spoke in detail.

'Never a problem, either of them,' said Ron. 'Except to other people.'

'That's what I was wondering,' I said, telling him about the conversation I'd had with Bob.

Ron shook his head and his face furrowed into a tight smile at the idea of some sort of prison vendetta extending outside. 'Crims are very self-righteous,' he answered. 'Neither of them would have lasted long in the main yard so they were kept apart and served out their sentences in a strict protection area, a cage within a cage. We let them mingle among others of their kind, the rock spiders, the paederasts and child-killers. We tell them if there's any trouble, they'll all be locked up in their separate cells again. They get along all right. Probably entertaining themselves swapping fantasies and the details of their conquests.'

I thought about that for a moment and wondered if they also made up other fantasies, about how 'rehabilitated' they were, to seduce the parole board. We walked around the sterile area and sparrows chirped in the stone walls under a perfect blue afternoon sky. 'Nesbitt spent a lot of his time drawing,' Ron said. 'He got quite good at it.' I recalled the obscene drawings hidden in the Bible among the pages of Jeremiah. We waited while the officer in charge of the entrance area came with his keys to let us in. I asked him whether they might have incurred the wrath of some gaol heavy who wanted them dead. Ron Herring considered. 'I know of several cases where there've been killings associated with gaol fights, but Nesbitt and Gumley just weren't in that league,' he said, 'and the others were killed inside. It was because they were such model prisoners that Nesbitt and Gumley were both released in the minimum time.'

From somewhere high above me came the sound of a muffled yell. I looked up and around. It was impossible to see into the banks of narrow, fortress-style window slits. 'They're always calling out,' Ron said. 'They're carrying on because they know you're here. They know everything that goes on. The minute something different happens or someone new comes in, they know. They're all watching us now.' The way he said it reminded me of the way a father might speak of the exploits of his seriously wayward children, proud despite everything.

'But those two, Nesbitt and Gumley,' said Ron, returning to his earlier conversation, 'were both grey little crims. Hardly noticeable. They knew it was best to lie low.' He was supervising my way through the padlocked door of the steel entry cage and I was feeling I'd wasted the trip and a tank of petrol when he suddenly answered my question. 'If anyone in our system had wanted them dead, they'd never have walked out of here alive.'

In the cage, I picked up my belongings, and stood waiting for the small door in the main gates to be opened by the supervising officer. 'I heard from one of my mates out at the Bay,' said Ron, referring to the old gaol at Long Bay whose high sandstone wall I drove past every day. 'They've got an old sex offender due for release in a few days. He's really starting to worry. When two old rock spiders get castrated and killed within days of going outside, it gives the others something to think about, even in different gaols.'

I was immediately interested and turned back. 'Who is he?' I asked.

'Don't know the name off the top of my head,' said Ron, 'but I can certainly find out for you.' I shook hands with the assistant superintendent and as I stepped from the steel cage out into the sterile area, another voice yelled obscenities down at us. Abuse me all you like, you poor bastard, I thought, as I walked into freedom. You've got to stand on a table and squint sideways through bars. I'm walking out into the late evening sunshine and the scent of roses.

Before driving back to Sydney, I took a styrofoam cup of very bad coffee into the municipal gardens and sat on a green park seat. You can't grow roses in Sydney the way you can grow them here. The deep clay soils, the cool nights and the dry inland air all combine to make Goulburn a heaven for rose-growers. A magpie picked over the soil to feed its two noisy, grey-collared offspring and I could hear the whispering of wrens in the dense hedges that ran along one side of the park. For a moment, I had a stupid fantasy that I could just leave my life, the mess, Genevieve's hostility, my lost daughter, perhaps even the past, and settle into a country cottage in a town like this. Just turn my back on the whole sad mess, breed roses and improve my watercolour skills. But as I stood up, throwing the rest of the coffee away and headed back to my car, I knew that would never work. Wherever there was a deep green garden, or a camphor laurel tree, and enough empty time to just sit and be, there was always the chance that a little figure from the past might slip through in her yellow sundress, whispering my name. Reminding me of a promise.

•

When I got home, I dug out my easel, brushes and tubes of watercolour, taking them and a seat from the kitchen out onto the paved area. I set up and quickly, in the remaining light, I started wetting the paper, blocking in the dense green shadows of the cypresses down one side of the paper, and the brighter green and occasional red leaf of the camphor laurel tree. I worked quickly and stood back, examining the composition. Using a touch of black in the greens, I washed a background in and found a soft brown stain for the foreground. When this dried, I'd overlay another, darker one. But the light had gone and I left my easel and the damp painting there, going inside to make a bit more order in the stacked folders and the packed boxes until I looked at my watch and saw it was nearly eleven o'clock.

Before going to bed I took out the anonymous letter again, holding it with tweezers. There was a moment when I almost threw it out, but both my policing and my scientific training got the better of me. Instead, I copied out the words on a slip of paper and put that in my wallet, replacing the anonymous missive in its drawer.

My bedroom is at the back of the house, its window looking out over the back garden. It took me a long time to go to sleep and I kept waking, thinking I could hear someone walking around outside. Once I even got up and looked out the window. But I could see nothing except the line of tall cypresses that divided my eastern side from my neighbours.

•

Next day, Ron Herring faxed me the necessary information. I picked up the mug shot of the convicted pedophile with his dropped eyelids and compressed mouth from my in-tray and studied the details of his convictions and sentencing. Frank John Carmody, I read, fifty-one, due to be released next Wednesday after serving the minimum seven years of a ten year sentence for the killing of an eleven-year-old girl, Suzette Carter, who lived across the road from him. I remembered the case because our lab had worked on the physical evidence. I remembered that the girl's body had been flung from the roadside down a steeply wooded mountain slope miles away from anywhere and accidentally found caught in the branches of a tree by two timber workers clearing below the road. I also recalled that Carmody was described as a 'family' man, with young daughters of his own. His blank eyes stared out of the mug shot at me. Most of us have children, I thought. But when it comes to the men who murder children, it doesn't seem to make any difference that they have kids of their own.

I rang Ron Herring to thank him for his trouble. 'He's going to live with a sister at Camperdown when he gets out,' said Ron, in response to my question. 'She's his only visitor. Nice old bird, they told me, who sees him once a month. The staff at the Bay think she's a bit eccentric because she's always lecturing them on her brother's innocence.' I remembered the saying that there are no guilty people in prison. No rich people either.

'Carmody told the duty officer he doesn't want anyone to know that he's getting out,' Ron Herring was saying. I recalled the terrible stripped gashes between the legs of the other two men and found that very easy to understand. I thanked Ron, and rang off.

Then I rang Staro and asked him if he'd like to earn some honest money. It was about half standard rates, but he jumped at the chance. It's not so much the money or the work that he likes, or doing something that's a bit more legit than selling Eccies or Rowies, but I know he likes the feeling of working for me. He looks up to me. I wish he didn't, but he does.

'There's a crim,' I said, 'due to be released from the Bay in a few days. I want to keep an eye on him. And I could do with a bit of help.'

'Sure,' said Staro. 'Why do you want to watch him?' I could hear the excitement in his voice. There are a lot of people like Staro who find this sort of fringe dealing with the law irresistible. Murderers even bring themselves undone because of it. They are usually people with no power of their own and it's as if they need to rub up against those whom they perceive as having it in order to get a piece of it for themselves.

'That's confidential,' I said, and Staro was hooked.

Frank Carmody had the trifecta that had proved fatal to two

others: he was a convict, a sex offender and due for release. And if a Corrective Services officer had noticed Frank Carmody's release was coming up, someone else surely had. And that someone, as we already knew, was very handy with a knife.

Later that morning, I went into the city and spent hours going through archived newspaper files. I read up everything I could on the murdered men, Gumley and Nesbitt. I noticed that their respective sentences had caused a lot of outcry and were considered far too lenient by both journalists and letter-writers to the papers. On a hunch, I looked up the references to Frank Carmody. Sure enough, the same thing appeared in the several stories around him. In fact, as I checked further, I found that Gumley, Nesbitt, Carmody and someone called Anton Francini, whose story I didn't remember, were the four cases always trotted out whenever a story about leniency in sentencing appeared. Further checking revealed that Anton Francini had raped and killed a young girl and been sentenced to nine years with a non-parole period of five years, because he'd been drinking at the time of the killing, and was otherwise 'of good character'. While I was making a note of Carmody's details, the heading of another news item underneath the convicted men's stories caught my eye.

'*I will never forget,*' I read, '*No matter how long or how short his sentence, I will never forget. He will pay for this,*' father of murder victim Suzette Carter said today. '*And when he gets out, he wants to watch his back. Men like this aren't fit to live.*' The accompanying photograph captioned 'Peter Carter outside court yesterday' showed a stooped man in his forties. I made a note of his name and jotted down a bit more information, then stood up, feeling that at last, I was getting somewhere with this case. Here was the possible link—apart from their crimes—that connected these four men. Frank Carmody was right to be fearful. Had Peter Carter taken note of these four names and decided that their sentences weren't enough? Or someone else with a similar brief? Bob had told me that the relatives of the dead had all been checked out, but I wanted to talk to this Peter Carter myself.

I rang Bob, told him what I'd discovered, how those four names and the relatively light sentences they had scored were the basis for several newspaper articles. Then I asked him about Peter Carter.

'Carter,' he repeated after my question. 'Yes. I do remember him. We had to restrain him during the trial on a couple of occasions.'

'I want to check him out again,' I said. 'He made threats that were reported at the time of Carmody's sentencing. And I want to watch Frank Carmody. See where he goes, who he talks to. I want a surveillance team.'

'Not possible. We haven't got the manpower to keep tabs on someone like Frank Carmody. Nobody cares whether he lives or dies.'

I rang off. It had been worth a shot. And what Bob had said wasn't quite true. Someone out there seemed to care very much.

•

I drove round to Charlie's place at Little Bay after a quick phone call and found him hidden under the bonnet of his car in the driveway, shirt off, surrounded by tools. On the ground near him lay several intricate bits of gearing, a little fly-wheel, a tiny gasket and other small and delicate mechanisms. He looked pleased to see me and wiped his hands on his trousers before trying to grab me. Where I'm tall and solidly built, Charlie is narrow and whippy. All his energy goes into his brains. I pulled back from the bear hug he always tries on, and he patted my arm instead.

'What's up with the car?' I asked him as we walked into his place, passing one of my less successful watercolours of Jervis Bay.

'Buggered petrol pump,' he said. 'I just put a new one in. You can buy the little kit. It's all finished now.' As he washed and wiped his hands, I recalled the bits of machinery I'd noticed lying on the driveway.

'But what about all the bits you left out? Lying on the ground?'

Charlie shrugged. My young brother, as well as having a doctorate in psychology, was also a great bush mechanic. He could pull a car apart, put it back together, have all sorts of parts still lying around and the bloody vehicle would still go like the clappers. The minute I tried my hand at mechanical repairs, something worse happened. Charlie says it's because of my state of mind and suggests that I should examine the deeper implications of quantum physics. I shake my head when he says things like that.

'Siya's gone to her mother's place for a few days,' he offered by way of explanation as he opened the fridge and peered in. 'I can only offer you a beer or a glass of orange drink.' Charlie lives with a succession of girlfriends, none of whom seems to last more than a year or so and at the moment he was cohabiting with a wild Cypriot, Anastasia, who trained as a commando in the Cypriot army before coming to Australia. Charlie works very hard as a psychologist for the Health Commission and also takes some private clients.

I took the drink and followed my brother outside onto the back deck. Charlie bought this cottage just before Sydney prices went crazy and built the extra room and decking out the back. It was shaping up into a hot day with the humidity already sticky and sapping despite a weak nor'easter. We sat together in front of a display of pansies, gardenias, lavender, geraniums of every colour, gladioli, and fabulous tropical hibiscus. Bees buzzed around lavender banks and a huge black butterfly flapped through the air. Somewhere, I could hear a spangled drongo calling, its metallic polyphony chiming in the distance.

'What's it like, living at Lapa?' my brother asked.

'There was a white-faced heron fishing in next door's lily pond last week,' I told him.

'You and your birds,' he said. 'Is the snake man still there?'

When we were kids staying with our aunt in Sydney, we went to see the famous snake man of La Perouse and his collection of reptiles in hessian sacks. I shrugged. I didn't know.

I always liked being with Charlie. He was alive and alert, and they are two attitudes that I don't meet very often. Sometimes I'd see it in the very rare smart crim I was interrogating; I'd notice him watching and waiting, scanning me in every way to see how much I knew. Charlie notices even more than I do. I told him about my investigations into the two murders, and what I'd just learned from the newspaper archives.

'Interesting,' said Charlie. 'You think someone is waiting for them? Someone like Peter Carter?'

'I do,' I said. 'It wouldn't be hard to find out when someone's due for release. It wouldn't be hard to cultivate someone from Corrective Services. Find out the exact time and date of release. Then follow the victim to find out where he lives. Find a way to strike up a conversation. In a bar. In a shop. Maybe the killer pretends to be someone of similar interests.'

But Charlie shook his head. 'There's no time for all that cultivation,' he reminded me. 'These buggers are killed within days of their release. What you're describing takes time. Especially with men like these. Deception is their game. They're paranoid about discovery. About who they take into their confidence.'

Charlie was right and I told him so. 'We've learned so much more about aberrant sex in the last ten or fifteen years,' I said to him.

'Now you're getting closer to my territory,' said Charlie. 'But,' he added, 'people don't go wandering about in those dark places late at night unless there's a reason.'

'A trap,' I said to my brother. 'He must lure them into a trap.' I was starting to feel the buzz of progress, of getting a sense of the pattern, the means and the way the killer might think.

'What sort of trap?' said Charlie.

Ideas started racing around in my head. I turned to Charlie. 'I don't know. This third guy's going to be really cautious,' I said. 'He knows what happened to the others. And not only because of that. There've been a couple of recent cases of pedophiles being murdered in their homes by erstwhile victims. This third guy's going to be very, very careful where he goes and who he meets.'

I got up and went to the edge of the timber deck. I could hear the *zissing* of wrens. I surveyed the garden, noting the tomatoes ripening on their vines and a wandering cucurbit of some sort waving its huge leaves up and over the back fence. I thought of the vegetable garden in our childhood home and the scarecrow wearing Mum's old purple and blue dress and hat. Scare anything away, that thing would. I remembered the day I'd found her in that same dress, smashing everything in the kitchen cupboards because Dad had thrown out all her supplies and she couldn't find a drink anywhere. I'd run away and hidden down the backyard in the shed.

'I drove up and visited Dad yesterday,' Charlie said, somehow patching into my thoughts like he can. I grunted. Our father still lived in the self-contained quarters he'd built for himself at the back of the big old house in Springbrook where we'd all grown up, while the house itself was rented out. 'He said it's a while since he's seen you. He's given me a whole box of Mum's stuff. You should have it. You're the oldest.' He indicated a carton by the doorway near the kitchen. 'There might be interesting family papers.'

'Great,' I said. 'Just what I need.'

Charlie knew very well I never went near the place. I hated going back there, to that house. Even though it looked very different now, it was still the same place, the same street, the same road of my memory. I had enough trouble keeping away from the past without going back to the very place where it would jump out and hijack me. 'And right now,' I added, glancing at the carton, 'I don't need another box of paper to sort through.'

'I know how you feel about going back there,' Charlie said, getting up and leaning over the railing, grabbing at a marguerite daisy that was just out of reach. 'But you *have* to go back,' he said after a pause. 'You *know* you have to some day.'

My breath caught at the back of my throat. The very idea of returning to that place horrified me.

'You look like shit,' he remarked, noticing my expression. I thanked him for his observation and almost told him about the anonymous letter I'd received. It would have been a relief to debrief with my brother. 'One day,' Charlie was saying, 'you're going to have to look at a number of things.' Then he immediately raised his two hands in mock surrender. 'I know, I know,' he said. 'It's not my business, not my life. But I happen to love Greg and I can see what all this is doing to him. And I don't only mean the bust-up. Or what happened with Jacinta.'

'Greg wants to come and live with me,' I said finally.

'Let him,' said Charlie, 'if that's what he wants. He'll be eighteen next year. He needs you now.' Charlie's tone was very serious. 'And I'm not saying that because of the way things are between me and Genevieve,' he added. Genevieve couldn't stand Charlie and they'd had a terrible fight some years ago. But Charlie has always had the capacity to put personal issues aside when discussing any topic or making a decision. He has the sort of mind that sees the big picture and can override his own feelings. No wonder my wife dislikes him so much with his detached way of seeing things—the opposite of her need to take everything personally. It's an enviable trait.

'Look,' said my little brother, 'Genevieve hates you and she's going to take you to the cleaners whether you're a bastard or not. Greg coming to live with you can't make her any worse.'

As usual, Charlie had homed straight in on a large part of my rather badly hidden agenda. I felt exhausted by Genevieve's grievances and wanted it all over.

'I don't want to do anything that'll stir her up. I don't want to have to deal with all that.'

'Why?' asked my brother in his reasonable way. 'What are you scared of? All she can do is yell.'

'You are a rational and reasonable person,' I said. 'Genevieve is not. Her discontent was always a problem. Now it's changed to hatred. And I can feel it coming at me whenever I'm with her. I get the feeling she only wants me back so she can punish me. I know she blames me because Jacinta was the same age—'

I couldn't say any more, but Charlie picked it up straight away and continued with the words I couldn't utter. '—Because,' he said, continuing my thoughts, 'Jacinta was the same age as Rosie was when *she* disappeared.'

There was a short silence filled with the twittering of a bulbul in the garden. 'Those sorts of patterns repeat in the next generation if they're not examined,' Charlie said, not addressing me, but talking to the garden. 'It's not anybody's fault. It's just the way things go.'

I couldn't say anything about that. I'm really just a chemist. The stuff I deal with is solid matter. It might be microscopic, but it's there, in front of me, waiting to be found, fixed on a slide, or pinned in a fume cupboard. The stuff Charlie talks about, even though his very elegant doctorate was well received, is a mesh of metaphors and inferences—coincidences, I call them—that disappear like mist when I try to examine them scientifically.

We went indoors and Charlie made me a coffee in his flash new Italian espresso machine while he considered my question.

'I think she left because Genevieve was so hostile towards her,' Charlie finally said.

I knew what he meant. 'I never understood it,' I said. 'Why would a mother be constantly criticising her own daughter?'

Charlie shrugged. 'That happens to lots of kids,' he said, 'but every kid's reaction is different. Some just withdraw. Others pretend to comply. Some kids rebel against it. Jacinta couldn't endure it.' The conversation was getting too close and personal for me and I could feel the discomfort tightening.

'Another character mightn't have been so affected,' Charlie was saying. 'Jass was super-sensitive. Something she said to me once indicated she felt she couldn't talk to either of you.' Charlie's tone was neutral—just a professional observing something. Charlie likes to talk about issues that I find almost impossible to articulate.

'But she could've rung me,' I said. 'Any time.' As soon as I heard my own words, I realised how pathetic they sounded. Charlie frowned at me.

'It doesn't work like that, John,' he said, perching himself on the counter. 'Then there was the whole business around Rosie. And Genevieve's policy about that. All the silence.' The way Charlie can talk of Rosie in that airy way makes me feel angry. As far as he's concerned, she's like some dream figure, or a character from a novel or a play. But he was a baby and never knew her. I quelled the irritation I felt and remembered that Genevieve's policy meant that neither of my kids even knew we'd had a sister, let alone what had become of her, until they were nearly adolescents themselves. And I myself found her very hard to talk about. Sometimes it seemed that I was the only person in the world who cared about her, who remembered her.

I stood up and walked out and down the steps into the garden. I heard him behind me and we wandered about in that weird silence that surrounds people who deliberately *aren't* talking about something that's an issue between them. I made an effort to remove both Jacinta and Rosie from my mind by concentrating on the investigation leads that I'd just gathered from the newspaper archives. I could hear music coming from the radio in the lounge room behind us. I was standing in front of some hanging baskets, throwing down the last of the coffee when the music stopped and I heard her. I swear my arm froze in mid air and I could not lower my cup. There it was again, that pinot noir voice, deep and husky, with the tremulous grainy underlay and the soft richness '... played by Glenn Gould,' she was announcing, 'on a digital remastering of the original Polygram recording.'

'What is it?' I asked, hurrying back up the steps and into the lounge room.

'A Bach prelude,' said Charlie, who had followed me indoors.

'I mean the station,' I snapped. 'What station are you on?' I was already over there, peering at the radio, unable to see where it was tuned. Charlie came over to join me, frowning. He put his glasses on and glanced at the radio.

'2LSM,' he said, straightening. 'Why?'

'Local?'

'Yes.'

While Charlie looked on with great curiosity, I found the phone number and rang the station. It didn't take me long to find out what I wanted to know. Pretending great interest in the content of the program, I listened while the woman on the other end of the line, as well as explaining that it was a listener-supported radio station, told me more than I wanted to know about the weekly Bach program I'd been listening to. With careful questioning, I discovered that the presenter, Iona Seymour, normally did the program live, but that this one was taped because Iona's car had been out of action for some days. The woman I spoke to assured me that the music Iona had selected was representative of her usual taste and then pressed me to become a subscriber. Within a short while, I was all signed up and ready to go.

'But there's something about a live presentation...' I added.

'Indeed,' said the woman. 'And we prefer that as a rule. Iona will be back from ten to eleven presenting her program again on Friday. Sometimes it can't be managed and then she tapes it.'

The minute I got off that call, I rang Bob. He wasn't in but I left a message asking him to check the name 'Iona Seymour' on police records.

Charlie stared at me while I made the two calls. 'What are you up to now?' he asked.

'A woman,' I said, 'rang the police anonymously with a tip-off about Jacinta. I heard the tape. That was her voice just then.'

'That presenter?'

'I'd swear to it.'

And in a few minutes, I'd told Charlie the whole story. Now I had a name and that's really all an investigator needs to get started.

'Nice bit of synchronicity,' he said. 'It happens.' He turned his head away for a few moments, busying himself with finishing his drink. When he turned my way again, I was surprised to see that he was gazing intently into my eyes.

'A body in uniform motion,' he said, 'will remain in uniform motion until it is acted upon by a force.'

I wondered why he was quoting the first law of motion at me and asked him. My brother was silent a while.

'What's it going to take to make you see—' he finally started to say but I quickly interrupted him.

'If you're going to give me advice about how I should be running my life,' I said, 'or tell me that I should see a counsellor or something like that, just don't.'

I could feel things stirring in my guts, old, heartbroken things, and I wanted to be out of there. Charlie shrugged, put his cup down and, seeing that I was already walking towards the door, he came with me. I felt his arm gently around my shoulder. 'Okay,' he said, 'It was just a suggestion.' I dismissed it with an impatient wave. 'And just be aware that you've ended up living at the back of a big house now, just like him.'

There was nothing I could say to this so I thanked him and hurried to my car.

'Hey!' I heard Charlie calling out after me as I climbed in. I stopped and turned, wondering what he wanted. As soon as I saw him, my heart sank. He was hurrying over, carrying the carton that I'd seen by the door. Our mother's stuff. 'Don't forget this.'

'Charlie, I don't need another carton of paper.' Especially this one, I thought.

'You're the oldest. You must.' He was stowing it on the back seat as he spoke. 'Besides,' he added, slamming the door, 'you've got to do something.' He came round and stood at my window. 'Can't you see what you're doing? You're hurting everyone around you. I've never been a fan of Genevieve, but I've got to tell you I don't blame her for having an affair. And I see why Jacinta had to run away. And it wasn't just because her mother's impossible either.' I stood there, stunned by what he was saying. 'Either let go of Rosie absolutely—do something...I don't know...bury a photograph or something. Finish it. Say goodbye and walk away— *or* devote your life to tracking the truth. Go back over the records. Reopen the case. Do it! Because the way you're living now is like you're already a ghost, too. Is that how you want to live?'

As I drove away I realised Charlie was the second person in a matter of days to tell me that I had to 'do something' about the past. I wanted to yell at him, and at Genevieve, too: 'What is this something I'm supposed to do—dig up the past and all its anguish? Reopen old wounds? Will it change the fact that our mother was a crazy alcoholic? That our father was the way he was? Can it change the events of that night in November '75 when Rosie disappeared? Will it bring back Jacinta? I took a corner too fast and realised I had to concentrate. I came up through the gears and settled into driving home. The past is a country I had no desire to revisit. And yet, somehow I understood what my brother was telling me. There's an old saying a police sergeant once used with us: 'Piss, or get off the pot.' Charlie was right. One way or another, I had to make a decision about Rosie—either reopen the case and throw myself into it one hundred per cent, or forever let her go.

FOUR

The drive south to Canberra next day gave me plenty of thinking time. When I got to Forensic Services, I gave the bagged anonymous letter to Sarah Witticombe, our in-house document examiner. Nothing misses Sarah's clear eyes.

'I'll do a full report for you,' she said, standing near the door of her bright examination room, her white coat spotless, her skin polished. 'I can tell you what sort of paper it was written on, what sort of laser jet printer printed it, where the envelope came from.' She turned the letter over carefully in her gloved fingers. 'I can't tell from looking if it's a "sticky" or a "licky" stamp, but we might get some saliva from that. Looks like a press-seal envelope.' She sounded dejected. 'But we still might get something trapped in the adhesive.'

I thanked her and walked down the hall, confident that soon I'd know where it had been posted, and that Sarah would pass it on to be tested for any DNA material she might find. Eventually she would tell me every possible fact about that letter and its envelope. Except what I really wanted to know: the name of the person who wrote it. Until I had the culprit and we could say 'perfect match', which we never do anyway, all I could do would be to file her report.

•

In the afternoon I drove over to Alix's townhouse, pressing the doorbell, taking in the familiar scents of *eucalyptus nicholii* and its spicy fragrance, hearing the bees in the bottlebrush. When the door opened, I was about to say something flirtatious until I saw the stranger behind the mesh screen. 'I'm a friend of—' I began, but was rudely interrupted.

'I know who you are,' she said. 'Alix deserves better than that.' A plump young woman with her hair wrapped up in a towel and a brilliant silky robe tightly held together scowled at me.

'I beg your pardon?' I said, puzzled at her animosity. 'I've been trying to ring but there's been no answer.'

'And there won't be,' said the young woman, wrapping her dressing gown tighter around herself. I smelled soap, powder and perfume. 'She's had to move in with someone else. She couldn't keep up with the rent here because she lost her job.' She scowled harder at me as if somehow I'd sacked the girl myself.

'Do you have her new address?' I asked.

She didn't move. I could see her that she was thinking overtime, trying to decide what to do. Finally she disappeared out of sight, returning with a piece of paper. The scowl was still there, too. 'Here's the phone number,' she said. 'I suppose you can have that.'

'We are...' I started to say then changed it to, 'We were quite close friends. I've lost touch with her because I've moved, too.'

The young woman's scowl eased a little. 'I thought you were just being a typical male.'

'And what's that?' I couldn't resist asking.

Without another word, she opened the screen door just enough to give me the piece of paper in her hand. Inside the house, the phone rang. The scowler glared at me again then closed both doors vigorously. As soon as I was in the car I tried the number. It rang out.

•

Friday morning found me back in North Sydney in the enclosed area surrounding FM Radio 2LSM at about ten to eleven, listening to Iona Seymour's program. I was parked in an area about the size of two tennis courts, shaded by a couple of big Moreton Bay figs. To me, what Iona Seymour was playing sounded a bit like merry-go-round music, punctuated as it was by the high-pitched song of the fig birds nearby. But every now and then, the harpsichord would fade out and the burgundy voice would point up something of interest before allowing the music to demonstrate.

One of the things I enjoy doing is matching people to vehicles and once her program was finished, I watched the people in the carpark coming and going, getting out of their cars, or getting into them. There was always the chance that she'd stay on and do some work at the station, but I had nothing to race back to. Nesbitt and Gumley were dead and there was nothing doing on Frank Carmody until his release. I surveyed the cars once again, trying to match the voice with the means of transport. I tossed out the black Saab, two BMWs, several Japanese cars, a large utility and a sprinkling of Commodores. I wondered what my blue station wagon said about me as I got out of it and walked around, tossing up between a fifteen-year-old dark blue Merc 280 and a white Jag. I adopted the air of an expert, walking around the Merc in what I hoped looked like an admiring manner, leaning close to examine the interior. I was right—on the passenger seat I spotted several envelopes and could read her name and an address in Annandale quite clearly. I didn't have to make a note of it. Something told me I would never forget it. Then I looked up. A woman had come through the automatic doors of the radio station and was walking down the steps towards the carpark. Quickly and casually I walked back to my car. I couldn't explain the surge of excitement that pulsed through my body when I saw her. I knew immediately that she was Iona Seymour.

I remembered it from stake-outs, this current that hums between the hunted and the hunter. People could come and go and even though I couldn't see them properly, I'd know they weren't the target. Then along would come another figure and I'd suddenly sit up straight, sensing, yes, this is the one. I can't explain it, but after many years, a cop develops extra senses around this sort of thing. Quite possibly there's something in quantum physics to account for it and that notion would certainly delight Charlie. Does the target's nervous intention meet up with the investigator's determination and does this create some quark-spinning turnaround where the observer becomes the observed? Even though I'd never give Charlie the satisfaction of saying so, I think about these possibilities more than he gives me credit for.

Inside my car I made myself as invisible as possible and watched the woman who was walking towards the old Merc, a briefcase in her hand, frowning despite the sunglasses. She was tall, with an athletic build, dark hair, pale face and red jacket, just as I'd imagined. Then something happened. Just as she stooped slightly to put her key in the lock, she raised her head to look over the top of her car and our eyes met. I dropped my gaze and turned a page of the newspaper I was pretending to read.

By the time I dared peer over the top of page, she was reversing the Mercedes, and driving out of the carpark. I noted the rego number and started to follow her. I couldn't let her go just now. She had claimed to know something about my daughter, and I was determined to speak to her.

The big old Merc was easy to follow, even in Friday's heavy traffic. We drove from North Sydney back into the city and she took the Macquarie Street exit. In Macquarie Street she slowed down and I could see she was looking for somewhere to park. Someone ahead of her vacated a spot and I overtook her as she backed in. I looked around for somewhere myself but couldn't find anything and made a highly illegal U-turn, coming back to pass her. She was sitting with her hands over her face, slumped over the wheel. I imagined I could see the sobs shaking her shoulders. A car pulled out ahead of me and I darted into the vacant spot, causing the car on my back bumper to lean on the horn. I made a mollifying sign to him and while I straightened up, I could see the red jacket getting out of the Merc in my rear vision mirror. She started to walk south towards College Street. I desperately scratched around looking for small change for the meter and by the time I'd found it, she had walked past the barracks and was now waiting to cross the road to St Mary's. I sprinted down the street just in time to see her mount the stairs on the western side of the cathedral and vanish through the heavy doors.

I crossed the road, raced up the steps and pushed open the doors, peering around in the dim interior. For a moment, I couldn't see a thing and I wondered why it is that the house of our God is always so dark.

People pressed around me in the gloom, some with cameras round their necks, others wandering, then pausing to look at the intricate stained glass windows and the various shrines and icons. I stood there, wondering if she was really smart and, knowing she was being followed, had taken counter-surveillance steps and was already disappearing out of another door. I felt a disproportionate wave of desolation, but then I saw her tall figure on the left-hand side of the raised and fenced-off sanctuary with its interlocking polished brass shamrocks. A large copy of a Byzantine icon hung there, with a slotted wooden box in front of it. I knew that what was written in faded typescript next to the box was an invitation to post prayers and requests for divine favours within for the Virgin's heavenly lobbying. I have to admit it's a beautiful image of the Madonna and Infant known to the faithful as 'Our Lady of Perpetual Help' and I remembered it from my very early school days with the Sisters of Show No Mercy.

Iona Seymour was now kneeling in front of this, oblivious to the movements around her as people brushed past and Japanese tourists took flashlight photographs. She seemed to have something in her hand and for a moment, I thought she was about to post a prayer. But instead, she stood up, blessed herself as the devout do, and hurried down past the sanctuary to a roped-off area at the northern end. I followed, trying to stroll casually just like the other tourists. The sign hanging on the red rope informed me that the area set aside was for private devotions only and cameras were forbidden. I had been here before on occasions with Charlie when he was doing his PhD and collecting images of mothers and sons. I saw Iona Seymour seating herself in front of a small chapel. As I drew nearer, I saw that there were two other altars on each side, but only the central one had the winking red sanctuary lamp, symbol of the presence of the mystery.

I sat in one of the pews behind and to one side of the woman. I felt awkward there, although the iconography was familiar from the territory of my childhood. In the stained glass above this private sanctuary, the Blessed Virgin was being crowned in heaven. I was wondering what I was doing there, and was just about to leave when Iona Seymour stood up, genuflected and started walking back the way we'd both come. I bowed my head as if in prayer and waited as she passed by me, feeling the movement of air as she moved, listening to her footsteps echoing on the marble floor. Then I slid out of my pew and followed at a discreet distance. As she approached the entrance we'd both used, she paused and, instead of going towards the heavy doors, she stopped in front of a huge marble statue. I stopped in my tracks when I saw what she was doing. The marble in question is a huge copy of Michelangelo's *'Pietà'*, the powerful image of the desolate Virgin holding the dead weight of her son's corpse across her knees. The whole massive work is supported by a huge block of stone, and it was into a tiny gap between the bottom of the weighty sculpture and the pedestal that formed its base that Iona Seymour, unnoticed by anyone but me, was pushing something small. Then she looked around and hurried away, her tall figure pressing against the heavy doors to open them.

I let her go, turning my attention to whatever it was that she'd hidden at the base of the statue. My breathing, already heightened by the intrigue of following this unknown woman, became even faster. With practised unconcern, I wandered over towards the sculpture, pretending great interest in its polished surfaces. People milled around behind me, and I realised that there was no need for any pantomime. I could just see something sticking out from under the statue where it rested on its sandstone base. Casually, I dropped my hand, took the corner of it with my fingers and quickly drew it out. It was a wedge of folded paper. I palmed it smartly into my pocket. Amphetamines come packed like that, and sometimes small deals of coke, except this packet was narrower than the usual dealers' folds I'd handled over the years. I walked outside, blinking in the sudden brilliance of Sydney summer sunlight. Indian mynahs screeched on the steps, pecking at rubbish. Bach preludes, drug drops, the pinot noir voice and the hidden eyes of a dark woman swirled around in my mind as I tried to second-guess what she'd hidden under the *Pietà*. Carefully, I moved away from the people walking in and out of the cathedral and out of the breeze to open the folded paper. Almost as soon as I'd done it, I regretted it, feeling ashamed of my intrusion. But I couldn't stop there. I had seen what was on it and something happened again. In the same way that our eyes had connected over the top of her car, Iona Seymour and I were inexorably drawn together. I had now become intimate with this woman. I knew things about her that I shouldn't know. That no one should know unless confided in by a trusted friend. I refolded the small square of paper, and tucked it into my inside coat pocket.

I ran down the steps and back to my car. My meter had expired and a parking fine was already tucked behind the windscreen wipers. I swore as I ripped it off my car and shoved it in the glovebox, noticing the large amount. But the strange exhilaration I was feeling soon established itself as the dominant mood and I drove away, feeling something like an adolescent boy when he first falls in love, holding two things in my mind: the contents of the little message in my pocket, and the memory of her address from the envelope on the passenger seat of the dark blue Mercedes.

Number 293 Reiby Street, Annandale, was a dramatic old stone two-storeyed house, hidden under thick Boston ivy and complete with leadlights, a tower and other neo-Gothic follies. The odd architecture, the overgrowth and the air of dereliction, put me in mind of Edgar Allen Poe's dark tale 'The Fall of the House of Usher'. I could see Iona Seymour's car parked in front of a tumbledown car shed down the back, at the end of an overgrown driveway. I felt a deep sense of satisfaction that I'd run her to her lair and that I had something very personal of hers in my possession. I put my hand in my pocket to touch the folded paper and the strange sense that the woman was mine grew stronger. Now I had to decide how I was going to approach her and whether it would be in my official capacity, or whether I might be better served by observing her habits and routines for a while and then setting up a 'spontaneous' meeting somewhere likely. I've learned to defer decisions rather than make them without due consideration, so I decided to sleep on it and drove home.

•

On Sunday afternoon, Chris Hayden went round to Iona Seymour's house and suggested that he had reason to believe she'd made two anonymous phone calls to the police concerning missing teenager Jacinta McCain. She denied all knowledge of any such call. When I heard that, I was very pleased I'd hung back.

'What impression did you get of her?' I asked him on the phone.

'She was very nervous,' said Chris. 'Rattled.'

'More rattled,' I asked, 'than you'd expect, given the circumstances of a uniformed police officer asking her questions?' I could hear the silence on the line while Chris considered my question and my fingers closed round Iona's little piece of paper in my pocket.

'I could practically read "how the hell did you find me?" in the way she was looking at me. Deadset the woman was lying.'

We talked a little longer and when Chris hung up, I considered my next step. Sure, I could come the heavy cop with her, tell her that we had her on tape and that we could prove it was her voice. But Iona Seymour had done nothing illegal—in fact, she had been trying to be helpful in an anonymous way, and if I went down that road, I'd alienate her completely. Far better, I thought, to hasten slowly, and discover everything she might know.

I pulled out the piece of paper and opened it again, reading words no human eye was ever meant to see, *Please help me*, I read, betraying her deep secret as I did so. *Please help me with this terrible business.*

'I reckoned she was lying,' Chris had said just before he hung up, 'as if her life depended on it.'

And now I was thinking, maybe it does.

•

Three days later, child-killer Frank Carmody was released from Long Bay and driven by his sister to her place at Camperdown. Ron Herring from Corrective Services had given me the tip so I was already waiting for them, my car parked discreetly opposite and up the road a bit from the address when they arrived in Miss Carmody's Festiva. I'd already checked round the back of the property to see if there was another exit to the small terrace, in a row of eight similar houses, and found that a stout metal fence ran along the back boundary of the Carmody residence and three others. Unless he jumped the fence, and there seemed to be no reason for him to do that, there was no other way in or out of the place.

I watched Carmody go inside with his sister, a plump short woman in a striped skirt. He was in his fifties with thin, greying hair and a slight stoop, carrying an army kitbag. In his creased white shirt and dark trousers, he could have been a harmless accounts clerk coming home from work, and almost as soon as the door on the one-storey terrace had closed loudly, I rang Staro.

'I want you to keep an eye on Carmody,' I told him, giving him the address. 'Midnight till dawn patrol is the crucial shift.' I didn't tell him I'd be checking on him from time to time. No way I'd trust Staro to do a good job of anything and lately I'd rather be out and about in the hours of darkness than sleeplessly tossing in my bed. But it's always helpful to have an extra body on the job, even if that was only Staro.

'Sure,' said Staro, 'I like working normal hours. Night fishing. Rock-spider bait to catch the shark.'

I looked at the time. It was too early for lunch although I was feeling hungry. Beside me on the passenger seat, I'd packed an expanding file full of papers and folders from my recent move that I planned to sort through during the hours of idle surveillance. I heard a door slam and looked up to see Carmody coming out of number 117. But I didn't even need to start the car because he was only going down the street to the newsagent, where he bought a newspaper, then he crossed the road, went to the TAB, finally going home again after buying some beer on the way back. Again, he had to slam the door noisily to get it to close. I stared at the closed door for a long time and then turned my attention to the expanding file.

I pulled out the first folder. I'd started reading it before I could stop myself to find it was my own statement from a November night in 1975. I put the badly typed papers down and turned away, staring at Frank Carmody's closed door. I was sitting here, watching the house of a convicted child-killer all because of the events of that night. I'd made a vow to find out what happened to my sister, to track down whoever had taken her. And when I was fifteen I'd had no doubt that I would succeed. For a long time, I even thought I'd find Rosie, too, and imagining our reunion as I freed her from her captor was an image that had sustained me through those dreadful days. But it faded. Nevertheless, Rosie was the reason I'd joined the New South Wales police in 1980, in the youthful belief that if I became a detective, I'd be able to solve my sister's disappearance and bring the perpetrator to justice. It was also because of Rosie that I'd spent several years in the Child Sexual Offences Squad, becoming aware of the sorts of men that targeted kids for sexual use. I wanted to examine the physical evidence surrounding Rosie's disappearance myself, with my own hands and eyes, so I'd taken up part-time study and eventually graduated in Science. Even though the evidence was old and stale, I'd gone over and over it. It was all recorded in various files and folders and I'd transferred much of it to my computer. And even though I knew it was completely unreasonable, I still found myself looking through the old files on occasion, just in case there was some thing, the *one* thing, that would make all the difference.

Rosie's abduction had affected Charlie, too, even though he'd been only a baby when it happened. Although he can barely remember her, believing that his memories are mostly reconstructed from photographs and my recollections, his life, too, has been shaped by that event. When Jacinta ran away eighteen months ago, he didn't say anything, but I knew what he was thinking. That was when he changed his thesis to a wider investigation into the patterns and repetitions that occur in families. Like Charlie, and despite my hasty attribution of coincidence, I couldn't help wondering, too, in what way the loss of our sister might have echoed through to the next generation. And I was certainly a bit shaken by Charlie pointing out that I, too, was living at the back of a big old house now, just like our father. I shivered. Since that summer night in '75 and because of it, my life had followed a certain trajectory so that now, on this sunny afternoon a quarter of a century after the event, here I was, sitting off the house of another child-taker.

And there was something else. I knew why Rosie had been outside on the roadway on that evening twenty-five years ago, and not playing with me down the backyard like she normally did. Something that Charlie, for all his brilliant insights into human behaviour, doesn't know. So it makes it all the more difficult for me to hear the things that he says because the parallels between Rosie's loss and Jacinta's disappearance are even greater than he suspects.

A feeling like nausea welled up from my guts to my head, and I got out of the car, going round the back, pretending to get something out of the boot, because the pressure was building up and I needed to move. Please God, I was praying, don't let Jacinta be dead, too.

I'd been buoyed up by the recent tip-off, even if it had fizzled out. And I was determined to question Iona Seymour as to what had made her call the police. People don't do things without reasons, even if those reasons are difficult for an observer to understand.

I walked down the street, constantly looking back over my shoulder to make sure all was quiet at number 117, and bought myself a chicken sandwich and a tin of fizzy drink.

I worked away through the boring hours sorting out the

contents of the file and putting all the material relating to my lost sister in a large envelope. I knew I had other records concerning her in other boxes at La Parouse and I was determined to put it all in order again. Moving from the marital home hadn't been a very organised retreat: I'd thrown things together. The information on Jacinta was more sparse and I separated that out as well. I sat there a moment, looking at the two files. My memories of Rosie were strong and vivid, but I wondered how much of that was because of constant reworking, like the too brilliant colours sometimes used to touch up the works of old masters. Then I thought about my daughter Jacinta and remembered how she would climb up onto my lap when she was tiny and put her arms around my neck, looking deep into my eyes as if she could find something there she needed. It had always made me uneasy, because I didn't know what it was, and I remembered how I'd bear it for a while, then gently undo her arms and put her down beside me. Even then, she wanted something from me that I didn't understand. Did she do the same with her mother, I wondered, and did she find the same gentle rejection? I closed my eyes against the pain of recreating something that could only hurt me. I tried making plans for my future, but couldn't get anywhere with them. I opened my eyes again and stared at the closed front door of number 117. I had to confess I didn't really care whether Frank Carmody lived or died. I got out of the car and stood there in the noisy road staring at the tiny terrace house. Phillip Street, Camperdown, is so narrow that cars can barely pass in opposite directions. That was why I didn't realise Staro had arrived on the scene until he almost ran over me. I showed him the house and Carmody's photograph.

'He looks like my grandad,' said Staro.

'Just be thankful he's not,' I said. 'You'd probably be even more twisted than you already are.' Staro seemed to take the remark in good humour. 'The only other person living there is his sister,' I continued, taking the photo back and describing the stout woman in as much detail as I could remember. 'Just keep on him,' I said, 'especially if he goes out tonight.'

Staro looked anxiously around and lowered his voice. 'There's really no wolf-man out there,' he whispered, 'is there?'

He was just like a kid, I thought, and wondered if I was

dragging him into something way over his head. Then I remembered where Staro had come from, what he'd endured and survived. I shook my head. 'I promise there's no wolf-man.' But that was hardly a comfort, I reasoned. 'That doesn't mean it's any less dangerous than it is,' I said. 'You understand that?'

Staro nodded. I took a closer look at him. 'You're different,' I said to him, noticing something I couldn't quite put my finger on. His features seemed sharper somehow, and he was edgier, more fidgety. He pulled out a packet of cigarettes and offered me one automatically. I declined, and Staro lit up with trembling fingers.

'I'm straight. This is the only drug I'm using,' he said, waving his cigarette at me. 'And I haven't been straight this time of day since I don't know when.'

'When you say "straight", Staro, what exactly do you mean?' I said.

Staro looked hurt. 'What anyone means,' he said. 'That I'm not using.' He looked at the cigarette. 'Apart from nicotine.'

'But methadone—,' I started to say.

'I'm off that, too,' Staro said. 'I want to come back to life.'

'Are you getting some support?' I asked. 'A counsellor? Some sort of help?'

Staro shook his head. 'Don't need it,' he said. 'I can do this. I've got the willpower.'

'Staro, Staro,' I said, 'willpower won't work. Addiction is not amenable to willpower. You need to come at it quite another way.' I meant by way of surrender but I didn't think Staro or indeed most of the world's population outside Twelve Step Fellowships would've had a clue what I meant.

He nodded vigorously. 'You're right, you're right,' he said.

I surprised myself by patting him on the shoulder as I got back into my car. 'If you're serious about this,' I said, 'you know you can't drink either? Or use pills.'

Staro raised his almost invisible eyebrows at this. 'I'm serious about this. I know that I can't switch the witch for the bitch.'

His terminology gave it away. 'You're going to NA?' I said, astounded.

Staro nodded, fiddling the cigarette between his fingers. 'The meetings help a lot, but I keep getting these memories,' he said.

'They just jump out at me. Things I want to forget. The reason why I used drugs in the first place.'

I knew what he meant. 'That'll happen,' I said. 'Have you got a sponsor?'

'There's a bloke there who hasn't been using anything for fifteen years,' said Staro, holding up his cigarette. 'Not even these. He said I could ring him when I needed to talk.'

I remembered how difficult it had been for me to let down the defensiveness that had become second nature. Staro looked at me with his bruised, grieving eyes.

'You don't think I can do it, do you.'

'I was just thinking how hard it is to be straight and honest with another person,' I said.

'But you did it,' he continued. 'I was talking to a bloke who used to know you in the old days. He goes to both fellowships. Ross from Randwick.'

I nodded. I remembered Ross from Randwick.

'Yes,' I said, 'I did it. But I only had one drug to deal with, not three.' I paused a moment before starting up the ignition. 'Take it easy, Staro,' I said. 'You can give me a ring if you can't get hold of anyone else.' His whole face lifted and lightened at that and I wondered for a minute if I'd made a serious error of judgment, changing up a gear from a purely business relationship to something more.

'It's the things I'm remembering,' he said. 'Things I've done. Things been done to me.'

I nodded. I knew what he was talking about it and he knew I knew.

'That happens,' I said, 'as the anaesthetic wears off. Talk to someone about it.' I waved goodbye and drove home.

•

It was a beautiful summer evening and the drive back to my new home was a pleasure, with the sun warm on the sandstone walls of Long Bay and the water cerulean blue off Congwong Beach. I often had moments where I felt enormous gratitude that I was clean and sober and this was one of them. Sobriety had given me back my edge, my sight and clarity. In most areas. Grey-white piles of fair weather cumulus lined the horizon and the sliver of a new moon rose in the east. Wattlebirds swooped among the scrub and clucked and chimed as I looked in the mailbox, but there was nothing much today, just some toy shop announcing a pre-Christmas sale and something from the council. I screwed up the flyer and threw it into the rubbish bin, opening the other envelope as I walked in.

I couldn't quite take it in at first. Les O'Neil from the council had pleasure in informing me that I'd won second prize in the local section of the art competition and this letter was my invitation to the official opening next week where I would receive my certificate and a cheque for $150. For a few moments I was absurdly pleased with myself and I stuck the letter up on the fridge where I could see it. I wanted to ring and tell Charlie, but felt too self-conscious about making such a boast. It was the first win I'd had in a long, long time.

With a lighter energy, I turned back to the job in hand, and put the two files, my lost sister's and Jacinta's, in the bottom of the built-in wardrobe in my little bedroom, picked up another box piled high with paper, cleared a spot at the table in the main room, and made a start on it. On the very top was a large folder containing glossy black and white police photographs of the white wooden railings that used to run alongside the roadway in Springbrook when we were kids. I knew these long shots and close-ups off by heart: the scraped marks on the posts, incomprehensible to a casual observer, were as clear to me as if I'd seen the whole incident. I hadn't looked at them in many years. I studied the first one again. It showed gouge marks on a wooden railing where the metal badge on the fender of a car had collided violently with the timber of the railing—the gouge marks left by the suspect vehicle when it skidded and struck the railings of the fence. The car had then reversed into a tree on the rear passenger side and accelerated away. Rosie had been snatched off the street in front of our house by 'a person or persons unknown'. Mrs Bower, the vicar's wife, had run from the rectory on the corner of the T-junction at one end of our street when she'd heard the crash. It had all been too fast for her, she said in her witness statement, and she hadn't seen anything. What *was* known was the fact that the height of the fenders back and front and the marks they had both left on the white fence and on the tree behind, were consistent with the suspect vehicle being a 1967 or '68 Holden sedan. We knew for a fact that it was tan and white, with some sort of badge on the back fender and at least one decorative stud in the shape of a chrome-plated, five-pointed star probably fixed to the front fender. We knew this because the Crime Scene police found the fat silver star in the dirt on the roadway among the scattered paint flakes. It was likely to be one of several decorating the chrome.

Because of the contents of all these folders and manila envelopes, I'd come to know a great deal more about that Holden sedan. The paint flakes gave us more information: they told us that the vehicle had undergone several changes of colour from the time it had come off the assembly line. Like the levels of an archeological dig, microscopic examination of the paint layers gave us the history of the car's colour changes. Starting off with one of Holden's standard colours of those years—a pale blue enamel—it had later been spray-painted a dark blue and only after that did it acquire the two-toned tan and white of the top coat. In spite of a massive police search, that car was never found. It simply vanished, together with my sister, off the face of the earth.

I pulled out another of the photographs showing a flashlight photo of the tree the car had backed into, with a long indentation cutting transversely across its trunk, revealing splintered, sappy wood. In a smaller manila envelope were the earlier drawings I'd made from the photographs, showing possible interpretations of the marks left on the tree by the shield-shaped badge. I'd spent a long time trying to match this and had concluded that it was most likely a car rally badge. Car clubs and rally clubs are still popular and there must have been hundreds of different badges around in the 'seventies. These days, windscreen stickers are used instead. In the early days when I was first examining this physical evidence, I used to look at that star as if it were the mark of the Beast itself because I knew it came from *that* car, and in that car at the time of impact was my beautiful terrified little sister. I used to hold the star in the palm of my hand and close my eyes like I'd heard psychics did, willing myself to know where the car was now, where Rosie was. But all I ever saw was the darkness of my own failure.

Under my sketches were photographs of the tyre marks left near the roadside as well as pictures of the plaster casts made up from their indentations. Tyre marks are like fingerprints. Every little imperfection in the manufacturing process, every notch or cut created by usage, leaves a distinctive mark in the rubber, and a corresponding imprint in soft soil. No tyre, even those from the same batch, is exactly the same as any other. When that is taken into account, together with the tyre's unique pattern of wear, a profile is produced that is unique. But I had little hope of ever deriving anything useful from those tyres now. After all these years, they would no longer be in existence.

I sat back, reminiscing. Thinking about the quiet leafy street I'd lived in back then had started a rush of powerful memories. On one side was the local headmaster's residence. He had three children, several years older than me and Rosie. On the other side lived Snotty Kirkwood and I clearly remembered his freckled face and tufty hair and the dark hydrangea bushes that ran down the side of his house, perfect to hide in. I'd had a crush on his sister in Third Grade and I tried to remember her name. The only other kids in our street belonged to Rev Bower and his wife who lived down at the corner, but they were always away at boarding school and never a part of the kids' community. Mrs Bower had a vague, anxious manner and was always looking at us as if she didn't quite remember who we were, even though we lived only a few doors away.

It was a long time since I'd allowed my mother any head space and, for a moment, I was nearly drawn into revisiting my family home, my father in his office, my mother fumbling around trying to make dinner. As soon as my memory saw the glass of wine in her hand, a shutter came down fast.

I gathered up the photographs and replaced them in their envelopes. I put everything back in the box and leaned my elbows on the table. I noticed one envelope still lying beside the pile in the box and I thought again of the empty envelope among Nesbitt's gear. I picked it up and shoved it in with the others. I heard someone banging on the door and went to it, peering out the back window to see who it was before opening it.

'Hi, Dad.'

Greg's lanky seventeen-year-old frame filled the doorway, his light, bronze-flecked eyes like his mother's, now wary and self-conscious, looking away as he stood fiddling with the keys to the old Corolla he'd bought last birthday with some help from me.

'Come in, son,' I said, stepping back to allow him to pass me. His hair was plastered flat with whatever gel it needed to kill the curl. He hated his hair. He walked in leaving the door open and looked around. I felt the tension in him ease.

'This isn't too bad,' he observed, walking to the table where all my stuff was piled. He glanced at it, then turned to me. 'Please, Dad,' he rushed on, 'I can't stay with Mum. You know what she's like. I know she tries to be helpful but it just...' He threw the keys down on the table. 'I know she'll be hurt but I just have to get out of there. I've come to stay.' I glanced outside and saw that he'd brought an overnight bag with him, left lying on the paving outside.

Greg went to the fridge, paused and turned round to me. 'How come you won second prize in an art competition?'

'I entered a painting. The judges must've liked it.'

'You didn't say anything about it.' He raised his eyebrows and opened the fridge, peering in with adolescent hope, slamming it closed again on my pathetic bachelor collection of left-over take-away, various cheeses and a half bottle of flat ginger beer. I knew the bread was two days old.

'I can make you a jaffle,' I offered. 'Toasted cheese.' Greg nodded and I set about buttering the bread on both sides, slicing cheese and switching the electric jaffle iron on to heat up while he went outside and brought his bag in.

'I haven't got much room here,' I said, while the jaffle toasted. 'There's this room'—I indicated the living area in which we were standing, with its neat little kitchen area that folded away behind louvred cupboards—'my bedroom and that poky little room in here.' I showed him the other bedroom, to the right of the tiny bathroom, stacked almost floor to ceiling with my boxes and folders. Greg looked it up and down.

'If you get rid of your stuff,' he said, 'there'll be enough room in here. I can leave the big stuff with Mum.'

We walked outside and sat in the paved area on the kitchen furniture I'd dragged out there. As soon as the jaffle was ready I went in and turned it out on a plate for him.

'Do you want anything to drink?' I asked. 'Tea? Coffee?'

My son shook his head and fell on the jaffle as if he hadn't eaten for days.

'What does your mother think about you moving here full-time?' I asked, already knowing the answer.

Greg gave me a look. Then continued to demolish the toasted

bread and cheese, wincing a little as molten cheese dripped down his chin.

'She's a great lady, Mum,' Greg said when he'd finished eating, 'in her way. But I want to live with you. It's weird without you. It's like when Jacinta first went. Real quiet as if we were all waiting for something to happen.'

'We were,' I said. 'We still are.'

Greg moved to say something, then stopped.

'Go on,' I said, 'say it.'

He shook his head.

'You were going to ask me if I thought Jacinta was still alive.'

'Well,' he capitulated, 'do you?'

'Yes,' I said, 'as it happens.' We sat a while in silence after that, Greg going back inside and making himself another jaffle, and pouring himself the last of my milk. I made a mental note to remember to buy some more before I went to bed tonight. He came back out, towering over me and then collapsing into his chair, folding himself up like some great skinny pelican, all elbows and angles and flapping long limbs.

'I do believe your sister is still alive,' I said. 'It's a gut feeling. I know a lot of people would say I'm refusing to face the truth. But the truth is that no one knows. There are many more runaways than murder victims every year. The odds are in my favour. I think somehow Jass has made another life for herself.'

I stopped, thinking what sort of life a fifteen-year-old girl could have made for herself. I needed to turn my thoughts around. 'I'm involved in an investigation,' I warned him.

'Yeah, Mum said. Those guys who got cut.'

I looked at him. I didn't want to frighten him, but for some reason I couldn't let this cool, adolescent minimisation go past without saying something. 'Greg,' I said, 'they didn't just get cut. Whoever kills them cuts all their external sex organs right off. Penis, scrotum, the works. Plus inflicts deep lacerations to a major artery. They bleed to death in minutes.'

He looked at me and I wondered if I'd made a moralising blunder.

'Mum reckons it's about time men start to cop it. It's always women who get hacked up, she said. She said men had it coming to them.'

He looked at me and I could see the pain in his eyes. His mother's hostility towards me had been a constant in the household he grew up in. For years, Greg had breathed air heavy with resentment against men. No doubt Genevieve had good reasons much of the time. I was not a model husband or father. But I had been sober for fifteen of our eighteen years together although Genevieve could never acknowledge that, preferring to blame all her woes on me. I brought my attention back to my son. 'Statistically,' I said, not wanting to put her down in her son's eyes, yet not wanting to go along with her shit, 'she has a point.'

'I'm not crazy to hear her points lately,' said Greg, looking away. 'Especially the ones that put men down all the time.' He gave me a hard look when he said that, forbidding me any further comment, so I made him yet another jaffle and he chomped into it like a ravenous creature. I watched the way the shadows in his temple changed at the movement and the way his jaw lifted, and the lovely pure line of it. I looked around for something to sketch on, but there was nothing suitable and I resolved to buy charcoal and drawing paper next time I went into the city.

'Just because I'm on leave at the moment,' I told him, returning to the conversation in hand, 'doesn't mean I'm here much. You know I'm working with Bob Edwards. You'll end up spending a lot of time on your own. And you're not used to that.'

'Cool, Dad. That's great. That suits me heaps.' He swallowed the last of the jaffle and for the first time since he'd arrived, he grinned. 'I can really turn the sound system up.'

'You'll have to think seriously about this move,' I continued. 'Whether you can study here successfully or not. It's much more convenient for you at'—I nearly said 'home' but couldn't quite manage that word now—'at your mother's place—your nice big room, your desk. Everything laid on.' My mobile rang from inside and I went to get it, then chickened out. I was pretty sure it would be Genevieve.

'Aren't you going to get it?' Greg said as I walked back out again. He can't bear leaving a phone unanswered, fearing that he's going to miss out on the message that will change his life forever.

'No,' I said, 'I'm not.' I smiled at him, at this long, lovely youth, my first-born son. Inside, the phone suddenly stopped. There were things I wanted to say to him, but I could not. I had no skill in this sort of thing. Maybe Genevieve had a point or two and there was a lot I didn't know. More than I'd like to admit to myself. 'I'll come over on the weekend,' I said instead. 'And help you move some stuff. We can do it in stages. And now, you'd better ring your mother. Tell her where you are.'

'Won't you? She'll just yell at me.'

'She'll do exactly the same to me. It's your decision. Your life. Your phone call.'

'How come you talk like you know everything?' he said angrily as he stomped inside. And I could hear his mother. I was suddenly reminded of a childhood scene with my father, where I said almost exactly the same words to him, but try as I might, I couldn't remember what the situation had been. I could see myself standing in front of him, yelling, and him freezing me with his look of utter contempt. Then the memory abruptly stopped and I was left there, listening to my own son trying to explain something to the mother who didn't want to hear it. I could hear Greg's voice becoming more distressed, then more placatory. Eventually, he came outside, holding the phone out to me. 'She wants to talk to you.' Slowly, I took it.

Genevieve was about as bad as she could be, screaming down the line that I'd destroyed her life and taken both her children from her. What did I plan to do next? she shrieked. Completely destroy her? Because I might as well. She also had some choice things to say about Alix in Canberra. Despite the rules of never admitting to anything, I'd been stupid enough to admit to this once months ago, when she confronted me with mere hearsay from a mutual acquaintance. I remained icily polite, but my hard-won control only enraged her more.

'When are you going to stop being so bloody superior,' she screamed, 'and join the human race?'

I said goodbye and that I'd ring her back when she was more able to discuss things rationally. I was very aware of Greg in the erstwhile spare room, making space for his things. And I was shaking a bit when I put the phone down. I know I've been often remiss as a husband and father, but the level of her venom took me by surprise. At least, I thought, the gloves are off in her corner now and I won't have to endure any more of those awful visits with her in her slinky dress and perfume trying to get me into bed again.

Greg walked out as I hung up. 'Why does she have to be like that?' he said. 'Why does she have to see everything in the worst light? Why can't she just…?'

I walked over to my son and put my hands on his shoulders, looking into his eyes. There was nothing I could say about his mother in that moment that would have helped. 'How about I take you down the street and shout you a proper meal?' I said.

We walked down the street to the waterside Italian restaurant where Greg became engaged with the blackboard menu. I was thinking of Genevieve's accusation of superiority. Fifteen years in AA had taught me that I didn't have to react with anger to an angry person. If Genevieve saw this as superiority, there was little I could do, so I dismissed the thought as we sat down at a table on the veranda. It was a still night and the canvas awnings were rolled up high, allowing a good view across the bay. The derricks and cranes of the airport were etched against the sky like crouching skeletal creatures. The conversation with my estranged wife had upset me so I didn't feel hungry and ordered an entree which more than served me, but my son, with the endless appetite of seventeen, had a huge meal: lasagne with lots of garlic bread and a side salad that he didn't eat. We didn't talk much until my coffee arrived with Greg's lemon squash. With the straw still in his mouth, Greg was checking out the other diners in the restaurant, and I saw him staring at a family at a table across the room, mother, father and two kids, almost the same as our fragmented family might have been. They were animated, talking and laughing, taking genuine pleasure in each other. I glanced away, heartsick.

'I want you to tell me,' Greg said, 'exactly what happened the night Jass ran away. Exactly.' He put the lemon squash down. 'You can tell me now, can't you?'

'Greg, it was pretty bad. I can't see much point in going over it. Why do you want to know?'

'Because Jass is my sister and what happened is what happened. And I *should* know.'

I stared at him, the sound of his words echoing in my ears, activating memories I'd thought were lost forever. I remembered saying almost the same phrases, word for word once. About Rosie. I could almost see Charlie smiling his 'told you so' smile.

'What? What is it, Dad?' my son was saying, concerned. But I still wasn't sure where to start, or how honest I should be. 'Did Mum hit her?' Greg was asking.

A few weeks prior to that night, Greg had grabbed Genevieve's arm as it swung back in an arc to strike Jacinta across the face. I'd heard the altercation and walked in to see my wife clamped tightly by her strong son, screaming, 'How dare you raise your hand to me!' I remember thinking at the time that she'd come tops in drama.

'No,' I said, shaking my head, 'she didn't actually hit her.'

'What do you mean, "actually"?'

'Your mother—,' I started to say, when the mobile rang. I swore and grabbed it with immense relief, hurrying outside, aware of Greg's eyes on my back.

I felt sure it would be Genevieve, conjured up by this conversation about her. But it was Staro, overwrought and over-excited.

'Frank Carmody's heading into the middle of Centennial Park,' he said, speaking too quickly, 'and I'm right on him. Hurry up and get here.' He told me his bearings. He was approaching the straight palm-lined avenue that bisects the park into two hemispheres.

'Staro,' I said, 'be careful. Wait outside for me or Bob to get there. I don't think you should go in any further.'

'But I can't lose him,' he said. 'Deadset he's meeting someone.' His voice had a raw edge and I knew he'd be feeling strung out. I was concerned.

'Remember what this killer does, Staro. I don't think you should go in there. You've done a great job. Now go home.'

'I'll be right,' said Staro too brightly and rang off.

I was aware of Greg standing behind me with the bill. I paid and we left, hurrying home past the street lights.

'Where are you going?' he asked as I unlocked the house and let him in.

'Work,' I said.

He gave me a very particular look and I realised that having my son living with me was not going to be straightforward. 'Look,' I said, 'this is urgent. I'll be home as soon as I can.'

'Yeah yeah yeah,' he said and I knew he was angry with me. To my astonishment, I felt a powerful rage rise up in me and for a second, I had to fight an urge to lash out at him. This shocked me so much that I went over and slammed his door shut and in the time that bought me, I was able to bring things under control again.

FIVE

I drove up fast to the York Road entrance of Centennial Park, still rattled by the fury that Greg had provoked in me. The elaborate Victorian gates are closed to cars in the evening so I hurried through the pedestrian gate, clutching my heavy torch.

Centennial Park was dedicated to the people of Sydney in the nineteenth century and although developers would love to get their hands on it, and there's been some open land lost, in the main, it provides hundreds of hectares of parkland, native and exotic trees, wetlands and waterlily lakes with islands for waterbirds to nest on and raise their young with reasonable safety. There are also formal gardens and a central drive lined with ancient, dying palms. It's a magic piece of Sydney by day, with large family groups enjoying picnics and barbecues around the lakes, and youngsters rolling the circuit on in-line skates, horse-lovers practising dressage and lunging in the central paddocks, or walking and trotting round the circuit, as well as walkers and talkers and babies in strollers. In the old days Bob and I had investigated some very nasty murders in the same park. All sorts of things go on—kids losing their virginity, married men having homosexual liaisons, adulterous lovers sneaking out to rendezvous while they pretend to walk the dog, and even the odd intrepid jogger who either doesn't mind, or isn't aware of what else is going on in the shadows around him. Or, more dangerously, her.

I'd rung Bob from the car to tell him what was happening.

'I'll be right there,' he'd said. 'Looks like he's going to meet someone.'

So now I loped along as quickly as I could in the starlight to the place Staro had designated. I'm not easily spooked, but I had to admit that the blackness of the huge Moreton Bay figs with their buttressed and snaky trunks and the weird alarm calls of waterfowl disturbed by something made the hair on the back of my neck start to prickle. Staro's whispered message on the mobile now told me that Carmody was standing, apparently waiting, near the stone summer house in the middle of the road that runs through the park's centre. Further phone contact was out of the question because of my increasing proximity to the summer house and the deep silence of the night, and I wished I'd taken the time to dig out a certain prohibited item I knew was packed away in one of my cartons at home.

Above me, the sky was clear with a waning moon low in the west ahead of me. My eyes had adjusted to the dark and I could see reasonably well now, so I increased my pace, thinking of who might be in the long shadows and impenetrable blackness of the trees. I jumped with fright when a startled plover screamed, '*Shit shit shit!*' and its partner joined in, their high-pitched calls shattering the silence.

So when the first of the terrible screams started, I didn't recognise them for a second. When I did, I froze for a moment, immobilised by fear, shock and uncertainty. The shrieks were coming from the central area where Staro had said Frank Carmody was waiting. An eerie night breeze rustled the leaves of the palms above me and I started running as fast as I could. Never in my life had I been at a crime scene while the offence was being committed and it was years since I'd been to one at all. And back in those days, I had an armed partner with me and the knowledge that back-up was available. Here, I was apparently alone in the dark in the middle of deserted parkland with Bob probably just pulling his trousers on a good five suburbs away.

I raced across the car bridge over the central pond, flashing my light ahead of me. At first, I could see only innocent lawns and garden beds, then the summer house and the closed-up ice-cream vans. 'Stop!' I called out as I ran closer, 'police!'

The words sounded empty and stupid in the dark. I was close enough now to hear the sounds of a struggle and horrible choking noises.

'Staro!' I yelled, 'Staro! What's happening?' There was no reply, just the dreadful sound that had fallen away to gasping sobs and, further away, the thud of running footsteps. Then the beam of my torch turned the corner of the northern side of the summer house and my body stopped automatically in shock at what I could see. In the same automatic state, I whipped out my mobile and dialled emergency. Carefully, I moved closer, finally squatting beside the wretched man, the smell of blood thick in my nostrils. I registered the sound of a motorbike revving up and then fading in the night. I stood up. 'Staro?' I yelled again.

I waited, but there was nothing. Just the now distant sound of the motorbike and soft, tentative night sounds returning after the explosion of violence.

Now all my attention was concentrated on the man slumped against the wall, his head and upper shoulders propped up, the rest of his body splayed out along the ground. His blood-soaked trousers revealed terrible gaping injuries and the dark flood surrounding his lower body was pooling and thickening. Eyes stretched wide in terror and shock and his mouth also gaped in a silent scream. I could see a slight rippling movement in his neck, but I knew it was all over for Frank Carmody. His body slumped in the deflated collapse of death. I stood, looking around, picking up the odours, the slight movements in air, the ambience of this red-hot crime scene. My skin prickled with goose bumps. A sense of dark and heavy hatred swirled around me like a miasma, infecting me, so that I swung around. But there was nothing to see, just the dim outline of the dark island in the middle of water only slightly less dense and black, the city stars above me and the distant hum of the traffic.

It seemed only minutes before that same dark place of death was brilliant with police lights, the video unit, photographers, paramedics, the scrambled voices of police and ambulance radios and one or two people from the papers. I've always said you can believe two things in the newspapers, the date and the price. But the press can be helpful in certain investigations and this was one of them. In the distance I could see Bob squatting beside the corpse, deep in conversation with Bradley Strachan. Journalist Merrilyn Heywood saw me and came over. 'What can you tell me?' she asked, with her notebook and pen ready.

'I'm not the person you want,' I told her. 'You need to talk to the officer in charge. I'm just a blow-in really, doing a mate a favour.'

Merrilyn winked at me. She's a nice woman and there's always been a bit of chemistry between us. Merrilyn and another journalist had collaborated on a successful book a few years ago, *Portrait of Murder*, about a painter turned murderer, and I'd helped her with some of the scientific research. 'Come on, Jack,' she said. 'Off the record. You can just be "reliable sources".'

I shook my head. 'I haven't been back in town very long. I've got to keep sweet with these people. Give me a ring tomorrow and we'll chat.' I scribbled down my details and she took them, thanked me and walked away. I called after her. 'And Merrilyn!' She turned. 'Make sure you do something to kill that wolf-man nonsense once and for all!'

She nodded and started walking away. I was on my way to catch up with Bob when it was my turn to swing round as I heard Merrilyn call my name. I turned straight into a flashlight. As I swore and blinked, she lowered the camera. 'Thanks, Jack,' she said. 'You're a darling.'

Staro, it seemed, had vanished into thin air. I borrowed a police car and drove around for a while looking out for him and calling his name. But apart from the pool of brilliant light in the middle of the park, there seemed to be only the darkness of the night. I drove out to where he lived. His insomniac landlady let me into his room and I left a scribbled message for him on his bed to ring me as soon as possible and went home at three.

When I crept in, I saw that Greg had made a bed up for himself in the spare room and was sound asleep, curled up as he always was, on his right side, his hated curls springing everywhere. I covered him with a light open-weave blanket because the night was cool now, and stood looking down on him for a few seconds. I fell into my own bed, still in my underwear. I've been to too many violent crime scenes to let the images from the park keep me awake. I had no doubt Bradley Strachan would tell us it was the third killing in the series; I'd seen enough to know that. Then I was asleep.

•

Next morning, after giving Bob my statement about the night before, I drove to Staro's address. The newspapers were having a field day with huge headlines about the third murder. I grabbed the *Telegraph* and glanced through it in the car. A photograph of the group around the covered body and a close-up of Carmody's sister closing the door on reporters took up the bottom of the first page. Merrilyn Heywood's by-line showed under a 'Death Targets Sex Predators' article. I'd read it later, I thought, as I knocked on Staro's front door but he still wasn't in and when the landlady let me into his room again, it was clear he hadn't been there since my visit last night. My scribbled message lay where I'd left it, so I placated the landlady whose main interest was the rent, leaving another message for Staro to call me urgently. I felt some concern for him. But I reminded myself that he'd been looking after himself on the streets of Sydney for the last twenty-five years, starting from an age when most kids are still playing with Lego.

Merrilyn Heywood rang while I was driving to the Collins Club in Flinders Street. 'I can tell you this much,' I said, responding to her questions. 'Looks like it's the same person who killed Gumley and Nesbitt.' I described the wounds I'd seen on the dead man the night before. 'Same pattern of attack. Excision of the external genital organs.'

'What was he doing at Centennial Park at that hour?' Her voice was incredulous.

'That's what we'd all like to know,' I said.

'An assignation?' she suggested.

'Quite possible,' I said. 'But not quite the assignation he was expecting.'

'Do you think it could be a woman?' Merrilyn asked. 'Someone reclaiming the night?'

I considered. 'Almost certainly it's not a woman,' I said. 'The knife in general is not a woman's weapon. Unless the first blow renders the victim inoperable, and that's very unlikely with a stabbing injury, she'd have to deal with a very pissed-off person who is now also in pain and shock as well. Perhaps if there was evidence of bludgeoning first, knocking the target down and then using a knife, it might be possible. Or working with a partner. But there's no evidence to suggest that.'

'Surely the attacker would get blood all over himself in the process?'

'I would think so,' I agreed.

'Well?' she demanded.

'There are steps he could take to prevent that.'

'Like what?'

I shook my head. 'Look,' I said, 'the crims are smart enough these days. I'm not going to give them any tips in the daily press.'

There was a silence as Merrilyn changed tack. 'And anyone might come along and interrupt?'

'Yes,' I agreed. 'He's certainly a high-risk operator.'

'I want to finish this story for tomorrow,' she added. 'Is there anything else? I heard a rumour that this last victim was being kept under surveillance.'

'Oh?' I said casually. 'I don't know anything about that.'

'You see,' she said, 'a lot of people out there think this killer is more like an agent of justice and not just the usual evil bastard.'

'You'll write a great story, Merrilyn,' I said. 'Good luck with it.' And I rang off.

I was pulling up outside the Collins Club when Bob rang. 'Can you come to the morgue?' he said. 'Bradley's found something you should most definitely see.' As Bob was speaking I suddenly saw Pigrooter's bright aqua Bufori sports car, notorious around the Sydney traps, parked in a laneway. My target was here. I couldn't leave just now.

'Half an hour,' I said to Bob, 'I'll be there.'

The Collins Club, for all its pretensions, bore the same stink of stale beer, stale cigarettes, disinfectant and last night's perfume and chunder found in any bloodhouse. I looked around. Only hardened drinkers and shift workers were there at this time of day, but then I saw the massive figure of Pigrooter sitting at a table probably checking his shares in the newspaper. Another of his interests was hunting feral pigs. I'd heard it said in the old days that when the wild boars heard that Pigrooter was after them, they just rolled over and died of fright, to be gathered up like nuts in May. Pigrooter had a phenomenal memory bank. Which made his dismissal some years previously from the New South Wales Police puzzling. He'd been charged with accessing confidential government records, and thereby sinning against the Privacy Act. This was odd, because the way I'd heard it, Pigrooter didn't need to break into records. He had the dirt on everyone and everything in town and I wondered why he hadn't simply sold his memories. But right now, this nemesis of renegade pork was sitting with his customary eccentric drinks—black tea with cognac chaser—applying himself to the stockmarket report. He looked up as I approached and I saw in his shrewd eyes that he was searching his memory, and then locating me. Marty Cash made to get up, but the effort was too much. Instead, he put out his hand and pulled a chair out for me.

'Jack McCain,' he said. 'Well, root me.'

I ordered a lemonade and we chatted a bit about the old days before he'd blotted his copybook and I'd become a scientist. And then I got to the point.

'I was told,' I said, 'that she'd been working at the House of Bondage in Darlinghurst. I checked it out. Nothing doing.'

'That was a bad business,' he said, shaking his head, 'losing your daughter like that. A lot of coppers' daughters get into strife.' There was a moment's silence as we both got back on track. 'So who gave you the info?' Pigrooter wanted to know.

'Anonymous tip-off,' I told him, keeping Iona Seymour to myself.

'Someone said your lass was working at the House of Bondage, eh?' he said, looking away from me and out the window. I nodded. Pigrooter suddenly took a long drink of his tea, finished it, wiped his mouth and came in close. 'Of course you know,' he said, 'that there are two establishments in Darlinghurst that cater to those hooked on the pleasure–pain complex? One of them much more extreme than the other. And they both go by the same name?'

I didn't, and my face would have revealed it to the sharply observant fat man opposite me. 'And so I can't help wondering,' he continued, 'which House of Bondage your informant meant?'

•

As I drove to the morgue, all I could think about was the other brothel. Pigrooter had been happy to give me the street name and a clear description of the house which I'd written down on one of the Collins Club coasters. I felt elated, but reminded myself that

I'd been here before. Many times before. And disappointed just as often.

I got to the morgue about fifty minutes after Bob's phone call to find that Bradley Strachan, gloved and gowned, was about to clean up. Bob and one of the Crime Scene photographers had already bagged and labelled the late Frank Carmody's bloody clothes and shoes. When I walked in, Bob looked up and wordlessly picked up an envelope with the tips of his gloved fingers and passed it to me. I pulled some gloves from the dispenser box on the counter and carefully took it from him.

'Bradley found it tucked away in his inside pocket,' Bob said as I examined the opened envelope. It had been slit along the top and dark blood glued it together along one edge. I tipped the folded letter it contained onto the bench, carefully opening it as Bob passed me a plastic sleeve and I housed it, studying the letter through the plastic. 'This makes things much clearer,' he said.

Dear Mr Carmody, I read, noting that the letter was written in black ink in a strong, somewhat backhand copperplate: *Thanks so much for replying. It makes everything easier for me and also makes me feel that you are interested in my friendship. There was an expression in your face when I saw the photo of you in the newspapers that made me want to contact you. I know how dreadful it is to be locked up, year after year, at the mercy of your gaolers. And I'm lonely and I would so much like to be your friend.*

I looked up at Bob and Bradley. 'This handwriting,' I said. 'I've seen it before somewhere.'

'Where?'

I thought, but couldn't bring it to mind.

I returned my attention to the letter, reading on: *I'm twenty six-years old, and work as a dancer in a nightclub. I have long blonde hair and blue eyes and I live with my brother in Potts Point. I've cut out your photograph and it sits on my bedside table. Please reply as soon as you can because I'm looking forward so much to hearing from you. One day soon, I hope I can dance for you.*

It was when I came to the signature that the writing seemed to waver as I blinked several times. My eyes locked onto the name at the bottom of the page.

'Did you notice the signature?' Bob asked. I blinked again. I hadn't made a mistake, or seen something that wasn't there: *Yours sincerely*, the letter was signed, *Rosie McCain*.

My sister's name, signed in slightly bigger writing than that contained in the body of the letter. Beneath it, was a one line postscript: *Please destroy this. I don't want any other men reading what I write for you alone.*

Neither Bob nor Bradley said anything for a moment, then they both went to speak together.

'It's not a unique name,' I said, speaking over their mutual apologies. 'There must be hundreds of people called that.' I was rallying fast. 'The important thing,' I said, 'is that I've seen this writing on an empty envelope when I was going through Nesbitt's stuff.'

'Was there a letter?' Bob asked. I shook my head. 'I didn't find any letter. But this is the best explanation as to how he'—I paused—'or she—does it. Writes to the victim while he's still in gaol, and then presumably a meeting is arranged shortly after he's released.' But even as I was saying these words, some part of my mind was thinking, *it could be*. It just *might* be Rosie. Had Rosie, after twenty-five years' silence, come forward as some sort of avenging angel? The idea was insane. If she was going to come forward, she'd come to us, to her family who had missed her for so long, and longed so desperately for her return. 'Note that she thanks him for replying,' I said, bringing my full attention back to the letter in my hands. 'And yet it seems to be the first letter she's written to him.' Bob nodded, getting my point.

'So we need to find out,' he said after a thoughtful pause, 'exactly what he replied to.'

The three of us looked at each other. Carefully, I picked up the envelope by a corner and turned it over, looking for any identifying marks. It was postmarked Potts Point and dated January, a year ago and, like the letter, it was addressed in the same strong, slightly left-leaning hand.

'It's the first physical thing we've had,' said Bob, 'that gives us somewhere to start. Someone writes to him in prison. Someone who says they want to meet him.'

I thought of the corpse lying in the next room, the long medial opening now neatly zipped back together, there because someone with my lost sister's name had wanted to meet him last night.

•

Driving over to Phillip Street we found the house empty—Miss Carmody was away staying with a friend—and it didn't take us long to locate another three letters, carefully wrapped up in brown paper among her brother's scant possessions. Only the one that Bradley had found on the victim's body had an envelope, the rest were folded together in the order of their arrival, all written in the same distinctive backhand in black ink. We took just about everything we found in his room back to the Police Centre. Bob and I read the letters carefully, handling them only at the very edges, gloved up and replacing them in order in plastic sleeves. As I read them, I started to realise the nature of the trap used by this killer to lure his—or her—victims. For over a year, this person had planned. The letters were sent at monthly intervals, starting with the first one dated June the previous year. Each letter grew steadily more provocative, more openly suggestive. *'Tonight,'* Bob read aloud, *'I undressed in front of your photo. Then I touched myself, calling your name. I am aching for you. I can't wait to meet you. But my brother is so jealous and suspicious of me. He never lets me go anywhere alone. I'll let you know a good place we could meet.'* Bob's grey eyes looked over the top of the paper. 'It's signed the same way as all the others,' he said. *'Until then, I am yours only on paper. Rosie.'* It was hot and heavy gear for a sex-starved sex offender, locked up for years.

I started thinking about the scenario the letter-writer was creating and Bob stood up, hands in his pockets, and walked over to look through the partition at the rest of the office. 'Maybe there is a brother,' I said, 'and maybe they work in a team. "Rosie" arranges the time and place of the meeting, then she goes, seemingly alone, to the pre-selected meeting place and while she distracts the victim, out jumps the brother with his knife.' Bob nodded slightly, still standing with his back to me, gazing out through the glass. But I knew he wasn't seeing anything out there. He turned round to me again, shaking his head.

'I can't really see why the killer would mention the existence of a brother, if there was such a person and that person was part of the killing. It's giving too much of the game away. That's why I don't think there is a brother at all. This brother business is part of the character that "Rosie" is creating for the victim to believe, that she's a naïve, lonely, beautiful, highly sexed, over-protected young girl—'

'—who dances in a nightclub?' I said, incredulous. I knew the sorts of kids who ended up dancing in nightclubs, and although they might be young, they were hardly naïfs. 'Bob,' I said, 'what does the picture that Rosie is painting of her situation really suggest to you?' The reason Bob and I have been close associates for so long is that his way of thinking is very similar to mine.

'Actually,' he said, a slight frown lowering his bushy eyebrows, 'it reminds me of the kind of letter that you might read in *Playboy*.'

'Exactly,' I said. 'The whole set-up smells like one of those porno movies that attempt to weave a plot and some other characters around Miss Fanny and the Ramjet. It's bullshit, Bob. It's fantasy.' I thought a bit more and refined my conclusion. 'Male fantasy,' I added. I looked through the letters again, frowning. 'That's definitely the last one?' I asked Bob.

'Yes,' he said. 'Why?'

'Because there's still no mention of where and when they're going to meet. There's the mention of a meeting, but nothing's planned.'

'Maybe she contacted him in another way?' said Bob. 'Maybe a visit?'

I shook my head. 'I'll check that with Corrective Services,' I said, making a note to myself. 'I think there's a missing letter.'

Bob smiled one of his rare smiles. 'Let's say there *is* another letter somewhere, naming the time and the place.' He tapped the letters. 'At least now we know how the killer does it. The poor bastards showed up all right. Who could resist these?'

'I think I could,' I said. 'Especially if I'd known what happened to two other sex offenders. I'd be very wary of meeting anyone unknown.'

'But Rosie isn't unknown,' Bob pointed out, speaking from the victims' point of view. 'She's probably the closest friend the poor miserable bastards had in the world. As far as they're concerned, she's a twenty-six-year-old blonde nightclub dancer who's hot for them. It's a different set-up to what's happened to those other men who, after all, are only names in a newspaper.'

Long blonde hair. And a red jacket.

'Those notes,' I said, 'on the envelope with Nesbitt's gear.'

Bob waited, not following me, but hearing the excitement in my voice.

'He'd written, "Long blonde hair, red jacket," and I'd assumed it was some poor kid he was targeting, like they do. But it wasn't. It was a description of someone he was going to meet.' Bob nodded and I realised I was doing the same. We were starting to build up the picture. 'Do you think it could be a woman?' Merrilyn Heywood had asked me and I'd said no.

For the next little while I dictated and Bob typed up a transcript of each letter. That way, we could go over and over them without harming any delicate traces of physical evidence on the originals. The transcript I'd give to Charlie as well as our forensic linguist. The originals we'd send over to Document Examination. The State Government lab, just like the one in Canberra, would give us the type of paper, the type of pen used, the name and possibly even the batch number of the ink and just about everything you could think of about those letters except for the one thing we really wanted—the name and address of the writer.

'I'll run them over to the lab myself,' Bob said, 'then Fingerprints can have a go at them. See if there's anything interesting.' Police had learned the hard way not to send questioned documents to Fingerprints first. Some of the processes used in that department render the document useless for further examination.

We went over the events of the night before one more time, with Bob questioning me about my statement, trying to get me to identify what sort of motor cycle I might have heard leaving the crime scene. But all I could really say was that it sounded high-powered and that it was going like the clappers.

'We need Staro,' said Bob. 'We've got to find him. He might have seen what happened.'

'If he did, and the killer knows that he did, I can understand why he'd just want to disappear for a while,' I said. 'Staro values his equipment as much as the next man.'

'Staro hasn't got the form this killer targets,' said Bob. 'And we have no reason to assume the killer saw him.'

'We don't know what sort of form Staro might have,' I reminded him as I picked up the bagged clothes of the lately dead Frank Carmody and wondered how Staro was handling his new sobriety in the face of last night's incident. 'Staro has the sort of past that could easily involve sexual abuse. Of him, and by him,' I said. 'Poor old Staro's been for sale for a long time.' Thinking of the selling of sex reminded me about the second House of Bondage. And,' I continued, 'you should know that there are two establishments that go by the name "House of Bondage".'

Bob raised one of his wild eyebrows. 'Is that so?' he said. 'I wonder why we haven't heard about it.'

'Maybe it's new,' I said. 'I plan a visit and I may need to organise a warrant later.'

More words on paper. Words on paper were starting to feature too much in my life lately. And I couldn't entirely shake the feeling that maybe the anonymous ill-wisher was somehow connected with the letters that now lay on Bob's desk, awaiting examination. According to my unknown correspondent I was going to be 'made to' care. And soon. Were the 'Rosie' letters related to that threat in some way? They had been printed, not handwritten, but I knew I had to come clean with my erstwhile partner about this business, much as I hated doing so.

'Bob,' I said, as he moved to leave, 'I've had an anonymous letter.'

I told him the gist of it. Better than that, I quoted it because I knew it off by heart. Bob frowned. 'You'd better bring it in and show me,' he said.

'Sarah's looking at it,' I said. Before I left, I asked him for the address of Peter Carter, father of the girl Frank Carmody had murdered.

•

At Long Bay, I went through the records with a helpful young officer. Apart from his sister, the only other visitor Carmody had was a Father Dumaresque of St Kilian's, Padstow.

I wrote the name and address in my notebook and went back to my car. Then I drove to the Schofields address Bob had given me and found Peter Carter's house, a small timber cottage set on a large block. I walked up to the front door, passing a derelict henhouse on my right and a neglected garden. I knocked at the door and waited. After a while, I knocked again. I waited a little longer, then walked round the back. On a long open veranda, a man was sitting smoking.

'Hullo,' I said, 'I knocked but maybe you didn't hear me.'

'I heard you all right,' said the man. I thought it was Carter but needed to be sure. I pulled out my ID card and waved it at him.

'Peter Carter?' I asked.

The man nodded.

'I never answer the door,' he said. 'I think you'd better leave now. I've got nothing to say to any of you people.'

'I'm a scientist, not a cop, Mr Carter—' I started.

The man stood up. 'No,' he said, 'don't you Mr Carter me. I used to have some respect for the law. For the police and the government of this country. Not any more. My little girl was killed and the animal that did it ends up spending less time in gaol than the poor bastard down the road who knocked off a few service stations. I lost my daughter, I lost my marriage. I've got nothing. That's all I've got to say to you. To anyone. Except that I'm glad someone with more guts than I've got has done the right thing by society and killed that scumbag. It's not murder, it's execution.' He walked towards the screen door. 'So now get off my property.' With that, he threw his cigarette butt over the railing, went inside and slammed the door.

I went over to where he had thrown the butt and gently crushed the hot end with my shoe, carefully picking it up on a leaf, and slipping it into an envelope. Peter Carter had just given me everything I needed from him.

•

Next day I left a note for Greg saying I'd be away all day, and left before sunrise, with my anonymous letter and the cigarette butt, arriving in Canberra before nine. When I arrived at Forensic Services, the people I met in the corridors just nodded to me, or ignored me, or did whatever they usually did when we passed each other or met in the central kitchen area. Only Florence frowned at me. Despite her wild hair and denim skirt, there was something in the expression of her mouth that always reminded me of the woman in *American Gothic*, that painting of the Puritan farm couple. Today, her bushy hair was clipped into two semicircular wings looping each side of her face, fastened in a chignon.

'What are you doing here?' she asked, her intense blue eyes sharp and watchful. Then she apologised and tried to explain that she didn't mean to sound unwelcoming, but she thought I was on leave.

'I am,' I said, 'but I'm involved in a Sydney case. So here I am with a few items to search.'

She still seemed uneasy, pulling at her hair where it had come out of its comb. Florence's hair is a rusty colour, with salt and pepper grey. 'Florence,' I said, 'would you mind testing this cigarette butt? I want to eliminate someone.'

'Or implicate them,' she offered. 'Are you in a hurry?' I shook my head. 'I'll get it done as soon as I can,' she said. 'Just for you.' Then she actually snatched the packaged butt out of my hands and ducked away. I watched her solid figure vanish into the corridor near the lab.

I put Frank Carmody's bloodstained clothes in the huge walk-in two-way fridge and prepared myself for the Search Room. Gloved and space-suited, I covered the surface of the search table with sheets of white paper. I teased out Carmody's shirt and trousers, turning them over, carefully examining them through the big overhead microscope under the bright lighting. The trousers were drenched with dried blood and I saw straightaway I wouldn't get much off them. But the shirt was clean apart from two large blood splashes. Two buttons were missing, and one of the buttonholes was pulled and stretched, possibly damaged by someone grabbing the shirt violently at the front. Looking down the microscope, I saw where the fibres of the fabric had been bunched up in a way that supported my suspicions. Then I found a prize, caught around the first remaining button on the pale green material. A long blonde hair that I gently removed with tweezers and slipped into a small plastic packet. I continued shaking out the dead man's clothes until I was satisfied that anything caught in the fabric had fallen off onto the paper beneath. I looked again at the shirt. Under the microscope, I could see creases on the upper parts of each sleeve. I imagined someone grabbing Carmody, pinning his arms, leaving something of himself behind after that deadly embrace. However, there's no telling with the collecting of potential DNA samples. Some people are great 'shedders'. Others don't seem to spread themselves around much. I 'posted' the clothes through the hatch into the Biology Lab next door for the next stage in the process.

It didn't take me long to mount the various fibres and particles I'd retrieved from the surface of the paper and give them to a couple of the younger blokes to take to the examination rooms. With great care, I handed the long blonde hair over in its bag. I couldn't help thinking of the twenty-six-year-old nightclub dancer. Maybe she was starting to materialise. Bob would be amused, I thought.

A change of suit and gloves saw me in the Biology Lab, taking tiny samples from the creased areas of both sleeves. I placed these in the small plastic containers, shaped like tiny amphorae, to be screened for any DNA material that just might be there.

SIX

The screening process told me that there was DNA material on the shirt front and also on the sleeves. Of course there would be: a human being had worn the shirt. A profile generated from Carmody's lifeless body would eliminate him from the search. What we needed to find was a trace left by the killer. Deoxyribonucleic acid, the genetic material that makes each one of us the individual that we are, is a highly complex chemical chain found in the nucleus of cells. I once explained it to Greg by asking him to imagine that everyone in the world was each given three billion different coloured beads with which to make a necklace. And then to imagine the chances of two people arranging the beads in exactly the same sequence. A person's DNA is their genetic blueprint and it shows up in almost every cell, the exception being red blood cells, which lose their nuclei during production. DNA is remarkably durable if it is protected from sunlight. Grains of wheat found buried with Egyptian mummies have been successfully sprouted, the genetic material safely stored in those dark places for thousands of years, just waiting for the right conditions to germinate. DNA has been extracted from the tiny bodies of dead lice found on the same mummies. The extraction process moves through complex stages where everything that is not the protein we're after is stripped away. Then, positively charged ions, which can cause DNA degradation at high temperatures, are mopped up by a suspension of tiny beads, kept moving by means of magnetic 'fleas', so named because they jump around. Once we've extricated the DNA from everything else around it, what we have is the biological equivalent of fingerprinting. And just as crims have attempted to alter their fingerprints with acid or surgery and failed, they've also tried to obliterate body fluid traces after their crimes with bleach or vinegar. But criminals as a rule are not patient, meticulous, discerning people. Good scientists are. And we only need a few cells. Theoretically, one cell would do the trick. By means of a 'biological amplifier' we can detect the tiny traces of nucleic matter, 'printing' and 'reprinting' them, over and over, until we have enough to extract for a profile. The first amplification test tells us whether we're dealing with a male or female, and there are nine others. These combined tests give results that print out in a graph. Once I'd run the tests, known as the 'amps', I'd know whether or not someone other than Frank Carmody had creased that shirt up around the sleeves. There was nothing more I could do here, so I left and drove back to Sydney.

•

I went to the address Pigrooter had given me and drove up and down the street a couple of times, pretending I was looking for parking, which was the truth. The house I was interested in was in a row of small nineteenth-century sandstone terraces, many of them covered in cement render or unfortunate paintwork. Just as Pigrooter had described it, number 42 had the traditional red light, now unlit, and a weird cactus bursting out of its pot in the tiny concreted front yard. Pigrooter had said the place was white, and I suppose it had been once. I drove round the back, checking the lane that ran behind it. East Sydney is one of the oldest suburbs, built in the earliest days of the settlement at Sydney Cove and the houses almost always back onto lanes where the dunny cart once made its way. I parked the car some distance away and walked down the footpath on the other side of the road from number 42. The cottage was the same as its neighbours except that it had a closed circuit security camera just visible above the front door. I crossed the road and walked past it, noticing the blind was drawn on the front window, went round the corner and then into the rear lane. Some of the cottages still had the outhouse down the back, covered in vines. Some had been removed, others rebuilt as part of a backyard shed. I stood up on the fence and peered over into a small overgrown backyard and a closed-in back veranda with a wooden staircase down the side. A dog started barking furiously so I stepped down again and rang Bob.

With Bob and a warrant, I attended the raid on number 42 Marian Street. Within minutes, it became clear that the joint specialised in 'advanced' S & M. My heart sank as we went through the place, collecting and recording the various illegal substances we found in cupboards and drawers. The bedrooms were decked out like medieval dungeons, with shackles hanging from the wall and whips, handcuffs, and various other items of restraint. As I walked into a bathroom, a girl sitting on the toilet screamed, swore and pulled up her black lace panties. Before she could say anything, I held up my ID card.

'You bastard,' she said, 'you could've knocked.'

The thin, pretty girl in the black lace slip could have been seventeen or twenty-seven. I noticed several tiny sores on her chin and suspected too much cocaine. Her bronze-rimmed eyes were busy, watching, flickering, working me out.

I looked around the tiled area. Manacles and chains, baths and basins and shower areas were set up with every type of hose, nozzle and enema bag. I picked up and squeezed a rubber bladder. 'People find *this* a turn-on?' I asked, incredulous. To me, it was about as sexy as a bowl of cold cat sick, but even cold cat sick, I realised, probably had its afficionados.

'You should try it sometime. You never know.'

'No fear,' I said, as I followed her to one of the rooms while she fetched her driver's licence. Renee Miller, aged twenty-three, of Rushcutters Bay, stared out at me from the licence photo, and in reality a few metres away.

'I don't know who owns the place,' she said, in answer to my question, worrying at one of the sores with a short painted nail. 'You need to speak to Pam. I only do my shifts here and then go home. It's got nothing to do with me.'

'Pam who?'

Renee shrugged, pushing her long hair behind her ears. 'She's the woman who comes round for the rent.'

'What about the other girls who work here?'

I pulled out a photo of Jacinta with her hair pulled back taken eighteen months ago, just before she left. Her shining features and intelligent eyes gazed clear and straight at the camera.

'Have you seen her?' I asked Renee.

Renee stared hard at the picture. Then she looked up at me. 'You're a bloody cop. Why should I tell you anything?'

'I'm not a cop, I'm a scientist and Jacinta is my daughter,' I said, keeping my voice on an even keel. 'I want to take her home.'

Renee looked at me. 'Why did she leave in the first place? Kids don't leave home unless they have to.'

'She had a fight with her mother.'

Renee was unimpressed. 'Everyone has fights with their mother. They don't leave because of that.' I was starting to feel annoyed at having to explain and justify this painful complex subject to a sharp little moll.

'Listen,' I said, 'she ran away because of an argument. Happens all the time.'

'When was this?'

'Eighteen months ago.'

Renee stepped back at that, looking at me as if I was retarded. 'Eighteen months ago? And you're looking for her now?'

'I've never stopped,' I said. 'Just look at the picture and answer my question.'

Renee looked at the picture of my daughter and then back at me. 'If she'd wanted to come home, she'd have done it a long time ago. You just don't get it, do you?'

It was then that realisation dawned on me. 'You know her,' I said. 'You know Jacinta. And you know where she is.'

There was a long moment. Then she nodded. 'I might do,' she said. 'But she looks different in this photo.'

'She *is* different,' I said more savagely than I meant to. 'When this was taken she was barely thirteen.'

Renee shrugged. 'We were all thirteen once.' She turned away.

'When did you last see her?' I asked.

Renee's face went blank. 'Sometime. Maybe a few weeks back. She comes and goes here. Works other places, too. She's like me. Pretty fussy about what she does.'

She must have seen the look on my face because she burst out angrily. 'I know that look. You think you're better than me! Bastards like you drive your kids away but you still feel superior to everyone else. You're just like my bloody father. You're *shit*, people like you.'

I took the photograph from her in silence, carefully replacing it.

I'd handled this very badly and now I didn't know how to go about redeeming the situation.

'Look,' I said, 'I've got off to a bad start with you.'

'I don't believe it,' she said, with a hard, sarcastic laugh, 'a copper trying to be diplomatic. A police raid isn't a very diplomatic occasion,' she said. 'And anyway, Miss Manners hasn't done that chapter yet.'

'You're working in an unlicensed whorehouse,' I said. 'Miss Manners hasn't dealt with that topic either.' The mutual joke softened the atmosphere a little.

'I'm not a copper any more,' I said.

She shrugged. 'Once a copper always a copper. People like you, they never change.'

'Why do you do it, this sort of work?' I asked, trying a new tack.

Renee took a step back, put a hand on a hip, and gave me a contemptuous look.

'Where've you been?' she said. 'Are you some sort of fundo?'

'What?'

'You know. A religious nut. We get them sometimes. After they've fucked me, they want to save me. They're disgusting.'

'I just want to hear in your own words why you do this work.' I was hoping I'd get some insight, some way to understand or accept that my daughter worked in this world.

She raised her eyes to heaven.

'I do it,' she said slowly so that I'd understand, 'because I can make ten, twenty times the money I'd get working a cash register.'

'Fair enough,' I said.

But she hadn't quite finished. 'And,' she added, 'because it gives me power over men.' I waited in silence, thinking of Jacinta.

'And how do you work that out?' I asked.

Renee came in closer and looked up at me. Without the tiny sores and the garish make-up, she'd be a very pretty young woman.

'Because,' she said, looking at me straight with eyes that blazed hatred, 'if I'm ramming a dildo up some bastard's arse, then he's not fucking me over, is he?'

She had a point. I turned away to leave. But just before I went, I had one last shot. 'If you'd just tell me whatever you know about my daughter, we'll call it quits,' I said. Renee gave me a knowing look.

'You people never call anything quits,' she said.

I didn't reply, just waited as the silence went on.

'I'll pass a message on,' she finally said. 'That's all.' She paused. 'Then it's up to her if she wants to take further action. How do I know you weren't screwing her or something?'

In spite of myself, tears sprang to my eyes. I blinked quickly and shook my head. 'I wasn't,' I said.

The tears surprised both of us. They were partly because of the nature of Renee's suggestion, partly because of what had become of my child and partly because I knew well enough that too many fathers betrayed their daughters in this way. But they were also tears of excitement. Because, I thought, as I scribbled my address and phone number onto a torn-out page from my notebook, if Renee could give Jacinta a message, it meant that she knew where she was.

Renee took the piece of paper, glanced at it and then at the fifty dollar bill I'd taken out of my wallet. She cocked her smart little head to one side. 'There's a real dungeon here, the original cellar of this place. I could chain you up down there and do what I liked with you. No one would hear you.'

'Help me, please,' I said.

She snatched the fifty from me with one hand, yanked my zip undone with the other, and had my cock in her hand before I realised what was happening. 'I love it when men beg,' she said.

I jumped back, knocking her away, taken completely by surprise, not only by her move, but also her strength. I jerked my zip up, and straightened my belt.

'Renee,' I said, 'I'm begging. Where my daughter is concerned, I'd do anything. 'Please help me.'

After the others had left, I sat off the house in Marian Street until Renee left. A pair of currawongs called to each other, *'To me! To me! To me!'* as they circled and landed in a large fig tree down the street from the brothel.

Three male visitors had been and gone by the time she appeared, wearing a funny little tiger print coat, closing the front door, looking around the street, then heading off west towards a smart red Golf. I followed her to her address in a large block of white apartments at Rushcutters Bay and watched while she drove into the underground carpark and the automatic door closed after her. Even after I was sure she'd settled in for the night I stayed sitting there. Something Renee had said about my absent daughter came back and I couldn't help applying it to my sister. Maybe Rosie, like Jacinta, hadn't wanted to be at home either. Maybe being stolen by a stranger was better than what was going on at home. Memories from those days started surfacing. My mother drunk, half-sitting, half-falling from her chair at the dinner table. My father, white with anger, furiously carving a roast, serving the vegetables as well, his mouth a compressed line, Rosie shrinking away from him as she passed me my plate, baby Charlie crying down the hall in his cot. No one saying anything. I made a mental note that sometime soon Greg and I would have to have a father/son talk about how things were in this family of ours.

I started the car up and drove to the big supermarket at the top of Kings Cross, did a week's shopping for myself and my son, remembering to stockpile milk, bread and various breakfast cereals. Greg could clean out a well-stocked fridge in forty-eight hours. He ate a loaf of bread most days, what with toast, sandwiches and other snacks.

When I got home, I went straight to the mailbox. I knew immediately I looked at it that the envelope I could see inside housed another of the anonymous letters. This time, I left it there until I'd gloved up inside and returned with a plastic bag. Leaving it unopened, I carefully transferred it to the bag and put it away with the other one. This one, I decided, I'd open myself in the lab. I didn't want to miss anything. That way, too, it was more impersonal: I could pretend that I was simply doing a job and that the malice was not directed at me. I was very tired, but checked on Greg, to make sure that he was covered properly. Greg is the most restless sleeper, usually waking up with his head at the foot of the bed and the covers in a twist somewhere on the floor. He was sound asleep, lying across the bed with his head hanging over the side and the pillow bunched up under his hips. There was little I could do without waking him, so I backed out. My mobile rang and I snatched it up, pleased to have this distraction. 'McCain?' I snapped.

'Jack McCain?' said a voice I didn't recognise. 'You don't know me,' he said, and for a moment, I thought the anonymous letter-writer was on the line, 'but I was a young constable at Springbrook at the time your little sister was taken—'

'Who is this?' I interrupted.

'Detective Inspector Colin Swartz,' he said. 'I've just been talking to Bob Edwards in Sydney. He thought you'd want to hear what I have to say.' I waited, bewildered at the way Rosie was suddenly appearing everywhere, signing erotic letters to convicts and now remembered all these years later by a strange police officer. 'It was my first big investigation,' Swartz was saying, 'your little sister and the circumstances surrounding her disappearance. I've never forgotten.'

'No,' I said finally, bringing my emotions under control. 'Neither have I.'

'I went along with some of the young blokes to a suicide here at Blackheath yesterday,' said Colin Swartz, 'and, to cut a long story short, we found something out the back. In the car shed.'

I listened while he continued and when I heard what had been found I became very interested in what he had to tell me. We arranged to meet the next day.

•

Even though I was tired, I couldn't sleep. As well as the sense that I was getting closer to Jacinta, there was the promise of what Colin Swartz had told me about the suicide at Blackheath. I was wide-eyed and restless. The second anonymous letter was worrying at me, too. And my mind couldn't let go of those letters signed with my sister's name. Rosie McCain is not a common name, I kept telling myself. But it could be nothing but coincidence. So round and round my mind went until I was almost considering trying to find the couple of sleeping pills I recalled lying somewhere at the bottom of one of the cartons. Finally, however, the mayhem between my ears stopped, so I think I must have slept. But then I was suddenly awake again. I sat up with a start. There was someone in the room. 'Greg?' I asked, 'is that you?' But I had a strong sense that it wasn't him. Indeed, without knowing why, I had another equally strong sense that there was no human being in that room, and yet I continued to sit, bolt upright, aware of a presence that charged the atmosphere of the pitch-black room. Gradually, I could make out an almost undiscernible line of less dense blackness under the curtain.

That was when my disbelieving eyes saw her standing silently near the door. My breathing stopped. I think my heart stopped. She stepped closer from where she'd been, dressed in the yellow linen sundress I'd last seen her wearing in 1975. I could even see the blue and yellow enamelled silver necklace that I'd given her for her thirteenth birthday, three days before her disappearance. I shivered.

'Rosie,' I said stupidly, 'you can't be here. You're dead.'

I checked that I really was sitting up in bed and that the dark contours around me were those of my bedroom. I knew that out through the doorway, past the impossible figure near the door, was the living area and, off that, another room, where my son Greg lay crookedly across a bed. I knew all this with perfect clarity. And at the same time I knew also that his aunt, my sister, presumed dead years before Greg was born, was standing in my bedroom near the door, here and now. The figure seemed to move closer to me. Her voice sounded different from the way I remembered it, yet when she spoke, the words seemed very familiar to me.

'We've learned so much more about aberrant sexual behaviours in the last ten or fifteen years,' she said to me and I was about to ask her where she'd heard this, but she went on. 'Why aren't you using everything to find me? Apply the new knowledge to the old. You promised me. Apply the new to the old.'

'Jesus, Rosie,' I said 'tell me, are you dead or not?'

And then she just wasn't there any more and I realised I must have got out of bed without noticing and was now standing in the dark in the middle of my bedroom. I stood there for I don't know how long. Maybe it was only a few seconds, maybe it was minutes. I tiptoed over to the place where Rosie had stood. I even put my hand out, as if there might be something to touch. But there was nothing near the door that might have remotely resembled a human figure, no shirt hanging on the back of the doorknob, no towel. Nothing behind the door when I looked. I'd heard that sometimes the air is chilled at the time of a ghostly apparition, but the temperature near the door felt normal for the time of night and the month of November. And in my mind's eye, I could still see her, clear as day, the way she'd stood there just a second ago, in her cute yellow dress.

I stepped back and nearly tripped, hitting the bed and falling back on it. I lay there. This was getting serious. I recalled the awful moment when I'd felt rage at my son and almost hit out at him. Now, on top of everything else, I was seeing things, hearing things. Had Rosie appeared to me, as a vision or a ghost, or was I going insane? For a few panicky moments, one of those two completely unacceptable positions seemed to be the only possible choice. I recalled my brother's warning that I was going to have to 'do something about myself'. If this was a stress response, things were a lot worse with me than I'd believed. Maybe I *would* have to do something. But what that something was, I had no idea. Then I recalled the phenomenon known as a waking dream, a projection of the unconscious, seen 'out there' as if it had a separate, solid, three-dimensional existence. Charlie and I had discussed this years ago in connection with a woman who claimed to have seen apparitions of the Blessed Virgin.

I went out to the kitchen and switched on the light, taking comfort from the mundane scene of the untidy table and my cartons of gear stacked around. Out here, with the little table lamp casting a friendly glow over familiar objects, my sense of what had just happened seemed to change, the clarity and immediacy of it to lessen. I made myself some bread and butter which I ate without tasting, sitting at the table among the files from the three investigations in my life—Rosie, Jacinta and the murdered sex offenders. No wonder, my brain rationalised, that I'm starting to see things in connection with my sister. Even without having any qualifications in psychology, I could see that my emotions and my mind had been stirred up by the conversation with Renee and Jacinta's possible reappearance in my life. In the stillness of my kitchen, with my heartbeat returning to normal, it was starting to seem inevitable that Rosie might arise in such a visible way. Add to that the call from the Springbrook cop, and it seemed almost inevitable to me. I sat there and the world was hushed. I could have been in the middle of the bush, so quiet was it. In the stillness, the words Rosie had repeated to me—*'Apply the new knowledge to the old'*—re-echoed in my mind. Did she appear to tell me that? It seemed platitudinous now, a bit like the brilliant instructions written down after a dream that turn out to be stupid and banal in the light of day. What did I know now that I hadn't known then? Only just about everything, I thought bitterly. I looked around and the little green digital clock on the amplifier told me it was two fifty-one, the time when the human spirit ebbs to its lowest point and the darkness is at its most dense. And there I was, in the centre of it.

•

Greg was still asleep and the magpies carolling when I left him a note on the kitchen table saying I'd be back later in the day and that there were bacon and eggs in the fridge. Not that he'd need a note to track them down.

It felt like November hadn't quite made it to the Blue Mountains yet, and a mist covered the distant mountains and ridges. I drove with the heater on, despite the bright sunshine, and when I arrived at Springbrook police station, Colin Swartz was out but he'd left an envelope for me with a note and a rough map. I was about to leave with these when a police Commodore pulled up and a portly man in his fifties got out and introduced himself.

'I've actually met you before,' he said, 'but I wouldn't expect you to remember.' He patted a paunch. 'There wasn't so much of me then.' He wasn't tall enough to carry the extra weight well and the fat had also collected round his jowls and neck. 'You gave a lecture years ago when you were still with us.' I knew by that he meant the NSW police.

'Must have been a long time ago,' I said and complimented him on his memory. I followed him into his office, noticing how he'd unsuccessfully combed his hair over a bald patch. He pulled some black and white photographs out of a manila envelope, turning to me with them.

'I didn't notice anything till after we'd cut him down,' Swartz said, as he passed me the photos. I quickly went through them, seeing the skinny dead figure, trousers almost falling off the narrow hips, bunched up in the rafters hanging from a rope, the other end of it looped over and fastened to an engine block that had been levered from a workbench to the floor. *Bevan Treweeke*, I read on the envelope in front of me, *DOB 29.8.43*. Now very dead over fifty years later.

'That old engine block acted as the counterweight,' he said. 'It pulled him right up to the roof as you can see.' The rest of the photos were different angles of the same scene. 'He was one of our old pervs,' said Colin. 'We've always known about him. All the local kids were told to keep away from him but he'd been behaving himself for the last few years. As far as we know, anyway. I'm really puzzled that I can't find any record of interview when your sister disappeared, but we must have it somewhere. He'd be on any shortlist.'

'And it was definitely suicide?' I asked, the memory of three murdered men large in my mind.

'No doubt about it,' said the paunchy inspector. 'He left a note, and the way that engine block was rigged up shows he was taking no chances. I think the murder of those men in Sydney stirred something up in him. I couldn't use the word "guilt" because I don't think these pricks know what that means. But something wasn't right for him.'

'Or maybe,' I said, 'he recognised the style of the killer, knew that whoever it was would be coming after him next and was so frightened that he preferred to do it himself in his own way, rather than face the knacker's knife.'

'Can't say I blame him,' said Colin Swartz, adjusting himself awkwardly and then flashing me an embarrassed look. 'But when I saw that car, I forgot about him. And I immediately thought of you. I remember the whole state was looking for that frigging car twenty-five years ago.' Swartz passed me the photograph of an old Holden. 'It's beyond me why we wouldn't have found it back then. We'd have searched any place belonging to a bloke like this bastard.'

The photograph in front of me seemed to waver, as if it were underwater. I realised I was just about to faint. I grabbed at the desk top, my fingers skidding past paper, until I had a grip on the edge of it. It was the 1968 Holden that took my little sister.

'It's okay,' I managed to say to Swarz who stood beside me looking concerned, too awkward to say or do anything. Then I noticed the registration plates. In the same moment, Swartz spoke. 'The last person it was registered to was'—he fished around on his desk and picked up a scribbled note—'Bradley John Wheeler of 189 Allan Avenue, Blacktown.' He passed me the piece of paper. 'If he's a friend of Bevan Treweeke, he'd be worth a bit of a look.' I looked at the piece of paper. *Out of rego 25 years* Swartz had added underneath.

Shortly afterwards, he walked me outside. 'Reckon this just about wraps it up,' he said. 'Bevan Treweeke must've taken her. Years later, the guilt gets to him.' I got into my car, hardly hearing him. 'She's probably buried out there somewhere.' I started up my car and Swartz stuck his head into my window, too close to my face. I started winding up the window. 'Still, it must be some sort of relief,' he said to me, withdrawing his head fast. I managed to say goodbye and drove away.

I followed the road to Blackheath, past the newer subdivisions and onto a dirt road where, after about five kilometres, I found what I was looking for. It was a property where the homestead was set back off the road with a large, dark garden of dripping trees. Blue and white checked Crime Scene tape decorated the front gates. I drove past the mailbox, noting the freshly painted name on it and up the corrugated driveway. The day was warming up but in spite of that I shivered. It seemed that everything was happening at once. Rosie, Jacinta, the murders and now the suicide of a man whose garage housed the car that abducted my sister. The house itself was in great need of repairs with broken boards in the veranda that ran around two of its sides, although a ladder was propped against the side of the house and the upper weatherboards had been scraped back, prior to repainting. I introduced myself to the uniform who'd been left to secure the scene of a suspicious death, and together we walked down the back towards the car shed. The dank gardens felt wintry and bleak, despite the sunlit dapples on the long grass. I saw that the old timber double doors I'd seen in the photographs were open and I peered into the cobwebby interior. The uniform walked back to his house-sitting job and I was alone in the place where Bevan Treweeke had spent his last living moments. I looked up to the rafters and could clearly make out the marks of the rope that he'd slung over a beam. On the floor on the other side of a dusty workbench lay the rusting engine block.

But I was hardly thinking of the pathetic man whose death had brought me to this place as I squeezed past another old car body. Behind this was the car Colin Swartz had noticed and photographed. An old canvas cover lay on the ground beside it. Now I just stood there, stupidly staring at the cream and tan 1968 Holden with the chrome bumper bar and the touring club badge that had left its imprint on the tree. It looked like it had been parked here forever and the scientist in me rejoiced. Sheltered here, the vehicle would have been spared the environmental conditions that can destroy evidence so quickly. DNA deteriorates rapidly in the presence of radiation. Automatically, I started examining the outside of the car. The four tyres were brittle and perished, crumbling away. I walked round to the rear of the vehicle where I could plainly see the indentation created when it had reversed into the tree during its getaway, and when I examined the front bumper bar, I could see the shorn-off place where once a fourth chrome star had been fastened in line with the other three, still safely fixed to their moorings. Rats had chewed the upholstery and thick cobwebs curtained the windows on the inside. But physical evidence, provided it is in a dry, cool environment, remains silently ticking away, waiting to be collected and analysed.

I peered further into the car's interior. My sister had been in there, restrained, terrified. Maybe even assaulted. If there was any trace of her, I would find it. I saw two old-fashioned beer bottles lying in the back amid some other rubbish, but none of it was rubbish to me. It was like finding pure gold. I straightened up, realising I was emotionally numb with the shock of this discovery. Then, as the numbness started wearing off, I could feel my anger and bewilderment mounting. If Bevan Treweeke was a known pedophile, who should have been on any shortlist for interview, as Colin Swartz had said, what had happened? Why the hell hadn't he been pulled in? Why hadn't his place been searched? Why hadn't this car been found? And why hadn't he been charged? I knew corruption had been part and parcel of the old police force of twenty-five years ago and I'd been aware of it during the time that I was a serving officer. It was known that in the past pedophiles had been able to buy themselves out of trouble with certain corrupt police officers. But surely not out of abduction and murder.

My legs were shaking under me and I had to lean against one of the workbenches that ran the length of the side wall. My mind was running ahead of itself. If someone turns out to have been corrupt, it started telling me, I'll track him down and I'll— But I stopped this sort of thinking in its tracks. I reminded myself I was a man of science with a lifetime of law enforcement behind me and that at this stage, I could make no assumptions. There was a process and I would follow it, step by step. The thought of my familiar methodology calmed me down and I pulled out my mobile and rang the Crime Scene people at Parramatta to discover that they had left an hour and a half ago and should be arriving at any minute. When they did, I explained who I was and, because of my old association with Bob Edwards, discovered my presence would be tolerated when they went over the house and garage.

The two Crime Scene officers and I systematically searched Treweeke's little house, but we found nothing except that he'd had a passion for plastic flowers. Dusty bunches decorated every surface in cut glass vases, or nailed into position over doorways. I washed up at the kitchen sink and Treweeke's old cat wailed around my legs wanting a feed. I found some milk in the fridge for it. You poor bugger, I said to the cat as it lapped up the milk. I looked around the kitchen. An arrangement of blue and yellow plastic flowers put me in mind of the blue and yellow enamel necklace I'd given to Rosie. I went closer to them and saw they were covered in spider webs. In fact, the plastic was so old and brittle that the cobwebs were practically holding them together. With my eyes now tuned to cobwebs, I could see them everywhere. Treweeke had not been a good housekeeper. They darkened each high corner of the ceiling and covered the edges of the dusty windowpanes.

I heard my sister's words of the night before: 'Apply the new knowledge to the old.' Looking at the cobwebs and the way they interconnected and threaded around the dusty fake flowers, I had a realisation of what she meant. In the last few years, we'd come to know so much more about the activities and proclivities of men like Bevan Treweeke. They were like spiders with interconnecting webs building little networks for themselves comprising others of their ilk. They exchanged information. In certain cases, they even exchanged children. We found nothing in the house, but I knew enough about men to know that often their most important secrets were hidden in the shed.

I went back to the shed where the Holden lay, followed by the old cat. I started looking through tool boxes and drawers of spanners and fasteners. It was right over in a corner under the dirty sink that I found it. A small address book, wrapped in a greasy rag, hidden in a pile of old towels, shoved right at the bottom of the plastic basket. There was nothing to identify its owner in the front pages. I quickly went through it. Under the heading 'Birdwatchers Club' I saw a list of names and numbers at the front: Tony S,

Julie B, Bobbie T, Sandy M, Robyn Mc, JoJo A. Except for 'Julie B' they were all androgynous names that men like these often adopt between themselves. It was the phone numbers I was really interested in. I had a horrible feeling I knew exactly what sort of quarry these birdwatchers stalked. I put the book in a plastic bag and turned my attention back to the car. By tomorrow night, this car and its canvas cover would be wrapped up, crated, freighted and delivered to the dock beside the Forensic Services Division where I would go over it inch by inch. This was the first lead we'd had in twenty-five years. I would apply all the knowledge we now had regarding these men and their habits and then I'd reapply myself to my little sister's case. I closed my eyes and briefly prayed that this might be the end of it. Then maybe I could close the book on Rosie and get on with sorting out the rest of my life.

Colin Swartz had loaned me the case records of Bevan Treweeke, and I was hopeful I might be able to find something that would cast more light on her abduction and her fate. Just before I left, he called round to the damp old cottage.

'Thought you'd like to know someone from Blacktown went round and had a chat to that fellow the Holden was registered to, name of ...' He frowned, reaching into his memory.

'Bradley John Wheeler,' I reminded him.

'Christ, you've got a good memory,' he said.

I shook my head. 'Only in certain cases.'

'Turns out he's an alderman now,' he continued. 'Pillar of the community.' He must have seen my face because he added, 'In the old days,' and his voice was plaintive, 'things like that used to mean something.' He paused. 'He's a cleanskin. Says he remembers the Holden very well. It was his pride and joy when he was a youngster. He sold it after a rally in the Blue Mountains. Some young bloke. Gave him the rego papers all those years ago and never heard a word from him after that.'

•

I drove back to Sydney with yet another folder to add to the pile on my dining room table.

I was intending to go straight home when I noticed the sign to Annandale and almost without knowing what I was doing, I found myself taking the turn-off to the road where Iona Seymour lived.

I parked unobtrusively and sat there, leaning back in the seat, tired from the driving, wondering what the hell I was doing sitting off this woman's house while I ran different scenarios for inserting myself into her life. I was wondering what it would be like becoming a volunteer at an FM radio station, when I looked up and saw her walking to her car. Because the afternoon was quite hot now, she was dressed in shorts and a sleeveless checked shirt, tied in a knot at the midriff, and I was surprised at the muscles in her calves and thighs and, more especially, by her well-developed shoulders. She drove down the road and I pulled out, following her to a cross road where she took a right-hand turn and then a hard left. She parked and got out as I went past her and around the corner of the short lane she'd stopped in. I hurried back to find her making her way up a ramp beside a graceful Anglican church.

Another desperate prayer, I wondered. Is that what she's up to? I was curious and excited as I watched her walk past the side entrance and head for the drab hall behind the stone church. For many years some time ago, I myself had spent hundreds of hours in places like this and I wondered if I now knew her secret. I have never forgotten the wretched early days of sobriety, learning to live without the only thing that had made living possible at all. If Iona Seymour was an alcoholic, we had a lot in common. It would certainly explain the strong attraction I felt towards her. It is a fact that addicts seem to be drawn to each other.

The doors of the church hall stood wide open, and I could see people sitting in a circle inside. Because those present were mostly women, I suspected it wasn't, in fact, an AA meeting, where the ratio of men to women is at least sixty to forty, and I was about to turn away when a young woman standing in the doorway whose grey-blue eyes matched her shirt, suddenly reached out and took my arm.

'It's okay,' she said, with a kindly smile. 'A lot of people want to run away when they first arrive. Are you here for the meeting?' I couldn't think of any response, so I just nodded. 'I'm Nell,' she said, extending her hand. 'We only go by first names here.'

Suits me, I thought, since I already know the surname of the member of your group that I'm interested in. 'John,' I said automatically, reverting to my real name and giving her hand a vigorous shake.

Nell drew me inside, found an empty chair and sat me down in it. Almost immediately, I realised I'd walked into one of AA's several offspring: Twelve Step groups dedicated to almost every problem associated with being human. Banners on the wall declared this to be 'Relations Anonymous' with the Twelve Steps slightly adapted. I knew of Twelve Step groups for compulsive overeaters, for smokers, for narcotics users, for pill-poppers and for gamblers, and I'd heard of similar groups for people with HIV, sexual compulsions and even for those whose credit card use was completely out of control. Someone had once even tried to convince me she'd been to a Vampires Anonymous meeting in LA.

My arrival had interrupted a woman speaking from her place in the circle.

'I'm sorry,' I whispered to her. She acknowledged me and continued speaking.

'—so now I'm trying to stand on my own two feet for the first time in my life. I've always expected a man would do it for me. Not that I was aware of it. I thought I was pretty independent until the divorce. Now there's just me.' As she spoke, I looked around the group, careful not to betray too much of an interest in the dark-haired woman in the checked shirt and shorts who was only a few chairs away to my right. The format felt very familiar and it didn't take me long to work out that Relations Anonymous seemed to have its focus on those who were suffering because of difficult relationships with other people. Even though I was here somewhat under false pretences, the irony of my position was not lost on me. I certainly had the right qualifications to be a member of this group and I didn't feel so much of a fraud as I might have. With the exception of Bob and Charlie, I thought to myself, all the relationships in my life have been problematic. As memories of Genevieve, my son and daughter, and earlier memories of my father and mother stirred, I forgot for the moment the hanged suicide and the Holden as I focused my attention on what was being said. The next speaker was describing how she'd finally kicked her boyfriend out after he'd told her she was fat and ugly and would never find another man.

'I told him I disagreed with his assessment of me,' she recounted, 'but that he'd most definitely have to find another woman. And I walked away,' she said. 'That was last week and I'm still a bit shaky, but on the whole I feel pretty good about it.' As she sat down, the chairperson looked straight at me.

'John,' she said, and I realised Nell must have added my name to the list in front of the woman who was chairing the meeting. 'Would you like to tell us something about why you're here?'

'Not today, thank you,' I said, using a familiar formula. 'I'll just listen.'

And I did, sometimes listening as speakers described the difficulties they were having with some of the people in their lives, but mostly going back over my memories of Bevan Treweeke's place, recalling the freshly painted name on the mailbox, the poor condition of the cottage, the ladder against the wall. These inconsistencies might be telling me something important. I wanted to know why no one had found that Holden twenty-five years ago and I realised I'd been miles away when I suddenly heard her name being called.

'Iona,' the chairwoman was saying, and I was now completely alert and present in the long hall with its dull floorboards and tall windows. The voice I knew so well now was very low, and though she was only a short distance away I had to strain to hear.

'It's getting worse,' she said. 'I simply don't know what to do. I've learned from coming here that I'm not responsible for things I have no control over, but in this case, I feel that I am. I feel lost. I don't know what to do. There is nowhere I can turn except here. I tried talking to someone about my situation, but he doesn't really understand.' She broke off and I felt an unreasonable dislike of the man who had failed her. 'I'm trying to find some clarity in all the confusion.' She stopped and, after a lengthy pause, the chair invited another speaker.

As the next speaker outlined his strategy for dealing with a challenging daughter, I was wondering what it was that Iona Seymour had no control over. I kept her in my peripheral vision as I helped to stack chairs away against the wall after the meeting. Several people had gathered around the refreshments table and I glanced across in time to see that Iona was hurrying towards the door. No chitchat for her. So there was not going to be an easy way for me to insinuate myself into her day. But she was stopped by the sociable Nell who drew her to one side and made two cups of instant coffee, passing one to Iona, all the time engaging her in conversation.

'John,' she said, noticing me, 'Coffee?' And before I could say yes or no, she had poured one and was holding it out to me.

'Thanks,' I said, taking it from her.

'Your first meeting?' Nell asked.

'Of this fellowship,' I said, trying not to look too interested in the tall woman near us, drinking her coffee fast, almost edging away.

'I've found these meetings very helpful,' said Nell. 'You might, too.'

'I'm sure I will,' I said, as Iona put down her unfinished coffee cup and turned to leave.

I put my untouched coffee down and exited fast, smiling an apology at Nell, and hurried back down the ramp to see Iona Seymour walk to her car, climb in and pull out.

I raced to my car and followed her down the road, where she stopped at a small local supermarket a few streets away from her house. Perfect, I thought to myself. This might be the opportunity. She went inside and I followed her, took a trolley and set off down the aisles to find her. She was working from a shopping list and I watched what she selected. The strange intimacy I felt with her, although she didn't know of my existence, increased as I became familiar with her choices: a large pack of natural muesli, a sugary processed cereal, soy milk, full cream milk, cheeses, sweet biscuits, free range eggs, bacon, tins of weird health food and fruit and vegs from the chilled racks near the door. I bought a couple of things I needed, and followed her to the checkout area, taking one of a number of bags of oranges from a hook near the exit. As the Lebanese proprietor operated his till and Iona's goods were pushed towards the end of the checkout, I ripped open the bottom of the bag of oranges with the penknife I've carried with me since my days in the Scouts so that oranges went everywhere, into her trolley, around our feet, or rolled away towards the door.

'I'm terribly sorry,' I said, attempting to pick them up. 'The bag burst.'

While the proprietor clucked and grabbed the oranges on his counter, Iona Seymour fished some out of her trolley and handed them back while I picked up the ones I could see on the floor. 'Here,' she said, in that voice. 'I think that's all I've got. Oh no. There's one under the checkout.'

We both stooped at the same moment, and our faces were very

close and at eye level. I wanted to know who or what had caused the terror I could see hiding in her eyes. We straightened up together.

'You were at that meeting,' I said, pretending surprise. She smiled.

'Yes. And so were you.'

We were so close that I could feel the tension and the strength of her well-built body. Her shoulders and upper arms showed well-defined muscles, and the hand collecting the runaway oranges was square and powerful. She reminded me of Charlie's latest girlfriend, Siya; this woman had the same sinewy strength. I took the orange from her and added it to my purchases.

'Can I buy you a decent coffee?' was out of my mouth before I had time to think. 'This bag bursting has been the latest in a series of domestic disasters.' It sounded pathetic and I regretted the words the moment I said them.

Her smile was a surprise because it lit a face that seemed created for seriousness, even sternness.

'They're the worst sort,' she said. Her dark eyes looked straight into mine. 'A decent coffee would be good,' she said.

I was feeling stupidly self-conscious and I had to deliberately reason with myself as I carried the two coffees back to where Iona was sitting, in the cosy little weatherboard café next to the supermarket that seemed more like some dear old auntie's front parlour than a commercial enterprise. Just for a while, I left behind my failed marriage, my lost daughter, my vanished sister. I knew they were all safely waiting for me and I'd be picking them up soon enough, but just for this hour or so, I was a man with an attractive woman and I was feeling as awkward as hell.

I put the coffees down and went back for the sandwiches I'd ordered. Iona sat gazing out the window. She seemed miles away, but turned and there was a slight smile as she looked at me. I got the sense she was really trying.

'Please have a sandwich,' I offered, moving the plate closer to her. She shook her head. 'It's a really nice double smoked ham,' I said, feeling stupid. Iona recoiled.

'I'm vegetarian,' she said, with some distaste. I'd have to do better.

I bit into the sandwich and little pale green streamers of lettuce fell onto the tablecloth while Iona watched the steam swirl from her long black.

'Have they helped you?' she was asking me and for a minute I didn't have a clue what she was talking about. 'The meetings?' she said. I nodded.

'Very much,' I said. And because of my past, it wasn't a complete lie.

'I haven't seen you before.' She was looking intently at me and I revisited that powerful moment when our eyes had connected over her old blue Mercedes in the radio station's parking area, and I prayed she wouldn't remember. Avoiding eye contact with the target is the golden rule. I felt guilty for what I knew about her: that I'd read her desperate prayer, that I'd followed her like a stalker. If she'd known any of this, she wouldn't be sitting here with me now.

I was creatively evasive. 'I don't live round here. I just came to this one for a change of scenery.'

That seemed to satisfy her, and she sipped the coffee, still looking at me with her steady dark eyes. The fear I'd seen earlier was no longer obvious as she leaned behind her to pull a white cotton jumper around her. I saw the muscles move in her arms and shoulders.

'And you?' I said, remembering the old days of AA meetings and intimate conversations with strangers that were only made possible because of a mutual, dangerous obsession. 'Do you go to other meetings?'

She shook her head. 'Just this one.'

I'd forgotten how to be social and light with a woman. Things had been so difficult with Genevieve for so long, and conversation hadn't been a priority with Alix. Also, I had to admit to myself that I'd been very shaken by the apparition, or whatever it was, of Rosie in the night. Whether or not she was a figure of my imagination, or whether she had somehow 'materialised' in time and space, hardly mattered. Nothing like that had ever been in my experience and there was a new place created in my mind because of it.

But I knew well enough from my years in the job how to make others feel either relaxed or threatened. So I asked her harmless questions about music and books, what films she'd seen lately, and we were able to have a discussion about a film we'd both seen.

But I wanted more than that, so after a bit of this sort of talk, I tapped the chromed steel name plate attached to her keys.

'It's an unusual name, Iona,' I said. 'Is there a story?' Again, the slight smile moved her face. Her beauty was very fragile; some times her face lit up, at other times she looked anguished and her features stern and forbidding.

'Oh yes,' she said in her rich voice. 'It's an island high up the west coast of Scotland—only a few miles long and about a mile and a half wide. My mother met my father there. He was studying for the priesthood but meeting her changed all that.' She frowned momentarily and sighed at some memory of her own. Then she came back to the subject in hand. 'The island of Iona is in darkness from October to February. The sun barely touches the horizon. So most of the inhabitants go to the mainland then and everything closes down. It's very beautiful in that windswept way. The north wind blows without ceasing and summer is about three weeks long.'

I repeated her last sentence silently to myself. The words flowed like a poem. I knew a lot about her already, although she knew nothing about me. I knew she lived alone, but had no doubt that there was a man somewhere in the picture. She'd as good as said so at the meeting. Some difficult man who was causing her grief. Most people live in couples, I thought, with singleness only occurring when something goes wrong.

'And you?' she was saying, putting her cup down. 'Tell me something about you. What did you do today?'

I couldn't really say right now that I'd looked at marks on a timber beam caused by a suicide's rope, or that I'd checked out the car in which my sister had been taken to her doom twenty-five years ago. 'Me?' I said, buying time. 'I've driven up and back to the Blue Mountains. Work,' I added.

She frowned. 'What sort of work is that?'

'I'm a scientist,' I said, hoping she'd leave it at that. I didn't want to reveal my true colours nor did I want to lie to this woman. The awkward position I was in brought me back to the reality of my situation and that broke the spell. I threw back the remainder of my coffee. Iona took my cue and picked up her keys and purse.

'Has your scientific background given you a special insight into the human condition?' she asked.

I thought of my police work, the lab, the way we added to the body of knowledge about death and crime, but I doubted if that was the part of the human condition she meant.

'In a way,' I said.

'Science was a sort of enemy in my household,' she said.

I wanted to ask her what she meant, but she was suddenly restless. She started digging into her purse and her eyes glanced at the little folded-up bill under the plate.

'I'll get it,' I said, picking it up. I hadn't done anything like this for years and I knew I wanted to see her again, but didn't know how to make that happen. We stood up and I knew I should make a move now.

'Is it appropriate to ask you for a phone number?' I said.

She hesitated. 'Do you want my number because of the meetings or do you want my number?'

I knew exactly what she meant. In Twelve Step programs, phone numbers are exchanged so that when a person feels the familiar pull to the old, compulsive behaviour, he or she can make a phone call to someone who's gone through the same crises and found new ways to deal with them. I didn't know what would be the best answer. 'Both,' I said. That seemed to have the desired effect. She pulled a business card out of her wallet and passed it to me.

But suddenly something changed. Her face become hard and closed and I could sense stormclouds gathering around her. 'I've got to go,' she said, the shimmering voice even more beguiling under pressure. I remembered that tone. She had spoken my daughter's name in just that way. 'I'm sorry. It was a mistake'—she looked around at the coffee things—'this...this socialising. I shouldn't have agreed in the first place.'

I was aware of her power and, at the same time, her fear. 'What is it?' I asked. 'What is frightening you?'

She stared, shocked, into my eyes and for a moment I thought she was about to burst into tears. Then she turned away, picked up her shopping and started walking swiftly towards the exit. I hurried after her.

'Please,' I said, 'don't go like this. I've offended you in some way. I've been too pushy. Please forgive me.'

'No, no,' she said, 'it's not that.' But she didn't stop, calling the words back at me as she continued to hurry away. I didn't want to make a pest of myself, but nor could I afford to leave her like this. It wasn't just that I was strongly attracted to the woman, she had some real connection to my daughter and I wanted to know how and why. Otherwise, there was only Renee.

'I'll ring you,' I said, touching the business card she'd given me.

She looked at me briefly and nodded, but perhaps it was just to get rid of me. She paused for a moment before she got into her car and I saw her take a deep breath, as if she had to steel herself. Then she drove away in the bright afternoon. I watched her car as it turned out of the street. I know a lot more about you, Iona Seymour, than you know about me, I was thinking. And I had to admit to myself that the more I knew, the more I wanted to know. I was not going to let her get away.

•

Back home, I looked up St Kilian's, Padstow, and rang the number. A man answered.

'Father Dumaresque?' I said. There was a pause.

'Who is this?' asked the voice at the other end of the line. I told him who I was and found I was speaking to Father Cusack.

'Mr McCain,' said the priest, 'is this a professional or personal call?'

'Professional,' I said. 'I just want to ask him a question or two.'

'Ask me,' said the priest.

Somewhat impatient at his nosiness, I went on to explain. 'Father,' I said, 'sometimes priests deliver messages to people when they visit.' I also remembered that the letter Frank Carmody had received in gaol thanked him for *replying*. But to what?

'That's so,' said the priest.

'I want to ask Father Dumaresque about whether he's done such a service. During a particular visit to a particular prisoner at Long Bay last year.'

'Do you now?' said the priest. 'Then I'll have to tell you that Father Dumaresque went to his heavenly reward over five years ago.' He must have sensed my surprise because his voice was gentle when he next spoke. 'I only asked all those questions,' he said, 'because I thought you might be pulling my leg. We get mischief calls a lot of the time.'

I rang off and immediately called Bob. He reminded me that

anyone visiting any of Her Majesty's prisons must furnish the administration with their name and date of birth which are checked. Anyone with a criminal record is refused admission.

'I'll check that the priest is really dead,' Bob said. 'Some reverends do tend to take the moral crusade very personally.'

'Priests show up as perpetrators,' I said, 'rather than revenge takers.' But someone had availed themselves of the name and identity of a dead priest and I wanted very much to know who this person was.

SEVEN

I put Iona Seymour and the priest from the dead out of my mind by reading through Bevan Treweeke's miserable record. It went back thirty years. He'd first come to the attention of the local cops for an indecent assault on a little girl when he was sixteen. There'd been lots of complaints about him hanging round schoolyards, there were several charges of indecent exposure and even some convictions for burglary and peeping. But no serious charge had got past the committal stage. The year Rosie went missing, Treweeke had been thirty-two. This man certainly had the previous form I'd expect for a child abductor. But when I looked more closely at the earlier witness statements and records of interview, I understood why there was no record of interview with Bevan Treweeke concerning the disappearance of Rosie. In November 1975, when Rosie was taken from outside our house, Bevan Treweeke was at Devondale Correctional Centre, serving the second of a four months stint for Break and Enter. I turned my attention to the address he'd given in those days and saw that Treweeke hadn't lived at the address where he'd hanged himself and where we'd found the car, but in Springbrook, where we'd grown up. As I flipped back through the records again, the Blackheath address I'd visited earlier in the day caught my eye. It was given as the address of his grandmother, Mrs Marjorie Selwick, his next of kin. I put the papers down and stood up, needing to move. As a general rule, the abduction of little girls is not a crime involving grandmothers. And yet Bevan Treweeke had ended up living there, and the Holden had also ended up there. Grandmother Selwick may have even bought it at some stage, in all innocence, and it was just a coincidence that her grandson hanged himself near it many years later.

I went over the facts that I knew by heart. Rosie was taken from outside our place. The car had raced down the street, skidded on the corner, reversed into the tree, and taken off at speed. Mrs Bower on the corner, who admitted hearing the crash, hadn't been able to give the police much information. It had been days before the police had come out with a possible description of the car and by that time, anyone could have taken it anywhere.

I found Mrs Bower's statement from my own records and read it. 'I was cleaning the louvre windows,' she said, 'when I heard the sound of a crash. I couldn't say what sort of car it was because everything happened so fast'. I threw the folder down in frustration and kicked it across the floor, further irritated. Until I felt the weight of the deflation and hopelessness that now pressed down on me, I hadn't realised how much I'd had riding on this new connection. Then I reminded myself that my position had improved and that as far as the Rosie investigation went, I wasn't back where I'd always been. Now we had the car that took her. And Bevan Treweeke's little black notebook. I opened it up and started copying out the phone numbers in it. Discovering who these belonged to would be a start. I'd hardly written the first one when my mobile rang.

'I'm sorry to have to be the one with the bad news.' It was Florence from Forensic Services. 'But I'm afraid the results on Frank Carmody's clothes were NR.' The disappointment hit me hard: Not reportable. 'Even the amelogenin test?' I asked. The first marker on the DNA profile gives us the subject's sex.

'Like I said,' said Florence, 'all the loci were NR. Sorry.'

I felt the heaviness of disappointment. All my careful searching and combing of the dead man's clothes had come to nothing. But there was still my prize from the buttonhole.

'What about the long blonde hair?' I asked, and a fantasy image of the nightclub dancer twirled in my imagination.

'Ah, that,' said Florence. 'No follicle. No DNA. We had a good look at it even so. Either Carmody came into close contact with some crazy knife-wielding Asian who bleaches her hair then dyes it again or...'

I sighed, knowing what she was about to say. 'Okay, Florence. That's unlikely, so I'll settle for the obvious.'

'Yep,' she said, 'someone was wearing a wig.'

Most wigs are made from Asian hair which is straight and strong, then bleached and dyed to the required colour.

'That elimination sample from the cigarette butt is here ready for you,' Florence was saying.

'Thanks,' I said. There was a pause on the line. 'So we haven't really got anything,' I said finally, 'on the killer.'

'Oh I don't know,' she said. 'Sarah's got some interesting results from the letters. She said she'd be faxing them through to you sometime soon.' The 'Rosie' letters had taken a back seat because of my preoccupation with the hanged man and the Holden, and the recent unsatisfying interlude with Iona Seymour.

'I'll be in Sydney day after tomorrow,' said Florence. 'I'm coming up for a three day mini-conference.' I remembered the Forensic Society was running a program at Sydney University and Florence and several others had been invited as speakers. 'I'm not doing anything any of the nights,' Florence was saying. 'I'm staying at the Holiday Inn at Coogee. That's only a little way from where you're living.'

'That's nice,' I said vaguely, wondering why she was telling me all this and somewhat surprised that Florence would know or care where I was living. 'I hear it's quite comfortable. Great views.' I didn't quite know what to say next. 'The weather's been good,' I offered. 'A bit sticky but you could have a dip when you're not busy.'

'And I thought,' she continued, 'that it might be nice to ask you if you wanted to meet up with me for something. You know...'

I didn't. I had no idea what she was talking about. 'I'll be back down in Canberra by the time you've returned. There's a document I want to look at,' I said, thinking of the packaged anonymous letter that I still hadn't opened.

'I didn't mean about work.' Her voice was raw and stricken and I suddenly realised what she meant.

'You mean a get-together?' I said, quickly trying to restore the situation. 'Grab a coffee or something?' But it was too late.

'Oh, for God's sake,' she said, 'it doesn't matter.' She rang off abruptly and I was left standing there, the strained voice ringing in my ears. So that when the phone rang again, I didn't immediately pick it up. I was dismayed at the realisation that Florence Horsefall had some sort of romantic interest in me and I simply hadn't seen it. I had the deepest respect for her professional and her scientific ability, but as far as anything personal went, she was just Florence who'd been a work colleague for as long as I could remember. Now her odd, self-conscious behaviour, the flustered manner, the embarrassment that she'd displayed when she was in my company made some sort of sense. Not only had I failed to see this, I'd also just failed miserably in dealing with her in an intelligent or decent way. The anger in her voice had been the anger of a woman who feels herself wronged. I knew that tone too well to ever mistake it.

Slowly, I picked up the mobile and saw 'Missed call' on the screen. I pressed the message bank. When I heard the voice at the other end, so familiar and yet so different, I froze. The voice in my ear was a woman's voice. Eighteen months had softened and thickened her child's voice. My daughter's voice.

'Dad? It's Jass. Where are you?' There was a pause. I heard her swallow. Was she nervous? Frightened of me? 'Dad?' Her voice less sure of itself now. 'Dad. There's something that's happened.' There was a pause. I wondered if she was crying. 'I'll call again.' Then came the click as she rang off.

I was stunned, rooted to the floor for a second. Then I almost threw the mobile to the floor in frustration. Fucking hell, I'd missed the most important call of my life. I felt an unfair hatred for Florence Horsefall and her fumbling embarrassment and her romantic delusions. In that moment, I felt all the anger with all the women who had ever offended me. Damn you, Jass. Damn all of you. I wanted to cry. I played the message again and again. Slowly, I geared down and the fury left me. My daughter was alive and talking to me. She had responded to me. Renee had done her bit fair and square, earned her fifty bucks. My daughter had called me. She'd said she'd call again. All I could do was hope and pray and trust that she would. I picked the mobile up, willing her to ring again. Please, Jass, I whispered to myself, ring again. Now.

I walked outside and down the back, the mobile still in my hand. I peered through the bushes at the end of the yard. The playground over the back fence was deserted as always and the little swing hung stiff on its iron fittings, moving slightly as if someone had just left off sitting there. I stood there, remembering again the night my daughter ran away, the stupid argument about pierced ears, the screaming, the confusion, the sitting up all night and waiting for the police to take it seriously. I went back up the yard, automatically pulling the odd weed out of the tomato pots, seeing the yellow flowerets setting fruit the size of peas. I went back into the house, wondering where Greg was. I rang Charlie and in a few minutes I was at his place.

•

'I'm in trouble,' I said to him, as he let me in.

He looked at me closely and I could see concern in his features. 'Yes,' he said, 'I can see that.'

I put my hand on his arm and wondered where to start. So much had happened in the last twenty-four hours. 'Charlie, Jacinta just rang me. A few minutes ago.'

Charlie sat up very straight. 'What did she say? What did you say?'

I told Charlie about the fact that I'd missed the call because of Florence. Then I had to tell him something about the Florence mix-up. 'I think she's got a crush on me,' I said. 'I've never even noticed her. In that way, I meant.'

I told him about my visit to the suicide's car shed and the finding of the old Holden. 'If I sound all over the place,' I said to my brother, 'it's because I am. The last twenty-four hours have just exploded around me.'

Charlie made a soothing noise and led me into his living room and made me sit down, pouring me a lemonade while he had a brandy. I was vaguely aware of Siya in the kitchen and the smell of rosemary and lamb roasting. I described my meeting with Iona, and my growing attraction.

'Ah,' he said, remembering, 'the woman with the voice.'

'Yes,' I said, 'the voice. Bob and I both think she might have been about to say something about the murders of Gumley and Nesbitt, then changed tack. It's only after she'd changed direction that she mentioned Jacinta.'

I put my head in my hands. 'I don't know. There's just too much happening for me to deal with properly,' I said finally. 'I'm overloaded.'

'You've been overloaded for a while,' said my brother in his serious voice. I sat there, nursing my lemonade.

'And Charlie, there's something I want to tell you. Maybe you can help me explain it to myself.' I paused, gearing myself up to say the words. 'I saw Rosie last night. In my bedroom. Just standing there near the door, as plain as I'm seeing you now.' In the kitchen I could hear Siya singing about love in the only Greek words I knew. 'I feel like my life is coming unhinged from its moorings. Now I'm seeing things that aren't there. And not seeing things that are. I should've noticed what was going on with Florence.' Charlie just sat, watching me attentively and listening to my litany. 'But the thing that really worries me,' I said finally, 'is this. If I couldn't see that a woman I work with, that I see most days of my life up close, was sweet on me, how many other things aren't I seeing? Things that I need to see?' I looked over to Charlie, but he was just sitting there, still and quiet, listening intently. I waited for a while but the silence just grew longer. I inhaled deeply, realising I'd been holding my breath. 'I knew I was a bit stressed out,' I said, 'but now I'm really alarmed. My job depends on me seeing everything, noticing what's there, reporting, recording, analysing. You know and I know I can't afford to overlook anything, not the tiniest thing.' Again I was silent, then I looked at him. 'You said recently that I needed help,' I said. 'Well, here I am. Help me.'

Charlie smiled. 'It doesn't quite work like that, Jacko. I can't be involved with you like that.'

'Why not?' I asked. 'You've got the letters after your name.'

'Yes,' said Charlie, 'and I've got the same letters *in* my name. I'm your brother. I can't be a counsellor to you.' He relented a bit. 'In the most casual way, perhaps,' he added. 'I mean in the broad picture. But if you want to talk to someone, it really can't be me.'

'Why not?'

'Because I'm emotionally involved with you. I'd be compromised. Biased. Not seeing things clearly either.'

I sat there thinking. I knew this already, but I hadn't realised that I'd need to be told like this.

'It wouldn't do you any good,' he added. 'Besides, you'd probably take no notice of anything I recommended.'

'But you must be able to do something. Tell me something.'

Charlie got up and went to the sideboard, pouring just a finger more brandy and a lot of mineral water. 'Go home,' he said. 'Go home and have a look at that box of our mother's stuff. Start thinking about the past. Start letting it in. Draw a picture of our house and a map of the rooms. Start thinking about the similarities between our mother and the woman you married. The similarities with you and our father. The fact that our sister and your daughter both left home at thirteen.'

'But they were totally different incidents!' I said. 'You can't compare them.'

'I'm not comparing them,' said Charlie, 'I'm simply noting them. And asking you to do the same. I'll have a think and get back to you with some names and phone numbers.'

As if on cue, Siya came out of the kitchen, her dark eyes in their shadowed sockets glancing from me to my brother, taking in the scene.

'Please will you stay for dinner, Jack?' she asked. She laid her brown hand on my arm. I shook my head.

'Greg,' I said. 'I need to be home for him.'

'Ring him. Ask him, too.'

But I left in a few minutes.

•

I was cutting potatoes up and getting the broccoli ready when the back door banged open and my son came in. He went straight to the fridge and started making himself sandwiches. I could see that he'd had a tough day. He was pale and his eyebrows met together in a frown.

'Don't fill up too much,' I said. 'Dinner won't be long.'

He wandered into the living area and collapsed onto the lounge, upside-down, with his head hanging down, looking at me with his legs hooked over the back of the settee. 'This is a daggy place to live,' he said. 'Why can't we live somewhere decent?'

'Like where?' I asked.

He swung himself up the right way. 'I don't know. Just somewhere with a bit of life. None of my friends live out this way.'

'I know it's hard for you, Greg. I didn't know you'd want to come and live with me. I just grabbed this place because it was quiet and I could afford it.'

I was about to tell him about his sister's phone call, but hesitated, wanting to find the right time.

Later, we had an almost silent meal together, both preoccupied, both unused to talking to each other about the things that ran deep in us. Finally, he asked me about the investigation and I told him what I could about Bevan Treweeke's suicide, glad to be talking again, even though we were avoiding the huge subject of his sister.

'Do you think his death is connected with the three mutilation murders?' Greg asked me.

I shrugged. 'I really can't say one way or the other,' I said. 'He's another sex offender, and he's dead, but that's as far as you could take it.' The conversation bridged the gap between us somewhat. I felt I should tell him about his sister's call. I couldn't put it off any longer. 'Jacinta rang a while ago,' I said, 'not long before you got home.'

Greg put his knife and fork down, staring at me, open-mouthed.

'But I didn't get to talk to her,' I continued. 'She said she'd ring again.'

My son just sat there. 'What did she say?' he managed eventually.

'That was it, really. That's all she said on the message.'

Greg stood up and walked away into his room, his half-eaten meal lying on the table.

'Don't you want this?' I asked, picking it up and taking it in to him. He was lying on the bed, staring at the ceiling, eyes brilliant with tears. I put his meal down on his desk, not knowing what to say or do.

'Can I get you anything else?' I asked, feeling stupid.

My son looked me in the face as he spoke. 'I've got used to her not being around. I've forgotten her.'

'It's been a year and a half,' I said. 'That's a long time for someone your age.'

'I don't even feel I've got a sister any more. I don't know what it'll be like if she comes back.'

I sat on the bed with him, feeling the distance between us. I hadn't been in this situation with him, sitting on the edge of his bed, since he was a little boy, and obsessed with a story about a little red engine. He turned over, away from me.

'What is it, Greg?' I asked. He didn't move for a moment, then he rolled back to look at me.

'I don't feel anything,' he said finally. 'Like, she's my sister and she's rung and I don't feel anything about that.' He turned away again. 'There must be something wrong with me,' he said in a muffled voice. I patted him awkwardly and stood up, leaving the room.

I went to my table and sat down. Though I hadn't been able to articulate it, I knew exactly what my son meant and I was feeling some of it myself. In the last eighteen months, we'd all done what we needed to do to protect our hearts and our egos from the pain and the guilt of Jacinta's loss. Now, the reality of her reappearance, in spite of the excitement it raised, and the potential for very real relief and joy, also brought with it all the other business: my sense of failure as a father, as a husband. Then there was all the business of what she'd been doing with herself over the last year and a half, what had happened to her, how she'd lived, what sort of people she might be involved with. If she came back to us, she'd bring all this with her, swirling around like black shrouds. I returned to Greg's room and sat in a chair. Eventually, he rolled over and looked at me.

'I know what you're feeling,' I said, 'because I'm all confused, too.' It was the humblest admission I'd ever made to my son, to anyone. It was the end of the all-knowing, father-knows-best charade.

'Geez, Dad,' said my son. 'What are we all going to do?' He looked away, blinking, and I could see he was on the verge of tears. 'Our family's a real mess,' he said, in words that were little more than a whisper. There was nothing I could say to that so I touched his arm, left the room, steeled myself and phoned his mother.

Genevieve was almost hysterical, demanding to know why I hadn't traced the call and what was I going to do, just sit there till Jacinta decided to ring again. I told her, yes, pretty much.

I suddenly remembered a scene between my parents from my childhood, with my mother screaming at my father, and my father standing there, sounding just like I had then before I'd put down the phone.

My fax machine started humming, so I cleared away our meal and stacked the dishes in the sink. Then I went to the overcrowded corner table where the fax machine was and tore off a letter from Sarah.

Hullo Jack, Sarah had written. *I'm sending Bob Edwards my official report but I knew you'd like to hear the basic points. In my opinion, the three 'Rosie' letters are indistinguishable from each other,* —Sarah was using the formula she used in court, rather than stating that they were written by the same person—*and they are each written with a fountain pen that catches the paper on the upstrokes, using an imported French sepia black ink. The most interesting element is the paper. I've never seen this stuff before and when I asked Warren Austin about it, he says he hasn't seen it for ages. It's an expensive linen-based paper, manufactured by Liberty Mills. According to them, production of this line ceased about ten years ago when it became too costly to produce in small quantities. Hugh Fullerton had a look at them, and he reckons the use of this expensive ink and the fine paper suggests someone fastidious, eccentric, maybe even crankish. I've passed the originals over to Fingerprints and made a copy of the text for Hugh to study. No doubt he'll venture a few learned opinions concerning the character of the letter-writer in due course. How's life on leave? Bye, Sarah.*

I put the fax down. Eccentric, fastidious and crankish, our lingo expert had said. And, he could have added, 'homicidal'.

•

Next morning I was in Bob's office looking through Sarah's official report. It gave detailed descriptions of the chemical make-up of the ink and the paper used and was signed with her official seal. It was highly technical so I turned to her summary and read pretty well what she'd faxed me last night.

'It's not uncommon to have boxes of stationery hanging round for years,' said Bob, putting down the report. 'When I chucked out Sheila's stuff I found boxes with teddy bears on it. Stuff she'd had since before we were married.'

'So all we need to do is find out who's got the box that paper came from,' I joked.

Bob picked up a note from his desk. 'I checked on the priest. Father Dumaresque died over five years ago.' Just as Father Cusack had told me, I thought.

'But he's still walking,' I said. I stood up, wandering around the room, picking things up, putting them down, my mind playing with different ideas. 'Impersonating a priest is a good one,' I said. 'It's not the sort of thing that anyone's going to check up on. Anyone could do it. I suppose they'd have to know a bit about what priests do.'

'And keep out of the way of real ones, who might smell a rat.'

'That wouldn't be hard,' I said, 'especially on a brief prison visit.' I sat down on one of Bob's spare chairs, but I was restless and stood up again. 'What do you make of it so far?' I asked my old colleague, who looked quite comfortable, sitting back in his chair, hands folded behind his head, legs stretched out and crossed in front.

'It's someone who likes good things,' he said, 'like Hugh suggests. Good paper, French ink. Someone's putting a lot into these letters.'

'Hell, yes,' I said. 'Not your average vigilante. After all, he's got to convince these men. Got to get them to meet him.'

'We're both saying "him" quite automatically, aren't we?' said Bob.

I considered his remark. 'If it's a woman,' I said, 'it's someone who's very strong, and handy with a knife.'

'Not many women like that around,' said Bob.

'My brother Charlie is currently living with a woman who trained as a commando in Cyprus.' Bob raised an eyebrow.

'We got a result on the hair I found caught on Frank Carmody's shirt,' I went on.

'And?'

'It's most likely from a wig,' I said. 'Florence found bleached, dyed hair, probably Asian in origin, the sort that's used in the manufacture of good quality wigs.'

'He dresses for the part, then,' said Bob, referring to our theoretical killer. Like an image from Hitchcock's *Psycho,* the grotesque figure of a man wearing a wig and women's clothes loomed out of the shadows of my imagination.

My mobile rang and I snatched it up. 'Yes?' I said. There was a long pause and I was starting to wonder if it might be a heavy breather. Then she was there again, very faint.

'Dad? Is that you?'

'Jesus, Jass, where are you?'

I felt Bob's alertness. The air in his office was charged and both of us stiffened.

'Dad? Please come. I've done something really stupid.'

'Where are you? What's happened? Just tell me where you are!'

'I don't know the address. I'm at Renee's. I've been straight for seven whole days, I'm booked into a Rehab and then just a while ago...' Her voice faded away.

'I know where Renee lives. I'll be there in ten minutes. What's the flat number? Stay on the line. Jass? Jass?'

But there was no response. 'Sounds like she's overdosed.' Panic was rising up to my throat. 'I know where she is but I don't know the address to give the ambos.'

'I'll get them to follow us,' said Bob, calling them as I raced out of his office. 'Get me a car!' I heard him yell, in between talking to the emergency operator. 'Who's got the keys?'

'Richo had them last,' someone said. 'Here they are. Catch.'

Bob caught them deftly in midair. 'Yes,' he was saying to the ambulance operator, 'we're on our way now.'

We ran to the lifts, taking the stairs when we saw they were both stopped floors below. I was hardly aware of the people who gawked after us as we raced down the stairs, round and round until we finally pushed open the heavy fire door to the basement carpark. 'Seventy-one,' said Bob as we ran towards it. 'Should be here.'

It wasn't. I looked around despairingly. 'Shit,' I said. 'Where is it?'

We wasted more time running up and down looking for the car among all the others. My daughter had done something stupid. Her voice had faded away. In spite of everything, part of me was feeling angry with her. Here we go again, this part was saying, just as I'd imagined, I was being drawn into her horrible mess. While at the same time, another voice was saying, for Godsake, she's only a kid who's been out on the streets. Give her a break, have a heart.

Bob was opening the driver's door of seventy-one and leaning over to fling open the passenger door for me.

'Okay,' he said, 'tell me where to go.'

We got to Renee's apartment block with the ambulance hard on our heels and Bob pulled rank and got past the security system. One of the ground floor residents told us that Renee Miller's apartment was on the thirteenth floor so we ran to the lifts. Bob and I and the two ambos raced along the parquet corridors, slipping and sliding on the corners until we came to apartment seven.

'Jass?' I hammered on the door. Bob took a running jump and kicked the door once, twice, to no avail. The next-door neighbour opened her door.

'What's going on? she demanded. It didn't take long for her to realise things were serious and, best of all, she had a spare key.

I fumbled it in the lock then ran inside, looking around. I stopped, taking in for just a second all the stuffed animals that sat on every surface and piece of furniture, or hung from shelves and cupboard doors. In the second bedroom I found my daughter. I knew her straight away even though she was much longer and thinner, and her hair was bleached white spikes. Her face, collapsed by unconsciousness, was sharper and bonier than I'd remembered, and there were blotchy patches on the skin around her mouth. Even the little cleft in her chin had a bluish shadow in it. She was lying on the floor near the bed, the phone still in her hand, wearing only pale blue underwear, an empty bottle of brandy beside her, clutching a white fur bear. I wanted to pick her up and hug her, but the ambos pushed me out of the way. I could feel tears building around the back of my throat and I couldn't help noticing the tracks on her arms.

'Bloody junkie,' said the older ambulance officer, with the impatient manner they had towards addicts.

'She rang me, she's been clean,' I explained.

'Yeah,' said the older man, checking her vital signs, pushing her sleeve up past the track marks, hitting her with Narcan to counteract the heroin. His gloved hands picked something up off the floor. 'And what do you think this is?' It was a spent disposable syringe. He let it fall. 'There's a new shipment on the streets. This is the fifth one today. They're dropping like flies.'

'I'm her father,' I said and they both looked at me, their professional impassiveness not quite concealing their embarrassment, pity and disgust. 'It might happen to you,' I said, feeling angry. 'You might find one of your kids like this.'

I felt Bob's hand on my arm and he patted me in the way men pat each other as he gently drew me aside.

'Take it easy, Jacko,' he said, 'let the experts do their job.' It was the same tone and voice I'd heard him use with dozens of other shocked and hurt people over the years.

Neither of them said anything as they stretchered her. I knew their training program well enough to know they were both obeying the chapter that instructs them not to buy into the problems caused by aggressive or shocked relatives and friends. The older one reached in under the bed and brought out an empty pill bottle. 'Rohypnol,' he said, noting it, then passing it over to me. 'She's lucky to be alive. That's alcohol, heroin and a hypnotic. So much for clean.'

'Is she going to be all right?' I couldn't help asking, although I'd sworn to myself I wasn't going to ask that question. I'd heard it a thousand times in the job, coming from distressed parents, lovers, spouses. I knew from experience that there was only one true answer to this question, and it was the younger ambulance officer who said, 'Can't say at this stage.'

Before Bob drove me to St Vincent's Emergency, we had a quick look around the flat. I found a large batik printed bag that proved to be Jacinta's and searched through it. Some underwear, a few clothes, some papers in an envelope, an address book, make-up in a leopard skin case, a novel and some NA pamphlets with phone numbers scribbled on them sat on the top of a gift-wrapped package that took up the bottom of the bag. It wasn't clear how long she'd been staying with Renee. Maybe she'd been here all the time, even when I'd spoken to Renee at the brothel. Bob helped me gather my daughter's belongings together because my hands were shaking so much I kept dropping things. Then he drove me to St Vincent's.

My daughter was processed in a rush through Emergency and hurried off to be cleaned out. I went to the little hospital shop and bought toothpaste and brush, soap and shampoo for her. I spotted a little doll, dressed in knitted pink clothing that I bought for her as well. I kept thinking of how she'd climbed up to gaze into my eyes when she was little, searching for something, and how I'd always lifted her back down again, distracting her with a toy or a book because I didn't know what she wanted of me. Now I was starting to understand. She'd wanted *me*. My time. My attention. She just wanted me to sit with her, to be with her, to chat, to listen. But I hadn't known that then. I hadn't known a lot of things. I remembered the way Genevieve would charge me with behaving as if I knew everything.

I rejoined Jacinta as they wheeled her into the lift, to take her to an upper ward. As the lift ascended, I looked at her, lying there dead to the world, her lips a little apart, a green-blue vein pulsing slowly on her temple. There were bruises on her shins and the bones stuck out around her thin shoulders. Her ears were decked with dozens of plain silver rings and her left eyebrow sported a silver knob. The sister in charge told me they'd ring me when Jacinta came round and that while she was in Intensive Care, visits would be very restricted, if permitted at all. I handed over the toiletries I'd bought, as well as some underwear and the make-up case I'd found in her overnight bag.

Bob left and I hung around for a while but there wasn't much point so I left my details and then hailed a cab, directing him to Genevieve's house. During the ride, I examined the gift-wrapped parcel in my daughter's bag. I peeled back one of the corners and when I saw what was inside I was stunned. Then afraid. Carefully, I tucked the wrapping paper back and repacked everything on top of it. I zipped it up and held it close to me.

The cab pulled up outside the house that had once been mine. When it drove away I stood outside for a few minutes, not only dreading the next stage, but also very concerned for Jacinta's safety. I took a deep breath, straightened my shoulders, took a strong hold on the batik bag and knocked on the door. Genevieve opened it and let me have it, both barrels.

'What do you think you're doing here?' she yelled, trying to slam the door closed on me. I pushed myself halfway through and glimpsed someone else in the house. Over her shoulder I saw the large figure of John Cleever Kapit standing in the lounge room.

'It's about Jacinta,' I said. 'She's in hospital.'

All the fight went out of her. I walked in past her. The infestation of little figures in pantaloons had worsened, and worst of all, the large figure of John Cleever Kapit stood in front of the mirrored mantelpiece, practically smiling at me as if we were at some social gathering. It was weird standing there, my estranged wife in between two men doubled by the mirror, both of similar height and build. I couldn't help noticing he was wearing a blazer just like the one Genevieve had bought for me years ago. She wasn't very original when it came to gifts.

'Always nice to see you, Jack,' he said, and I wasn't sure if he was being hypocritical or ironic. But at least he made no attempt to put out his hand. I ignored him and anyway, my hand was occupied with Jacinta's bag.

'Genevieve, I need to talk to you in private,' I said. 'This concerns our daughter. The situation is critical.'

I saw Kapit look over to her for a cue and was relieved when she gave it.

'I'm sorry, John,' she said to him. 'I'll ring you as soon as practicable.' She gave him a glance that seemed to say 'as soon as I've got this loser of a husband of mine out of here' as she accompanied him to the door, drifting too close beside him in her purple silky outfit and gold high heels, and I wondered, still smarting from her look of contempt, what she now did with the memories of all our years together, the good times, the love-making of our earlier days, the occasional fun, the births of our children, the shared history. She turned back to me after she'd closed the door after her boyfriend and her face had darkened. But before she could say a word, I got in first.

'Jacinta's just been admitted to St Vincent's.'

I watched her face change yet again. She raced to grab a coat. 'I've got to go there,' she said. 'Where is she? What ward? What happened?' In her face, so drained of colour, her mouth with its dark lipstick looked like a wound.

'She's in Intensive Care. Accidental overdose. They may not let you in to see her. I suggest you ring first.' Genevieve suddenly stopped her manic rushing, one hand still raised like a statue.

'Overdose?'

I nodded. 'Visits are restricted in the ICU so ring first,' I said again. 'She may have taken Rohypnol as well. She'd also been drinking.' I quoted the ambulance officer. 'She's lucky to be alive,' I repeated.

As I said all this, I was aware of my desire to punish my wife, to make her feel what her behaviour eighteen months ago had caused my daughter. My vengefulness backfired.

'This is you,' Genevieve screamed. 'This is your disgusting

alcoholism! You brought addiction into this family. You brought that to my child.'

I grabbed her arm, pulling her close to me, aware I was very close to losing it.

'Genevieve,' I said, hating her in that moment. 'I *did* something about the way I was!' I pushed her away from me, angry with myself for this display. 'It's just a real pity you never have.'

She stood in front of me, eyes blazing, rubbing her wrist where I'd grabbed it. I waited for the explosion.

But she took me by surprise instead with her sudden tears.

'Oh Jack,' she sobbed, 'what am I going to do? I'm her mother and I don't know what to do.' Her heartbroken cry touched me, despite the distance I'd put between us. This was the first time I'd ever witnessed such unguarded humility in Genevieve.

'She's in the best place possible,' I said and my voice was gentler. 'They'll do everything they can for her. Ring the hospital—they'll keep you informed. And I'll keep in touch.'

There was a moment when I might have stepped closer and said I was sorry about everything, the awful muddle we'd made of it, but I couldn't. The moment passed and I let myself out of the house and ended up walking for a long time, carrying Jacinta's bag, thinking about my daughter, my marriage, my mother and my wife. None of the thoughts were happy. Finally, I hailed a cab back to Renee's apartment.

•

I slipped in behind a resident who gave me a very suspicious look until I held up my ID card. When I got to Renee's door, it was off its hinges and a locksmith was drilling around the old lock. Renee herself, unpainted and wearing only a man's shirt and thongs, had a few things to say to me.

'It was an emergency,' I protested. 'My daughter was in a bad way. There wasn't time for niceties. I'm sure your insurer will pay up.'

'I heard from next door what happened,' said Renee. 'I see you've already got her stuff. Is she going to be all right?'

I shrugged. 'She still hasn't come out of it.' I looked around the flat with its sad little stuffed animals. 'How long had she been staying with you?' I asked.

Renee lit a cigarette. 'It feels weird,' she said, 'with my door lying flat on the floor and everyone looking in.'

'No one's looking in,' I said.

'Feels like it,' she snapped.

I repeated my question.

Renee gave me a long look. 'I don't have to answer your questions now or any time. The only reason you're in my flat at this very minute is because I haven't got a fucking door. Thanks to you.' She threw the lighter onto the counter, inhaled deeply and walked to the window where she looked over Rushcutters Bay and across the Harbour, exhaling smoke like a skinny little dragon.

'Renee,' I tried again, 'Jacinta is fighting for her life up the road. Can't you help me just a bit? You claim to be her friend.'

She frowned, threw me an odd, sideways look, tapped her cigarette and went to a sideboard where decanters of spirits gleamed in a row. A familiar squat figure in Chinese pottery carrying a long weapon next to the decanters made me look more closely. It was Kuan Ti.

'That's my patron saint,' said Renee, noticing my interest, pouring herself a Scotch. 'He's the Chinese god of hookers.'

'He's also the god of detectives,' I said as she flung herself on the white leather lounge, kicking off the thongs. Renee looked at me in disbelief and I saw enough to realise that she was naked under the oversize striped shirt.

'He assists police in difficult investigations,' I said.

'Not in this house he doesn't,' she said shortly.

'Please, Renee. This isn't an investigation. This is about my daughter.'

Renee stared at me as if she couldn't care less. But I knew it was an act. She glanced over again at the god of hookers and detectives and her voice was less spiky when she spoke.

'Jass lobbed here a couple of days ago,' she said, returning her attention to me. 'Said she was in trouble. Needed a place to stay. Just for a little while till she'd worked out what she was going to do.'

'Where did she live? Before the "trouble"?'

'Some dealer boyfriend. I never met him. She had this fancy idea she was going to kick the junk.' Renee shook her head and ran her fingers through her hair. 'Imagine having a dealer boyfriend, and then going and getting clean! Gear laid on and not using it. Makes no sense at all. That sort of put a strain on the marriage.' Renee rolled her eyes. 'True lerv flew out the window, would you believe.' I waited for her to continue. 'See, Jass started going to NA a few months ago and it gave her ideas.' Renee raised her eyes to the ceiling. 'It's an organisation full of losers.'

'She was going to Narcotics Anonymous?' I said, remembering the pamphlets she'd had in her bag. Renee stubbed her half-smoked cigarette out, nodding. 'She's been trying to get clean. She wanted to get away from Sydney. Go to a new place, start again. Go back to school. Reckons she'd been off the gear for a few months now. But, hell, we all say that.'

'Where did they live?' I asked Renee.

'Look,' she said, 'you're taking up my time.'

I pulled out my wallet, and showed her I only had ten dollars. Renee moved closer and, remembering the occasion at the brothel when she'd grabbed me, I put Jacinta's bag down and took a step backwards. She smiled at that, took off her shirt and stood naked in front of me. She had a neat, thin body, with almost no breasts and a tattooed leopard that curled from her groin around her pubic area, and up onto her stomach, showing its claws and teeth under her breasts.

'You can look for ten dollars,' she said.

I picked up her shirt from the floor and threw it at her. Sex was the last thing on my mind just now.

'Keep your shirt on, darling,' I said. 'I've seen it all before.'

'Suit yourself.' She shrugged.

I repeated my question and she shrugged again.

'I don't know where they were living. Somewhere in the city. But she'd moved out a few weeks ago and was just staying with people. Moving on every couple of days. The guy she was with, the dealer, wasn't happy about her leaving. You could ask around the streets. I mean, Jass and I see each other around, but we're not in each other's faces.' She put the shirt on again and tucked my money into the pocket.

'Renee,' I said, thinking of the contents of the gift-wrapped package in Jacinta's bag as I took hold of it again, 'there's something you should know. You could be in the shit.'

Renee's light blue eyes narrowed. I saw several things move

through her face in quick succession but the expression that stayed was annoyance. 'What's new?' she said.

My mobile rang and it was Florence calling from Canberra. 'A 1968 Holden's just arrived,' she said, in a cold voice. 'I believe you want to check it out personally. I heard it was involved in the disappearance of your sister many years ago.'

'I certainly do want to look at it, Florence,' I said, 'but I'm not claiming absolute rights to it. There should also be Crime Scene evidence from Parramatta bagged with it. Will you check and make sure that's arrived, too?'

'I can't personally,' she said, 'I'm just about to drive up to Sydney. But I'll ask someone to do it. I don't shirk my responsibilities.'

'Thank you, Florence,' I said. 'I'm pleased to hear it.' She rang off without further conversation and I stood there a moment, staring past Renee out to the Harbour lights. Rosie had intruded again as she always did. But I put her little ghost aside for the moment.

'You have to help me, Renee,' I said. 'Find me the boyfriend. Just leave me a message.' And I scribbled my phone number again for her to keep.

'Why should I help you?' she demanded. 'What have you ever done for me?'

I stood there thinking about that. 'There are about ten things I can think of that I could get you booked for right now,' I said.

'Like what?'

'Like anything I fucking well feel like,' I said, the sudden anger taking me by surprise. 'Just don't push me.'

Renee knew that I could do what I threatened. She shot me a look of pure hatred and I felt ashamed that I'd stooped to bullying this skinny little kid. But I was desperate for my daughter's sake.

'Jass had this dream,' she finally said, 'that she could get out of this life. But it was only a dream. No way she was going to get clean.' She stared defiantly at me as if to say, OK, you can make me talk, but you're not going to hear anything that will give you any pleasure.

'I believe she was intending to make it happen,' I said. 'Did you know what she had with her when she turned up on your doorstep?'

I could tell straightaway that Renee didn't know, so I told her.

The colour in her face drained even further so that she looked like the ghost of a ghost.

'And whoever she took it from is going to be coming after it,' I warned. 'And her tracks lead straight to what's left of your door. You are in real danger. Get a good deadlock.'

'I'll just point whoever it is in your direction,' she said coolly. 'You'll be the one in trouble. Not me.'

'You help me and I'll own up. Otherwise, I'll deny knowing anything about it.'

'You copper bastard,' she said.

'I need your help, Renee. Jacinta needs your help. I'll do whatever it takes to keep my daughter safe.'

She gave me a look of withering contempt. 'Oh sure you will. You've had such great success so far, haven't you, Daddy dearest, with your daughter on the street.'

Renee walked into the bedroom and slammed the door.

EIGHT

The minute I got home, I rang the hospital again, putting the bag down under the table. There was no change in my daughter's condition. This sort of thing, the doctor told me, can go on for a day or two. Or longer. There's no pattern. We just have to be patient. I put the phone down and looked in on Greg. He'd crashed out and was upside-down again on his bed, with bedclothes everywhere. I covered him as best I could and went outside, restless and unable to settle down to sleep. The scorn and contempt in Renee's voice were still with me. Outside, all was quiet. The scent of the cypresses filled the night air and I walked down into the darkness of the garden. Starlight ridged the leaves of the camphor laurel. I was turning back towards the house when I heard the odd metallic noise again. It wasn't anything living, I was sure of that now. And I knew that I'd heard that sound a while ago, but I couldn't for the life of me remember where or what from. I had a sense that I was not alone. I strained to see or hear whatever or whoever was around. I went down the backyard again, peering into the dark recesses, standing perfectly still, willing the sound to happen again so I could finally identify it. One more time and I'd have it. I remained standing in the darkness a few more moments, then I walked around to the front of the house and tried to discern if there was anything or anyone in the front garden. I was a bit spooked. I went back inside and locked up carefully, aware that I needed to find a secure place for the contents of Jass's batik overnight bag.

It was impossible to sleep, so I picked up the carton of my mother's papers Charlie had forced on me and put it on the table next to the documents and papers about Rosie and Jacinta. Now the three absent females in my life were lined up in boxes on my table. I couldn't face them just now so I pushed them all aside and on a piece of plain white paper from my watercolour block, I did one of the things Charlie had recommended and drew up a plan of my childhood home. It was a rambling brick and tile cottage, and I drew the tiled veranda that ran around in an L-shape from the front door area, down the right-hand side where another door, this one from what we called 'the good sitting room', opened onto the same maroon and cream tiles. I drew the hallway that ran half the length of the house with my parents' room to the right of the front door, Charlie's room on the left, with Rosie's bedroom adjoining his. Next to my parents' room was a fourth room, opposite Rosie's, that had french doors opening onto the veranda and that we used as a dining room.

At the end of the hallway, the house opened out into 'the good sitting room', rarely used except when we had special visitors, a room that we only walked through to get to the kitchen and the smaller sitting room next to it. Then I drew the doorway to my bedroom, an erstwhile small veranda that had been enclosed, so that it no longer gave onto the garden but had frosted glass louvres running halfway down the external wall. I remembered it had been very cold in winter, the glassed-in area losing heat on chill mountain nights, and the tiny gaps between louvres allowing wind to whistle through them. It had been many years since I'd thought of that bedroom. On a table in front of the louvres, I'd had a collection of birds' nests and eggs, small creatures in glass tanks and various pets, some of them rodents, that had caused my mother, when she was sober enough to take notice, a lot of concern.

My love for and interest in native birds had started then, as I came to know the birds of the mountains, the black cockatoos, the coucals and the rare satin bowerbird. I remembered how I'd thought I could understand what they were saying when they called. It wasn't such an outlandish claim, I realised. The alarm calls of birds are easily identifiable as such: urgent, repeated on the wing as they flee the threat or drive off the predator. The whispers and cooings of mating calls, too, are obvious, as tiny feathered bodies flirt and tease. Even today, I can't help hearing words when I hear the cries of birds. I've never told anyone this; I suppose I'm a little ashamed at such a childish habit.

Behind the door was a large poster of Merlin, and I suddenly realised twenty-five years later why I'd identified so closely with him. Merlin had been given the gift of understanding the language of bird and beast. There was a large table with my books and treasures stacked on it. I studied and read at that table, being called to dinner at about six thirty if my mother was still upright at that hour. I recalled my deep reluctance to put the book down, usually some gothic tale or other of death, decay and forbidden love. I remembered the odd formality of those dinners in the bare dining room presided over by my parents, before my father moved out to his shed, my father carving and my mother serving the vegetables while we pretended not to notice her swaying in her chair, or that the potatoes were almost raw, the beans blackened on the side that had stuck to the pot, or the carrots so salty they were inedible. I think my mother was the worst cook in the world even when she was sober. Anything she made was disastrous. Even as a kid, I could tell she had no love for food, no interest in it. She regarded everything she did in life as a chore and a waste of time. She was the only mother I knew who bought butcher's schnitzel, in the days when the butcher sold this ready rolled in breadcrumbs to hide the second-rate cuts. Every day Rosie and I took vegemite or peanut butter sandwiches to school. Every night we had tinned fruit and ice-cream for dessert. Some nights there was a fight that ended when my mother left the room, leaving my grim-faced father and us two kids sitting in a terrible silence. Other nights, there was only the ominous silence. Either way, we couldn't wait to excuse ourselves and leave the table. My job was to wash up while Rosie wiped. She was always nagging me to let her do the washing up and I never let her. Somehow, washing up seemed slightly more desirable than drying.

Thinking of how my father vanished from the dinner scene by the time I was about twelve made me remember his shed in detail. How could I have forgotten the shed, I thought, as I sketched it in at the bottom of the backyard. It was painted fibro, with a corrugated iron roof and had been the garage before he'd had the big brick and tile one built in the driveway. Over the years, my father had created an alternative household down in that shed, gradually taking everything he needed for his secret life down there. A black and white television, radio, electric jug, jaffle iron, lounge chairs, standard lamp, desk, chests of drawers, even a strip of floral red carpet to put down on the cement floor. The 'kitchen' was nothing more than a couple of spirit burners on which he seared his steak and onions. Spade, shovel and tools all hung on the walls that he'd lined over the years and drawers and boxes of bits and pieces were stacked on the benches he'd built. Eventually, he slept down there on a fold-up bed covered in army disposal blankets. In the last couple of years before my mother died, my father practically lived in the shed. He made his own meals down there, he discouraged us visiting him, although sometimes he'd tolerate us if we were quiet and just read or looked at books in silence. The smell of kerosene always pervaded the place in winter because of the old heater he had down there. I remembered the funny gurgle it made, like someone's stomach rumbling, as the big upside-down bottle of blue kero fed into the housing under the radiant mantel.

My mother knew better than to enter that shed. The only time I'd witnessed physical violence between them was the day she tried a forced entry. No wonder, I thought to myself, that I married a woman like Genevieve. Although she hadn't always been so difficult. It's hard to look back and wonder what it was that drew us together twenty years ago. Perhaps it was just sex and sentimentality as Charlie used to say about men and women. My thoughts turned to the woman to whom I was now attracted. Was she just another in the procession of witches? I recalled her seductive, grainy voice, the muscular arms and strong hands, the haunted shadows around her eyes. The fact that she was in some way connected to my daughter. The fact that she'd made an anonymous phone call to the police, changed tack halfway through, swerving away from something in her mind and giving information about Jacinta instead, and then denying doing so, made her complicit in intrigue at best, and something far more dangerous at worst. I thought of how she was named after an island off the wild west coast of Scotland, where a long night fell from October to February.

I walked outside again, restless, agitated. It was very late now, the distant roar of city traffic long ceased. I could smell salt from the sea on the breeze. I thought again of the tapes Chris Hayden had made for me. What was the information that Iona Seymour had almost told the authorities before her mind and voice detoured to something else? My fingers closed around something in my pocket and I remembered the desperate, mysterious words of the prayer she'd pushed under the statue. I knew enough about the workings of the human mind to understand that there must have been some connection in her thoughts between what she stopped herself from saying and what she eventually said. I went back inside to where the cassette player was still sitting on the sideboard with her taped voice on it. I stood listening intently as I played the start of it one more time. 'I want to talk to someone in charge of the investigation dealing with those two'—I stopped it there. Those two what? I pulled out the prayer she'd written and read it: 'Please help me with this terrible business.' I recalled her powerful presence and the stormy energy around her. I put the small folded piece of paper on the table next to my diagram of the family home, sitting and staring at the rooms I'd drawn.

Eventually, I went to bed, but it was a long time before I slept and even then dreams of my mother swirled around together with Rosie, Jacinta and Iona Seymour and it seemed no time before I heard Greg in the shower, and groggily looked at my bedside clock. It was almost seven and outside was another Monday morning. I lay there for a moment while all the world rushed back into my consciousness. The memory of the contents in the wrapped package that I'd found among my daughter's meagre possessions took hold of me. I'd have to find a secure storage place soon.

•

I had a shower and rang the hospital. Jacinta had passed a quiet night, the sister said, but her situation hadn't changed. They didn't use the word 'coma'. Greg stood opposite me towelling his hair dry while I spoke on the phone. Then I cooked him bacon and eggs, feeling as if I hadn't slept a wink, a tea towel tucked round my waist. I moved the bacon in the pan so it wouldn't get stuck in the cooking egg white and had a weird feeling, like a premonition, that there was something I needed to know, and that it was looking up at me from this very pan.

'How is she?' Greg asked as he watched the toast. He'd flattened his hair down with some gluey substance and looked like a slick baby gangster from a thirties' B grade movie.

'Nothing's changed since yesterday,' I said. 'She's still

unconscious.' I turned the heat down under the frying pan and searched the drawers for the egg slice.

'I've got a bit of business to do this morning,' I told him, 'then I'm driving to Canberra.' I found the egg slice and lifted the eggs onto his plate. 'And I won't be back until tomorrow night.' One egg broke and Greg grabbed a piece of toast and cut a little toast wall, placing it beside the break in the egg to dam up the runny yoke. One wayward tress of hair had broken free of the gel and stood up on the top of his head like a tidal wave. I leaned over to flatten it, but he ducked away.

'That's cool,' he said. 'Paddy's asked if I can sleep over at his place. Is there any more bacon?' Again, the strange feeling descended. 'What did you say?' I asked him, disoriented for a split second.

'I said two things,' replied my son logically. 'I asked if there was more bacon and can I sleep over at Paddy's place?'

'Paddy?' I said. 'Who's he?'

Greg frowned, looking at me as if I had two heads.

'You're truly weird.' Then he spoke in a deliberately patient voice, as if he were speaking to a child. 'Paddy is like only my best friend since Year 10, Dad. And his dad got all of us good seats when we flew to Queensland year before last.'

I searched around in my memory, then I nodded. I remembered Paddy and his family. I'd done my usual predator check on them a couple of years ago when Greg first started spending time with the fair-haired boy whose father was project manager for Ansett and whose mother was a teacher. Neither of them had a police record and they sounded pleasant and friendly on the phone.

'That'll work out well then,' I said. 'That means I'll be back before you get home from school tomorrow.' We finished our breakfast and I thought how Jacinta's friends had also been subject to my enquiries. I cleared away the breakfast plates. In many ways, I haven't been much of a father, but at least I've done that bit for them, I thought. Then I recalled my bruised daughter lying in Intensive Care and had to admit that even that hadn't worked in the long run. I felt suddenly wretched and leaned into the washing up, and then Greg surprised me by coming up behind me to give me a hug. He hadn't done anything like that in the years he'd been at high school. I didn't know what to say so I patted him and gave him thirty dollars.

On the way out the door, Greg turned to me. 'You look pretty cool wearing that tea towel,' he said. 'Even if you're freaky.'

'Have you got your keys,' I asked, 'just in case?' He touched his pocket, turned to go, then paused on the doorstep.

'Dad,' he said, 'do you think Jass will be okay?'

'I know that everything that can be done is being done, Reg,' I said, using his old nickname. He nodded.

'Do you think I can go and see her?'

'As soon as she can have visitors, I'll take you.' His face didn't change from its expression of concern. 'We just have to wait, Greg. And hope.'

A long time ago, some kind policeman had said almost the same words to me and I shivered at this merging of memory and reality. Greg waved and was gone to catch the bus but I was still back at my childhood house with my father, drawn out of his shed because of this terrible, unthinkable thing that had happened, as we sat opposite each other on the old velvet lounge and the two detectives spoke to us. I tried to remember where my mother had been, but could find no memory of her at that time. 'We just have to wait,' said the older detective. 'And hope.'

After I'd cleaned up the kitchen and searched in vain for whatever memory had been triggered by the frying pan, I grabbed my shaving gear, some clean clothes and the plastic packet containing the two anonymous letters, packed my old overnight bag and locked up. My mobile rang as I was walking to the car and I stopped in the darkness of the palm jungle.

'McCain?' I said.

She only had to say hello and I knew who it was.

'I was wondering,' she said, and her voice trailed off. Overhead, I was aware of the rustling of palm fronds and the rich compost smell of rotting fungus in the dimness of the thick grove.

'Yes?' I said, trying to keep the excitement out of my voice.

'I was wondering,' she said, 'if you'd let me buy you a coffee this time?'

I kept my voice steady and polite. 'I'm sure that could be arranged,' I said. 'When did you have in mind?'

'Sometime to suit both of us,' she said. 'I'm free most days.'

Days. She wasn't free at night. The man in her life loomed at me so that when I next spoke, the coolness in my voice was genuine. 'I'm away until tomorrow morning. What about tomorrow afternoon?' I suggested. 'Same place. We both know that.'

We agreed on four o'clock and I rang off. Despite all the weight of my various concerns and my irritation about the anonymous bastard who'd caused her to seek help from Relations Anonymous, I found my spirits had lifted as I drove to the Collins Club.

•

Pigrooter was already installed with his *Fin Review* and other newspapers, his cup of tea and his cognac when I asked if I might briefly join him. He extended an open hand and indicated the chair opposite him.

'I found my daughter via the illegal House of Bondage,' I said. 'I suppose I'm here to thank you for the tip. But my daughter's in Intensive Care this very minute. Heroin overdose.'

Pigrooter nodded. 'A lot of them do that,' he said finally. His pen was poised over the crossword and most of the little squares were filled with his large, slanting printed letters.

'I'm out of touch in this city,' I said. 'I want the name of the dealer she's been associating with. Get me that. I can do the rest.'

Pigrooter looked steadily at me.

'I have reason to believe,' I said, 'that she could be in all sorts of trouble.' I thought of her lying comatose in the Intensive Care bed and thought how silly those words sounded. To be in worse trouble, my daughter would have to be dead. And that was a distinct possibility if she'd ripped off a dealer. 'I'll owe you one,' I finally said.

'You're with the *Federales* now,' Pigrooter noted, saying that word in a mock Spanish accent. He leaned back in his chair and his belly lifted like a huge, deflating beach ball. 'Not much use to me. I say that with respect,' he added.

I knew what he meant. I wouldn't have the local knowledge that he traded in.

'You never know, though,' I said, 'when you might need something analysed. Some trace. Some tiny thing. Could make all the difference.'

Pigrooter considered, sipping his black tea and knocking back the last of the cognac. 'Still off the booze?' he asked me. I nodded. 'Commendable,' Pigrooter grunted, staring at the crossword as if I'd suddenly ceased to exist. I waited. This was all part of his game. 'Getting anywhere with the mutilator?'

'We've got some leads,' I said. 'It's a confusing sort of case.' I thought of the dead priest.

'I'll ask around, have a chat.' He picked up his pen again, filling in a vertical word. Then looked up at me again. 'It'll cost you,' he said, 'one way or the other.'

I called in at St Vincent's and sat beside my daughter. I could see that her mother had been there by the two little ceramic donkey vases, their tiny carts holding flowers on the table beside the bed. For years they'd sat on a shelf over the television set with Red Riding Hood and Little Bo Peep and a silly fellow in yellow pantaloons beside them. I leaned back in the chair, willing Jacinta to get better, to wake up. What were you up to, Jass? I asked her. Whose money is it? What's going on? But these were only superficial questions. Beneath them lay the mystery of eighteen months' absence and I wasn't sure how much of that I wanted to unravel.

Jacinta's pale face was turned towards me, her breathing slow and deep. With her hair now soft and brushed forward over her forehead, no make-up, and her lips softly open, she looked like a little kid again. Hell, I thought to myself, she *is* a little kid. What do you know at fifteen? A lot more, I thought a while later as I walked back to my car, than I did at the same age. I remembered the gawky youth I'd been, inarticulate before, and even worse after the loss of my sister.

•

I had to go back to Canberra to complete several tests and sign reports that were needed by the police in cases that were about to hit the courts so I drove south again. As I swung through the gates, I noticed the doors to the hangar-like building we use to house large exhibits were open and I caught a glimpse of the 1968 Holden. The sight of it sent a shiver through me. I signed myself in and went straight to my office where I made a cup of coffee and finished and signed the reports. Then I took out the plastic packet with the second anonymous letter and Rosie's old bear. I took the battered teddy to the Biology Lab where it would be screened and tested for her DNA so we'd have a reference sample to match against anything found in the Holden. Then I gowned and gloved myself and took both anonymous letters into one of the well-lit examination rooms. I opened the second one carefully over the white paper lining I'd placed on the table and gently unfolded it, spreading it with gloved fingers. It looked pretty much identical to the first one I'd received, except for the wording: laser jet print on bright white copy paper.

You think you're so smart, I read, *but you're so full of shit you can't see the forest for the trees. People like you have to be made to see the truth about yourselves. And it won't be long.*

I put the two letters together. Since the advent of white copy paper, those examining questioned documents have gathered a formidable array of tests in the composition of paper. Sarah would be able to determine if these two sheets of paper had come from the same ream of A4 paper and if they'd been close together or separated in the ream. Refined investigation, but until we found *that* ream of paper in the possession of the very person from whom these letters had originated, all we'd have would be some very fancy results. We'd check them for fingerprints, naturally eliminating our own in case we touched anything injudiciously. Even if the letter-writer had worn gloves, there was a still a chance we might discover latent prints.

I took off my coat and hung it in the anteroom, thinking of my daughter lying in another very different sterile environment. I'd found a couple of minuscule flakes on the letters that looked like some sort of metallic substance and I fixed them for further examination. It was impossible to deduce what they were although I didn't think they were paint. I handed the tiny traces over to Nigel who did most of the particle and fibre examination. 'Don't sneeze,' I warned him. Although it was a joke, there wouldn't be a bench worker alive, myself included, who hadn't spent a fair bit of desperate time on hands and knees crawling around a laboratory floor, searching for the speck of evidence that had somehow jumped off the slide. And on which an entire prosecution case might well depend.

It was time for lunch and I didn't feel like using the staff facilities, so I drove into town and ate a sandwich at a milkbar. I felt some apprehension about meeting Iona Seymour and realised I was what the Americans call 'dating' again. I was still surprised at my strong, personal interest in her. But from the moment I'd heard that voice on the tape at Kings Cross police station, I'd been attracted. This reminded me that I'd have to encounter Florence sooner or later. She'd be the person who would determine what if any DNA profiles or sequences might be derived from the Holden. I was very hopeful that there might still be something adhering to those old beer bottles.

I went out to the big garage and walked around the Holden. After all this time there was little likelihood of any fingerprint evidence remaining, though I could see where Fingerprints had dusted with red fluorescent powder. An alternate light source and filtered goggles revealed what could not be seen by the naked eye. I bent over and looked into the interior. Careful vacuuming, using a brand-new vacuum cleaner bag before anything else was done, ensured that the interior contents could be microscopically examined. Now red dust adhered to the steering wheel, window sills, interior and exterior door handles, the dash, gearstick, brake handle, anywhere, in fact, that a human hand might fall. If the abductor had left anything of himself in the way of clothing fibres or hairs, we'd pick them up. And the same went for Rosie.

I returned to my office and tidied up, putting the finished reports in the tray for posting. A tap on my door and Florence was suddenly there. Her reddish hair was pulled back from her face and she looked sombre in a black trouser suit.

'I thought you'd want to know that we got lucky on the beer bottles. Saliva. It's being amplified now. I did your sister first. She was all over that car.'

So, after all this time, there were still infinitesimal fragments of Rosie. I felt the wave of hope rise within me, mixed with sadness. I hated to imagine my sister's time in that Holden. Rosie would have left skin cells, possibly hair with the follicle attached, other traces that I didn't like to think about too much. I stopped myself going down that road by turning my attention to the traces left by the abductor or abductors. Saliva, by itself, has no nucleic component, but yields plenty of shed epithelial cheek cells.

But there was something else I had to address first. 'Florence—' I started to say.

She raised a hand. Her strong face was forbidding, mouth in a tight line, eyes narrowed. 'I don't want to discuss anything with you apart from work-related matters. Okay?'

Several thoughts flashed through my mind but the easiest thing was just to agree with her. 'If that's what you want.'

'That's what I want,' she said, turning away. 'I'll let you know when the amps are ready.' I heard her footsteps faintly tapping along the vinyl corridor and out of hearing.

I stood there, perplexed. But the wave of hope was sustaining me, lifting me above the awkwardness of Florence and her responses. If they'd got saliva from a bottle neck, there was a good chance we'd get a profile.

Before leaving for the day, I tried the number given me by Alix's flatmate. This time I got an answering machine. But at least it was her voice. 'Hi,' I said, 'it's me. We've lost touch and I just wanted to say hello. I hope everything's okay.' I was about to leave my new phone number but I knew in that moment that it was too late now. The 'convenient association' had come to an end. I thought of Alix lying back naked on her dark red satin sheets, lazily watching me as I sketched her, alternating sunlight and shadow striping her fair skin through the venetian blinds of her bedroom. Despite everything, I felt a sadness and a chill somewhere near my heart. Another ending. Another connection severed. In that moment, it seemed that my whole life had been created out of negative forces—loss and the absence of loving women. But I couldn't quite throw the phone number in the bin. I stashed it in the odds and ends bottom drawer on the right-hand side of my desk.

As I walked out of the building, I met Nigel, the particle man. With his slicked back dark hair and tiny moustache, he looked like a villain in a melodrama, rather than one of the smartest young scientists in the country.

'I'll have a result for you on those bits and pieces from that FU you gave me,' he said, relishing the acronym for 'forensics unknown', 'in the next couple of days.' He ducked back to his room. 'Smart time to take leave, doctor. The crime wave is supposed to be over,' he called, 'but we've had the busiest month on record.'

I decided not to stay overnight as I'd planned, but to drive back, even though I felt quite tired. I'd done this drive so often in my married days, I could do it asleep.

•

In three and a half hours I was in Sydney and although it was nearly eight, I called in on Jacinta on my way home. Genevieve was there, hunched in a chair beside our daughter and she whipped around when I walked in. The last few days had started to take their toll on my pretty ex-wife. She looked haggard and drawn and there was something new in her face I'd never seen before.

'There's been no change,' she said to my unasked question. She turned away from me, to gaze on the still face of our daughter. 'I lost Greg,' she said. 'I'm not going to lose this one.'

'You haven't lost Greg at all,' I said, impatient. 'He's decided he wants to live with me for a while, that's all. Sons often do that, for chrissake.'

As soon as I spoke, I regretted my reaction. Let her interpret the world in her negative way. It was no longer my business. It never really had been, except when I'd crashed into one of her interpretations. I walked around the other side of the bed. I could see Jacinta's eyelids flicker and the shadow of something like a smile moved across her face, like the lightest of breezes. I touched the hand that lay across her chest.

'It's Dad, Jass,' I said to her. 'I'm here.' I leaned over and kissed her, noticing a vein pulsing slowly at her temple. I stayed for a little while, but the atmosphere in the room was filled with Genevieve's hostility so that when Bob rang, I was relieved.

•

I had no difficulty finding the Edgecliff crime scene because the police had cordoned off the entire street and even righteous citizens trying to get through with the shopping were having a hard time. Bob must have given my name to the uniform whose car blocked the road because as soon as he saw my ID I was ushered through. I noticed Bradley Strachan's Audi double-parked outside number 389 View Street, a Tuscan-style mansion with a row of dwarf citrus trees in pots running each side of the flagstone path that led up to the entrance, and I heard his voice as I stepped through the handsome double doors of the entry. There seemed to be acres of softly lit marble and my eyes were drawn upwards to see the concavity of the dome high above, crowning the entrance area and suffusing it with greenish light. I became aware of a woman's intermittent screaming upstairs, and the high-pitched repetitive sound reminded me of spurwinged plovers startled at night.

'It's like the other three murders in certain respects,' I heard Dr Strachan saying as I approached one of the rooms off the entrance.

'There you are,' Bob said, beckoning me over. Through the half-opened door I could see hundreds of books on shelves from floor to ceiling behind him, and the sombre, rich colours of a traditional gentleman's study. As I came in, Bradley Strachan straightened up from where he'd been stooping and for the first time I was able to see the dead man lying in his blood on the marble floor, the bloodied, crumpled Persian rug under him. His clothes were disarrayed, trousers around his ankles, and bloody wounds at the groin and lower belly gaped in the brilliant lights of the police video unit. It all looked sickeningly familiar until I looked closer. Maybe this time the killer had been interrupted. The murdered man's balding head was turned to the left, looking away and I saw a severe laceration on the side of his head. He had been a solid, even portly man, but I've noticed that some corpses look as if they've been deflated after death and this was one such. I was aware of Bob leaving the room and as I studied the details of the victim, ideas began forming in my mind. And some questions.

'Let's get him back,' said Dr Strachan, 'when you fellows have got all you need.' He left the room, peeling off his gloves, loosening his Tyvek spacesuit, looking back at me. 'Jack, see you back at the morgue. Bob will fill you in.'

I followed him out into the entrance area and looked around for my colleague, but couldn't see him anywhere in the large open plan expanse.

'We found this pulled out of the shelves.' Dr Strachan indicated a CD cover, already labelled and safely housed in plastic by the Crime Scene people. It sported a black and red rose design across it, and written in decorated script the title: *The Last Castrato*. The killer was sending us a message, even if it was hardly subtle.

'He's out the back on the phone,' said a tall young Physical Evidence detective, answering my question of a moment ago. 'Couldn't get a signal in here.'

I walked across the wide marble stretch, pondering the CD cover. Was our killer now turning to irony?

I walked through a flagstoned cloister that gave onto a magnificent swimming pool outside, surrounded by classic pillars and urns of flowers tumbling from a high wall. Bob was coming towards me, hooking his mobile on his hip.

'Who was he?' I asked, referring to the bloodied corpse inside. We walked back into the house together and I paused to admire the magnificent terracotta tubs of gardenias that lined the flagstoned area between the house and pool.

'Dr Jeremy Guildthorpe,' said Bob, 'and Bradley reckons he was killed sometime after midnight. Knife wounds. A head injury. There's no sign of forced entry and his wife said she didn't hear anything. She found him when she went to see why he wasn't coming to bed.' I realised the staccato screaming from upstairs had stopped.

'That,' he said, tapping the mobile riding his hip, 'was one of the brass from the Commissioner's office demanding to know when we're going to pull our fingers out and get a result on these killings.'

'These killings?' I said, indicating the room behind us, 'or this killing? The bloke in there still has his equipment.'

Bob didn't answer for a long moment. 'The thing is,' he said, 'that this guy is well connected. He's a distant mate of the Premier's. Not exactly A-list, but top of the Bs.'

I looked around at the dark paintings in heavy gilt frames, the graceful silver epergne standing on a carved cedar table. Opposite me, a huge pre-Raphaelite oil painting of the destruction of Pompeii took up the length of the wall under the curved staircase. Men, women and children in classical attire looked back at fire in a dark sky. Behind them, Corinthian columns crumbled and the earth was split near their sandalled feet, reminding me of the words of Jeramiah I'd read under the obscene drawings.

'"A whirlwind of the Lord is gone forth in fury",' I misquoted, enjoying the expression on my colleague's face.

'I didn't know you were of a religious bent,' said Bob in his mild way.

'I read it in Nesbitt's Bible,' I told him. 'It's stayed with me.' We walked back into the study and I turned my attention to the dead man.

'Recently released from prison?' I asked, already knowing the answer.

Bob shook his head. 'Cleanskin.'

I pondered this. 'What sort of doctor was he?' I asked.

'Doctor of theology,' said Bob. 'The study of God.'

Behind me, Dr Jeremy Guildthorpe, now secured in a body bag, was on his way to his final thorough medical examination. Several people went out at the same time and the house felt less crowded.

In my pocket, in a heavy envelope, was the little black book I'd found in the garage where Bevan Treweeke had suicided. 'Can you get someone reliable in Child Protection to run a check on any names and phone numbers in this?' I half pulled the notebook out before slipping it back inside the envelope again. 'In connection with the abduction of Rosie McCain? And let me know the results?' I briefly told him about Colin Swartz and the Blackheath hanging. Bob nodded and took the envelope.

Behind me I could hear a conversation and I looked around to see a plump woman in floral slacks and a pale blue coat that reminded me of something a dentist might wear, talking between two Crime Scene detectives.

'It's not my job,' said the woman. 'I'm not touching it. I was hardly ever allowed in there anyway.' She looked from one man to the other. 'Vacuum and damp mop. No hands and knees. Dust and wipe all surfaces. Windows, venetian blinds and ovens by arrangement. That's what it says in my contract. Not this sort of thing.'

'We'll need to ask you a few questions,' the shorter detective said. 'Just routine.'

I moved over to join them. The woman hadn't been here when I arrived.

'How did you get in here?' I asked.

'I live here, sonny boy,' she said smartly. 'I could very well ask the same thing of you.' After a bit of sparring, she settled down and I noticed that her blue eyes were filled with tears. 'He was such a nice man, you know. Always thinking of others.'

I remained silent, a technique I had always used to good effect during interrogations. 'He helped lots of people, you know,' she said. 'Young ones. Very generous with his time. Now look what's happened. It's a disgrace. What's happening in this world?'

She hadn't heard anything or anyone last night either, she told me, in answer to my questions, but, as she pointed out, the house was spacious and the bedrooms tucked away from the entertaining areas, especially hers, right at the other end of the upper floor. I took Mrs O'Neil's name and phone number for future reference.

'That's two out of four you've attended now,' said Bob, when we were alone again.

'Anything spring to your mind?' I said.

'You go first.' I'd worked with Bob long enough to know what this meant. He wanted more time to digest what he'd seen. Possibly he'd wait for the PM results before he'd say anything. We were making our way back towards the entrance and behind us I could hear the video unit dismantling lights and joking.

'Did you see that piece in yesterday's paper? You looked like a startled rabbit.'

'Me?'

'That woman journalist,' Bob was saying, 'did a big spread on the castration killings and the use of science in analysing physical evidence.' I remembered how I'd turned straight into Merrilyn's flashlight that night in the park. He noticed my face. 'What is it?' he asked. 'The photograph?'

'Shit,' I said. No one in our game likes to be photographed. You never know who might see a photograph. Might remember your face next time. I reminded myself I was no longer in the job, but was now just a hidden technician.

'It wasn't a bad piece as they go,' Bob said. 'At least she put the record straight about the canine DNA. I won't have to put up with people like the fellow who rang today to tell me that the killings were UFO abductions that had gone wrong. Reckoned his group had found abnormally high levels of phosphorous at each crime scene.' He leaned in closer as we stepped outside, past the uniform at the door and around the blue and white tape.

'Anything more on those anonymous letters of yours?' Bob asked. I shook my head. 'Should hear something in a day or so,' I said. 'But you know how it is. Refined results aren't worth a damn without something to match against.'

'How's your daughter?'

'Still unconscious.'

'But you've got her back.'

'Yes. And I want to talk to you sometime,' I added, 'about something I found in her possession.' I lowered my voice and looked around. It'd been a long time since we'd been partners in the old days but that's what it felt like now. I had to tell my partner something this big. 'Jacinta had an accounts book and a lot of money with her in a bag.'

'Jesus,' said Bob. 'Whose is it?'

'At this stage I've no idea,' I said. 'She'd been living with a dealer. Don't know the name. Pigrooter's looking into it for me.'

'How much is a lot? And you be careful of Pigrooter.'

'Well over two hundred. He's not my cup of tea, Bob,' I said.

'Who else knows you've got it?'

'Only you,' I said.

'Let's leave it like that,' said Bob. 'I'll talk to Stan Lovell in the Drug Squad. He might've heard something. He's usually on the money.'

'I'm going home,' I said. 'I'm buggered.'

'Call me in the morning,' said Bob.

'Where can I get some decent take-away food round here?' I asked as I climbed into my car and slammed the door. I said I would call him and drove home.

•

Greg wasn't there and I remembered he was staying at Paddy's place. He'd even left the phone number written for me on the dining table. My son was growing up into a responsible adult. He'd also made another note under this. *Iona Seymour rang. Wants to change the meeting place. Can you meet her at her place same time? 293 Reiby Street, Annandale.* Under this, my son had drawn a great big question mark followed by several exclamation marks. Who is this woman, he was asking. I had to admit to myself that it was a good question.

When I'd eaten my take-away satay chicken I searched through my bag of tools and found the pliers. In my bedroom, I took the torch out of the drawer and put it down next to me. It was easy to pull out the tacks that pinned the section of new floorboards into position. As I lifted them away, the scent of musty earth arose, reminding me of something I didn't want to think about—the cubby house down the backyard of our old place in Springbrook and the smell of its earthen floor and rotting timber frames. I flashed the torch around the cavity under the floorboards. Beneath me was the dusty ground; nearby, I could see the sandstone pillars that supported the house. I went back to the living room and brought Jacinta's bag into my bedroom. Kneeling on the floor, I counted and stacked the money. Two hundred and thirty three thousand dollars in large denomination used notes. I leaned back on my heels, surprised at how little space it took up as I stowed it in the floor cavity. I took the large maroon accounts book out to the living area and flicked through it in the better light. A criminal organisation runs just like any other big business and I was holding the records of a drug distribution enterprise. Orders, deliveries, bets, payoffs and payments all have to be recorded. Although I knew I was looking at a coded system, there were people down in Canberra with sophisticated software who were capable of busting any code. The names were obviously nicknames, but the mobile numbers were very real. And very traceable. Someone would be looking for this accounts book even more than the money. I put the book back with the money, replaced the floorboards and looked around. If I moved the bed from its current position and put it up against the wall, the whole area was further hidden. I washed my hands. I needed more information before I could make another move but whoever was missing their records and their money would soon be making a noise about it.

•

Next morning, I went down to the council art exhibition to see my *Morning Mist* in all its glory. There were only a few people wandering around and I took the single sheet printed catalogue from a table near the entrance with me as I joined them in the foyer of the library. I walked around, noting the wide variety of talents and subjects collected here. Most of it wasn't very good, lots of hackneyed scenery, Harbour views with yachts, flowers in vases, and the occasional strong work jumping out at me. *Morning Mist* had a reasonably good position in a well-lit area of the hall and I felt pleased when I saw the second prize certificate pinned underneath it. I kept wandering around and was about to leave, barely looking at the catalogue when I was drawn to a monochrome triptych of three young girls, portraits in oval frames, set in a wide frame. Something about the middle girl seemed familiar. I scanned the catalogue and found it: number 15 was titled *Murdered Girls*. I studied the art work more closely. I swallowed hard. My vision seemed to waver and for a second I thought I might overbalance. Now I understood why the middle girl looked familiar. I stopped breathing. My heart raced and I could feel it thumping under my ribs. On her right was Amanda Smith, a girl whose murder had galvanised Sydney twenty years ago and on the left, Tiffany Jo Bentley, murdered by Warren Gumley less than a decade ago. Smiling at me from a quarter of a century away was the girl in the middle, my sister, Rosie. I realised my knees were weakening and I leaned back against the wall. There she was, with Amanda Smith, whose murder had been one of my first investigations, and Tiffany Jo Bentley. The rational part of my brain kept telling me it was surely just a coincidence, but another voice inside was becoming insistent. What's going on, it was asking. Everywhere I went, Rosie seemed to be popping up. I'm doing the best I can, Rosie, I told her. I'm doing what you want. I'm getting the Holden examined, I'm going to chase up the names in Bevan Treweeke's nasty black book. What more can I do?

I stayed there against the wall, pretending to be studying the painting opposite, a beach scene with loads of cobalt blue taking up most of the canvas. The girls in the triptych wore summer dresses, and the high contrast between light and shadow on their faces implied the Australian summer sun. Amanda Smith's hair was tied back with little clips. Tiffany Jo smiled coyly, looking around to face the artist, and I remembered that photograph from the newspapers. Then I looked more closely at the figure of my sister. Around her neck was a tiny necklace. My breathing stopped again. Although the triptych was in black and white, I knew that necklace. It was the blue and yellow enamel flowers on silver that I'd given her for her thirteenth birthday, three days before she disappeared. Nobody in the whole world, except perhaps my father, if he were pressed, knew about that necklace. Yet someone had painted her wearing it. That someone had only three days to do it in. I put the personal shock away in a box in my mind and called on my professional self. I noted the name of the artist in the catalogue: Jeffrey Saunders. Within an hour, I had the man's address from his application form and was on my way.

•

Jeffrey Saunders greeted me and glanced at my ID. I wondered for a split second if this was the man who'd stolen my sister, snatched her from the street, made off and murdered her. Until I realised he would have been aged about ten at the time.

'Is this business or pleasure or do you want to buy a painting?' he joked, indicating that I should follow him into the house. The Glebe cottage he lived in seemed too small to accommodate him with his belly and beard and the plump jowls and neck that go with too much wine and food, filled as it was with paintings, framed and unframed, stacked against the walls. The smell of oil paints was especially strong in the room into which he now ushered me, and I saw that he'd made this front bedroom with the large bay window into his studio because of its good light.

Murdered Girls, I said, as I walked in behind him. 'Where did you get the models from?'

He looked bewildered at my question. 'What do you mean?' he asked. 'I know my work's a bit confronting. Not very PC. People like roses and sunsets. But don't tell me someone's complained?'

'I'm not interested in your work at all,' I said, more sharply than I'd meant. 'And no one's complained as far as I know. I'm here because I want to know about the middle girl, Rosie McCain. I want to know where you got her from.' I swallowed hard. 'And how you know she was murdered.'

Jeffrey Saunders was taken aback. 'Look,' he said, 'you come barging in here flashing some sort of police identitification—'

'I haven't started barging yet,' I said. 'Rosie McCain is…was… my sister. I want to know how you knew about her. Why you painted her. What model you used. You must have got her from somewhere.'

I could see he was shocked. The bluster fell out of him. 'I'm sorry,' he said, 'I had no idea. It must have been distressing for you. To see your sister like that.' The angry energy between us changed.

'I recognised the other two girls,' I told him, 'and I know where you got their images from. I was actually involved in the investigation into Amanda Smith's murder. And Tiffany Jo Bentley's photos appeared in the newspapers, too. But that's not the case with Rosie. I remember the photo used for her in the press. And it wasn't anything like the image you've come up with for your masterpiece. I want to know where you got it.'

Jeffrey Saunders started rooting through trays and boxes of half squeezed oil paints, and plates used as palettes and daubed in mixes of colour. Unlike me, he was a messy painter, with old rags everywhere and paint on the floor. 'Somewhere here,' he said to me over his shoulder. 'They were here last time I noticed them.' I came over behind him and my heart sank. The mess in the corner he was searching was chaotic.

'I used to live in the Blue Mountains,' he said. 'I remember there was a piece on your sister in the local newspaper some years ago about unsolved mysteries.' Furniture had been pushed into the corner to make space for his easel and boxes, and trays of old, dried tubes and brushes were layered like an archeological dig. Jeffrey Saunders started unstacking some chairs so as to get close to the mess in the corner. 'The unconscious is a funny thing,' he was saying. 'I just started copying the middle girl in and it took me a while to realise that I knew her face already from the newspaper article.'

'What are you looking for?' I asked.

'For Rosie,' he answered. 'She was here. In a whole box of others.'

'Other whats?' I said.

But he didn't answer me directly. Instead, he reached in behind a pile of canvases and I could hear him grunting with the strain of stretching. 'I'm always buying these,' he said, 'in secondhand shops. They're full of stories and lives. Full of the past.' Finally he turned round and I could see now that he had hold of a shoebox filled with old postcards and photographs. 'I got this whole box for thirty dollars. She was in here,' he said. 'Just smiling out at me in her pretty summer dress.' He passed me the box. 'She was the one whose face I wanted in the middle. I didn't even know who she was until I was almost finished.'

I looked at him and saw that his face under the beard was soft and that his eyes were gentle. You've touched him, too, Rosie, I thought, and he's had to paint you. I'm doing the best I can, I told her. I'm following every lead you lay down.

Saunders put the box down. 'Damn it. She's not in there.' He looked around, remembering. 'I had her stuck up here with a thumb tack while I was painting her.' He looked dejected and I wondered if this was another wild goose chase. But he suddenly lurched forward in front of me. 'Ah,' he said, 'there she is.' And he reached over to the wall and took a black and white photo from a corkboard on the wall. He handed it to me and I stared at it.

There she was, my little sister, Rosie, standing somewhere in the November sunlight, smiling straight at whoever was taking the photograph, her brow clear of the anxiety that usually furrowed it. For a moment, I thought I might disgrace myself. I felt an almost overwhelming cry at the back of my throat. Instead, I turned the photo over and looked at the back. There were no distinguishing marks, no brand names. This looked as if it had been developed in someone's private darkroom.

'Can you remember where this box came from?' I asked.

'Most certainly,' he said, pleased to be helpful. 'I bought that batch in a little olde worlde shop at Blackheath. The one opposite the pub, just off the highway. There's always lots of stuff in that place.' I nodded, knowing the shop he meant, a rambling warehouse filled with old things. The sort of place where Genevieve could have happily spent half the day.

'You see,' I said, 'that necklace she's wearing. I'd given that to her only three days before she went missing. No one in our family took that photo.'

'Can I get you a stiff drink?' Jeffrey Saunders offered.

I shook my head. 'But thanks, anyway,' I said. 'I'd like to take this box away with me. See if there's anything else that might be related.' I looked again at my radiant little sister. There was something so like Jacinta in her expression. Two beautiful girls. One dead, one fighting to live and my life haunted by the two of them.

'Please do,' Saunders was saying.

I took the box from him, regretting my earlier rudeness. 'I paint a bit,' I said, 'but not as well as you. Mostly watercolours.'

'You sure I can't get you a drink? Anything else?'

'No,' I said, 'I have to go.' And I did. Another moment, and I think I would've broken out crying.

I was aware of him watching me with concern as I made my way back to the car. I put the shoebox on the passenger seat and sat there a while. Eventually, I drove away and found myself parked at the end of my street where the land rose, staring out at the blue expanse of the sea, watching the long swell coming in through the bay beneath the swirling gulls. I propped up the photograph of my little sister against the dashboard and stared at it. There was a stone wall behind her and the shadows of trees across the foreground and behind her seemed to indicate late afternoon. I started going through the contents of the box. It was a jumble sale of postcards, some with names and addresses from all over Australia, others grubby but unused, old photos and the occasional greeting card. Halfway through, I grew dispirited and put them all back with Rosie on top. Another box to add to the growing collection at my house. I glanced at my watch. I needed to start preparations for my date with Iona Seymour. I drove home.

NINE

As I made a sandwich, showered, shaved and patted on a discreet amount of a cologne I didn't know I had, the haunted feeling I'd had at Jeffrey Saunders' place lifted somewhat. The money under the floorboards was still worrying me. It wasn't a safe place. I was too closely connected to Jacinta.

My mobile rang and it was Bob.

'I've found a photograph of Rosie,' I told him. 'She's wearing a necklace that I gave her. Someone took this photo in the three days before she was abducted. It looks to me as if it's been developed at home.'

I heard the silence on the line as Bob took all that in. 'Any idea where it was taken?' he asked.

'That's my next step,' I said. 'I've got the whole box of cards and photos it came with. There might be something else in there. Something I can identify.'

'Have you heard anything from Staro?'

'No,' I said. 'Is there any talk on the street?'

'You know he'd been trying to clean up his act,' said Bob. 'One of his confrères thought he might have gone up the coast. There's a rehab place somewhere up Wyong way. A farm of some sort.'

I found it very hard imagining poor old Staro living the clean farm life, milking cows and gathering eggs. 'I think he's gone to ground,' I said. 'He's always been looking over his shoulder. You know how it is with informers.'

Then, because I was thinking about my pending visit to Iona, I said something to Bob that had been on my mind ever since she had denied making those phone calls. 'Bob,' I said, 'I've wondered a lot what the woman who left the message about Jacinta was originally going to say before she changed tack. She started off saying'—and I quoted the words to him that I knew by heart—'"I want to talk to someone in charge of the investigation dealing with those two" and then she broke off and her voice changed completely. Do you remember?'

'I do,' said Bob. 'I've been thinking about this. It was just after the first murder—Warren Gumley—that she rang the police. Early in the morning. And her second call was made the day of Nesbitt's murder.'

I paused to catch my breath. 'I'm wondering,' I said, 'if she was originally intending to say, "I want to talk to someone in charge of the investigation dealing with those two *murders*".'

There was a silence on the line, but I could hear Bob's presence in it. There's a quality to deep listening, even on the phone, that makes the silence rich. 'If that's the case,' said Bob finally, 'then we should be taking more of an interest in this woman.' We were silent together for what seemed a long time. 'And furthermore,' said Bob slowly, as if he were thinking aloud, 'if that *is* the case, and she then runs on to mention your daughter, then there's also some connection, in her mind at least, between those killings and Jacinta.' He was right. I had been trying hard not to make that connection myself.

'That's the part I really hate,' I said to him. 'That's the part of this business that I can't stop worrying about. Even though it's impossible.'

'Nothing's impossible in our game,' Bob said. Again, I knew he was right. 'And she denied making those calls,' he said. 'There's definitely something going on with her.'

Bob paused a moment. 'I've got the PM results on Jeremy Guildthorpe,' he said. 'I've also found out a few more things about the late doctor. Just give me your impressions of that crime. Off the cuff.'

I considered for a moment, my imagination back in that expensive house, studying the body on the Persian rug. Outside, I could hear the shrill whistling of a gang of honeyeaters gathering nearby. '*Quick! Quick! Quick!*' they urged.

'In comparison with the earlier three killings,' he added.

'Bob,' I said, 'every single thing was different. He was killed at home. He was a wealthy man, not a man with a battered suitcase living in a rented room. He had no form for sexual crimes. He hadn't done time and he hadn't just been released from prison.' I paused. 'And,' I continued eventually, 'even though there were serious injuries inflicted to the groin, he still had his penis and balls. Plus, there was a head injury that none of the others had. Looked like he'd been bashed, maybe rendered unconscious.' Again Bob waited, but that was all I wanted to say at this stage.

'So you won't be surprised,' my erstwhile colleague said, 'to hear that it was a different knife that was used. The wound measurements indicate a bigger, one-sided blade. The injuries are different as well. Many more stab wounds. Bradley used the word "frenzied".'

'There are too many differences,' I said finally. 'What else?'

'The housekeeper has made a statement for us,' said Bob, and I remembered the woman in blue who'd called me "sonny boy". 'She told me that Dr Guildthorpe used to sometimes bring young men home, for private studies.'

'Real private,' I said.

'And sometimes,' Bob continued, 'young men would be let into the house at odd hours.'

'Fancy that,' I said.

'When I heard that,' said Bob, 'I started asking around the right places and would you believe Dr Jeremy Guildthorpe was a very active man around town, and had a particular circle of friends who were quite unknown to his good lady wife.' Bob sometimes uses that sort of Rotary men's language for effect.

'That's often how it goes,' I said, remembering other widows weeping over things they'd found in bottom drawers.

'So Bruce Geldorf and Crime Scene turned that study and the rest of the house upside-down. The whizz kids copied everything on his hard disc.' Bob paused on the line. 'They found heaps of jpg videos, porn websites, dirty emails. Beats me where these blokes get the energy.' He paused a moment. 'Not to mention the bloody time.'

My mind processed the new information and I considered the Guildthorpe murder again. I was about to ring off, when Bob spoke again.

'Iona Seymour,' he said. 'Do you want to get on to her? I could bring her in to have a chat about something.'

'You needn't bother,' I told him. 'I'm having afternoon tea with the lady.'

•

I pulled up a little way away from Iona Seymour's house and took my time walking up to it. Despite its general air of neglect the front garden seemed tended, with several flowering rose bushes and petunias in terracotta tubs standing near the front steps. Something about the set-up reminded me of the house of my childhood. The driveway, just as ours had been thirty years ago, was in danger of being blocked by climbing roses whose wild canes curved over from the fence and, in some cases, touched the side of the house. It would require axes and chainsaws if anyone wanted to clean the place up. On the black and white tiled front veranda, hemmed in by rusted wrought iron, the ramblers and climbers had grown rampant and apart from an opening cut to allow passage off the veranda, almost all the railing was hidden from view, while vines sent winding tendrils across the chequerboard squares to curl around slim wrought-iron pillars supporting the top balcony. I pressed a doorbell that made no audible sound so then I knocked and stepped back. Nothing happened, so after a while I stepped back down and started walking round the other side of the house, ducking rose canes and stepping over knee-high summer grass.

Then I heard her voice calling me from the front, and hurried back to find her, flushed and flustered, standing on the doorstep, smoothing her dark hair.

'I'm so sorry,' she said. 'Please come in. I was doing something upstairs and didn't hear you straightaway.' She stepped aside to let me pass and I caught her scent, sandalwood and something deeper. 'Have you been here long?'

I had the distinct impression that she knew exactly how long I'd been here. 'Only a minute or two,' I said. I followed her down the central hall, past several closed doors on either side until we came to a large double room, divided by tall wooden doors that were now folded back against the wall. Dark old furniture lined the room, worn tapestry covered armchairs and there were redwood tables and a heavy cedar sideboard. A dark green wallpaper had once been handsome. Now there were water stains that indicated a roof leak at one stage. Heavy Regency-stripe curtains in green and cream kept the room cool and dim and the Victorian furnishings seemed original.

'It's very good of you to change our meeting place at such short notice,' she said, indicating a deep armchair, her voice warm and rich. I sat uneasily on the edge of it and it was then I noticed afternoon tea spread out on the dining table under a transparent cloth and jugs with beaded covers. It reminded me of long past teas with my grandmother. The room, the woman, the spread in front of me, seemed to belong to another age. 'I asked you here instead because I'm finding it harder and harder,' she said, 'to go out of the house.'

'There's a word for that, isn't there?' I said, playing dumb.

She nodded. 'Agoraphobia. It's awful.'

'I went through the opposite of that,' I said, remembering that we had the Fellowship in common and that intimate disclosures were not at all out of place. 'I couldn't keep still or stay home for about three years. I walked all over Sydney all hours of the day and night.'

'Did your partner have a problem?' she asked. I shook my head. '*I* was the problem,' I said. She seemed not to want to go any further than that and instead lifted the cloth off the table. I was touched to see that she'd made sandwiches and there were also little iced cakes.

'I made cucumber and tomato sandwiches,' she said, 'and some cup cakes.' She passed a plate to me and I took a sandwich. I'd never had a cucumber sandwich in my life.

'This is a feast,' I said, more to break the silence than anything.

Suddenly, she was sobbing—heartbroken, terrible, anguished sobs that shook her from head to foot. 'I'm sorry,' she kept gasping when she was able, 'I'm so sorry.' She took out a hankerchief. It was automatic that I got up and went straight to her and put my arms around her. She neither responded nor resisted, just stood there shaking, blowing her nose with her elbows squashed close to her body because I was holding her. 'I don't know what to do,' she sobbed. 'I feel so stupid. But you seem to be a kind man.' It was a long time since a woman had found me 'kind' or indeed to have any redeeming quality.

'I know you're suffering,' I said. 'Tell me what it is. I may be able to help.'

She stepped out of my arms and turned away, back to the afternoon tea things, pocketing her handkerchief. 'No one can help,' she said.

I remembered her prayer. I reminded myself that this woman knew a good deal more about two of my investigations than she was letting on. I thought that to calm her as well as give me more access, a bit of Twelve Step program-talk might be in order. 'You know what they say,' I said, 'that we're only as sick as our secrets. Isn't that why you go to the meetings? To deal with things you've never spoken about?'

'I don't know why I go to the meetings,' she said. 'A friend of mine said they might help.'

'Iona,' I said, and it was the first time I'd called her by her name. 'I've been through a lot of life. I know we've only just met, but we have a fellowship in common that brings people back to life by such simple methods.' She raised her dark eyes to mine and I thought I saw something desperate in her face. 'Life can be good,' I said.

'Come upstairs,' she suddenly said. 'Yes. Now. I want to show you something.' This was so unexpected that I followed her up the staircase, wondering what she could possibly be going to show me. There was a moment when I was seized with terror that she'd come at me with a knife, but I calmed myself, knowing that I could easily overpower her.

'Come in,' she said, holding a door open, 'I won't be a minute.'

I walked in and heard her close the door behind me. I looked around. It was her bedroom. I stood still in the middle of the wide, elegantly furnished room. Curtains in deep green and blue shades hung from ceiling to the floor all along the wall opposite the door, the dim light penetrating their heavy fabric indicating where the french windows gave onto the upstairs veranda. Was Iona Seymour about to seduce me? Had I been so blinded by my own need to know what was going on in her that I couldn't see a seduction in progress? I stood in the centre of the room at the end of her large double bed, taking in her subtle fragrance, the heavy cedar wardrobe, the creamy rugs on dark polished timber floors, her dressing table with its three mirrors in front of the rich curtains, reflecting me back in triplicate, the old-fashioned silver-backed brush and mirror set that lay on the polished surface. Seeing myself three times in the bevell-edged mirrors brought to mind the *Murdered Girls* triptych. I looked at the paintings on her walls. Dark oils in heavy frames from the early nineteenth century, and an oval-framed portrait of a beautiful woman with Iona's colouring and eyes hung on the wall next to the door.

I was wondering if I should leave when the knob turned and Iona stepped into the room, wearing only a silky robe. 'Tell me,' she said, 'if a man could find me desirable.' She let drop the robe and I made sure my practised professional mask was firmly in place. Her body was beautiful, toned and strong, but an angry red scar ran horizontally across the top of both girlish breasts.

'Who did that?' I said. 'What happened?' But she ignored my questions and came closer, putting her arms around me, looking into my eyes with the same look I remembered in my little daughter's eyes.

'Could a man still want me?' she asked, 'even with this?' She brushed her fingers lightly across the length of the scar. It was hard to determine how old the injury was, because now that I could see it more clearly, and despite its angry hue, it didn't look recent. 'Just tell me that,' Iona was saying. 'I'm asking you because I feel I can trust you.'

Iona, I thought, the feeling is not mutual. And this is not a good idea for other reasons that I can't express to you right now. I was about to step back but she'd already lifted her face to mine and was kissing me, soft lips parting. I was startled and immobilised. I couldn't have drawn back from her then. And, after a frozen second or two, I kissed her back slowly, deeply and fully. Her personal scent was very sweet and I remembered hearing that it is only meat-eaters who can be rank, remembering that she was vegetarian. 'You're a very beautiful, desirable woman,' I said when I could speak. 'The scar is simply an extra'—I groped for the right thing to say—'embellishment.'

She smiled at the word I'd used, and pleased, pushed me back onto the bed so that her silky hair fell against my face and neck, and her sandalwood scent filled my nostrils even more. Then she was undressing me and all the time my body was saying yes, my mind was saying no, asking questions. Was it a genuine situation, coming from the fear of rejection? Or was it just a way for her to get me into her bed? My interest in Alix had been purely physical, but the woman now in my arms had drawn me to her with more mysterious filaments. Finally, I got to the stage where my brain stopped its interrogation. Just for the moment, I no longer cared.

'There are condoms in the table beside the bed,' she whispered. We spent the rest of the afternoon in bed while our sandwiches staled and the tea turned sour and cold in the pot downstairs. Outside, in the old fruit trees and rose canes, noisy miners called, 'Careful! Careful! Careful!'

I lay back while Iona massaged every inch of my body with sandalwood oil. Again and again I returned to her, and each time she responded.

'I want you to know me,' she whispered, as our eyes locked together. 'I want you to see right into my soul.' No woman had ever said anything like that to me before and even though I was physically finished, my body felt light and weightless.

Later, we lay back, she with her head on my chest and her hair spread around while I stroked her back and her arm, and the room grew darker. It was then I noticed that there was something hidden behind the curtains to the left side of one of the french windows. A piece of furniture, I thought. A table and chair.

'I feel I've known you for quite a while,' she said. 'I felt that straightaway about you.'

I couldn't tell her the truth, that I'd been keeping an eye on her for some time, that I'd stolen a desperate prayer she'd left under a statue, that I knew she'd made two anonymous phone calls to the police. That even now, while she was believing that I was a kind man, she was, in fact, the subject of my investigation.

'I want to know what happened to you,' I said. 'That cut on your breasts.' She sat up, throwing her hair back, holding her breasts with her two hands, examining the scar that ran across them, almost like the line of an evening gown.

'Glass,' she said. 'I was running down some stairs and I didn't see a glass door. I ran straight through it. Stupid of me.'

I let that go for the time being. 'It must have given you quite a shock,' I said, smiling to myself.

'You're smiling,' she said. 'I can hear it in your voice.'

'I feel good,' I said, and it wasn't a lie although it wasn't the reason for the smile. 'I haven't felt this good for a long time.'

'I don't normally behave like this with men,' she said, but I turned over towards her and laid two fingers gently against her mouth, looking into her shadowed eyes.

'It's not my business,' I said, 'how you behave. You don't need to say anything.'

I reminded myself why I was here. Invisible interrogation, Bob used to call it. The mutual membership Iona and I shared in Relations Anonymous as well as the fact that we were in bed together gave me the right to make enquiries that, in other cases, may have seemed too probing. I rolled onto my back again.

'Tell me something about yourself,' I said casually. 'Do you have a family?'

She stroked my arm and I liked the feeling. 'I don't have children,' she said. 'And my parents aren't around any more.'

'No husband?' I asked, fishing. She shook her head.

'Why not?' I said.

'Let's just say I had another interest,' she said.

'A married one?' I asked, wondering if this was the problem in her life. Some women, I realised, put their lives on hold waiting, year after year, for some forsworn man.

'No,' she said. 'It's not like that.'

Now I *had* her. Her use of the present tense suggested to me that the situation was ongoing. I was thinking of how best to take this further when she sat up, modestly pulling the sheet across her breasts and most of the scar. 'Did I tell you already that my father was a clergyman?'

I nodded. 'You said he was studying for the priesthood. On the island of Iona, but he met your mother. When you were telling me about your name.'

She was silent for what seemed a long while, then she started stroking my neck and shoulder. It tickled a bit but I didn't tell her. I didn't want her to stop.

'It's a funny thing,' she said, 'but did you know that over seventy per cent of the members of those European terrorist organisations in the '70s like the Red Brigades and the Baader-Meinhof groups were the children of Protestant clergymen?'

I admitted I didn't.

'Oh yes,' she said, 'and that the great gunsmiths like Browning and Gatling were also the sons of clergymen?' There was a passionate tone to that voice of hers.

'Why do you think that might be?' I asked, still enjoying the half-irritating movements of her fingers on my skin.

'Because being a clergyman's child means that certain things are forbidden,' she said. 'Certain ordinary human things.' She paused a moment before continuing. 'Or at least the expression of them is forbidden.'

'Such as?' I asked, wondering why she was telling me this.

'Anger, for instance,' she said. 'Anger is one of the seven deadly sins. When I was growing up, childhood misdemeanours were offences against God. Everything was a sin. My mother was always telling me that things weren't "nice".' She moved away from me a little.

'It's quite true that a lot of life isn't nice,' I said to her.

Iona shook her head. 'That's not what my mother meant,' she said. 'She was referring to the ordinary everyday things'—she briefly covered my penis with her spread fingers—'things like this. Normal body functions. It was very difficult,' she said, taking her hand away, and I sensed from her voice that she'd closed a door on something. I lay there, wondering what Charlie would have to say about her conversational jump from parents to terrorists.

'What about yours?' she asked. 'Your family? Your father?'

I lay back, considering. 'My father was… is… a science teacher.' I thought of him in his shed behind the house at Springbrook and realised that soon I'd probably have to visit him.

'What do the children of science teachers become?' she asked and her voice had lost its serious undertone and was now more playful.

'They become kids who believe—this one believed—they can understand the language of birds.'

'Like Merlin,' she said. 'Where do you work?'

'I used to work in Canberra. For the government,' I said. 'I'm currently reviewing my life. I analyse things.'

'What sort of things?' she wanted to know.

'Particles,' I said. 'Fragments.'

'It sounds very refined work,' she said. It was a very accurate remark. 'And your mother?' she was asking. 'Did she have a profession?'

'Not what you'd call a profession.' It was an obsession, and one that I understood more than most people. 'My mother…'

I paused. 'My mother was also a teacher at one stage, but she had a drinking problem.' I was getting uncomfortable with this conversation. I had never liked talking about my family. 'What about brothers or sisters?' I asked, to move away from the subject of my family.

Iona stretched over, reaching to get her robe from where it lay, half on a chair near the bed, half on the floor. 'I have a couple of cousins,' she said, draping the robe around her shoulders. There's got to be a man around, I thought, creating a problem for her. An ex-husband. Or lover. I knew enough from my days in the job about the way some men can behave when a relationship comes to an end. And I knew first-hand how some women behaved in the same situation.

'It can be a real problem,' I said, fishing cautiously, 'when one party doesn't want the other to go. I've just been through that myself.' I rolled over to face her, stroking a shining strand of hair that glossed the side of her face. 'Something you said at the meeting,' I said, remembering her desperate prayer, 'made me wonder if you were going through that particular problem.'

She propped herself up on an elbow and looked down at me. Strike one, I thought to myself. Her whole demeanour had changed.

'I didn't think I'd end up in bed,' she said with a laugh that I didn't like very much, 'with someone from one of the meetings.'

It was a warning to keep my distance. She'd steered me away from the subject. It was like a dance between us, me seeing how close I could go before she'd deflect me.

'Do you have any kids?' she asked.

I realised I wasn't getting anywhere with the subtle approach, so I lined her up for a direct shot. 'I have a seventeen-year-old son,' I said, 'who is in Year Eleven.'

She nodded and murmured, waiting for more.

I moved closer and looked straight into her eyes; I didn't want to miss anything that might happen there. 'And,' I said, 'a sixteen-year-old daughter who is in Intensive Care.' I saw her flinch, and yet recover so quickly that had I not known already about her calls to Chris Hayden, I might have thought her response was no more than that of any compassionate stranger.

'Oh,' she said, 'how awful.'

'It is awful,' I said, carefully choosing my words. 'She was found unconscious in someone else's flat. She'd overdosed. So far, she hasn't regained consciousness.'

I thought of the money hidden under my bedroom floor and made a decision it had to go from there, and soon.

Iona was edgy now. She sat up and swung her legs out of bed but I pulled her down to be beside me again. She looked startled, unsure of what was happening. Her robe had fallen aside.

'You should have given me a better explanation for this,' I said to her, running my forefinger along the scar. 'Shark attack would be more credible.'

I watched her colour as she jumped up again, hastily grabbing the robe around her body. Contact injuries such as she'd described occur at the leading edges of the body—the forehead, the nose, the hands—and not in its concavities, under chins, in eye sockets. Just like people who lie about walking into doors to explain black eyes, Iona's story contained no element to account for how a recessed area, such as the area *beneath* her head could have been injured. If she'd really run into a glass door, she'd have had facial injuries and other cuts.

Now her voice was cold. 'I'm going to have a shower,' she said. 'Please feel free to have one when I've finished but then I'll have to ask you to leave. I have rather a busy evening ahead.'

I kept up the pressure. 'You said you trusted me,' I said. 'And in return you lied to me.'

She half-turned on her way out the door. In the dim light, I couldn't help noting that the curve of her powerful body as she twisted back, away from the direction she was moving, would have made a beautiful charcoal study.

'It's ancient history,' she said, 'and none of your business.'

I was about to say I wished in future she'd say just that, rather than insult my intelligence, but I seriously doubted now that there'd be any future for us. Was Iona one of those deeply masochistic women who stay with men who ill-treat them? I'd met some of them over the years when I was getting sober and I'd come to understand how they might derive feelings of superiority and even nobility from this distorted behaviour.

I sat up. A heavy feeling of depression and sadness enveloped me in the darkening room. I had a sudden moment of clarity and it was less than comforting. The whole Iona interlude, my strong attraction to her, the way I'd followed her, our lovemaking, was nothing but an escape from the sadness and confusion of my life. I tried to tell myself this with conviction. All I'd needed to find out from her was how she'd known the whereabouts of Jacinta. But now that Jass had come back, everything had changed. The need to know had dropped from absolutely essential to idle curiosity. It was just good fortune that Jass had turned up when she did because I'd allowed emotional issues to get in the way of business—a trap as old as law enforcement and I'd fallen straight in. It was humiliating.

I got up, listening to her shower rattling through the pipes of the old house, wanting to be out of the place as soon as possible. I pulled on my clothes and it was when I was searching for one of my shoes that I pulled back the curtain to reveal an elegant Victorian lady's desk in an alcove beside the windows. I found the shoe and was about to push the curtain back when something caught my attention. On the desk was an old-fashioned bottle of ink. Intrigued, I picked it up. I heard the silence as the shower stopped. She'd have to dry herself, I reasoned. I had a few minutes. It was then I slid open the shallow drawer at the front of the escritoire and saw the expensive, linen-based paper. I looked at the bottle of ink again. The manufacturer's name was printed on it in filagree lettering: *Les Frères Brunairds, Paris,* and before I'd even unscrewed the lid, I knew the colour of the ink would be sepia black. For a second I froze. Then I told myself to stop being paranoid. Lots of people have fancy notepaper. Lots of people like extravagant inks. There was nothing to say that this was the ink and this the paper on which the 'Rosie' letters had been written, except my imagination. And it was working overtime. This very minute, the killer could be on her way, with the knife.

First I froze, then I was frantic with terror. She'd lured me up here to kill me. I recalled how helpless I'd been in her bed and remembering that restored me somewhat. If she'd wanted to kill me, she'd have done so already. But my hands were still trembling so much as I unscrewed the lid that I thought I might tip the ink all over myself. Somehow I managed to press it upside-down against some of the stiff paper, pour some out, fold it up and safely take a sample. I scrambled to the cedar wardrobe and pulled it open. There in front of me was a red jacket and, lying on a shelf above the hanging space, was a wig of long blonde hair.

Almost in the same moment I heard Iona coming back down the hall. I barely had time to shut the wardrobe and bend down so as to be seen harmlessly tying my shoelaces when she came back into the room. I hoped she wouldn't notice that the curtain over the escritoire was hanging at a different angle. All the time I'd been trying to draw her out, had the shoe been on the other foot? She wrapped the towel around herself, then came over to me. I stood up fast.

'I'm sorry I lied to you,' she said. 'It's a painful subject.' I looked at her eyes, only a little lower than my own. But I was sure I could handle her. Particularly now that she'd lost the element of surprise. Ready for anything, I touched the scar. I recalled her words from the meeting.

'Is that a legacy,' I asked her, 'of the man who doesn't understand?' She looked away and I had the sense that she was considering something, but she started picking up clothes and slipping on underwear. The silence in which we both moved now had more than the usual awkwardness which occurs between people who have been inappropriately intimate. And, for me at least, there was a dangerous underswell. This woman could be the savage, hate-filled killer of at least three men. Is that what she'd been implying with her talk about clergymen's children, the terrorists of Europe and the great gunsmiths? Had that been a diagonal confession?

In silence, we finished dressing and she went to the wardrobe, took out the red jacket and put it on. We walked down the stairs together, with her a little ahead of me the way I was trained to do it. Halfway down, my attention was taken by a painting on the stairs. I think I stopped in shock, wondering why on earth I hadn't noticed it on the way upstairs with her. But I guess my mind then had been on other things. It was a small, simply framed watercolour and it showed a bright blue monkey hanging from a tree that grew just under the lip of a cliff. It was so much the landscape of my nightmare that I must have made some involuntary sound.

'What is it?' she said, swinging round to look at me, then behind me, up the stairs so that I couldn't help swinging round, too, wondering if the nameless predator of my dream was about to pounce on me. I was getting too old for this, I told myself.

'That painting,' I said, when my attention came back to it again, 'where did you get it?' The fear had vanished from her face and she smiled.

'I did that,' she said. 'I used to enjoy painting with watercolours when I was younger.'

I stared at her and she became uncomfortable, then angry. 'Surely it's not that bad,' she said, and just in that moment I couldn't imagine her as a killer. But the moment passed.

We continued to the bottom of the stairs, I mumbled something about it being an unusual subject, and then she was walking me to the front door and opening it for me, standing beside it, waiting for me to leave. There was another awkward moment when I stood on the step prior to saying goodbye and her eyes seemed to search my face, wanting some response from me. Just now it didn't seem possible that this was the same woman who, only a short time ago, had asked that I look right into her soul. As I looked into those eyes, again it didn't seem possible that she was a murderer. But I'd been party to the charging and conviction of beautiful women for serious crimes once or twice before in my life. I avoided her gaze as I said goodbye and hurried back to my car. I was dazed.

•

It was one of those days that just get hotter as the afternoon wears on into evening, and my mind was swirling around with all sorts of fears and projections. To give myself something ordinary to do, I found myself at the supermarket in Anzac Parade without even noticing I'd driven there. It was a good, if unconscious decision. I needed to do some shopping and going around the shelves loading my trolley brought me back into reality.

Half an hour later, I carried the groceries inside the house. A currawong flew overhead.

'Gimme a break, gimme a break!' it complained.

I found Greg lying in front of the television.

'Hey,' he said, jumping up as I walked in, 'I've got a part-time job. As a kitchenhand. At the Italian place down the street. Friday and Saturday nights. They're paying me nine dollars an hour.' He came over to help me with the shopping.

'That's great,' I said. 'You'll be able to save some money.'

My son looked at me as if I were mad. 'What's that?' he said, watching me as I now bagged and labelled the ink-stained paper.

'Just something that needs examination,' I said.

While Greg made room in the fridge for the food, I searched around for the folded piece of paper with Iona's prayer written on it, but it wasn't in the drawer where I was sure I'd put it. Then I started a full-scale search, alarmed that perhaps I'd lost it. It hadn't been of any importance before the events of today, except as a tantalising lead into her life. Now, if the handwriting showed similarities to the 'Rosie' letters, it could be vital evidence. With new information, the world of an investigation tilts on its axis and things once meaningless become priceless leads. I cursed because I couldn't find it anywhere.

'What are you looking for?' Greg asked, closing the cupboards on the last of the shopping.

I was still agitated and his question seemed a further aggravation. 'Shouldn't you be doing your homework?' I said.

'Why do parents always say that?' Greg frowned. 'You and Mum. Sometimes it was the only thing you'd say when you came home from work. Not "Hi, how are you? How was your day? Was it tough for you?" How come parents are so horrible? Kids never say, "Shouldn't you be parenting me?"'

I stopped the search and came over and sat down with him. Given everything that had happened to me that day, it took everything I had to bring my focus back fully onto my son. But somehow I did. 'Are you saying that to me now,' I asked him, 'that I should be parenting you?'

Greg shrugged, then nodded his head.

'Yes,' he said, 'I am.'

'Okay,' I said, 'here I am. I'm a parent. Be my kid. What do you need?'

'You could tell me a few things for a start,' said my son. 'Like, what are these?' and he held up some of the cards from the shoebox on the table that I'd taken from Jeffrey Saunders' place. I explained. It was a relief to be talking about this, rather than the frightening and confusing subject who was uppermost in my mind.

For a moment, I could put off examining whether or not I'd just been seduced by a violent killer.

'A photo of Rosie?' Greg started pulling cards out. 'Where is it?'

I found it for him and he studied it, looking at the smiling face, then looking up at me.

'She's a bit like you,' he said. Then he put the photo down on the carpet and for a few moments we both looked at it. 'Jass and I used to wonder why you never talked about her,' my son was saying. 'We knew she'd been abducted, but there was this forbidden thing all around her, like an electric fence. Mum used to freak at any reference to her.'

'Let me grab a shower,' I said, playing for more time to calm down, 'and I'll tell you all about it.'

'You're wearing perfume,' he accused, staring hard at me. 'What's going on?'

'I had a massage,' I said. 'A sports massage. He must've used a smelly oil.'

'Why?' he said. 'You don't play sports.'

I was aware of my son's suspicious eyes on me as I disappeared into the bathroom, where I had a shower and washed sandalwood oil and Iona Seymour off myself.

By the time I was out of the shower, Greg had peeled potatoes and put them on the stove. I rubbed the top of his head and he ducked away, trying to preserve whatever glue he'd used to flatten his curls on his skull. 'How's Rosie?' he asked

I shook my head. 'Nothing's changed. But thanks for asking. You're a good son, Reg,' I said, using his nickname. 'You're a good human being.'

'I'll do a bit of study,' he said, pleased and embarrassed.

I was rewarded by a half smile and now I, too, was feeling more settled. For the moment, I was just Greg's father again, preparing dinner. He vanished into his room, allegedly to do some study, while I mustered a mixed grill. Doing these ordinary kitchen duties gave me more distance between myself and the events of the afternoon. It was even possible to wonder if those events had really happened. But the ache in my lower back and gluteal muscles left no real doubts. While Greg was out of the way, I went into my bedroom, moved the bed, lifted the floorboards and took out the money, stashing it in a black and yellow gym bag. I didn't want it in the house.

'I'm going over to Charlie's,' I said, when dinner was finished. 'I've got something to give him.'

'Can I come?' Greg asked, but I shook my head.

'Work-related,' I told him and grabbed the box of cards and postcards and the gym bag.

'You said you'd tell me,' he said, pointing to the box, 'about Rosie. About my little lost aunt.'

'I will, I will,' I said. 'I promise. There are just a few things I must discuss with Charlie. It can't wait. I'm sorry.'

Greg shrugged and went to the doorway of the spare room. 'I thought I'd see a bit more of you,' he said, 'living with you.'

I was going to go after him, but there was nothing I could say except some version of 'don't you remember, I warned you about this' which is just a fancy version of 'I told you so.' I gathered everything up and went over to Charlie's.

•

'What do you think?' I asked my brother as we stood in his lounge room. Siya wasn't around so we had the house to ourselves. I put the box from the secondhand shop in Blackheath on the sideboard for the moment, the gym bag on the floor and I told my brother about how I'd visited Iona and what I'd found there. I didn't want to mention the rest of it.

A strong wind had come up and the night outside was wild, but it was a hot westerly and I could almost feel the thousands of miles of desert it had crossed to blow here. I looked outside but couldn't see anything past my own reflection and the reflection of Charlie's comfortable room.

'Lots of women have red jackets, and blonde wigs,' Charlie said. 'It has to be *that* red jacket and *that* blonde wig. Worn by *that* person. You know that.'

'That might be very hard to prove,' I said. 'Even with the paper and the ink.' And I told him about that, too.

'Do you think she's physically capable of the killings?' he asked. 'You've seen the damage.'

'Physically,' I said, 'I can't see a problem. She's very fit. And when you consider that surprise is the main element of these murders, I believe she could inflict those injuries.' I shivered at the thought of the knife slicing through my flesh, hacking off my penis.

'What's your sense of her?' Charlie asked. 'Would she be psychologically capable of doing it?'

I recalled the haunted shadows round her eyes, her sobbing in the dining room, the dramatic way she'd stripped down and shown me her scar, the strange mood swing on the staircase, the abrupt way she'd shown me out of her house.

'I think she's capable of a lot of things,' I said.

'Why aren't you talking to Bob about this?'

I considered the question. 'If I tell Bob,' I said, 'the whole machine might swing into action. Out of my hands. And I don't think that's a good idea.'

'Why?' Charlie came over and peered into my face. I looked away, fearing he would read the true reason there. There was a silence broken by my brother's disbelieving voice. 'Jack, you haven't, have you?'

I didn't say anything. I didn't have to. My brother looked at my face again, noted my silence and whistled slowly as he formed the right conclusion. Then he shook his head.

'Oh dear, oh dear, oh dear,' he said. 'You've broken the first and last investigator's commandment. What *were* you thinking of?'

Not much, I thought to myself as I remembered, thinking of the shocking scar on her chest.

'She has a long scar across the top of her breasts,' I said, now that he knew everything. 'She gave me some bullshit answer about how it got there. But someone's cut her. I reckon she's involved with a violent alcoholic partner.' I paused before saying something I didn't want to say. 'It's also possible that the injury was self-inflicted.' I stopped before voicing my third conjecture.

'I can't believe you've been so stupid,' said Charlie, 'so compromised.'

'Look,' I said, pissed off, 'I'm a chemist. I work at a bench in a sterile environment. I search for particles and fibres. I work with physical evidence and little amps. I look down binocular microscopes and I mop up positively charged ions. I can't *be* compromised because I don't work with people like an investigating police officer. It's not an issue.'

'Until now,' said Charlie. He went and poured himself a brandy and lime soda. 'See how it's already gone murky,' he said. 'Already you're not taking your partner into your confidence.'

His words stung and I defended automatically. 'That's not the way it is,' I said. 'Bob's not my partner.'

'I thought he was your friend.' I couldn't argue with that and there was nothing I could say. But my brother hadn't finished with me. 'And now, worst of all, your *professional* judgment is compromised. Now you've got sex mixed up with everything else.'

These words hit me hard. To lose one's scientific objectivity is to lose everything in my world where reputation equals livelihood. In my mind, old Dr Brouardel's words jumped off the screen in my office: *If the law has made you a witness, remain a man of science. You have no victim to avenge, no guilty or innocent person to convict or save.* But now everything was shifting around...

'Charlie,' I pleaded, 'there was absolutely no question of Iona being a suspect in this investigation when I first became'—I hesitated, finding the right word—'*personally* interested. All I knew then was that she knew something about Jass. It was my business to get involved. And that was light years away from sex offenders getting murdered.'

'Okay,' said Charlie, 'and now Jass is back. Well, physically back. And you don't need Iona Seymour's information any more.' He walked outside into the windy night, leaned over the timber railing, then turned back to look at me. A waxing moon had risen to treetop height and skeletal branches bowed against its brightness. A wagtail wittered away, *'Teach, witty preacher,'* it called, agitated by moonlight. 'Didn't you tell me not so long ago that you thought there was something in her voice when she phoned with the tip-off?' said my brother. 'That there was a dramatic change in both her manner and what she was talking about? Didn't you tell me that you and Bob thought there was the possibility of some connection in the caller's mind between Jacinta and the murders of the first two men?'

I nodded.

'And haven't you considered that if she knew something about Jacinta,' said Charlie, 'she might also know who you are? Might have known all along?'

This hit so hard that I sat down to consider both this suggestion and the fact that something so obvious hadn't occurred to me until now.

'And if she didn't know me all along,' I said, 'my bloody photo was in the paper two days ago. She rang the day after and changed the meeting from the café to her place.'

'Where there was a nice big double bed,' said my brother drily. 'Mate, you've been done like a dinner.'

My cool, logical brother, who never let personal issues confuse the truth of how things were, stood there, looking at me. What could I say? Charlie had me cold. I'd really stuffed this up. My brother came indoors and flung himself down on the floral couch opposite me, hunched forward over his drink.

'It's no good crying over spilt milk,' he said. 'Let's just do damage control, go over what you've got. First, what do you think will come of the ink and paper examination?'

'I can't really say until—' I started to say, but he brushed that aside.

'I'm your brother, so forget the scientific niceties,' he said impatiently. 'Just tell me the likely outcome.'

'Sarah will examine it,' I said, 'and from what I saw, she could find that it's indistinguishable from that used in the "Rosie" letters. But that's not enough.' I couldn't bring myself to tell him about the prayer I'd taken from under the *Pietà* and subsequently lost. 'Even if we could get a sample of handwriting, and it looks similar, it's still not enough.' I thought ahead further. 'Just say we get ESDA enhancements—'

'What are they?' Charlie asked.

'It's one of our magic boxes with flashing lights,' I said, 'originally invented in order to bring out latent fingerprints though it isn't much good at that. What it is good at is enhancing slight impressions, especially the sort left by the pressure of writing on a pad of paper. We've obtained clear readings five pages down from the written-on surface.' Charlie nodded and I continued. 'So even if we could actually *read* the last "Rosie" letter on the piece of paper that I've taken, that still wouldn't be enough. Because all she has to do is deny writing it, deny owning the pad, and she's established reasonable doubt. It's still only circumstantial.' I paused. 'But if she *is* involved, and we've pulled her in prematurely over evidence that is inconclusive, then we've alerted her and destroyed the possibility of her further implicating herself.'

'Like killing someone else?' said Charlie.

'I somehow doubt—'

'—that she's implicated? Why?' my brother demanded.

'Look,' I said to my brother, 'maybe this will sound strange.' I took a deep breath. 'She doesn't fit the profile of a savage killer,' I said. 'She's a bloody vegetarian and she goes to a Twelve Step group.'

Charlie looked at me as if I was a lunatic. 'Are you serious?' he asked. 'Are you suggesting a negative correlation betwen vegetarianism and murder? Do I have to remind you, of all people, that men and women who go to Twelve Step programs are *addicts*! They're capable of anything.'

'It just doesn't fit,' I said. 'It's not right.'

'You know that practising addicts hate themselves deep down— *and* everyone else,' Charlie said.

I shook my head. 'It's still not right,' I said. 'She doesn't fit.'

'This killer may well see himself,' Charlie said, 'or herself, as some sort of avenging angel. With a moral dimension. The worst are full of passionate intensity,' he reminded me, quoting Yeats, and I remembered Merrilyn Heywood's remarks and the words of Jeremiah. *A whirlwind of the Lord is gone forth in fury, even a grievous whirlwind.* 'Some sections of the press,' said Charlie, 'are suggesting that if the courts genuinely matched the sentences with the crimes these criminals committed, then these three men would still be alive. Alive, and locked up tight like they should be.'

I stood up. Now that the initial shock had worn off, I found I was unable to be still. If Charlie's surmises were right, I'd been badly burned. At the very least, it was looking more and more as if Iona was the most recent in the line of witches with whom I'd become involved.

'My taste in women hasn't improved,' I said. My AA sponsor used to say, 'For at least the first five years of your recovery, when you feel yourself attracted to a woman, *turn around and walk the other way. Fast.*' But I'd always felt safely smug, married to Genevieve. I couldn't see then that I'd already married the witch queen.

'I think your taste is getting worse,' said Charlie. 'Maybe the only reason you didn't end up sliced and dead is because you were in her house. I'd be very wary of future meetings with Iona Seymour, Jacko, if I were you. Especially if the invitation is for somewhere secluded late at night.'

I sat down again. It was like finding myself starring in a real-life *film noir*. 'There won't be any more meetings,' I said.

During the silence that followed, I pulled the photograph of Rosie out of my pocket and put it on the table between us. 'I found this,' I said, 'in a box of cards and postcards sold to an artist.' I filled Charlie in about how I'd tracked down the creator of the triptych and started pulling out the other photos and postcards from the box.

Charlie picked up the photo of our sister, holding it close to him, studying her. 'I don't remember her at all,' he said, 'although there was someone who used to play in the bath with me, swimming the face cloths around like fish.'

I remembered that, too. 'That was Rosie,' I said. 'Our mother was too sick by that stage to play with anything except the whisky bottle and Dad had pretty well moved into his parallel universe down the back shed.'

'What happened?' said Charlie in an odd voice and I was surprised to see his eyes were filled with tears. 'What happened to our family? In one generation, a young girl is abducted, in the next, she runs away. You make relationships with witches and here I am, in a combat zone with Siya.' He took out a handkerchief and blew his nose loudly.

'I thought things were okay with you and Siya,' I said, surprised. 'You always seemed happy—' I stopped because Charlie gave me a look and I remembered how we didn't talk about personal things until they were crashing down around us and there was no alternative. I leaned back in my chair, stumped by the enormity of the question. 'Christ, Charlie,' I said eventually, '*I* don't know what happened in our family. That's your territory.'

'But you must have memories,' he said, 'of what happened and how it all went to hell. Maybe you even remember a time when it wasn't?'

I considered. 'Sometimes I think I do,' I said, 'but I'm never sure. I remember always being anxious about Mum's drinking, and wishing she wouldn't. I remember always trying to impress Dad.

But nothing worked. He always knew more. He always competed with me and he always won.'

'That's how fathers destroy their sons,' said Charlie. 'Competing with them and beating them instead of being a good parent.' I wasn't sure what he meant and made a note that one day I'd ask him.

In silence, we pulled out the other black and white photographs and matched them with the snap of Rosie. These other images were all obviously from a different source, some of them the professional work of high street photographers, with their scribbled initial or other marks on the back and long defunct studio address, others of different sizes and print quality. We'd just about given up when I pulled out almost the last one, of a slight, adolescent boy standing near a stone wall.

'I think that's the same wall,' said Charlie, 'that Rosie's standing near in this one.' And he put the photo of Rosie beside the young man. Together, we studied the two pictures. 'Look here.' He pointed to something in the stone work. He went to a drawer and pulled out a magnifying glass. He studied the photograph and then passed me the glass. 'Take a look,' he said. With the aid of the glass, I could see part of a wrought-iron grille, cut off by the edge of the exposure. 'There it is again,' said Charlie, 'you can see a bit more of it in this photo.' I looked from one picture to the other. The wall was built of sandstone, well shaped and hewn and probably laid down in the late nineteenth century when stonemasons were affordable and not the rare and expensive artists they had become in our times, and there was at least one, possibly more, decorative grilles set in it, allowing light and air to circulate from one side of the wall to the other.

Charlie was staring at the two photos. 'I think I know this wall,' he said. 'I think I've seen it. It's from somewhere up there.' I knew he meant Springbrook and I picked up the photograph of the youth.

'So who's the guy?' said Charlie.

I studied the frowning face: young, good-looking in a sharp, thin-lipped way, but I shook my head. 'No one I know,' I said. 'Or knew.' I looked more closely. There was something. 'And yet...' I added, my voice trailing away. My brother waited, impatient for me to finish what I was going to say, but I shook my head. 'No,' I said, 'it's no one I know.' I put the photo down and picked up the one of Rosie again. 'Charlie,' I said, 'there's something I've never told anyone about what happened just before Rosie went up to the front of the house. It parallels almost exactly what happened to Jass.'

Charlie was all attention. 'Rosie had a crush on some boy. She'd written him a note and our mother found it and came down to where Rosie and I were playing. I'd seen Mum crazy and drunk before, but never as bad as this. She was screaming at Rosie, calling her a slut and a little whore. It was horrible. Even Dad came to the doorway of the shed, and nothing usually got his interest. I yelled at her to shut up and leave Rosie alone and when she turned on me Rosie ran away up the backyard and I thought she'd just gone into the house. She used to lock herself into her room when things were grimmer than usual. I ran up after her to try and comfort her, but she wasn't there. I didn't know where she'd gone. We didn't have any friends. We couldn't ever ask anyone home, not the way things were. So I thought she was just hiding somewhere and would come out when Mum had passed out.'

In my mind's eye, I saw my little sister stumble, crying, over the unmown grass in her pretty yellow sun dress, wearing the necklace I'd given her, running away into eternity. 'And that's what happened with Jacinta,' I said. 'Genevieve was yelling at her to go and wash her face, that she was wearing too much make-up, and that she looked like a whore. Forbidding her to have her ears pierced.' I stopped, recalling the ugly scene. 'Hell, she was just playing around with make-up like young kids do. I don't know what else had been going on, but it must have been the final insult. That's when Jacinta bolted out the door and we didn't see her again.'

Charlie was staring at the photograph of Rosie. 'Do you think,' he said, 'that our mother could have killed her?'

I was stunned at the idea. 'I've never thought of that,' I said.

In the silence that followed, I reviewed the past investigations I'd been involved with. Apart from cases of infanticide, women rarely kill older children. Fathers and brothers feature more prominently in the murder of their daughters and sisters.

'I very much doubt it,' I said. 'How would she have done it?' I recalled my mother and how towards the last days, she was barely capable of disposing of her own body, apart from staggering from the kitchen to her bed. 'She was skin and bone and bruises, as I recall.'

'We need to break the family spell,' Charlie was saying, as I came out of the trance of the past.

'If I can find out what happened to Rosie,' I said, bringing my attention back to the here and now, 'I somehow feel that we can.' I stood up, ready to go. 'I promised Rosie something a long time ago. If I keep the promise, I can redeem things.' I think I was as surprised as Charlie at my words.

My brother stood up, taking my cue. 'I hope so. Otherwise,' he said, 'we're going to end up two lonely old men living behind someone else's house with our girl children run away and our sons defeated and conflicted.' He flashed me the ghost of a smile. 'That's if we're not knifed first.'

I collected the box of postcards and the photographs and picked up the gym bag. 'I want to leave some stuff here,' I said.

Charlie raised an eyebrow. 'I'm always worried when a cop says that,' he said.

'I'm not a cop,' I reminded him. 'It's just some gear.'

'I don't want to know,' said Charlie, opening the tall built-in linen press in the hallway.

'Stick it up there,' he said, pointing to the top shelf where he'd stashed the boxes of cards containing the index for his doctorate.

I shoved the gym bag in as far as I could on the top shelf and closed the doors. I turned round and my brother was very close to me.

'What is it, Jack?' he asked. 'You look terrible.' I gently pushed him out of the way and went back to the living room. 'I've got the phone number of someone you can talk to. I've heard she's really good.'

I took it from him without looking at it.

I drove away and I hadn't felt so desolate since the earliest years of sobriety.

TEN

Next evening, after a day spent completing fiddly bits of paperwork connected to several cases I'd worked on, and chasing up reports, I got home late and Greg was lying in bed reading, with just the sheet over him. I stood at his bedroom door and he looked at me briefly, then his eyes went back to the book. While I was making the tea, I decided to talk to Greg so I opened a packet of hidden chocolate Montes and knocked on his door.

'May I come in?' I asked.

He lowered the book and looked at me.

'What is it?' he said.

I came in and sat down beside him on the bed. 'What you said to me the other day is right,' I said. 'I do need to do more parenting. So now I'm here,' I said, gently taking the book from his hands and putting it face-down on the bed. 'And this is the whole story about Rosie.'

I had all his attention and I told him everything, even the bit I'd never told anyone except Charlie. I told him about the terrible days after she'd gone, the police interviews, the nights of lying awake, and how, when Jacinta left us, it had been just like a replay of that earlier loss for me, only worse, because this time there were two losses to deal with, and the first still as raw and unresolved as ever. I told him about the murders I was involved with and the 'Rosie' letters, written by someone to lure these men to their deaths, and how I'd found the car that had abducted Rosie in a garage behind the hanged body of an old perv in Blackheath. I brought him up to date with everything, even the strange apparition I'd seen in the night. 'She was standing in that room,' I said, pointing towards my bedroom. 'I saw her as plain as I see you now. She said: "Apply the new knowledge to the old."'

Greg lay back, wide-eyed, listening without interruption. 'Wow,' he said finally, 'what a story!' For some moments he just lay there, taking it all in. 'A family ghost. That is heaps cool.' He sat up higher in bed. 'Do you think you really saw a ghost?'

'I don't know what I saw. All I can say is that it happened. Or that I had an experience. I don't know how it happened.'

'But what do you think she meant,' said my son, 'when she said that bit about applying the new knowledge to the old?'

'I thought I knew. And I've been trying to do as she asked.'

'Like how?'

'Like screening for DNA traces. Like not losing sight of the facts we now know about pedophiles. About how driven and compulsive they are. Once, I think there was a tendency to believe that if you gave one a good scolding, locked him up for a while and he promised to be a good boy in future, that was it. It was finished. It's taken us a long time to really see that they are slaves to a compulsion over which they have no control. They are devious, cunning and manipulative.'

'You mean they can't help it?' My son's face was incredulous.

'Charlie and I have talked about this over the years,' I said. 'They can help it in the sense that they know what they're doing isn't acceptable. But they project their desires onto the child and say that children have a "right" to be sexual. They say that community values are out of whack, and it's the community that needs to change its attitudes, not the pedophiles. And if a man's going around saying, "I'm a fixated pedophile and I'm proud of it," he's hardly going to see that *he* needs help.'

'You were always paranoid about those men,' said Greg, 'when we were kids. I remember how you used to point those weirdos out to us. It used to piss Mum off heaps.'

'I was a cop in those days,' I said. 'It was always in my mind then.' I stood up.

'But little kids are sexual,' Greg said. 'I remember mucking around with a little girl when I was about four.'

'Sure,' I said. 'Kids with kids. That's natural curiosity.' I tapped the book on the bed. 'It's late. Don't read too much longer.'

'I won't be reading at all,' he said, putting the book on the floor.

'I don't think I'll be able to sleep either. I come from a truly weird family.'

I tucked him in like I used to do when he was little and kissed him on his forehead. I remembered how when he was born I'd got drunk because I thought that's what fathers did and I felt a sense of sorrow that was seventeen years long. Genevieve certainly had grounds for serious complaint.

I searched through the box of cards and photos and found the picture of the youth again and studied his frowning face. I couldn't work out where he fitted in, what part he played in the combination. I don't know who you are, I said to him, but you're standing where my sister stood in the previous shot. And I want to know if you took her photo and then she took yours. I need to know how you knew her, and what you were doing when she was snatched off the street a couple of days later. I want to find you. I have to find you, if you're still alive. I found some blue tack in a box of odds and ends and stuck the young man's photo on the wall opposite the table where I worked.

Outside, it was still hot and the air was heavy. I walked down to the bushes at the back fence, wondering when I'd get the time to do the gardening I'd planned when I first moved here. I knew the invisible ocean would be flattened by the westerly and I could see the occasional flicker of a distant storm in the southwest. A terrible foreboding overcame me. I looked up at the night sky and felt myself to be a tiny, lost and unimportant dot on the face of the planet.

I walked back inside, my head filled with ideas, memories, regrets and sadness. I stared at the photo on the wall. Who are you, I asked him. Where do you fit in?

By the time I lay down on the bed, I'd reached a decision. Tomorrow, I'd go and tell Bob everything about my association with Iona Seymour. Then, as atonement, I had a plan. It was dangerous, but it might trap the killer. After my fall from grace, I felt it was the least I could do.

•

Next morning after Greg had gone to school and I'd cleaned up, the phone rang. It was Detective Senior Constable Debbie Hale from Child Protection.

'We've finished cross-referencing the phone numbers in the Treweeke notebook,' she said. 'They're mostly a group of peds in the mountains and western suburbs and we knew of most of them already. Springbrook police knew them too.' She laughed. 'Except for the clergyman.' I asked her to explain. 'One of the phone numbers in the book turned out to be one we had in our old records,' she said. 'Belonged to a reverend. An old listing, long before all the numbers were changed over to the new system.'

'Another dirty old clergyman,' I said.

'Not necessarily,' she replied. 'It turns out that one of the old buggers on our list used to talk about his problem to the clergyman there, the Reverend Bower. Didn't do him a scrap of good as it turns out.'

'Bower,' I said. 'That's a name from the past. I know the old rectory. I lived down the street from that place.' Immediately, the Bower rectory came to mind, the fateful corner where the Holden had skidded, but driven away again, with my little sister inside.

'Now you're showing your age,' said Debbie. 'We checked the Reverend out years ago and he was above reproach.'

'Well?' I said.

'That's about it, I'm afraid,' she said. 'He's dead now, and as I said, all the guys in the notebook were already known to us. Not to me, personally,' she said, 'but to the older guys who work here. Some are inside. Some we haven't heard a squeak from in years, so they've probably left the district. Some of them are dead. It's quite possible one of them had something to do with your sister's disappearance, especially considering the car was hidden in Treweeke's garage. He could've been doing a favour for a friend. Or maybe he genuinely didn't know anything about that car, though that's hard to believe. But after all this time, I just don't see how we could do anything anyway. You know how it is. Unless someone comes forward and gives us something. That's really the only way we get anything going in these old cases.'

She was right. 'Okay,' I said, 'just send the book back to me.'

'I'm sorry we couldn't be more helpful.'

Another dead end. It was very dispiriting and I hadn't realised that somewhere, I'd been pinning a lot of hope on the hanged man's notebook. He had been the only link I'd had to the car that had taken my little sister. And now that link hadn't connected anywhere.

I rang Bradley Strachan. 'You did the PM on a Bevan Treweeke?' I reminded him unnecessarily: Dr Strachan never forgets a customer. 'I did,' he said.

I wasn't even sure why I was asking him for this. It was just a gut feeling and because the Holden and Treweeke were connected, it had to mean something, somewhere. I knew that after his post mortem, bits of Bevan Treweeke lived on in bottles of formaldehyde.

'I want some tissue from him,' I said, 'in case I need to eliminate him from a crime scene.'

Dr Strachan promised to courier this to Florence at Forensic Services as soon as possible. I felt a little better. The disappointment of Treweeke's notebook going nowhere had hit me hard, and even though I was probably clutching at straws, the fact that I was doing something that might be useful one day cheered me up a little.

I had another plan in mind as well, and I rang Ron Herring at Goulburn Gaol. In front of me, I had the notes I'd taken from the newspaper archives.

'You've got an Anton Francini as a guest at your establishment?' I asked Ron.

'We do,' said Ron. 'Nice quiet-living old child-killer,' he said. 'Not a spot of bother. I'll bet he's pleased he's not due out for a while, too,' said Ron, 'considering what's happened to some of his friends.'

'I want to talk to you about that,' I said.

I told him what I was setting up and what I wanted and after a bit more chat he arranged a time for me to visit and interview the killer. Then I rang Merrilyn Heywood and put something to her. She said she'd speak to her editor, and let him know that Bob would be ringing him.

After that, I went to the hospital. I bought some pink roses from the shop and was relieved to find that Genevieve wasn't there. Jacinta lay, thinner and paler than I remembered from last time, and it crossed my mind for the very first time that she might not come out the other end of this, that she might be dying. I threw out the drooping yellow daisies and arranged the roses in the blue vase on the bedside cabinet. Then I sat beside my daughter and massaged her wasting arms. Her wrists were so thin now, and her fingers lay inertly in my own. I'd just got sober when she was born and so, unlike my behaviour at the time of my son's birth, I had clear memories of the feelings of fear I'd experienced as she was laid in my arms. This is a whole person, I remember thinking to myself, a whole new person who has to live in this world for perhaps another eighty years. It seemed an enormous and terrible thing to do, to bring a whole new person into being and I'd done it twice now, without any thought.

'I'm sorry, Jass,' I whispered to her unmoving features, 'that I was such an indifferent father. I didn't understand what I was doing. I didn't know what life was about. I'm seeing now I don't know much at all.' I thought of my irrational attraction to Iona Seymour. 'In fact,' I whispered, 'I've just done another stupid thing and I don't think I'll ever be able to live it down.' I heard a sound and looked up to see a plump, pretty nurse had come in and I felt self-conscious and foolish, caught out whispering to myself.

Afterwards, I drove to the Police Centre to tell Bob the whole story about me and Iona and to face the music. Bob took it very well, considering. He looked at me after I'd finished speaking, not saying anything for a minute or two.

'It wouldn't be the first time,' he said finally in his mild way, 'and it won't be the last that something like this happens to someone like you.' He looked up from the notes he'd been jotting down. 'But if it turns out she's a killer and the defence gets hold of this'—he tapped his notes—'and they bloody will, she'll walk.'

I nodded. There was nothing I could say so I showed him the ink-stained paper that I'd taken from her desk. 'I'll give this to Sarah,' I said.

Bob nodded. 'It's something to start with,' he said. 'In the meantime, we'd better keep a discreet eye on Ms Seymour.'

I saw again how my association with Iona had distorted my thinking. Bob hadn't wanted to pounce on her at all. He'd used the word 'discreet'. Everywhere I looked I saw only my own foolish misjudgment of everything. Including the wisdom and expertise of my old friend.

I stood up and went to his office door, looking around. A few other people worked at their desks and seemed out of hearing range, but I pulled the door closed, just in case. 'If you can get permission from the boss to do what I'm about to suggest, Bob, I might be able to redeem myself. Give the killer to you, red-handed.' I thought of that image and changed it immediately. '*Almost* red-handed,' I added. I told him what I intended to do. Again, my old colleague heard me out in silence.

'It just might work,' he said, 'if our killer is consistent.'

'So far, he has been,' I said.

'Or she,' said Bob, stressing the pronoun. He stood up and went to look out his window. There was nothing to see except another grey cement wall with windows in it just like his and I could dimly see my old friend's face reflected back at me. 'There's been a thirty per cent increase in the number of women in prison,' he said to the window. 'Nothing's like it used to be.' He turned round and sat down again, frowning. 'It's a dangerous plan,' he said. 'If anything went wrong you could get yourself cut up badly.'

'If you're in charge, I think I'll be pretty safe,' I said. 'I worked with you for years. I know how good you are.'

Bob looked surprised. 'I didn't know you cared,' he joked.

'OK,' I said. 'I'm going to gaol.'

•

Anton Francini had a crouching quality to him. He sat hunched in a chair opposite me, looking up at me because his head poked forward like a turtle's. It seemed impossible to imagine him harming anyone, let alone a kid. After I'd introduced myself and shown him my ID, he hunched up even further. He gripped the arms of the vinyl chair with fingers that were stained with nicotine. I'd bought a pack of cigarettes and offered him one. He grabbed it, and lit it immediately with his own lighter.

'What do you want?' he said, exhaling, and his voice had the dead rasp of a heavy smoker.

I decided to go straight in. 'I've heard you've had a letter. Maybe more than one,' I said, 'from a young woman called Rosie McCain. A dancer in a nightclub.'

His head jerked up. 'I haven't done anything wrong,' he said. 'You've got no right to poke your nose in my personal business.'

'And I'm willing to bet you had a visit from a priest. Father Dumaresque?'

Francini's face showed me I'd made a direct hit.

'You might as well tell me about it,' I said. 'You see, I have reason to believe that same priest visited other men with similar or related interests to yours. And as soon as they got out of gaol, those men were murdered.'

Francini paled. 'I read the papers,' he said, greatly subdued. 'You don't think the father killed them?'

'Tell me what happened.'

'You're right,' he said. 'The father visited me. Just the once. I didn't know him. He said he'd read I was a Catholic in the newspapers and might need some spiritual counsel.' Francini lowered his voice. 'He told me there was a parishioner of his, a young woman who wrote to lonely men in prison. He told me a few things about her. I was interested. I said I'd like her to write to me.'

'How long ago was this?' I asked.

Francini shrugged. 'About a year.'

'And?' I prompted.

'She wrote.' He shrugged again.

'What would she say to someone like you?'

Francini looked offended. 'She said she knows what it's like—'

'"—to be locked up",' I quoted, '"year after year, at the mercy of your gaolers"?'

Anton Francini's jaw dropped and he sat there, staring at me.

'I need to see those letters.'

'You can't,' he said. 'I've destroyed them. She said to.'

'We'll see,' I said.

He spun round in his seat and then stood up. 'I want to go back to my cell,' he called to the prison officer who was standing near the door.

But it was too late and he knew it. Ron Herring was approaching down the corridor. He gave me the thumbs up. 'We found what you said we would,' he said to me, holding up two envelopes.

Anton Francini looked first at the superintendent and then back at me, confused, angry and frightened.

'I spoke to Assistant Superintendent Herring,' I said, 'before I saw you, and he has guaranteed you a carton of cigarettes a week if you cooperate with something we're planning.'

'A carton a week?' he repeated, looking at Ron Herring.

'That's right, Francini,' said Ron. 'And a transfer to another prison.'

'All you've got to do,' I said, 'is let Mr Herring know the time and the place that Rosie suggests for a meeting in her next letter.'

'What letter?'

'The one I'm tipping you'll get in a few days,' I said. 'If you agree to do as we suggest.'

Anton Francini looked from one of us to the other.

'Like another smoke?' I asked.

•

Two days later found me driving south again, with two more 'Rosie' letters, this time in their envelopes, for Sarah to examine. They were franked 'Kings Cross' but now I wasn't too concerned about tracking the killer through the letters. Already the rumour mill was churning. Beside me on the passenger seat was the newspaper with Merrilyn Heywood's column. Ms Heywood was very concerned, she wrote, to hear that child-killer Anton Francini was due for release in the next few days.

When I knocked at Sarah's office door, she opened it and glanced through the items in their respective bags.

'See what you can get off these,' I asked her.

'While you're here,' she said, 'I talked to Hugh Fullerton about the content of the anonymous letters you gave me to examine. In his opinion, it's very likely a woman. She has a good educational level, yet feels aggrieved in some way.'

'How would he come to that conclusion?' I asked. Although certain people in our game and in the legal world regard both handwriting analysis and content analysis as something of a 'black art' and not to be taken too seriously, I knew how helpful these investigative tools could be. And very valuable later in court. I remembered the famous cross-examination of a revered document chief who, when asked how many qualified document examiners would reach the same conclusion as him, replied: 'All one hundred and thirty of them.'

'The use of "care", for instance,' Sarah was saying. 'It's usually a woman's word and rarely used in this context by a male.' The natural light of a summer afternoon flowed into the room while Sarah continued to educate me in the finer points of forensic linguistics and how these can give valuable clues about the sex, age and schooling of the letter-writer. Sometimes, even their profession.

Sarah picked up some notes and frowned as she read. 'He also said that letters that begin "You don't know anything about me but I know everything about you" generally come from someone who resents her perceived position *vis à vis* the recipient.' I tried to think of someone in that position relative to me, but failed.

Sarah puzzled over something Hugh had written, then worked it out. 'She perceives herself to be unfairly treated, humiliated even, by people—or a person—whom she believes see themselves as superior to her. Of course it's all her projection, but she doesn't see that.' Sarah paused. 'He asked me to ask you if the person who received this had employed babysitters or cleaners? People like that who can move around the home like a member of the family, but who are distinctly *not* a member of the family?'

'I'll have to check,' I said. We walked to the door of her office.

'You're very busy,' she remarked, 'for someone who's supposed to be on leave.'

'I can't keep away from the place,' I joked.

Then I felt something behind me. Years of living with Genevieve had sensitised me to the awareness of a hostile presence. I turned around. Florence, wearing a lot of black and silver, was standing in the corridor, just outside the door to her office, blocking my way.

'That's what I heard, too,' she said, 'except it wasn't work that kept bringing you down here. It was an extra-curricular activity. And this particular extra-curricular was young enough to be your daughter!' Her face contracted into a hateful glare and she disappeared into her office, slamming the door.

Sarah looked at me, embarrassed. 'What was all that about?' she said.

I shook my head, rattled. I suppose it hadn't occurred to me till now that Alix had been somewhat on the youthful side. It hadn't been her youth that had drawn me in, but rather her keenness.

'She's been really off lately,' Sarah whispered to me as we walked past the slammed door with its nameplate almost falling off, crookedly pointing downwards.

I left Sarah at the door of her room and continued outside into the hot day. The air was spiced with the scent of eucalypts and filled with noisy miners' alarm calls. I wondered if Florence Horsefall had it in her to write anonymous letters. I was seeing people in a different light these days. As, it seemed, they were seeing me.

On the way home, I found myself turning off at Annandale again, and driving down the tree-lined street where Iona lived. It was evening and I was tired from all the hours in the car. I got out and stretched my legs, out of view of number 293. Then, keeping well back and using the parked cars as cover, I made my way down the street until I was opposite the house. She wasn't there. The car was gone and the place was locked up, blinds drawn. I crossed the road and looked around. It was that time in the afternoon where the lull occurs just before everyone starts coming home. I ducked into the driveway and sneaked down the side of the house, wondering whether some good neighbour was already on the phone to the police. I walked right round the place, coming out at the front again, near the tiled veranda under the top floor balcony where I'd been put out rather smartly only a day or two ago. I had a sense that someone was watching me and I looked up suddenly, expecting to see a face at a window. But nothing disturbed the curtains behind their french doors upstairs and nothing moved apart from the slight breeze that lifted the rambling rose canes against the southern side of the house. I walked back to my car and drove to the Police Centre.

•

'Look what we've got,' said Bob, passing me a letter. I sat down to read it.

Dear Anton, it said, *I'm longing to meet you in person. I have to leave Sydney suddenly because of a family matter, but I can meet you straight after work on Thursday 27th November before I go. I like to go skinny-dipping at night to cool off, especially on these hot nights. Can you meet me at Coogee Beach, about 1.30 a.m? I'd love to invite you home, but my flatmate makes a fuss if I have guests that late. I'll meet you on the stairs behind the old fishing club at the north end of the beach. There's a chance for some privacy there. I can't wait to run my hands all over your body and feel your hands on mine. It will be so good.*'

It was signed, like all the others, with my sister's name.

'I've spoken to the boss,' said Bob, 'and he's okayed the overtime. We can get people into position well before.' He picked up the letter from where I'd placed it and looked at it again. 'I'm going down there tonight with Ross Llewellyn so he can have a look around. Find the good spots for his blokes. There's a tiny park there, as I remember, just north of the fishing club.' He paused and looked at me closely. 'Sure you want to go through with this?' he said. 'I could get one of the muscle-heads to do it. They'd jump at the chance.'

I shook my head. 'No one else knows what I know,' I said. 'If it's her, I'm sure I'll know it straight away. I know how she moves, how she walks. And I'll be waiting for her. I can wait till she's right on me. And I'll feel snug in the knowledge that Ross and his band of merry men are about to drop down out of the trees.'

'What is it?' Bob asked. He was looking closely at me.

'It's not this,' I said, touching the 'Rosie' letter. 'It's life. My life. Things are very complicated at home just now.'

'Take it easy,' Bob said.

'How do you do that?' I asked.

Bob didn't let me in on the secret but instead went back to his desk and picked up a folder. 'Fingerprints have picked up a partial from the Guildthorpe crime scene.' I remembered the doctor of theology lying in his blood on his Persian rug in his mansion in Woollahra and the staccato screams from the invisible woman upstairs. 'It's being enhanced. Smiley Davis reckons there's a good chance they'll get enough to run a match on it.'

'If whoever did it has a record,' I said, thinking of a woman who hid prayers under statues and made cucumber sandwiches. 'Where was the print found?'

'He'd been struck on the head with a heavy object.' I remembered the livid wound on the head of the murdered man. 'A brass firedog,' Bob was saying. 'It'd been wiped clean, but whoever it was missed some at the base.'

'Keep me posted,' I said.

I drove past Iona's house again and there was still no sign of her car. I got out and deftly lifted the lid of her letterbox. Enough of a build-up to suggest the mail hadn't been checked for a couple of days perhaps, but inconclusive. I was tormented by sexual images of her with another man, the violent man who'd driven her to seek the help and community of the Twelve Step program. My mind took over, running rampant as I imagined her in the 'making up' cycle of an ugly relationship, torrid love-making turning inexorably towards contempt and sometimes violence as the so-called 'love' aspect was replaced by the underlying hatred. I needed to talk to my brother.

•

Charlie made me lime and soda and sat down opposite me. The house seemed oddly quiet and the atmosphere was different, hot and oppressive despite the ceiling fan above our heads.

'Siya's staying with a girlfriend,' said Charlie. 'We had a fight last night.' He bowed his head into his hands, pushed the hair off his temples and leaned back in his chair. 'She actually picked up a knife. It was horrible.'

'I'm sorry,' I said, and even though it sounded stupid, I was. Sorry that he was suffering, too.

'I forget,' he said, 'that she grew up in a war zone. It's affected her. I think I'm the only one with family issues.'

'We're both having family trouble,' I said. Charlie went out to the kitchen and poured himself a black coffee from the percolator, switching off a Chistmas carol on the radio.

'The Christmas compulsion,' he said. 'Every year, mindless lemmings in shops. Christ, it's hot.' He came back and sat down again. 'You look shit,' he said to me, as if he'd just noticed.

'So you keep telling me,' I said. 'I'm not sleeping too well. And there's this whole Rosie thing. It's wearing me down.' I wasn't quite sure how to phrase the next thing I said to him. 'I hate the sense that there's something connecting our family with those mutilation killings. The name at the end of those letters is bad enough. Then Iona's voice on the tape, the way she swerved away from what I suspect she was going to say and then tacked on that bit about Jacinta.' I stood up and went down the short hall to the bathroom, ran the cold water and splashed it over my face and the back of my neck, trying to wash away the darkness that seemed to connect our family to violence and murder. I straightened up and groped for a towel and came back to where my brother was sitting. 'I'm starting to think like you,' I said, as I dried my hands. 'I'm seeing these resonances as you call them. And I don't like them at all.' I sat back down opposite him. 'I told Bob everything,' I said. 'Made a full and frank admission about me and Iona.'

Charlie looked at his watch then went into the kitchen and opened the fridge door, pulling out a plate of cold cooked sausages. 'This is all I've got,' he said, offering me a sausage. I declined. He took one and ate it in two bites. 'I've got a client in twenty minutes. I'm going to have to push you out the door.'

'I can't get the woman out of my head,' I said, hardly aware my brother had spoken. 'I keep seeing her. With another man. Or luring men to their deaths. I'm going crazy.'

Charlie stopped chewing the sausage. 'I think it's an escape for you,' he said.

'An escape?' I was incredulous. 'How can you say that?'

'I think your obsession with this woman is a way to occupy your mind with something that's non-essential. It stops you focusing on the real issues. Your failed marriage. Your kids.' He finished another sausage and wiped his hands on some kitchen paper. 'It's a distraction.' He patted me on the shoulder. 'Hell,' he said, 'I'm not blaming you. It's what we humans do. I do it all the time.'

'She's not a distraction, she's a suspect,' I said, 'in a series of violent and horrible killings.'

'Jack,' said Charlie in his conciliatory voice, 'I didn't mean to rub you up the wrong way. I agree there's *some* basis for your interest in her. But I think she's also carrying a heavy load. Your projections.'

He had a point and the subject was disturbing me so I looked for a way out and a way forward at the same time.

'Charlie,' I said, 'will you come to Springbrook with me? See if you can identify that wall in the photograph of Rosie?'

'What if I can?' he said.

'If we find out where the pictures were taken,' I said, 'it might give us something. It's a place to start from. Rosie was *at* that place, wherever it is, sometime in the three days before she disappeared.'

I could see my brother metaphorically shaking his head over me, as I tried to solve the impossible. But his good heart won the day. 'Day after tomorrow?' said Charlie. 'Siya and I were going to take a picnic to Centennial Park and feed the ducks.' He looked dejected at the thought.

'No ducks,' I said, 'but you can still pack a picnic.'

Greg was lying in a clearing on the floor when I got home, watching a video. He sprawled, seeming to take up much more room than was possible, inside a circle of school books, cassette covers, empty plates and containers and items of clothing pushed out of the way around him. He nodded when I came in, and turned his attention back to the movie.

'Charlie and I are driving up to Springbrook day after tomorrow,' I said. 'Wanna come?'

He paused the movie and two frozen lovers shimmered on the screen. 'I've got a history test and the swimming carnival day after tomorrow,' he said. 'Otherwise I'd go with you.'

'Can you do something about that crop circle you've created?' I indicated the messy circumference. Greg reluctantly started gathering plastic containers together and picking up empty packets, the lovers on the screen went back to their engagement and I looked around for something to eat.

As the hours passed, I was getting more and more nervous about the date I'd be keeping with 'Rosie.'

•

I went with Bob and the 2IC of the State Protection Group, 'Flat Line' Floyd, for a drive to Coogee next morning because Ross Llewellyn was otherwise engaged at a seige. Flat Line looked around, local map spread out on his knees, first from the car, driving along the streets that enclose the north end of the beach, and then on foot. He was very excited to find the solid little fishing clubhouse.

'Find the key holder of that,' he said, 'and we're laughing.' It was a small, well-built structure, a little bunker, with a door and barred windows high up, reminding me of Goulburn Gaol. 'And a few blokes up here,' he said, indicating the small hillock that rose behind it, with a brick amenities block off to one side, dotted with gnarled banksias, deformed from the prevailing wind. Wattlebirds rattled and scolded each other and a pair of crows called. 'Those boats are a possibility, too,' he said, squinting in the hot sun, indicating the upturned fishing boats beached some distance away from the low stone wall that separated the sand from the grassy verge. He walked across the park, checked buildings, made notes and eventually rejoined us. We drove away, with me in the back seat and Bob and Flat Line in the front.

'Unusual nickname,' said Bob, turning to Flat Line.

'I was killed in an operation about eight years ago,' said Floyd.

I noticed the wide scar that tracked through his hair and down his neck and vanished beneath the collar and I remembered my father had a scar like that.

'I was on the table with all the surgeons poking around like they do. Then they saw the flat line on that heart screen. I was just lying there dead. But they brought me back. When my mates heard about it, one of them said hey, how could they tell the difference?'

I was sweating, and it wasn't only the heat of the November day. I hoped Flat Line's mate was referring to his leader's *sang-froid*, rather than his intelligence. I looked back at the beach as the car climbed the hill and thought how in a few short hours I'd be here. And, if all went according to plan, so would 'Rosie'.

•

Midnight found Bob and me sitting in the dark in the deserted upper bar of the Beach Palace, surrounded by empty tables, watching the northern end of Coogee Beach, familiar companions to this sort of silence and each other. Bob had found this spot earlier in the day before meeting Flat Line and me, and we'd already been there for a couple of hours. Opposite us, and nestled in the curve of the rise, the little fishing club building showed as a pale outline against the darker wooded knoll behind. Time passed slowly. Occasionally, we'd say something to each other, but mostly we sat in silence. Sometimes Bob's portable spoke, as Flat Line and his mates checked in. Sometimes, I stood up and walked around the long room. It was times like these, I wished I smoked again. Anything to help pass the time, although it wasn't unpleasant being in this upper room which smelt of food and cigarette smoke. Occasionally a figure would walk along the path from the dark headland, coming out of the banksias and low heath brush of the small public park. I knew that many people took the path around the foreshores and these days, a person could walk from Bondi almost as far as Maroubra. Adjacent to the park were the outlines of flats and houses, the bright windows of insomniacs or shift workers.

Bob's portable crackled and Floyd's voice made me jump. 'Flat Line and company standing by. Five minutes to countdown. Copy that.' Bob acknowledged the call and I glanced at my watch. It was one twenty-five. Now the beach and its surroundings were deserted. The lights along the tiled promenade frosted the small waves as they uncurled along the sand. Gulls appeared brilliant white in their light, then vanished as if by magic into the darkness as they flew out of the powerful beams.

'You'd better start wandering down,' Bob said.

I picked up the coat and cap on the table. In case our target had studied the countenance and physique of Anton Francini, I dressed myself to look bulky, and I hunched myself, pushing my head forward, losing a couple of inches in height. I wore the cap that I'd been told was Francini's habitual headgear and a longish coat.

'How do I look?' I said to Bob, my voice hoarse with tension.

'Like a first class A-grade perv,' he said. I turned to go out the door.

Bob walked with me, touching my shoulder. 'There are a dozen blokes to make sure you don't come to grief.'

I'd felt this racing heart before exams, when waiting for a target to show, and, many years ago, sitting at the kitchen table in the old house at Springbrook waiting for my mother to come out of her room, knowing how nasty her mood swings could be. As I walked downstairs, I couldn't help recalling that someone handy with a knife can be faster and deadlier than someone armed with a gun. I tried not to think of that as I left the building and crossed the road, keeping my steps shorter and slower than my habitual gait. How would Anton Francini feel and behave, I asked myself. But I couldn't answer my own question, because, unlike the previous men who'd gone to meet 'Rosie', I knew what to expect. I wondered if I was going to see her hurrying across the sand to me, her red jacket covering her powerful body and the long, blonde wig hiding her dark hair. The low surf pulsed in and out and I could just discern the horizon line between the sky and ocean.

I shuffled over the paved promenade, heading for the fishing club, hoping I looked like a newly released murderer on his way to keep a hot date. It was in keeping with my role that I look around and I certainly did, more alert than I'd felt in ages, my eyes scanning the promenade and the darker area behind the fishing club house. Someone was walking straight towards me. I stiffened in fear, but it was a man. He had his head down and took no notice of me. We passed each other and I heard his footsteps moving away behind me. I knew that a dozen pairs of eyes were watching him, watching me. Somehow, this knowledge failed to keep me from feeling exposed and vulnerable out here alone.

I was leaving the beach now, stepping up onto the grass, heading towards the club house. I could see it clearly now, and I knew that there were armed men inside the locked door, waiting. An odd noise stopped me in my tracks and I looked around. There it was again, a low moan.

Then something like a scuffle. I tried to look unconcerned as I kept heading for the club house, but the noise was coming from near the group of upturned fishing boats. As I got closer, the sound stopped. Two heads bobbed up. A couple of kids were going for it in the relative privacy that the boats provided. They didn't move until I'd walked past and then they went back to what they were doing.

It was a perfect warm summer night, and overdressed as I was, sweat poured down my back and itched my skin. A wooden bench near the fish-cleaning sinks on the western side of the club gave me a place to sit and wait. My watch said it was right on one thirty, the time the spurious club dancer claimed she would meet me. I hadn't realised until I stopped moving how hard and fast my heart was beating. I moved away from the bench and walked around the little club house, climbing the rise behind it, looking warily at the brick toilet block, as if I was checking it out thoroughly, concerned that I might be waiting on the wrong side. Something moved in the bushes opposite the toilets and I stopped dead.

'Rosie?' I said in a low voice, 'is that you?'

Whatever had moved was completely still, but I had the sense of something waiting, biding its time. Even though it was probably one of Flat Line's boys, it spooked me and I backed away from the source of the noise, a long low bank of heath bush, and took up my place again near the fish-cleaning bench. Fishing knives became uppermost in my imagination and I stepped away from the shadow of the building so that the SPG people hiding in cars or up trees or in drains or wherever the hell they were could easily see me. Then I wondered if the movement I'd heard was one of the warriors adjusting his automatic weapon. This thought was not a comfort to me. I didn't want to become a casualty of some muscle-head's hyper-vigilance.

I peered over to the top of the Beach Palace building, where I knew Bob was watching and then I heard a car driving up towards me, along the short dead-end road that runs east–west along the northern edge of the beach. A small, late model white sedan was moving slowly and I walked up the path to where I could see better. The car had backed into a space and my heart started pounding even louder in the silence, as the driver's door opened and a tall figure stepped out. Red jacket, harem pants and long blonde hair. 'Rosie' was right on time.

All around me, the air was charged as hidden men held their breath and watched as 'Rosie', standing under a street light, slammed the door behind her, adjusted her hair and paused a moment, as if taking in the fresh air and the warm night. She took a couple of steps in my direction. I realised I was holding my breath. I exhaled and as I did, I heard something. From somewhere came the sound of a mobile phone. The figure in the red jacket heard it, too, stopped midstep and with a speed that took us all by surprise, jumped back in the car. Several men, including Flat Line, emerged from their hiding places, I joined them and we started running towards the roadside. The door of the fishing club house opened and three heavily tacked SPG men spilled out. But the small white car had already screamed away from the kerb, raced down the road, made a fast right-hand turn and was halfway up the hill before anyone reached a vehicle.

'What happened?' I yelled. 'Whose fucking phone was that?'

One of the heavily tacked figures ran up to Flat Line. 'What's going on?' he asked his leader.

'Someone's mobile rang,' I said, furious and frustrated. I pulled the cap off and threw it to the ground. I tore off layers of clothing and the heavy coat.

Bob ran up out of the darkness. '"Rosie" was on her way,' he said. 'Then her mobile rang.'

'*Hers?*' I said.

The three of us looked at each other. Then Bob kicked sand in one of the only displays of frustration I'd seen in over twenty years of working with him.

'We were *that* close,' he said. 'It was all going so well.'

I walked over to the light of the promenade area, and saw a

police car returning. As it pulled up, I saw the driver shake his head. 'Lost the bastard,' he said.

Bob came over to me. 'If I hadn't had you under my nose,' he said, and he was only half joking, 'I might start thinking it was you who tipped her off.'

I was speechless. I stared out at the sea. My feelings were very confused. We were no closer than we'd ever been to finding 'Rosie'. She'd come so close. Bob's jokey suggestion had touched a raw nerve. Somewhere, was I pleased that our target had escaped?

ELEVEN

'We shoulda grabbed her the minute she stepped out of the car,' said Flat Line at next day's debrief at the Police Centre. 'Not waited. Searched her, found the knife. Charged her with carrying a concealed weapon. Once you've got her, it's just a matter of finding the evidence.'

'It mightn't have been her at all,' said Bob. 'Just some woman coming home. There're a lot of blondes in Sydney. And a lot of red jackets.' He looked at me. 'What do you think, Jack? Do you think it was her?'

I looked up from where I'd been doodling a flower pattern on the pad in front of me. 'It seems like too much of a coincidence,' I said, 'that someone wearing a red jacket and blonde hair shows up right at the time "Rosie" arranged to meet Francini. I'd have to say the probabilities are that yes, it was her. Whoever that is,' I added.

As we left the room, Bob came close to me. 'Was it *her*?'

I replayed the memory of the woman stepping out of the white car, standing a moment in the streetlight, adjusting her hair—or was it a wig?—then jumping back in as the mobile rang.

'I can't say whether it was or it wasn't,' I said. 'There was nothing familiar. But, on the other hand, it could have been her. Same height and weight.' As we walked down the hall, I was aware of Bruce Geldorf, now Team Leader of Crime Scene personnel, coming towards us with his box of tricks and a camera slung over his shoulder.

'Neil Pritchard was after you,' Bob told him. 'I said you were at Rushcutters Bay.'

'I was. He found me,' said Geldorf.

'What were you doing at Rushcutters Bay?' some sixth sense made me ask.

'Young moll,' said Bruce, walking into his office and offloading camera and case. 'Bashed to death in her apartment.'

I stood there, thinking what a fool I'd been. I already knew who it was. And I knew why. Two hundred and thirty-three thousand reasons and an accounts book.

'Renee Miller,' I said. 'That was the name, wasn't it?'

'She's right here, starring in this,' said Bruce, surprised. He tapped his equipment.

'I'd like to see that,' I said.

Bruce unloaded the video cassette to prepare it for screening.

A little while later, in a narrow room with banks of screens, and with the slow-moving Crime Scene tape fast-forwarded on one of them, I saw Renee's slight, battered body lying on the floor of the apartment where I'd found my daughter. Her head was black with bloody contusions, arms bruised and reddened, slender fingers blue-white under the blood. She lay on her back with her legs half under the bed, her bloody face turned to one side. Around her, the slow, silent and methodical panning of the tape showed the destruction of her apartment, furnishings ripped and overturned, light fittings torn out, mirror smashed, bedclothes tattered, mattress ripped open to expose the springs. A chair had been thrown through the glass partition between the bar and the lounge room.

I pressed rewind, and the machine purred into fast action. 'I should have seen it coming,' I said to Bob, who'd stood by the door watching. 'Should've warned her to get out of the place.'

'No one could have seen it coming,' Bob said. 'And do you really think she would have taken any notice of any warning you might give her?' I remembered the skinny, cranky little kid only a few years older than Jacinta and I felt an overwhelming sadness that she'd died like that.

'Your daughter was the one involved,' Bob was saying as we walked into his office, 'and she'd moved out. And,' he added in his methodical, logical way, 'this murder may not even be related to that particular package. The package!' Bob reiterated. 'Where is it now?'

'I'm dealing with that,' I said, wondering how long it would take Renee's killer to work out who was next in the chain of custody.

Bob's desk phone rang. 'Send him up to me,' he said into the mouthpiece.

'Smiley Davis from Fingerprints,' he told me. 'On his way up.'

A moment later, Smiley came into Bob's office and stuck his hand out. 'Haven't seen you round for a while,' he said to me.

'I don't work here anymore,' I told him.

He nodded. 'I got a result for you,' he said, 'on that partial.'

I'd almost forgotten the partial handprint Crime Scene had found on the base of the brass firedog in the impressive study of Jeremy Guildthorpe, doctor of theology and other things. 'Anyone we know?' I asked.

'He's got a record,' said Smiley. 'Mostly drug offences. Some B and E's way back. Couple of soliciting convictions.'

I took the computer enhancement and analysis with its twelve matching points from him and stared at them, dazed, while my mind tried to absorb the name under it. 'All that fancy DNA stuff,' Smiley was saying with triumph as I stared at the name, 'and it's old-fashioned fingerprints that get your man.'

I was aware of Bob frowning at me. 'What is it?' he said. 'What've you got?' He put his hand out for the fingerprint enhancement I was holding.

Slowly, I passed it to him. This was the palm print of a person I'd worked with for nearly two decades, bought drinks for, listened to, formed whatever bond it is that develops within the confines of our strange, not quite professional relationship. I still found it hard to believe.

'Robin Anthony Dowzer,' I said to him. Staro.

'He's got the form,' said Bob, 'if you look into it. Kids who end up selling their arses at the Wall don't come from your average happy family.' He turned to me. 'You know him, Jacko. And it makes perfect sense when I think about it. Someone like Staro, on the fringes, drug user, small-time crook, decides to get even with the men—as he sees it—who abuse children. Someone stuck it to him when he was a little kid, so he blames that for his horrible life and then gets all stirred up about the short sentences handed down to these guys, guys who've done a lot worse, and then he decides to punish them. All he had to do was find a way of setting them up.'

I shook my head. It just didn't sit right with me.

Bob continued. 'He's talking about himself when he describes the nightclub dancer. He's done things in clubs over the years. You're the link. Remember how he idealised you. You've said something about your sister Rosie. That gives him another incident he feels he needs to avenge. That's where he's got the name he uses in the set-up letters. '

'Absolutely not,' I said. 'I've never discussed my family with Staro. You can forget that idea.'

'He would've known about Jacinta.'

'All of New South Wales knows about Jacinta. That's quite different. I've never discussed my sister with him.'

'I know how it is with informers,' said Bob. 'A few drinks and the boundaries get a bit blurred.'

'You don't blur on mineral water,' I said. 'It's not Staro.'

Bob tapped the enhanced print. 'We've got him. There's no way round this. This puts him at the scene. With his grubby hands around the murder weapon.'

I considered. 'Okay,' I said, 'I'll rephrase that. Staro must have been at Jeremy Guildthorpe's address at some stage and I'm willing to concede that Staro could have killed him. Maybe something happened between them that upset Staro. He lashes out, strikes Guildthorpe with the firedog, panics, thinks of the mutilation killings because he saw Carmody's murder at Centennial Park, so he whips out a knife and tries to make it look like another one in that series.'

Bob jabbed the print enhancement on his desk. 'We can put him at the scene of the Carmody murder not as a witness, but a killer,' he said. 'He rang you to say he was following Carmody into the park. Of course he was! He set up the meeting in the first place. He kills Carmody, knows that you're on the way. He can't be caught with blood all over him, so he bolts.'

'Sounds neat, Bob. But it doesn't make sense,' I said. 'If you were about to meet someone and kill them, would you phone one of the investigators and tell him where it was about to happen?'

'It's damn good cover,' Bob said. 'Especially if I knew I'd have it done and be out of there before he arrived on the scene.'

'It's crediting Staro with a complexity that he just doesn't have,' I said. 'I've worked with him for a long time. He doesn't think like that. The only forward planning an addict makes is about chasing it.'

'You told me he was clean at the moment.'

'If he's stayed that way, he'd be off his face with anxiety. He wouldn't be able to think straight, let alone plan and execute something like you're suggesting.'

'We've got him at two of the crime scenes,' Bob said. 'And a strung-out addict is capable of anything.'

'It's beyond any probability theory,' I said, exasperated, 'that of all the people in New South Wales I could ask to help me cover Carmody I end up asking the killer himself!'

'Don't let the coincidental aspects of it blind you. Weirder things have happened.'

'Bob, come *on*. We're looking at completely different crimes!'

'Killers change their MO,' said Bob. 'We know that. You know that.'

'Not in this case. I know you'd love to wrap Staro around these four killings, but it's not on. Someone killed Nesbitt, Gumley and Carmody. Staro saw who it was, and he's been on the run ever since.'

'He's been on the run ever since because he's the killer,' said Bob. 'He used to wear women's clothing. That could have been him we saw last night in the red jacket and blonde wig.'

'Could've been anyone,' I said. 'I *know* it's not Staro.'

'Like you know your wife? Like you know your kids? Like you know whoever it is that's sending you anonymous letters?' He moved closer and lowered his voice. 'Like you know Iona Seymour?'

'If you bring Staro in—' I started to say.

'—*When* I bring Staro in,' Bob finished for me, 'I'll call you.' He dismissed me by picking up his phone. I heard him putting out the bulletin on Staro and I knew the manhunt would be on. I wondered how long someone like Staro could stay hidden.

On the way to the hospital, I thought a lot about a lot of things. I'd been wounded by Bob's gibe about my lack of perception. Only once or twice in our long career as mates and partners had his mild nature been stirred sufficiently for him to talk to me like that. It was true I hadn't known what Genevieve was up to. I'd withdrawn, because that was easier for me. In many ways, I'd done the same with the kids. I thought of my daughter still lying unconscious a few suburbs away. What did I know about her? What had I ever known about her? And Greg? It was only in the last few weeks that I'd attempted to enter *his* world. I'd always expected that the kids would enter *my* world, value what *I* held dear, admire what *I* admired. I hadn't really allowed for them to be completely different from me in every way. And in someone else who I also didn't know, I'd aroused sufficient malice for them to carry out an anonymous hate-mail campaign against me. So, painful as it was for me to admit it, Bob was very right to question my judgment in these matters.

I went over the odds and ends I'd gleaned from Staro's rambling conversations. I knew he was a country boy originally who'd run away from various institutions and tried his luck in the big city. He'd gone the way of too many youngsters without a sane family. By the time I'd met him and we'd done the deal that roped in the drug dealers, Staro had worked as a rent boy, a drag queen, a courier for a dealer, had fathered a child, been locked up several times, and was trying to lose a very expensive heroin habit. But I couldn't imagine him as a killer. If he'd killed Jeremy Guildthorpe, there must have been strong provocation. Why would a person like Staro kill a man like that? In the last few years, men who were pillars of the community had turned out to be vicious pedophiles. We'd only found out about their secret habits when they were murdered by killers who turned out to be earlier victims. That set me thinking. Staro had been trying to get clean the last time I'd seen him, claiming the only drug he was using was nicotine. Someone like me, who's been there and done that, remembers what those early days are like. It's the time when all the reasons that a person drank or drugged in the first place start raising their ugly heads. And this time the erstwhile addict has to deal with them without the usual anaesthetic. At a time of minimum inner resources, we have to deal with maximum stress. It's the reason so few people get straight.

As I was stepping out of the lift in the hospital, my mind sparked and the connection fused. My imagination played the scene for me: Staro, in hiding in Centennial Park, petrified, waiting for me to arrive, witnessing the death of Frank Carmody at the hands of a killer in a red jacket with long blonde hair, Carmody sliding down the wall behind him, his life's blood spurting, his killer straightening up, the wig perhaps slipping, and enough light for Staro to realise he's looking straight at someone whose face he already knows from Twelve Step meetings. The same face filled my imagination: Iona Seymour. I saw the scar across the top of her breasts in my mind's eye as I hurried along the hospital corridor. Someone had hurt her once. Maybe a sexual assault. So she'd be set on revenge. But I knew I'd need more than this surmise for her to be charged. She would be smart enough to know that she's got the best cover of all for this sort of crime, I thought. Everyone will be looking for a man.

I looked into Jacinta's room. She seemed a fraction better today, I thought, with a faint colour in her cheeks. 'I'm here, Jass,' I whispered, taking her cool, light hand. 'I know I wasn't here much before. But I'm right here now.' Did I imagine it, or was there the slightest smile touching the edge of her lips?

•

I got home and checked the mail. The minute I saw the envelope, I ripped it open, no longer caring to keep evidence pristine. *Men are losing their balls in Sydney lately*, I read, *but you never had any. Now you're doing the same thing that you did to me to someone else. Watch your back, arsehole.* I put it back in its envelope. What on earth was I doing to someone else that I'd done to the writer? I stopped walking and stood, trying to work out what this person might mean. Then I got angry. I wasn't going to give this stupid, anonymous, spiteful person any more of my time. I scrunched up the letter and threw it in the recycle bin. I made a vow that in future I wouldn't even open the pathetic things, but throw them straight out. I took a deep breath and was feeling pleased with this decision until I saw that the door to my house was open.

Greg must have come home early. 'Greg?' I called. But there was no answer.

I stepped inside and stopped dead in disbelief and confusion. The place was like a bomb site. Everything had been tipped out on the floor, cartons, boxes, files, the contents of drawers, bedding, furniture, hurled around and trashed. The place looked like some of the premises I'd visited over the years, where nothing had been picked up from the floor for thirty years. The fridge door was open and spilled milk, melting ice and food covered the kitchen floor. Every cupboard was open, boxes of cereals torn to shreds, bottles opened and tipped out. Melted pools showed where the iceblocks had been hurled. I saw immediately that the television and a big cassette radio player were both untouched. This was not the usual robbery. Someone was searching for his money. Another thing I should have known. Thank God Greg hadn't been there. After Renee, I was next in the chain of custody. Standing amid the debris of my home, I made a phone call. 'Get Bruce Geldorf over here,' I said. 'And Smiley Davis. Whoever did Renee Miller and her place has just been here.' There was no way I could prove that, but all my instincts told me it was so.

I couldn't do anything about the mess until it had been fingerprinted and examined and I didn't want to hang around so I jumped back in my car and drove to 293 Reiby Street. On the way, I had a keen sense that I was being followed. But despite keeping an eye on my rear vision mirror, I couldn't find any particular culprit. The car radio was full of the Guildthorpe story and the man police wanted to find to assist with their inquiries. I wondered where Staro was and how long it would take for them to find him.

When I arrived at Iona's house, she still wasn't there. Reiby Street isn't very long and no other car pulled up anywhere in the street. No one was following me. However, I glanced around. In the telegraph wires near her house, two electrocuted magpies fluttered upside-down, each hanging by one foot, like gymnasts on a wire, feathers lifting in the occasional breeze. When things got too rough for her, I was willing to bet she went to stay with the man whose presence I'd deduced. I watched the place for a while in the late, hot afternoon. In its overgrown gardens, the house seemed diminished without the presence of its owner. Almost without wanting to, I found myself crossing the road and pushing rose canes aside as I walked down the driveway at the side. I felt guilty, intruding like this, but more than that I felt fear. At the back of the house was a small yard, enclosed by the paling fences of the adjoining properties. A neglected lemon tree, a mulberry and a wild plumbago hedge almost filled the area. Attached to the back of the house was an old laundry. I stood at the door and looked in. Big twin tubs, with a rotting clothes wringer of the sort I remembered from my childhood house in Springbrook, ran along one wall. I poked around in the cobwebs and dust, finding nothing more interesting than an old wooden dolly peg and several empty jars. I was bending down, opening a cupboard under the tubs, when I thought I heard a noise. I straightened up, thinking of what I'd say if challenged by anyone, especially Iona. She could take me by surprise, sever my arteries, add to her collection of wet specimens, slam the door on me in here and no one would ever know where I was or what had become of me. I shuddered at the thought and remained motionless a moment, looking through the dirty windowpane beside the tubs. No one came and nothing happened. I breathed again and stooped down to reach into the dark cupboard. There was an empty paint tin with a paint-stiffened rag thrown over it. I pulled the rag off to reveal three congealed paint brushes set in the skin of paint that covered the bottom of the tin. Further along the shelf I found a plastic container containing fish hooks, and an old hand line. I pushed them aside, hardly noticing them. Because hiding in the darkness between the containers was something wrapped up in an old pillow-case. Even before I'd uncovered it I knew what it was. A knife, double-sided. With great care, and without touching it, I examined it carefully. The blade had been wiped clean. But blood is very hard to remove without trace and I had no doubt that this was the weapon that had inflicted terrible injuries on at least three men.

I hurried round to the front again, trying to peer into the dim interior through the coloured glass of the front door. It was then I noticed the small yellow post-it note lying on the tiles. I picked it up and read it. *Please ring me. Michael*, it said. With great care, I placed it inside my jacket. Michael, I said to myself, I've got you now.

I drove straight to the Police Centre only to find Bob was out of the office. I decided to wait and spent an uneasy half hour, hanging around, until finally he appeared. I gave him the bagged knife and told him where I'd found it.

'My place has been trashed,' I said. 'They suspect I've got the package.'

'You've still got it?' said Bob. I nodded. I didn't say anything about moving it to Charlie's. Then I showed him the post-it note and we agreed I'd make some inquiries. This Michael could well be someone we needed to talk with.

'I'll drive down to the lab in the morning,' I said, 'with the knife. We can get a result in a day or so.'

'No you won't,' said Bob. 'I'll take that and send it to our lab, not yours. You've got to stay right out of the picture.' It took me a moment to realise what Bob was saying. 'Even if it turns out to be the murder weapon,' he continued, 'the defence will want to know who found it. That's going to cause enough of a problem as it is without you being involved in the scientific examination of the damned thing as well.'

My heart sank as I heard his words. That afternoon of lovemaking with Iona was costing me more all the time. 'You don't think—?' I started to say, but Bob interrupted me.

'It doesn't matter what I think, Jack,' he said. 'It's what a jury can be led to think. It's the sort of thing that can establish reasonable doubt.'

I sat down, feeling defeated. If things came to trial and this indiscretion of mine became public knowledge, it would be the end of my work with the government. A scientist's objectivity is his safety line. If there was even the slightest suggestion that I'd somehow interfered with the course of justice, my career was over. I might as well move to Goulburn and grow roses and as I got back into my car, I realised my hands were shaking. I sat there in the car until the trembling eased.

I went back to Reiby Street and called on Iona's neighbour in 291, flashing my ID. I asked the surprised woman if she'd seen a man around next door, visiting or otherwise coming and going. She shook her head.

'No,' she said. 'Never.'

'Have you seen her go out with anyone? Someone calling for her?'

The woman thought a moment. 'Once or twice,' she said. 'But I don't take much notice. She leads a very quiet life.'

I left my card and the woman promised to ring me if she saw anything unusual. I asked her not to say anything to her neighbour, and reassured her there was nothing criminal involved. Then I drove home again, picking Greg up as he was walking home.

'There's been an incident,' I said, 'at our place.'

I told him what had happened as we pulled up outside the house. I collected the mail, a little packet that turned out to be Bevan Treweeke's notebook returned from Child Protection, and then we walked round the back to where my door stood open onto the half-finished patio.

'Shit, Dad,' Greg said, carefully walking in and looking around, 'this is serious.'

I had to agree.

'But you seem really cool about it,' he said.

In reality, I was still shaky from finding the knife at Iona's place and this trashing of my home added to the menace that seemed to be surrounding me.

'Not really,' I said.

'What were they looking for?' he said after surveying every room. 'Everything's still here.'

Eventually I was going to have to tell Greg about the money. 'Maybe I've trodden on some toes,' I said, 'in this investigation.'

He looked at me in disbelief. 'You've been involved in lots of investigations and nothing like this has ever happened before.'

The photograph of the anonymous youth was still stuck to the wall.

'Who's that?' Greg asked, noticing me looking at the figure with his sensitive face and floppy hair.

'I don't know,' I said.

My son stood opposite me, looking around the wreck of our place. 'Why have you got it stuck up there? What's going on, Dad?' he demanded.

'There are a couple of things that I can't really talk about now,' I said to him.

He rolled his eyes heavenwards and stomped off into the wreck of his room, slamming the door.

I went to it and knocked. 'Come on,' I said. 'Come with me to Charlie's and we'll talk.'

For a while nothing happened, then I heard him slowly walk across the room and open the door. 'Come on, Greg,' I said. 'You'll just have to trust me on this one.'

How could I begin to tell him about the mess I'd landed myself in? About the fact that I might be finished as a scientist, out of work, my reputation in tatters? I could hardly bear to think about it.

I drove us to Charlie's place and told my brother what had happened.

'What are you talking about?' said Greg. 'What package?'

'An amount of money,' I said, carefully choosing my words, 'was found in Jacinta's gear. My feeling is that whoever owns it came looking for it.'

'Great!' said Greg, swearing and throwing down his school bag. 'This is exactly what I mean about Jacinta coming home.'

I went to say something but Charlie put a hand on my arm.

'Now *my* life's turned upside-down again,' Greg said, 'and *my* place's wasted because she's done some stupid thing and dragged all of us into it. That's just so typical of her! I'm sick of my family. I hate it.' He stormed out onto the timber deck.

I went to go after my son, but stopped short. Bob was right. There were a hell of a lot of things I just didn't know.

'Greg,' Charlie said, following him out, 'you look like you could do with a beer.'

Greg swung round on him. 'I don't want a fucking beer,' he said. 'I just want to belong to a normal family. And not one where my sister's a junkie in intensive care, my mother runs round with other men and my father lives at bloody La Perouse—in a daggy house that's just been fucking trashed heaps.'

'Reggie, Reggie,' said Charlie, 'sounds just like what I used to say. With a couple of differences. Your father and I are driving up to Springbrook to the scene of the crime. I think you should come.'

'What crime?' said Greg. Charlie put a cold beer in front of my son, a lime juice for me and waved his hands around. 'Just *the* crime. Every family commits crimes against their members. It's a well-known fact. I'm always listening either to the confessions of the perpetrators, or the misery of the victims. That's my work. We have to go back to the past to understand it. You should know that,' he said, turning to me.

Greg tore the lid off the beer can. I could see he was interested, despite his anger. He'd always got on well with his uncle.

'Families,' said Charlie, 'have rituals and spells. And enchantments and curses. So if you know where they come from, you're halfway to undoing them. Come with us and we can talk about the patterns in our family. And how to get rid of the witch.' He went over to Greg and put an arm around him. 'You're absolutely right to be pissed off. It is the rational response to a hostile situation.'

I felt irritated with my brother and my voice was sharper than I intended. 'Now,' I said to Charlie, 'you're turning our trip tomorrow into some psychological vision quest. Have you forgotten that the point of the trip was to see if you could recognise that wall behind Rosie in the photograph?'

'That, too,' said my brother. 'But we'll have to drop in on Dad.'

I went and sat down in a deep armchair. Our father. Not him, not now, not with everything else going on.

'No way,' said Greg, 'am I going round to visit that miserable old bastard.'

My mobile rang and I walked into the hall to take the call from Sarah, leaving my son and my brother in serious discussion, looking at the collection of scabbarded throwing knives Siya had fixed to the wall of the bedroom. They were an improvement on flying ducks, even if somewhat ominous given my present investigation, and my eyes took them in as I listened to Sarah's voice.

'Okay,' she said, 'I've tested that piece of paper with the ink stains on it.'

'And?' I asked her, remembering the panicky way I'd grabbed it from Iona's bedroom. Now, after finding the knife, I wondered what might have happened if the woman herself had come into the room and seen what I was doing.

'And,' Sarah continued, 'you'll be interested to know that I find them to be indistinguishable from the paper and the ink used in the series of "Rosie" letters.'

I wasn't surprised.

'Where did you get it from?' Sarah was asking. She usually takes no personal interest in the evidence she tests, just does her work then moves on to the next test sample. But the notoriety of the mutilation murders even had someone as cool as Sarah wanting to know more.

'At a house I was visiting,' I said.

'Golly,' said Sarah. 'Strike that address off your visiting list.'

'I have,' I said, ringing off. Even as I said it, I knew I didn't mean it.

I walked back down to join the others and when Greg came back inside with Charlie, he looked at me. 'I won't go up to Springbrook with you two,' he said. 'Like I've told Dad, I've got important school stuff on.' He slumped down in a chair and looked at the beer he'd been drinking. 'Don't know what you ever saw in this,' he said to me, putting it down on the table. I saw that he was joking.

TWELVE

Charlie drove us to the mountains early next morning, after dropping Greg off at school. I'd suggested he stay at Charlie's or at his friend Paddy's place. I'd wanted him to come with us, as a security measure as much as anything else—that two hundred thousand dollars plus was scorching all of us—but I knew it wasn't possible to force a six foot seventeen-year-old male to do something he doesn't want to.

As we turned onto the freeway, I told Charlie about the knife and the way we'd set up the meeting with 'Rosie' and me masquerading as Anton Francini. And how we'd lost the figure in the red jacket.

'It is very strange,' I said to him, 'about Rosie's name being used like that. If it's Iona, it's as if she's involved with our family in some way. Using our sister's name to set them up and ringing with information about Jass. We know the killer either impersonates a priest or works in tandem with someone who poses as one. And her father was a clergyman. She talks about how the children of clergymen figure in terrorism. What does all that say to you?'

Charlie kept his eyes on the road. 'It's your mind that's putting all these things together,' he said. 'Like when a woman's pregnant she suddenly sees that everyone seems to be pregnant. It's your own preoccupation that makes certain things stand out. Of all the possible bits of information you've gathered concerning our family, that woman and the investigation you're involved in, you've chosen these particular bits. It's like you've dipped your hand into a huge jar of beads and you've threaded a necklace out of some of them and you're saying to me, "Look, isn't it amazing! These beads make a pattern!"'

I shook my head. 'Charlie, I'm not making bloody necklaces. These are *facts* I'm talking about. Facts. Not your resonances and veiled inferences.' On the radio someone was talking about steam trains which I found unreasonably irritating.

'Okay,' said my brother, 'let's go at it another way. 'The name Rosie McCain is hardly unique. There must be millions of Rosies and McCains. Bound to get them running together more than once, so that one can be put down to coincidence. There's no fact involved. And if it's not Iona who's killing the men, then she's not writing the letters anyway. And if that's so, there goes her spooky connection with our sister Rosie. It's a fact that she knew Jacinta's name. But, Jack, so does most of Sydney.' He pulled out and passed a utility loaded with cartons, settling down in front of it. 'The story about Jacinta was widely reported. And there were several articles about teenage runaways and her name kept cropping up. There are probably tens of thousands of people who know about your daughter and know her name.' He turned to me. 'It's you that's putting it all together. Take one link away and the whole thing dissolves into a series of random events.' He concentrated on the driving again. 'And you know and I know that women almost never do serial killings. They have other ways of doing payback. They've got kids to knock around.' Over the years, Charlie and I had talked about these matters and he was absolutely right on this point. Women don't do so-called 'random' killings.

'But Charlie,' I argued, 'these killings aren't random. A very specific type of victim is targeted.'

'Only in the same way,' said Charlie, 'that some killers target prostitutes. It's not an individual he's killing, it's a *type*.' He slowed down as we came to the lights at Glenbrook. 'Women don't kill types,' Charlie continued. 'They go for a particular person.'

Most of the traffic was coming the other way and we had a good run, arriving there a bit after nine. It was a perfect mountain summer day, without the sultriness of the coastal heat, the air fragrant with pine and eucalypt. I was not feeling any easier than I had in the last twenty-four hours. The thought that my career was probably finished was bad enough. Now the idea of meeting up with my father again made my neck and shoulders tense up even more.

I pulled out Bevan Treweeke's little black book and looked again at an address that had caught my attention. I'd previously rung a retired medical practitoner whose name I'd found in Treweeke's book and asked if I could have a chat sometime and now we were driving to his house. Dr Arnold Gulliver lived in an old-fashioned mountain cottage, with a garden to match. Tall hollyhocks and digitalis speared up around the front door that I knocked on, while Charlie read the newspaper in the car.

Dr Gulliver was a brisk, white-haired gent in his eighties who welcomed me and seemed pleased with the distraction. He took me through the house to his living room at the back where I stood a moment in wonder, watching the brilliant red and green king parrots feeding at a bird table outside the window.

'I remember him well,' the doctor said. 'Poor, sad bastard. He always had some sort of lower gut complaint.' He offered me a cup of tea and I felt mean refusing. I explained to the doctor that this was business, not pleasure, but that if he invited me up again to watch the king parrots, I'd be happy to bring a sponge cake from Mrs Ferguson's cake shop to go with morning tea.

I opened Treweeke's address book and showed him his name. 'When was he your patient?' I asked.

'I saw him on and off over a few years,' said Dr Gulliver. 'He talked to me about the police charges against him. He tried to convince me that it was natural, that there was no harm in it and that the kids liked it. But I knew he wasn't convinced. I don't have the records here any more, but I can give you a rough idea of the years when I saw him. We talked about aversion therapy once or twice. Hadn't seen him or heard about him in years till I heard he hanged himself.' Dr Gulliver sighed. 'I wasn't really surprised. Some people have terrible lives.' Outside on the bird table, two black cockatoos had flown in, disturbing the king parrots who flashed away.

'You may also remember the abduction of my sister, Rosie McCain,' I said, 'in 1975.' Dr Gulliver nodded.

'Everyone who's old enough round here remembers that,' he said. 'It was a dreadful business.' He looked up at me and I saw the compassion in his face and the life in his eyes. Some people have good lives, I was thinking, and this man was one of them. We started walking back towards the front door, through the neat house.

'We can confirm that Treweeke was serving a four month sentence at Devondale Correctional Centre when my sister was taken,' I said. 'That's why he was never interviewed about her disappearance.'

'He damn well should've been,' said Dr Gulliver emphatically. 'Devondale was a joke in those days. The men used to go out of an afternoon to the pub. Some of them used to stay out all night. As long as they were back for roll call.'

I was stunned. 'So he could have been out when my sister was taken?' I asked.

Dr Gulliver looked at me as if I was stupid. 'From Devondale he could've been out whenever he wanted.'

I was still stunned after telling Charlie what I'd just learned. We both sat in silence as the implications settled in and I felt vindicated that my gut feeling about Treweeke was justified. If he'd been able to go over the wall from the correctional centre, he'd have to be a prime suspect in my sister's abduction. I felt like I was getting somewhere after all these years.

Finally, Charlie turned into a street I remembered well and I realised that it must have been nearly ten years since I'd been here because last time we'd visited Jacinta was in her first year at school. Then, I'd driven up in the middle of winter with a bleak sky and skeletal trees. But today the tall trees were in full leaf as they had been that other long past November when Rosie disappeared. All I could think of was Bevan Treweeke as Charlie cruised down the street, past the once familiar houses, now sporting renovations and additions and gardens top heavy with magnificent trees. He drove very slowly past our old house. Now it looked even more miserable than my memories of it: rented houses are rarely loved and it showed. It needed a coat of paint and the windows were closed, despite the summer day. There was no sign of life. Nor was there much of a garden anymore; a hedge almost hid the house and although on either side flowers bloomed in adjoining gardens, our old house had nothing flowering except some bushy daisies near the front fence.

Charlie continued down the road to the corner where the Holden had clipped the guard rail. The course of the road had changed since then, the corner widened and sealed, the new work cutting into what used to be a gradually rising grassy bank in front of the gates of the rectory, so there was no trace anymore of the timber railing that had been hit when the car skidded. Nor could I identify anymore the young eucalypt gouged by the rear bumper bar when the Holden reversed. Unless it was the giant that now stood a little to one side in front of the cutaway bank.

'Stop the car,' I said to my brother. I got out and looked around. I hadn't stood in this spot since I was a boy of fifteen. The bank hadn't risen so sharply as it did now since the corner had been widened, so I had to go down the road a way and find a place where the slope was navigable. I walked up past the low stone wall of the rectory garden, where a row of deep green native cypresses, had since grown up, hiding the rectory completely. I remembered a time when in place of those trees, beautiful orange roses bloomed in bunches, and the handsome stone rectory dominated the corner and the street. I looked in at the gates. The rectory was still well kept, although the gardens were simpler than they had been when I was a boy. According to her statement, Mrs Bower, the vicar's wife, had been cleaning the louvred windows when she heard the crash and had come running down from upstairs, just in time to hear a car disappearing left around the corner at the other end of the street. She hadn't been able to give any details, because she said she hadn't seen, only heard, the impact. I looked around and I considered. Then I looked again, imagining the place as it had been all that time ago. Finally, I turned to my brother. 'Charlie,' I said, 'come up here.'

My brother climbed up from where he was standing near the car and stood next to me expectantly, looking at the rectory through the gate. 'If you were up there,' I said, pointing, 'cleaning those louvred windows, and these cypress trees weren't there, tell me what you'd expect to see from up there.'

Charlie looked up at the second storey of the rectory where the white-painted louvre window frames that ran the length of an enclosed balcony faced down the road. 'I'd expect to see everything,' he said. 'We can see everything from here as it is, so the view would be even better higher up.'

'And this corner wasn't so deep then either,' I said. 'A person up there would see quite clearly anything going on down here.'

'Sure they would,' he said. 'What are you getting at?'

I wasn't ready to reply. We walked back to the car and drove into the Mall.

Fortified by a good country breakfast, we returned to the house of our childhood. Charlie parked out at the front and together we crunched down the gravel driveway towards the brick garage that my father had built and then converted to his living quarters. His battered utility was parked outside the roller door, so we knew he wouldn't be far. I walked round the side to the door, and knocked on it.

'Who is it?' he called.

'Your two sons,' I said.

Nothing happened and I thought for a moment he was refusing to acknowledge our presence. When he did finally open the door, I was shocked. Ten years makes a lot of difference at each end of a life. The powerful presence he'd been in my childhood and adolescent years was gone, and in its place was a frail old man with blue veins showing through skin transparent as an embryo's. He was wearing an old sports coat that I remembered from another lifetime, his nicotine-stained fingers rested on the door knob. He no longer towered over me.

'I didn't think I'd ever see you knocking on my door,' he said, looking at me with his pale eyes. There was no welcome in his voice, nor was there any hostility. Just the words without flavour. Like he was now, I thought, hollowed out, emptied and nothing much more than a shell.

'Here I am,' I said, feeling foolish and stating the obvious.

My father looked past me to nod at Charlie. 'You'd better come in, then,' he said. I stepped inside and looked around his world. Another, newer kero heater gurgled, because it was still chilly in here despite the month, with the cement slab floor and the trees shading the roof. He'd placed a few rugs and bits of carpet here and there, beside the narrow bed, in front of the bookshelves and under the sparse furniture. His worn old chair was covered by a crocheted rug I remembered once gracing the end of my mother's bed.

'Is that daughter of yours recovering?' he said. I was surprised. I'd never told him anything about Jacinta.

'I rang Dad,' said Charlie, turning to me, 'when Jass went into the hospital.'

I was stunned for a moment. I hadn't realised that my father knew anything at all about my family. 'No,' I said, 'Jacinta is still not responding.'

'How's Gregory?'

'He's good. Doing well at school.'

'What about that woman you married?' he said. 'The smart travel agent.'

'She's okay,' I said, not wanting to go into it with him.

'I suppose you'll want coffee or something,' he said. I shook my head.

'No,' I said. 'We just had breakfast.'

Charlie grasped our father's hand. 'How are you, Dad?' he said. 'Your hands feel very cold. Why don't you turn the heat up? Or wear some gloves?'

The old man mumbled something and turned away. I remembered how he'd retreated down here because he couldn't cope, leaving three children and an alcoholic woman to manage as best they could. He had failed as a husband. And a father. He went back to the old chair and it closed itself around him.

I suddenly felt something that took me by surprise. When I could speak I pulled a chair over and sat opposite him. He looked up at me and I saw that his eyes had filled. 'This damn cold,' he said, pulling out a grubby handkerchief and rubbing his nose and eyes. 'I can't seem to shake it.' Charlie was wandering around, looking at the books and magazines that lay around.

'Dad,' I said, 'I need to know about the Bowers. Mrs Bower.'

'The new viruses,' my father said. 'They just keep getting bigger and better.' He groped around for a science journal. 'They're smarter than we are. Much more adaptable. More flexible.'

Charlie looked up from the *New Scientist* he was skimming. He knew I was on to something and he was curious.

'The Bowers,' I repeated. 'Mrs Bower. Tell me about her.'

'Your sister used to like going over to the Bowers,' he said. 'She stayed over occasionally. She was a kind woman, Mrs Bower.' He cleared his throat. 'Sometimes she'd bring dinner down for you and'—his voice trembled only a little—'your sister.' He paused. 'She knew about the situation here.'

My father used words like 'situation' to describe the awful grief and misery of ordinary family suffering. 'What about the vicar?' I said. 'Reverend Bower?'

'Never really got to know him,' said my father. 'He was a great gardener. Best roses in the district. That's all I knew about him. I don't hold with all that God business.' He looked at me closely. 'Why are you asking about them after all this time?'

'And the children?'

'They were never here,' said my father. 'Those youngsters went to boarding school. A girl about your age and a boy a bit older. Lived in Sydney most of the time with relatives. Don't know what happened to them. There was some problem with the son.' He snorted. 'The vicar was such a snob. He didn't want them mixing with *oi polloi*.'

It takes one snob to recognise another, I forbore remarking, remembering how my father used to enjoy demonstrating his superiority and speaking the phrase in Greek, rather than using the Anglicised 'hoy polloy'.

'Do you remember anything more?' I insisted.

My father shook his head. 'She was a beautiful girl, your mother. I don't know what happened.'

'She was an alcoholic,' I said, suddenly angry at his vague denial. 'That's what happened.' It was years since I'd thought of her death, the way she'd been lying in the house for days without anyone knowing. It was the way a lot of addicts went.

My father picked up the packet of tobacco beside his chair and started rolling a smoke. I watched the stained fingers deftly tap it into shape and I reached over and picked up the lighter and lit it for him. He looked startled.

'Charlie thinks that certain things run in families,' I said. My father grunted.

'You could say that,' he said, and I remembered the old contemptuous tone he used to pull out, when he couldn't run away from a 'situation'.

'I'm not talking about genetics,' I snapped. 'The way I was brought up didn't teach me what I needed to know to be a father. I've failed my children.'

'We all fail our children,' he said and his voice was hard. 'So what are you going to do? Shoot me?'

I stood up and walked around a bit, letting the sudden anger dissipate. There were things I'd always wanted to say to him, ask him. Like, why didn't you do anything to help us kids? Why did you just retreat and leave us to face the madwoman alone? But I was starting to see how I'd done much the same thing, leaving the kids with Genevieve, living in Canberra during the week. It wasn't only about money. Living like that made things easier for me. I didn't have to deal with family messes. I could avoid all that business. And Charlie was doing it in his way, too. He'd stayed single. He hadn't married his commando girlfriend. Or any of his girlfriends.

'And it's easy for Charlie to say things like that,' I said, referring to my earlier remarks, 'because he hasn't got any children and he's not married. So he's safe, in a way. He can stay safely untried. He's not passing on the curse.'

'Yet,' said my brother.

My father's face had flushed red beneath the translucent skin.

'What curse?' he said. 'What are you going on about?'

Charlie threw down the journal whose pages he was flipping.

'Why did you just turn your back on us?' he asked. 'Why did you leave Jack and Rosie and me alone with her?'

'Your mother—' he started to say.

'Our mother was a sick alcoholic,' said Charlie, 'and shouldn't have been let within coo-ee of any sensitive living thing.' He was trying to keep it neutral, even light-hearted, but I could see the signs of strain in his face, hear the catch in his voice. I'd never seen my brother in this mood and I think I realised something more about projection in that moment as I heard Charlie voice the questions he'd always said I should ask. All the times Charlie had been pressing me to 'do something' about my relationship with our father, he was also speaking from his own need.

I turned back to my father. 'They're fair questions,' I said.

Charlie had his back to us and seemed to be concentrating on the tassel of a threadbare cushion, as if the answers might have been there. 'And what Jacko wants to say to you,' said Charlie, 'is that he's failed as a husband and father because he didn't know how it was done. On account of he only had'—Charlie swung around and pointed at my father'—*you* to teach him.'

The old man was staring at him, wide-eyed, cigarette forgotten on the ashtray.

'Our sister ran away, Jack's daughter ran away at the same age. He married a nightmare woman like you did. I've got a similar tale to tell. And now Jack's living alone behind a house like you.'

I interrupted. 'Not like him, Charlie.' I shook my head again. 'Not like him.'

There was a long silence. My father was staring into space, and his blue eyes seemed to be seeing something in the middle distance. The silence went on and on, punctuated only by the gurgling of the kero heater as it plopped from its tank into the mantle and the shrieking of black cockatoos. That was supposed to mean rain.

While my father relit the cigarette, I pulled out the photograph of the youth near the stone wall and passed it to him.

'Do you know who that is?' I asked.

My father studied it for a long time. Then he handed it back to me, shaking his head. 'Maybe I knew once,' he said, 'but not any more. It's not little Snotty Kirkwood, is it?'

I took the photograph and studied it again. I could see nothing familiar in the features. I remembered Snotty with a wide, snub-nosed face, not like the youth depicted here.

'Why do you want to know?' our father asked.

'I've found a photograph of Rosie,' I said, 'taken just a few days before she disappeared. This one's from the same series.'

My father squashed the narrow handmade cigarette out. 'Maybe your mother took them, the photographs.'

I stared at him, incredulous. 'The only things she was taking in those days, were scotch and valium.' It was an absurd suggestion.

It was time to leave but I had one last question. 'Bevan Treweeke,' I said. 'Does that name mean anything to you?'

My father shook his head. 'Never heard of it. Why?' It wasn't a good question. My father wouldn't have known anything much about what went on in our house by the time Rosie was taken. Our mother could have been renting the front parlour to Jack the Ripper and my father would've been none the wiser.

'Come on, Jacko,' said Charlie. 'We've done what we had to do.'

Our father sat in silence, waiting for us to go. We left him in his chair, with his cigarettes and the stink of the kero heater and I was about to pull the door closed behind us when I heard his shuffling steps. I turned and saw that he was coming towards us, his mouth moving as if he were trying to speak. I stood there, transfixed, Charlie close behind me. Finally, my father made a noise like a cough and pulled his handkerchief out again.

'My father was a miner,' he said finally. 'He left home when I was twelve. And the only thing I got from him was this scar on the side of my head. I thought that when I grew up, I'd know what to do. Well, I didn't.' Abruptly, he stopped, glared at me, then turned away.

My brother and I didn't speak as we crunched down the driveway on our way back to the car. I was still thinking about what had happened back there in our father's shed.

'I suppose,' Charlie said finally as he started up the ignition, 'that he gave both of us a great desire to *know*. That's something.'

I thought of our respective careers, both of them investigating human behaviour in their different ways, Charlie in the mind, me in the physical world. I turned to my brother as he drove. He was staring straight ahead and we drove in silence to the end of the street. 'I want to go back to the rectory,' I told Charlie. He turned with a slight smile. 'I know you do,' he said.

At the corner, Charlie stopped the car and we got out again, climbing back up to the top of the grassy bank in front of the rectory.

'Maybe she was cleaning the windows at the back of the house,' I said. Charlie shrugged and we both walked through the gates, with me leading, and up the path. I knocked on the front door and waited. An attractive woman with a warm smile opened the door, introduced herself as Mrs Veronica Bailey, and glanced down at my ID.

'I hope there's no problem,' she said, looking past me to Charlie as he came up behind me.

'Not for you, ma'am,' I said. 'Just a routine inquiry. I want to know if there are louvred windows anywhere at the back of this house.'

The woman looked even more surprised. 'No,' she said. 'There's a balcony at the back. No louvres. May I ask you why you want to know?'

'We're just checking some information received, ma'am. Misinformation, really. Sorry to disturb you.' I thanked her and was about to rejoin Charlie. 'I used to live in this street,' I said, 'when the Reverend Bower was the vicar.'

'That was a long time ago,' she said. 'We've been here seven years, and the Driscolls were here for ages before that.'

'Do you know where the Bowers went?' I asked, 'after Reverend Bower retired?'

She shook her head. 'I'm afraid I can't help you,' she said. 'I'm sure the office in Sydney would know, though. If you wanted to catch up.' I heard a butcherbird calling and then I saw him fly over the garden to sit on the branch of a tree.

Mrs Bailey noticed. 'That's Bob,' she said. 'The butcherbird.' As if on cue, the smart black and white bird started his melodious carolling. The three of us walked slowly across the wide front garden to get a better view. The phone started ringing from inside the house and Mrs Bailey excused herself and ran inside.

'What are you up to?' Charlie asked, strolling over to a sundial that stood near the vine-covered wall of the rectory garden.

'I want to know why Mrs Bower lied in her statement,' I said. 'Let's go and start looking for that stone wall in the photographs.'

Charlie straightened up from the sundial. 'Those things never work,' I said to him.

'Look here,' he suddenly said to me and his voice was charged with excitement. 'Come over here.' But it wasn't the sundial he was talking about. I came up beside him to see that he was staring past it. With a deft movement, he pushed up a dense curtain of the flowering clematis. And there it was, underneath the thick vine, running along the eastern side of the rectory building, a stone wall, with a wrought-iron grille. I stood there, amazed. Then I pulled out the photograph and tried matching it up. I looked from the photograph to the wall.

Gradually, things became clear. When certain patches of mosses and ferns were disregarded, and allowances made for the inevitable shifting of the years, the area of wall I was looking at seemed to be the section I could see in the photograph.

Then I felt the sting of disappointment. The sundial should be there, or part of it, because of the angle of the shot. 'Damn,' I said to Charlie. 'There's no sundial.'

Charlie came back and looked at the photograph. Then he looked at the wall again. He went over to the sundial and examined it. He straightened up again and beckoned me over.

'Look,' he said. Stamped in the metal was the date 1975. 'You're supposed to be the detective, dill-brain,' he said. 'It was a while ago. The sundial wasn't here when this photo was taken. Just leave it out and look straight across from where you are now.'

I did. It was a perfect match.

'She was here,' I said. 'Rosie stood here, wearing her necklace, while someone took that shot.'

I positioned myself in the place and looked back at Charlie. No cloud darkened the sun, no chill wind lifted vines. Nothing happened to suggest I was treading on sacred, dangerous ground. Just the warm summer day and the butcherbird singing. I looked up and there he was, perched in the upper reaches of a tall yellow gum, in his neat black and white suit, turning his six-note remarks.

Half an hour later, Charlie and I walked through the country cemetery with its peaceful gums and saplings. It took us a while to find our mother's grave. There was only a limestone header with her name and dates on the double grave site. Charlie looked around. 'Not a bad place to end up,' he said. I looked past the weathered tombstones and rusting iron railings to where an ancient Clydesdale and a fat pony grazed on a hillside.

'I want to find Rosie,' I said, 'and bury her properly. I want to have a place like this to come and sit beside sometimes, and just do nothing.'

We hung around the graveyard, reading the Victorian epitaphs.

'I need to find her,' I said, 'and bring her here. Put her to rest. That way it somehow makes up for something.' I looked around the peaceful resting place of the dead. 'I know I'm not making much sense.'

Charlie looked concerned. 'I didn't know,' he said, 'that that sort of thing was important to you.'

'It's not, really,' I said. 'But I failed her. I was her big brother and I failed her. I should have run after her and brought her back to the house that evening.'

'Chrissakes, Jack,' said Charlie. 'You were *fifteen*.'

We drove back to Sydney, stopping for lunch at a chintzy little café just before Emu Plains. I ordered a toasted bacon and egg sandwich. Again, I had that odd sensation that something was staring me in the face and I wasn't seeing it. Something to do with bacon and eggs.

'Tell me why you think people lie,' Charlie asked, interrupting my strange preoccupation.

'Tell me yourself,' I said. 'I know that when I lie it's out of fear. Fear of hurting someone.'

Charlie laughed and shook his head. 'Nah,' he said, 'that's bullshit. That's the cover story we feed ourselves. It's because we don't want to deal with the other party's anger when they know the truth.'

'Okay, I'm prepared to concede that.' I considered. 'But in this case, with Mrs Bower saying she didn't see the car, she's got to have had a strong reason. No one seems to have questioned the word of the vicar's wife.'

Our meals came with amazing speed and there was a lull in our conversation while we started eating. Charlie was hoeing into a plate of chips and a pie.

'There'd be no reason to lie,' said Charlie, eating a chip, 'if she was an innocent bystander.'

I stopped chewing and looked at my brother's intelligent, lively face. 'She wasn't innocent,' I said. 'Our sister was photographed in her garden by someone a couple of days before she was abducted.' I leaned over the table. 'Mrs Bower said in her statement that she couldn't give a description of the car because "everything happened so fast". How could she know that everything happened so fast unless she'd witnessed it?' I put my fork down, too animated to eat any more. 'Charlie, I'm convinced she saw that damn car. I'm convinced she saw the whole thing.'

Charlie had lifted the lid off his pie and was scooping out the contents, leaving the piecrust.

'She saw that car,' I continued. 'Then we find that same car in the garage of a suicided pedophile twenty-five years later. That car is a link between Mrs Bower and Bevan Treweeke,' I said. 'I don't know how and I don't know why. But there's a connection here and I'm just not seeing it.'

Charlie regarded me over the last chip. 'Or,' he said, 'there's no connection whatsoever, but your mind hasn't found a way to impose the connecting grid on it yet.'

It was true and it was irritating to be reminded. 'Why do you always eat pies like that?' I asked him, pointing to the discarded piecrust sitting like a little dish on his plate. I wanted to criticise my brother, cut him down to size.

'It's simple,' he said to me. 'I don't like pastry.'

I pulled out the photograph of the adolescent boy with the floppy hair. 'Which also leaves me wondering who he is, and where he fits in.'

Charlie wiped his fingers on his napkin and reached over to take it. 'Who could he be?' he said.

'I'm going to find out,' I told him. 'I want to talk to Mrs Bower.'

•

The minute I got home I started ringing around. Eventually, I learned that Mrs Elizabeth Bower was living at an Anglican retirement village in North Sydney. I was about to drive straight there, when I realised I hadn't checked my message bank.

'Hullo,' said Nigel's voice, 'I've got a result for you on those metallic fragments you wanted tested.' For a second I had no idea what he was talking about. Then I remembered the anonymous letters and the tiny particles adhering to the paper. 'We found traces of a water-soluble gel and the story's quite surprisingly romantic. I'll fax the full report if you like. Give me a call.'

The next message took me by surprise. 'It's Iona,' came the voice. 'Can we talk? There are some things I need to tell you. I'll be working from home over the next few days. Call me and make a time to drop in.'

Drop in? I thought. Or drop dead? But there was no denying the fizz of excitement in my chest.

I steadied myself and rang Bob to tell him about my suspicions regarding Mrs Bower and my sister's abduction. 'I think she saw everything that happened.'

'Christ,' said Bob, 'it was a long time ago, Jack. A lot of time and energy went into that investigation. Do you really think you're going to find anything new?'

'I can't say,' I said. 'But I can't rest easy until I've checked everything out.' I thought of the little ghost that kept rising in the midst of my other investigations.

'We still haven't turned up your mate Staro,' Bob was saying. 'Everyone in Sydney is on the lookout for him.'

I thought of the skinny man who'd somehow become more than just an informer to me. 'Maybe she's killed him, too,' I said, 'and that's why he hasn't been seen since the night at Centennial Park. Maybe she recognised him when he recognised her and took off after him.'

'There's a lot of maybes in your scenario,' said my colleague. 'I've got a palm print to support mine.' And he rang off.

Someone else had rung while I was talking to Bob. I checked the message and did what the caller said, driving to the Collins Club.

•

Pigrooter was in his usual corner, except by this hour of the day he'd already finished the *Times* crossword and was reading. He put the book down as I approached him. I went to the bar and ordered my soda, lime and bitters, bringing it to his table. He looked at me as I sat down.

'Well,' he said, 'I've got the information you wanted.'

I sat down and waited. Very fat people all have similar faces, I thought. They lose the edges of their features because fat is deposited in the same places on all of us.

'You're not going to be very happy,' he said. 'And I don't feel happy about handing you something for nothing.' He tapped the book and I read the cover upside-down. It was a book on alternative therapies, *Healthy Consciousness: Healthy Body* with angels and beetroots on the cover. 'People don't value things unless they've paid for them.'

'I'll owe you one,' I said. 'A big one.'

'I heard you've acquired over two hundred thousand dollars. I want half.'

I tried to keep my face from showing anything. 'What makes you say that?' I said, keeping my voice in neutral as I'd learned to do long ago.

'From the man himself. The dealer your daughter was living with.'

I felt a thrill of fear shiver through my spine. 'So you know who he is,' I said.

'You know him, too,' said Pigrooter, looking at me with his sharp little eyes. There was a silence until I wanted to scream, *'Just tell me!'* but I sat there, seemingly impervious as ever, watching the waxy face and the bright eyes. Finally, Pigrooter smiled. A lot of gold gleamed in the darkness of his mouth.

'Your girl's got herself mixed up with our old workmate and your one-time colleague, Kapit. He's been dealing for a couple of years now.'

If I'd been shocked before, hearing that name numbed me totally. For a second or two, nothing happened. It was like the nanosecond that elapses between slamming the car door on your thumb and the scream.

'That bastard,' I said, and my voice was low and hoarse with rage. I'd disliked John Cleever Kapit from the first day I met him in the job twenty years ago. I hated him for his affair with my wife. Now I had reason to hate him even more. Something like acid coursed through my blood—hatred, and the desire for vengeance.

'Scoring the double like that,' said Pigrooter disapprovingly, referring to my wife and my daughter. 'He's a vain arsehole, Kapit. Fancies himself. Thinks he looks like Harrison Ford. But you've got his money so you're ahead.' Pigrooter tossed back the last drops of his liquor. 'What's the prick going to do about it?' he sneered. 'Go to the police?'

'I don't give a fuck about the money!' I said, furious. 'My little girl—'

'She's not your little girl any more,' said Pigrooter. 'Don't be sentimental.' He picked up the book from where it lay face-down on the table. He put a coaster in to mark the page he was up to and closed it sharply. 'I want my hundred. I'm reduced to this sort of brokering,' he said, with a shrug that wobbled through his upper body, 'because I've lost my licence over a technicality with those fuckwits in the New South Wales police. Some jumped-up little arsehole inspector decided he didn't like my attitude.'

'Hundred grand?' I said. 'That's not brokering. That's robbery.'

'You can let me have it by the end of the week. Don't let me down.' He stood up to leave. 'I'm in touch with people who'd do your granny over for a packet of chips.'

I went straight to the Police Centre and took Bob up onto the roof where I hoped no one could hear us. Dirty Sydney pigeons infested the nooks and crannies and their droppings caked in grubby stalagmites under any sheltered areas. I told Bob what Pigrooter had told me while both of us stared out through the turbid afternoon pollution that dulled the city dirty bronze. Sydney was filthy and now I felt part of the dirtiness.

'Kapit's name came up when I spoke to Stan Lovell,' said Bob. 'He's been a person of interest to the fellows in the Drug Squad for some time.' I thought of my stupid wife and her crim lover and how much pleasure I was going to get when I put her right about her boyfriend. 'Kapit's too toey for physical surveillance and he keeps moving house,' Bob said. 'The technical people have been breaking their hearts trying to stay on him.'

'I want to nail the bastard,' I said. 'Get him put away for a long time.' I could feel my fists clenching as I spoke, nails digging into my palms.

'It won't be easy to get him. You've got to get him with the gear. People like Kapit are too smart to handle it themselves.'

'I'll fit him,' I said. 'I'll buy heroin and spread it through his flat. I'll stick it under his house, up his chimney. There'll be no way he can get out of it.'

'You'd better split the money with Pigrooter,' said Bob. 'He took Larry Askin out with him pig-shooting last year. He lost most of his head in a shotgun accident. Turned out Askin owed him.' A Boeing airliner flew past in the east, heading for the airport. The sky was darkening, fast-moving storm clouds rolling in from the south-west while I planned my dream of revenge. 'It's only dealer's money,' Bob was saying. 'Put it away somewhere safe. Sit tight. It's not as if it's hurting anyone to keep it.' A lot of police officers over the years had formed that conclusion, I knew only too well.

'I wasn't thinking about the money,' I said. Bob leaned his back against the wall.

'Genevieve's been having an affair with Kapit,' I told him. 'That's why I left.'

My friend's face registered the shock, heavy eyebrows angled. 'I knew you were going through a hard time,' he said.

'First, he's involved with my wife,' I said. 'Then he's got Jacinta living with him. And using.'

'You could have him charged along those lines,' Bob suggested. 'She's only a kid, for chrissakes.'

We walked back towards the exit. 'I'm having a couple of days off,' Bob said as we parted. 'Ring me at home if you need me.'

I went straight to the hospital where my daughter still lay in her other world. The physio was with her, and I took over after the woman showed me what to do, moving the thin arms and legs in a counterfeit of lively movement. I brushed Jacinta's hair over the pillow and straightened the ribbon someone had tied in it. Somewhere, her mind rested and her narrow body was becoming freer of the addiction that had taken her hostage. I looked at her emaciated face and my heart melted. I laid my head down on the pillow next to hers, remembering the beautiful child she'd been. Get well and strong, I told her, come back to me and help me be your father. Teach me what you need from me and I'll be a willing learner. I sat up and kissed her goodbye.

•

Next morning I drove to the retirement village, a quiet, leafy place near the Lane Cove river. A tiny young Asian nurse, neat in her uniform, took me to Mrs Bower's room.

She was sitting on a long closed-in veranda with an untouched cup of tea cooling at her side, her misty eyes staring straight ahead. As I approached, she looked up at me and I recalled the woman of twenty-five years ago. Now, all that remained of her was the slightness and the anxiety. But the deep-set eyes seemed very familiar.

'When does this ship leave?' she asked me, slightly querulous, not quite focusing on me.

'I don't think it will be too much longer,' I said as I sat beside her.

She seemed satisfied with that, lost interest in me and we continued to sit together in silence for some time. Around me, old people waited patiently in their chairs, or shuffled past on frames. Opposite us, a woman plucked distractedly at the rug covering her knees, picking at things that weren't there.

'Mrs Bower,' I said finally, 'my name is John McCain. Our family used to live near yours. In Wentworth Street, Springbrook.'

She turned to me again, studied me closely, then frowned. 'This man is not my husband,' she said in a loud voice.

'That's right,' I said, 'I'm not your husband. I used to live down the street. When I was a kid. The McCain family. My sister Rosie…' I stopped, startled by the spasm that had galvanised the frail body.

Mrs Bower started rocking, moaning. 'Oh no, oh no,' she cried, 'it was a terrible thing to do. Oh no, oh no.' Her whimpering became more agitated and I looked around for a nurse but could see no one in charge, just the patient old people, some watching us, others sleeping in their chairs, mouths open.

'Mrs Bower,' I said, 'is there something I can do for you?' But she was weeping loudly now, tears running down her face, her hands with their almost transparent skin clutching the sides of the chair. 'Please, Mrs Bower,' I said, 'don't distress yourself like this.'

I stood up and looked around, desperate and then thankful to see a woman in a pale blue uniform heading in our direction. 'She became distressed,' I said to the nurse as she came up. 'I wasn't sure what to do.'

'Oh, we do that from time to time, don't we, lovey?' the nurse said. Then she squatted and pushed the cup of tea closer. 'Not having your lovely cup of tea, dear?' The nurse sat back on her heels. 'Mostly she's like this.' She indicated the weeping old woman. 'But she has her moments of complete lucidity,' she explained. 'Don't you, darling?' she asked Mrs Bower in a louder voice.

As if to prove the nurse right, Mrs Bower gave her a look of anger, and pushed herself back in her chair, pointing at me, speaking in a strong, loud voice.

'I know who you are,' she said. 'You're the brother. I didn't know till it was too late.'

I was riveted. Not only had the name 'Rosie' elicited a strong reaction from the old woman, but now she was referring to me as 'the brother'. She certainly did seem to know who I was. Maybe I'd be able to ask her some questions after all. I was standing there, wondering how to go about this when she spoke again.

'Ask my daughter,' she said. 'Not me. My daughter will make it all right.' Her face was still more familiar to me than a twenty-five-year-old memory could allow—deep-set, shadowed eyes, and large hands.

'Your daughter?' I repeated stupidly.

I looked at the frail figure. The skin around her eyes was so dark it looked bruised. 'Please, Mrs Bower,' I said, 'I need to ask you some questions. It's very important.'

But Mrs Bower was lost again. 'I used to have a son once,' she was saying. 'But he's dead now. He's dead.' Her grief overwhelmed her and I sat there, feeling helpless and useless.

I took her old brown hands in mine. 'What's your daughter's name?' I asked, suddenly knowing.

'Iona will make it better,' she sobbed.

I leaned back in my chair, shocked at this confirmation. A nurse swooped down on us, briskly offering practical support, re-propping the old woman up in her chair, busy with distractions. Slowly, I walked away, leaving Mrs Bower repeating her daughter's name and the nurse trying to offer comfort.

I hurried past the other old sentinels waiting lined up against the wall of the veranda and almost ran back to my car.

I drove back on automatic pilot, my mind trying to make sense of this new information. But I had witnessed a series of events that were incontrovertible. My sister's name had had a profound effect on Mrs Bower. And in the next breath, she'd mentioned her daughter, 'Iona'.

There it was again, the connection with my family. Rosie and Iona. 'Rosie' and the letters. I thought again of the strange conversation about terrorism and the children of Protestant clergy.

I drove straight to her place and even though the car wasn't there, banged on the door. Iona Bower Seymour, killer or not, owed me some answers. I lashed out as hard as I could, deriving some relief from kicking her door. 'Iona!' I yelled. 'Iona, talk to me!'

I stopped banging on the door and felt like a real idiot. I don't think I'd ever behaved like this in my life. I tried to look in through the front windows, cupping my hands so as to cut out reflections. I was peering into the heavy Victorian room she'd sat me in with her cucumber sandwiches. There was nothing on the table now except a newspaper and I was about to turn away when I peered closer, willing my eyes to make out the newsprint. My own startled face stared back at me, all stark contrast and shadows. The newspaper was opened at the page of Merrilyn Heywood's photograph, the one she'd stolen of me that night at Centennial Park, with Frank Carmody still oozing his life away against the wall and me like a rabbit caught in the shooters' spotlight. I wanted to smash the window and take my picture away from her, out of her house. I came away from the window, not knowing what to do next, and sat on the worn black step while the breeze moved the rose canes and shadows played on the chequerboard tiles of the mossy veranda. But then I thought of her praying in the cathedral, her face and dark hair glowing by candlelight. How many killers leave prayers in churches? I recalled conversations with Charlie and shivered. The world was full of malignant psychotic zealots who prayed as they primed their bombs.

I walked back to the car. I wanted to know where she was, who it was she hid out with. I wanted to know who he was, the man to whom she always returned. I suspected his name might be Michael, maybe even Michael Seymour, and that was something to go on.

Two hours later I was back in the mountains, in the registry of the Springbrook church, going over the marriage entries with the woman we'd already met at the rectory, Veronica Bailey, who was also treasurer of the local historical society. As we crossed the garden from the house to the church, I felt my own history and the history of my family curling around me and it wasn't a pleasant embrace. I made a donation to the historical society and Mrs Bailey, after pulling out the volumes that she felt would contain the dates I was interested in, left me to my own devices in the quiet sacristy. Slowly, I turned the big folio-sized pages over, my eyes scanning the various handwritings, bold or feeble, the different coloured inks, blue, black, blue-black, even the occasional sepia. I'd tried narrowing down the time when I imagined a youthful Iona Bower might have married a man called Seymour. She was only a little younger than I was, I thought, so I concentrated on the books from the early 'seventies to the 'eighties.

I seemed to search for a long time. The light in the small stone room was fading and the air was getting colder. Iona could have been married anywhere. Some fashionable Sydney church like St Mark's at Darling Point, or the Garrison Church at the Rocks. Anywhere. Maybe even overseas, maybe on the island whose name she bore.

I was about to give up and leave when her name jumped out at me. I leaned forward to read the entry. Iona Bower, music teacher, married Peter Seymour, general practitioner, in August 1988. I didn't need to write anything down. I'd never forget that name. I slammed the book shut, put it back on the pile, closed the door of the reading room after me as requested by Mrs Bailey and went to my car.

Medical Registrations told me that Dr Peter Seymour was presently working with Médecins sans Frontières in West Africa. Even though I knew from my past investigative experience that ex-spouses often maintained some sort of relationship, Iona's man problem didn't seem to revolve around him. And there still remained Michael.

THIRTEEN

The door of number 293 swung open as Iona let me in and she stood back while I stepped inside. The heavy Victorian furnishings seemed larger and darker and I was very aware of my emotionally exhausted state. There was no time for niceties, and anyway, I'd come to the conclusion that Iona Seymour was not a nice woman.

'Can I get you anything?'

'Yes,' I said. 'Some plain speaking, Mrs Seymour. Née Bower.' I paused, watching the effect this had on her. 'I want the truth.'

She looked startled and the beginning of a blush spread from around her neck and up through her cheeks until her face was pink.

'You haven't been honest with me.' I raised my hand to stop her speaking. 'Those phone calls you made to the police,' I said, 'about my daughter Jacinta. Don't tell me you don't know what I'm talking about. I heard the tapes. It was you. I know your voice like I know my own.'

She swung suddenly around, walking down the hall towards the back of the house. I followed her, wondering if she was leading me towards the laundry, towards the knife in the cupboard that was no longer there. But she didn't go outside. Instead, she stopped in a little narrow kitchen, took a glass down from a cupboard and got a drink of water from the old-fashioned tap over the pebblecrete sink. The colours were unredeemed 'fifties—cream and green—and there was the slight odour of leaking gas and dampness. Then she walked wordlessly past me, head down, back to the front room. Again I followed her and stood while she sat in one of the old Victorian chairs, perched at the edge of the faded tapestry upholstery.

'I... I...' She started to speak, then faltered.

'You were saying?' I said. She put the glass down and looked at me. I could see her marshall her resources. Or was she getting her story together?

When she spoke, the voice was low, with a grainy edge to it, as if she was close to tears. 'I made those phone calls because I was concerned about someone as young as your daughter—'

'So you know—you knew—who I was all the time. You lied about your parents being dead. I've recently visited your mother.'

Her eyes looked terrified. 'I didn't say that. I said they weren't around. She's Alzheimic. She says strange things.' I waited, letting the pressure of silence build. Finally, she could stand it no longer. 'What did she say to you?' she whispered.

I decided to let her stew a bit. I stood up and walked to the window so that I had the light behind me and her upturned face was exposed. What I saw was very interesting. Iona Seymour was terrified.

'She was extremely helpful,' I said quietly. What could a poor old woman in a retirement village have to say that might cause this personality change from seductress to fearful child? Iona was fidgeting with the glass, her fingers nervously tapping.

'And Michael?' I asked. 'Where does he fit in?'

Her face was a picture of dismay. 'That's private,' she said. 'My personal life has nothing to do with you.'

'I think it does, Mrs Seymour. I think your personal life and my personal life have started to get very mixed up together and I want to know why. And how. Why did you pretend you didn't know who I was?'

She shook her head. 'I swear,' she said, 'I didn't know who you were.' Her voice choked. 'Apart from a kind man I met at one of the meetings. It wasn't until I saw the piece in the newspaper with your photograph about that terrible murder in Centennial Park...' Again, she stopped and I waited for her to regain her composure. 'I was concerned about a child of your daughter's age working in that place. Anyone would be concerned.'

I watched her very carefully. 'Iona,' I said, maintaining whatever vigilance my drained state could muster, 'let's say for the time being I accept your story—'

'It's not a "story".' The shimmering voice was suddenly hard as iron. 'I did *not* know who you were when I rang the police about your daughter. I knew about Jacinta because I read the newspapers like anyone else. But when we bumped into each other at that Twelve Step meeting, I had no idea you were the same person.' She was very convincing, I had to admit, the wonderful voice rich with truth.

'Okay,' I said, prepared to let that go for the time being. I stepped a little closer, still with the light behind me, using my advantage to interrogate her. 'I have reason to believe that when you did make that phone call, you originally wanted to talk to the police on another matter.'

I thought I saw her flinch. It is hard to lie in close-up; indeed, hard to lie at all. The mind is filled with the truth that mustn't be said and the face reflects this. And each false statement could be plaiting the rope with which a liar finally hangs herself.

'What could you possibly mean by that?'

Questions are the safest tactic, and that's what Iona was using. I went straight for the kill.

'I have reason to believe you know something about the mutilator murders,' I said.

The colour drained from her face. She looked sick.

'And you were going to tell the police something about it, but you changed your mind mid-sentence, and instead gave the information about my daughter.' Bob would kill me if he knew I was here saying this, but he had no jurisdiction over me and I was free to lead the inquiry the way I wanted. This woman owed me.

'I know nothing about those killings,' she said, but her resonant voice was strained.

'You're lying,' I said. I stood up, ready to go. 'You got me into your bed, knowing that the existence of a prior relationship would compromise any evidence I might have concerning you.'

'What are you talking about?' Her voice was quite sharp. 'Are you such a pathetic, passive thing that you can talk like that? That I "got" you into my bed?' She flung away from me in disgust. I grabbed her arm. She looked at me, looked at my hand holding her.

'Let go of me,' she said in a low voice. Her dark, wounded eyes filled with anger. 'God, you men make me sick!'

I tightened my grip on her. 'Sick enough to stick a knife into them?' I asked her. 'Sick enough for you to cut a man's balls and penis off?'

I let her go. She remained in front of me, immobilised by my words.

'Why are you saying this?' she said, but her voice was faint, the anger gone, now only terror in her eyes. Her lips trembled and I felt like a brute. This had not been part of my plan at all and I hated myself. I'd bullied her, pushed her around. And now I wanted to make it up to her. I was a seething mass of inconsistency. Bob was right. I should be right out of this particular picture. But I'd never been in a picture like this, where a suspect had become a secret obsession. There were no protocols that I knew of for this scenario. All I could do was follow my instincts. I admitted to myself that I was exhausted and that exhaustion had drained everything from me except desire. I was feverish with it. I wanted to comfort her, kiss her, but I managed to collect myself.

'Letters were written to the victims,' I said harshly. 'On notepaper that came from this house.'

Her eyes widened further. She'd moved closer to me and I grabbed her hands. It was self-defence as well as what I wanted to do. 'And I found a knife,' I said, 'in your laundry. It's with the lab now.' By this time, I reckoned, the amped traces Jane had discovered would be delivering their information via the PCR replication process. 'Right now,' I said, 'there's a graph about to go up on the screen at the forensic laboratory. It's a DNA picture of the person who held that knife.'

'You had no right to come here. To take things from my house. You had no right!' Everything had changed. Her voice had a desperate edge now. Her reactions were erratic and unpredictable and I remembered the wild mood swings of early recovery and wondered again if this woman had an addiction of her own. I picked up the glass she'd emptied. 'All I have to do is compare this'—I brandished the glass '—with the graph on the screen and we'll have the person who's killed at least four men.'

She shrank back at this, shaking her head.

'Your DNA picture is here.' I pointed to where she'd drunk from the glass. 'I'll compare it to the sample we already have.'

'It won't be mine,' she said. 'It can't be.'

I was becoming more convinced of her guilt. Innocent people

don't behave like this. After many years of dealing with the guilty and innocent, I knew how innocent people deny the charge outright. 'No way,' they yell. 'I didn't do it! It wasn't me!' Anything else is tactics and this woman was using every tactic known. Anger overcame desire. I pulled her roughly back to me, squeezing her wrists, looking down into her white face.

'You found out who I was,' I said. 'You knew I was working with the Sydney police. That's why you rejigged our date here so you could get me into bed. You knew you'd be safe then. Once your defence counsel knew about that you knew you'd walk like O.J.—no matter what sort of evidence we had!'

Anger flashed through her eyes. 'You don't know what you're saying!' she cried.

'I think I do,' I responded. 'You thought you'd use me, find out what you could about my investigation.'

'And did I?' she asked scornfully, her voice charged with a new energy. 'Think about it! Did I question you about these murders? I didn't say a word about them.' She lunged at me, grabbing for the glass in my pocket but I blocked her arm, grabbing her close. 'That's my property,' she said. 'You have no right to it. You come here to my house with these wild accusations. I can have you charged with theft.'

'By all means do so,' I said. 'By that time, we'll have enough to convict you.' I wasn't at all sure about that, but I was quite prepared to bluff it. 'You told me about the children of Protestant clergy,' I reminded her, 'how they represented a huge percentage of European terrorists. What was all that about?'

'Did I?' she said, still angry. 'I don't remember. And you're crazy to hear a confession in some anecdotal remark of mine. It just shows me how desperate you are to charge someone. Anyone!'

'You were trying to tell me then that you are a killer,' I said, 'in some strange, oblique way. Killers do. Murder is a huge thing. It's hard to hold a murder in your mind. Let alone several.'

'I wouldn't know,' she said. 'This conversation is ridiculous.' She pulled her hands away from mine and went to the long french windows. Standing there, half-turned towards me, she could have been the subject for a Pre-Raphaelite painting. She opened the sideboard, took out two glasses and poured a dark red liquid from a crystal decanter.

'Drink this,' she said.

I shook my head and she slammed the decanter down.

'Oh for God's sake!' she said with irritation. 'Do you think I'm going to *poison* you?'

Despite everything, I almost laughed. 'I hadn't thought,' I said. 'I don't drink alcohol.'

Comprehension dawned on her face. 'Oh,' she said. She sipped at one of the ports and stood there, facing me squarely. 'From my point of view, you've behaved atrociously, and here I am, pouring you a drink and comforting you.'

Now, I wasn't sure at all. This woman no longer seemed the guilty party of only minutes ago. Suddenly she'd become dangerously interesting. It must be some reaction to adrenaline, I told myself, that made me want to take her upstairs again. I knew I was physically very tired and I knew that people made fatal errors in the state I was in. But my mind seemed more alert and fast-moving than usual and I felt I was in control of the situation.

Later, I couldn't really remember how it was that we ended up in her bed again. But there I was, lying beside her scarred body, kissing her, touching her, listening to her murmurs of pleasure, relaxing into the series of delicious moments that followed. Rich light shone through the heavy, decaying curtains and in the gloom, Iona's room and the woman herself had a preternatural quality of mystery and refinement. We strained together and I traced her scar with kisses. My climax was huge, and I collapsed across her body, barely aware of a different sound somewhere, unconnected to us or this room. Iona sprang up and pushed me off her as easily as someone might throw a sheet aside.

'What is it?' I asked, only half-present and shocked by the suddenness and vigour of her action.

She pulled her dress over her head and hurried to the closed door where she stood, listening.

'What is it?' I repeated.

But she waved me quiet with her hand without looking at me. She opened the door and without a word left the room.

I sat up. The magic had well and truly vanished and I dressed.

I went to the escritoire behind the fading curtains and was hardly surprised to see that the notepaper and bottle of French ink were no longer there. I waited in the room for a few minutes, then I opened the bedroom door and looked up and down the hall.

'Iona?' I called, and her name echoed through the house. I stepped out and walked down the hall, away from the staircase towards the rooms I hadn't yet explored. I called her name again, but there was no answer. I tiptoed down to the first door past her bedroom, pulling it open suddenly. A spare bedroom, dark and musty and very uninhabited. I could just see myself in the mirror of the dressing table opposite, veiled in dust. Visitors were not, it seemed, a part of this woman's life. I closed the door again. The door to the third room at the end of the hall was a little ajar. I peered in there, and found it was the junk room: old boxes and furniture, broken chairs, a huge chandelier in pieces lying partly across the worn carpet. 'Iona? I called again, wondering where she was.

There was one last door, right opposite me, one that closed the corridor off from the rest of the house. Perhaps it had once been the servants' quarters. I don't know what it was, some investigator's instinct firing, but I stopped in the hallway, drawn by the door. I came closer to it. It was a handsome, four panelled original door with a heavy crystal or cut-glass knob and with an etched glass fanlight over it. I don't think I'd ever encountered anything like this arrangement in the middle of a house and I wondered at the oddity of it. It wasn't locked, however, and neither was the steel security gate behind it which swung open to my touch. I stopped where I was, taking in what I saw.

I was standing in the middle of a library, with books reaching from floor to ceiling, lining the walls. This must be a most valuable cache of rare titles, to be hidden behind a steel grille in this way. I walked slowly, reverently, around the high-ceilinged room. The titles were forbidding. I pulled one out—a heavy clothbound edition with nearly a thousand pages entitled *Psychiatric Disorders and Priestly Orders*. I opened it at random. *A clergyman must take great care when dealing with the hysteric woman parishioner*, I read. *On no account allow oneself to be alone with this person. At all times ensure the presence of a third party.* I opened it at the front cover to find its author's name, Reverend Wesley Morton-Smythe, DD BA (Hons) Cambridge. I put the reverend gent's work back on the shelf and walked around, looking at the rest of them. The other titles were in similar vein. Books of sermons, books of biblical exegesis, prayer books, hymn books, different versions of the Bible, shelf after shelf of the sombre volumes, all of them many years old, dated, moralising, Victorian attitudes, now only curiosities. I couldn't imagine them having any value to Iona or anyone else for that matter. Maybe they had belonged to her father or the ex-husband. I couldn't imagine why anyone would bother to secure them like this, with a heavy duty security gate.

I was about to go downstairs to find Iona when I noticed a tiny annexe off the library. I peered in and found a narrow bed, a large old-fashioned trunk with P & O stickers fading and peeling from it and a small fridge with some toiletries on the top of it in the corner. I opened the fridge and stared in surprise. Several bottles of stout lined the inner door and the shelves were stacked with trays of meat, steak and chops on white plastic trays, covered in foil. I remembered the shopping I'd seen in Iona's trolley, the odd sensation I had when lifting eggs out of the pan. I stood, staring at the meat while things fell into place. What was all this meat doing here? Iona was a vegetarian yet that day when I'd contrived to meet her in the small supermarket, she'd had rashers of bacon in her trolley.

I shivered. A sudden chill had descended on the room and I was eager to be out of that sepulchral space. I hurried out of the library, closing the security gate and the crystal-knobbed door behind me. Every instinct in me was firing on over-drive and my white-hot mind strained to work out what was going on. Where was my hostess? Had she found another knife? Downstairs, I found that the bottom floor, too, was deserted, as empty as the *Marie Celeste*. I picked up the small port glass she'd drunk from and pocketed it.

The front door stood slightly ajar and I closed it on my way out. Her car was gone.

•

I crashed for an hour at home then had a shower and tried to make sense of what I'd seen. I was suddenly starving, and scrambled some eggs on toast, wondering why Iona had a fridge stocked with meat.

Did she creep into that library, gorge herself on flesh, read morbid psychopathology and fuel herself for murder?

I cleared away the plates and checked my messages. Florence's cool voice came first, with no greeting. 'I've got a male result from that FU from one of the beer bottles,' she said. 'Male. I'm doing the others today.' I made a note to myself to check this Forensics Unknown sample against the reference sample from Bevan Treweeke sent to the lab by Bradley Strachan. Then came the message that pushed everything else out of my mind and had me spilling the coffee I'd made all over my kitchen floor. I stood there, listening, my chest heaving, trying to keep my guts from going into spasm, while I played Kapit's words again.

'You've got something of mine,' he said. 'If you want to see your son again, do what I tell you.'

I listened as he told me what to do. I didn't need to write anything down. In my heightened state, his words burned into my mind like a brand. I played the tape over and over again. Then I raced out to the car and screamed around to the Italian restaurant down the road.

'Greg's not in tonight,' said the woman looking up from the till. 'His father rang up for him.'

'Someone rang?' I said stupidly.

'His father,' she told me.

I couldn't say anything. I ran outside, diving back into the car, driving the short distance home in black-out.

I ran inside again. My legs went weak and I stumbled against the table, then onto the chair. It really was true. John Kapit had snatched my son from me. For a second or two, I think I went blind as shock closed the world around me. Then my thoughts became tumultuous, spinning and racing. I'd dragged my son into this filthy world I work in. I should have been smarter. Covered my tracks better. A thousand 'if onlys' started playing in my head. I smashed my hand onto the table to stop them. I went to ring Bob, but my hand faltered over the mobile. I couldn't trust Bob. Not in this. He would want to follow the protocols, take the appropriate police action. I could even hear him agreeing with me not to take it further, but then putting the phone down and immediately organising an SPG operation behind my back, because it's exactly what I would have done had the situation been reversed.

All of my training told me to ring Bob. Don't do this alone, my instinct told me. But my training was not who I was in those frantic moments. I was only Greg's father, determined to bring him home, unwilling to do anything to jeopardise him.

I drove round to Charlie's, let myself in with the key that lived in the petunia pot, went straight to the hall cupboard and pulled out the gym bag. I opened it, checking the money. It lay dusty in its plastic coverings and I thought how meaningless it was compared with the brilliance and beauty of my son. That John Kapit could equate the two caused me to hate him even more and I swore that one day, I'd even things up between us. I re-zipped the bag, keeping my mind on what I was doing, because the hatred and rage building up in me seemed ready to explode. In retrospect, I understood what terrible danger Jacinta had been in, why little Renee had died, and what a blessing it was that my daughter lay comatose in a hospital, far away from consciousness, away from John Kapit. I had no doubt that it was only this contingency that had saved her life so far. Just for a moment I hated my wife more than I've ever hated anyone in the world—even Kapit himself. I longed to punish her, and hurt her with everything I knew.

It was in this mood that I drove back to my place, unlocked a box stashed at the bottom of one of my sealed cartons and pulled out a prohibited item. Many years ago, I'd taken the Colt .45 automatic pistol from under the passenger seat of a crim's car and never got round to handing it in. I knew I was breaking the law but right now I was very pleased that I had. I remember how I'd smiled at the gun amnesty, and the way many good citizens had handed in their weapons. I'd always kept it hidden and no one in the world knew of its existence apart from myself. Now, its blued surfaces cooled my sweaty hands as the eight rounds snapped into the magazine.

With the pistol carefully in position in the gym bag, between wads of cash, I drove to the Newtown address Kapit had given me. I could think of nothing else other than getting my son back safely. The other investigations currently in my life no longer existed. The loss of job and reputation meant nothing. On that drive, something deep changed in me and I knew I would never be the same again. I had crossed over into another territory where love, hatred, vengeance and justice were no longer abstracts, but a furnace that burned within me.

Going by Kapit's instructions, I recognised the 'For Sale' sign out the front of the narrow single-storey grey and pink terrace and pulled over. Aware that I was probably being watched, I waited by the kerb, gathering my resources. In that moment I realised something. Kapit hadn't mentioned the accounts book. I made a decision. I took the book out of the bag and stowed it under my car seat. This gave me leverage even though I was giving him back his money. There was no doubt in my mind that I would kill John Kapit if needed and that I would do whatever was necessary afterwards.

I got out of the car and picked up the bag from the passenger side. I crossed the road and went through the open gate of the cottage, past the long grass of the narrow front garden, ducking a thorny bouganvillea as I stepped up onto the veranda. I pushed the door as I'd been instructed to do and stepped inside. In the gloom of the deserted place, I saw the front room on my left where Kapit had told me to leave the money. I looked around. Dusty floorboards, stained plaster ceiling, a piece of masking tape holding the dirty glass of the window pane in position and a dusty table against the wall. I could sense the place was empty, but I knew Kapit's courier wouldn't be far away. He was probably watching me right now. You don't leave over two hundred grand sitting very long in a deserted house. I slipped the Colt out of the bag and into my pocket where its weight was a comfort. I could wait here until whoever was watching the place got curious about why I hadn't come out and jump him when he came in, force him to lead me to his master, or I could do what Kapit told me I'd need to do if I wanted to know where Greg was. I really had no choice. I had to be at the agreed place for the phone call.

I left the gym bag on the table and drove back to the house of my failed marriage. Genevieve wasn't home but I still had a key even though I'd never wanted to use it. I let myself in and waited in the kitchen, putting Kapit's accounts book on the counter beside the sink, looking through the archway into the living room, barely seeing the clusters of new china ornaments that encrusted every possible surface. I couldn't keep still. I picked up the book and put it down again. I walked from room to room, sitting briefly on Jacinta's shrine bed then visiting Greg's room which smelled of him and the gel he used to flatten his hair. On the wall were photos of him from the sporting successes I'd been too busy or too far away from to attend. I walked up to one where he was standing, sharing a soccer trophy with his team and the presenter, his face alight with joy. I could just see Genevieve in the background and Jacinta, small and sullen beside her. I couldn't remember where I'd been that day. Except that I wasn't there. I was rocketed backwards in time to the day I was in a car with a pennant or a certificate of some sort, and somebody else's father was driving me home. I had a terrible glimpse of something huge and dreadful: that because of who I was, of where I'd come from and what I had become, both of my children were paying in different ways. And so was I.

I waited, but the phone didn't ring. I looked at my watch. It was past the deadline Kapit had nominated. I waited more, prowling and pacing, glancing in at the bedroom Genevieve and I had shared for all those years, some part of me pleased that she had this coming to her for the way she'd played into Kapit's hands. I wondered if she was at the hospital or somewhere with Kapit, all unwitting and playing the sweet thing to him the way she used to do with me. I wondered how she'd feel when she realised how well and good he'd fucked her. And her children. But this triumph was hollow and empty. They were my children, too.

FOURTEEN

An hour passed before I came to accept that Kapit wasn't going to ring. Something had gone terribly wrong. I hunted through the phone book and eventually found his number, but all I got was his message bank. I smashed the phone down. Maybe I should have handed over the accounts book, too. I cursed myself for not having done it when I'd had the chance. How could I live with myself if anything happened to Greg? I'd have to ring Bob now. I should have done that in the first place, I told myself, and maybe Greg would have been here with me now.

I drove back to my place with Kapit's accounts book under my seat, the Colt in my pocket and a mind full of terror for my son.

The first thing I saw as I walked past the cypresses and the alarming noisy miners was that my unfinished watercolour was lying trampled on the ground. Someone had deliberately stamped on it and dragged it along with dirty shoes. Then I glanced at my back door and stopped in alarm. It was not quite closed. I could see the barest strip of the pale inner doorframe. My first thought was that my house had been broken into again. Or maybe Greg had come home in some miraculous way. My hopes lifted for a second. I put my hand on the weight in my pocket and crept towards the door. I stood there a moment, straining to hear anything. But nothing stirred inside. It was utterly still. For some reason, the crime scene at Centennial Park and Frank Carmody sliding down the wall covered in his own blood came into my head. When I realised why, my mouth dried in fear. The smell of human blood was in the air.

My heart contracted. My son. Dear God no. Please. Not Greg. Not my boy.

I remained frozen a moment or so longer, until I could bear it no more. Then with a roar, I bashed the door open, racing into the house, switching the light on, screaming his name, kicking out, my eyes frantically searching the room. Someone lay stretched out on the floor near the dining table. My heart lurched with terror, then relief. It wasn't Greg.

I remained where I was as the relief washed all over me. The man was lying on the floor, the shoebox of photographs and postcards scattered all over and around him, grotesque and oversized confetti.

I couldn't tell if he looked like Harrison Ford or not from the expression on his face, arms flung out, his lower body awash with blood, and legs drawn up as if to hide the terrible damage between his legs. But I knew what was there, or rather, what wasn't there. And even though I had detested the man who lay there on the floor, I'm not sure that I would have wished this death on him. I don't know how long it was before I grabbed my phone and hit the buttons with shaking fingers. As I talked to the emergency services, my eyes finally focused on the wall opposite. The photo of the unknown youth was gone from the wall.

Within minutes, my apartment was ablaze with Crime Scene lights, police and ambulance personnel. I didn't care about Kapit, all I could think of was getting my son back safely. Bob arrived together with Stan Lovell from the Drug Squad and I found myself making another confession to my friend about the deal I'd made with Kapit. 'He was going to ring me at Genevieve's place,' I said, 'to tell me where to find Greg. I waited and he didn't ring.' I was only vaguely aware of a Crime Scene officer squatting and labelling a small breaking tool that lay on the floor near the door.

'You should have told me,' said Bob. 'You know what the rules are. You can't do something like this by yourself.' He swung round on me and his eyes blazed. 'That is so typical of you,' he said. I'd never seen him like this before.

'I just wanted to get my boy back.' I felt my voice shake on the last few words. 'That's all I was thinking about.'

'That's why you should have rung me. You could have let us do all the other thinking for you, Jack,' said Bob more gently, 'that's our job.' It was the closest Bob got to an 'I told you so.'

'I waited and waited for his call,' I repeated, 'but he didn't ring.'

We both turned and looked back into the room where the dead man lay, surrounded by the professional attendants of violent death. 'Because he was here,' said Bob.

'He was here,' I repeated. 'And so was someone else.'

Bob didn't say anything, just made another cryptic entry into his notebook. Sometimes I think cops do that simply to have something to do with their hands, like smokers light up, and women used to flirt with fans in years gone by. I was awash with powerful emotions. Any pleasure that the bastard Kapit had well and truly got his deserts was overridden by my overwhelming concern for Greg. Bob suddenly put into words what I'd been trying not to think about.

'Whoever came here,' said my friend, 'didn't come to kill John Kapit.'

A thrill of terror shook me from head to foot and my agitation increased. I was the one who habitually sat at that table, tending my stored-up cases, my sad, boxed history. It should have been me lying there with my cock and balls cut off. I imagined the strong figure in the red jacket, the long blonde hair hiding face and features, creeping into my house, with no reason to think that the man at the table wasn't me. Maybe by the time she'd realised her mistake, it was too late to stop. Maybe in the struggle and the poor light, she'd never noticed.

'Take a look at this,' Stan Lovell called and we joined him at the door to see the shredded wood around the lock where the door had been prised open. 'Looks like Kapit broke in, left the door slightly ajar and sat down to wait for you. The killer only had to walk in.'

I wanted to be out of all the fuss and the stench of blood so I went out the back and paced up and down the unfinished brickwork of the patio while Bob asked questions of the Crime Scene people. Someone offered me a cigarette and I took it without thought, nearly vomiting on the first draught, throwing it underfoot and stamping on it, wondering what had happened to the fifty-a-day man I'd once been.

'Why was he here?' I asked.

'You don't fit the profile at all,' said Bob who'd joined me outside.

'I meant fucking Kapit!' I yelled. Bob edged over to me. 'If I were you,' he said, 'I'd be more worried about your other visitor.'

Bob's words shocked me into appreciating the danger of my situation. It wasn't the first time a killer had stalked an investigator. I recalled the rabbit-in-the-headlights photograph of myself. With a moderate amount of determination, anyone could have found out where I lived. At any another time, without the harrowing absence of my son, I'd probably have been terrified at this development.

'You must know something,' said Bob. 'Something so dangerous for the killer that you became a target.'

Frustration, fear and anger charged through my system. 'For Chrissakes, Bob, I don't know anything! We don't know anything about the killer—' I stopped, lost for words. 'It's a fucking joke to suggest that we do.'

'I'm not laughing,' said Bob, 'and you shouldn't be either.' His sober words calmed me somewhat, reinforcing my own conclusions, slowing me down. 'That dead man lying in there was supposed to be you,' he added.

I took a deep breath. I needed to stay sane and grounded, for my son's sake, and not to be spinning out like I had been over the last few hours. I desperately needed rest, although the idea of that seemed impossible. From inside my house, I could hear a burst of the laughter that accompanies grisly crime scenes, as investigators find a joke to relieve the pressures of dealing with violent death. I fought the urge to run in there and yell at them all, tell them all to get out, drop what they were doing and help me find Greg.

'Let's turn to Kapit for the moment,' said Bob. I tried to bring my whirling mind into line. 'Kapit knew you'd be out,' Bob said, looking up from his note taking. 'He knew you'd be taking the money back to him at Newtown.'

I remembered the book under my seat in the car. But I couldn't stay with the conversation. 'Where is he, Bob?' I said to my friend. 'What has the bastard done with Greg?'

I had an irrational urge to go in and kick the dead body. I understood how soldiers might want to tear an enemy's body to pieces in revenge for hurting the people they loved. Bob put a hand on my arm. 'Let's go to your place'—he corrected himself—'to Genevieve's place. You'll have to tell her what's happened. She might know where Kapit could have taken Greg.'

We walked down the side of the house and the scent of cypress and salt was strong in the warm air. 'I think you should seriously think about moving,' Bob said, as we climbed into his car. 'Or at least get some decent security at your place.'

On the way, we diverted to Newtown. The door of the 'For Sale' cottage was still unlocked and, not surprisingly, the bag of money was no longer on the table. Kapit or his cat's-paw would have struck within seconds of me leaving the premises.

At Lane Cove, Genevieve screamed and shrieked that I was lying about Greg and lying about Kapit and it was only Bob's presence that restored some sort of emotional order. I waited, trying not to say something I'd regret, focusing my attention on a little white and gold shepherdess with silly smiling sheep crowding around her legs and who was inexplicably carrying a watering can.

Eventually, when Genevieve had become half rational, Bob started on her. I made an attempt to question her, but Bob's look and half-raised hand in my direction stopped me.

'... anywhere at all,' Bob was saying. 'Any mention of a property, a flat, business?'

'John didn't discuss his business with me,' she cried. 'And he wouldn't have hurt Greg. He wouldn't. He *liked* Greg.'

'Yes,' I said. 'He liked Jacinta too. He liked her so much she's been living with him for the last couple of months. Your handsome boyfriend's a dealer. He probably started your daughter's using.'

The implications of this information were horrible and my estranged wife's face was stricken as she took it in. 'No,' she said finally, beyond hysteria. 'That can't be right. That's not true. You're making that up.'

'You'd better believe it,' I said. 'He tracked our daughter down all right, months ago.'

I let that sink in. I didn't want to ask myself why John fucking Kapit had found Jacinta when all my efforts had failed. 'He made a fool of you, Genevieve. And all the time, you're crying on his shoulder, thanking him for all the work he's doing searching for our daughter. Showing your appreciation.'

I couldn't help kicking the door of the bedroom and Genevieve jumped up in a rage that now included everyone as well as me. I walked outside, away from the explosion. Crickets shrilled in the darkness. I know I shouldn't have said what I'd said, but a bitter pressure had demanded release.

'I can't think! I can't think with all this going on!' I could hear my wife screaming inside. 'Leave me alone. Get out and find my son. If he'd stayed here with me, none of this would have happened.'

I waited till Bob came out, joining me with a nod. 'Let's get going,' he said.

•

Next day every property and known associate of John Cleever Kapit was visited. With Bob beside me, I talked to people who all had something to say about him. I spun from one door-knock to the next, my head swirling with crazy *déjà vu* feelings and scenes from eighteen months ago and twenty-five years ago. But we came no closer to finding where Kapit might have been holding my son. The newspapers published the 'grave concerns' police held for missing teenager Greg McCain. And it didn't take them long to link him with Jacinta McCain, who'd run away eighteen months ago. My fury rose as I read and then reread Merrilyn Heywood's piece, 'Lightning *Does* Strike Twice', about my children going missing. She had this all mixed up with Kapit's murder, and wrongly attributed Jacinta's return to his efforts, casting Kapit in the role of heroic PI who devoted his life to tracking down missing girls, as well as being the stalwart in the life of grieving mother, Genevieve McCain, abandoned by her philandering husband, and now facing the horrors of a missing child for the second time. It pissed me off that she'd taken this tack without talking to me. I made a mental note to forcefully disabuse Ms Heywood of her opinions at the next opportunity.

I went to the Collins Club but there was no aqua Bufori sports car and no Pigrooter in the corner. The freckled bar attendant put me straight. 'He's away for a few days,' he said. 'There's a big boar giving some cocky a hard time.' He tapped a colour snap stuck to the mirrored bar. 'Took Mountbatten with him.' The pig dog smiled out of the picture, its chest shielded by a studded leather breastplate, sitting cheekily on an enormous upturned tusker. I turned away.

'You Jack McCain?' the barman asked and for a second, I felt some foolish hope.

I turned and nodded.

'Marty said to remind you about that business arrangement if you came in.' How could I forget, I thought, as I walked away. I could hear Bob's voice from the old days saying, 'Cheer up. When things get really bad, they can only get worse.'

To counter the negative thoughts, I went to an AA meeting and came away feeling comforted by the wisdom I'd heard there. I knew I could face whatever the future held. No matter how difficult it seemed, millions of other humans had been there before me.

At home, I stood looking at the mess. I didn't want to stay here anymore, yet I felt I couldn't leave while Greg was missing. His pokey little bedroom here, his crop circle on the floor near the television, were palpable evidence of his existence. I couldn't move out, not just yet. The Crime Scene people had taken the bloodstained rugs away with them and had vacuumed the floor searching for trace particles. Bob had arranged for cleaning contractors. I picked up poor old Kuan Ti from where he lay awkwardly and straightened his pole-knife. As I set his heavy metal base in its accustomed place on the table I found myself thinking a pathetic prayer: Kuan Ti, I said, god of detectives, *do* something.

Someone knocked on the door and for a second I thought it might be my son. But it was Charlie who pushed the door open. He came in and put his arms around me. I've never been a hugger and always avoided this sort of thing, but now I stood there, letting my brother's arms encircle me, feeling bereft and helpless.

'Bob told me what's happened,' said my brother. He went to my cupboards. 'I know you can't,' he said, 'but I need a drink.'

'There's some brandy or something in the left-hand cupboard,' I said. 'Just near the soy sauce.' Charlie rooted around among the containers and found what he was looking for.

He poured himself a good one and came to where I was sitting. 'You look wrecked,' he said. 'Have you slept?'

'I've tried,' I said. 'But I can't. I keep thinking of Greg. What if Kapit's locked him up in somewhere only he knew about? Now the arsehole's dead, Greg might starve to death in some bloody dump.' The last words broke me and I slumped onto a chair, leaning my head on the table while the tears flowed over my face. I could sense Charlie standing behind me, and could just feel the touch of his hand on my shoulder. He didn't say anything or do anything and I was intensely grateful for that. He just let the storm come and go and when I could, I sat up, fished for my handkerchief and blew my nose.

'I've never really got to know my kids,' I said. 'I was just starting with Greg. I went in the other night and told him all about Rosie. And what happened the night Jacinta ran away. I even told him I'd seen Rosie standing in my bedroom. I felt we were just getting to know each other,' I said, 'and now he's gone.'

There was a silence and outside I could hear a bul-bul saying over and over, *'That's so typical, that's so typical.'* Charlie took a long swig of the brandy and I could smell it. 'Jass is lying in hospital in never-never land,' I said. 'Genevieve says she's lost her kids. So have I.' I felt completely helpless and hopeless. 'I just don't know what to do next.'

My mobile rang and I grabbed it. 'It's Jane,' said the caller. 'State Forensic Services. Bob thought you'd like to know we've got a result from the knife he sent over to us. I'm surprised you didn't take it with you to Canberra,' she added, reminding me again of how I'd compromised my scientific objectivity. 'I've heard your lab's better than ours.' I mumbled some reason as she continued.

'As you know, it had been wiped down but you know how it is with blood—all those microscopic pits and crevices on a forged blade. We found Frank Carmody all over it.'

That was the connection. The knife I'd found in Iona's laundry cupboard had been used to kill Carmody in Centennial Park. Despite the misery of my present situation, I felt something like interest.

'And,' she said, 'we also got an FU. A bonus trace of someone else. In a seam on the handle. We're amplifying it now. I'll let you know how we go. We could have a picture of the suspect for you.'

'Please fax me the result.' For some reason, I really wanted to see this killer's graph.

'If there is one,' she reminded me. 'It may turn out NR.'

Even with not reportable results, the amelogenin sex marker, the smallest segment of DNA used in profiling, is sometimes the only marker that can be determined, especially with trace samples. 'I'd give a lot to know whether you get a single or double peak,' I said, thinking of the female and male graph respectively.

'Like I say,' said Jane, 'we mightn't even get that.'

I gave her my fax number, but my thoughts kept swinging back to my son and I turned to my brother. 'Charlie,' I said, 'Greg could be anywhere.'

Charlie looked at me and between us some terrible unsaid fear arose.

I stood up again. 'I don't know what I'll do,' I said, 'if Greg dies.'

The phone rang again and it was Bob. 'We're talking to a bloke who says he saw Kapit at Darlinghurst with a youth who matches Greg's description at around five o'clock. I just thought I'd let you know.'

'I'm coming in,' I said.

'You're not,' said Bob. 'You stay right out of this, please. Let me handle it. I'll let you know the second we get anything.' He rang off and I told Charlie.

'Come and stay at my place,' he said. 'You can't stay here.' He looked around. A fine spray of arterial blood formed a red mist on the wall near the entrance to the living area. But I felt I had to be here, in the place I'd shared briefly with my son. I shook my head. 'I can't leave,' I said.

'Is there anything you want me to do?' Charlie offered. 'Anyone I could talk to?'

I racked my brains. I couldn't think of anyone. 'Could you wait here?' I said, 'while I go and visit Jacinta? Just in case. Greg might come here.'

My brother nodded. 'Sure,' he said.

As I reached the corner of Anzac Parade, a pair of magpies, locked in a squabbling black and white swastika, spun under the tyres of the car turning in front of me. One rose shrieking, the other floundered, dying, in the gutter.

I pulled up near the hospital and sat there a few minutes. I was staring out the window, unfocused, when I saw Genevieve walk to her car and drive away. Something moved in me and I felt some sort of compassion for her. She seemed such a distant person to me now, but she was still the mother of our children and I knew that whatever her faults, she was going through hell. More so than I was, because it was she who'd slept with the monster. Or, I had to admit to myself, another monster. Neither of us had very good taste. Perhaps we'd deserved each other.

In the room, Jass lay small and still under the pale mauve cover, her slow breathing almost imperceptible. I took her limp cool hand between both of mine and squeezed gently. 'It's me, Jass,' I said, in a low tone near her ear. I'd heard from nurses experienced in death and the dying process that hearing was the last faculty to go as a human being slipped away into the great mystery and I wondered if my daughter's mind was already somewhere near the border. 'Jass,' I continued, 'I need your help. More than anything. I need you to tell me where John Kapit might take Greg. He took your brother, Jass. And Kapit's dead now, so you're safe from him. But Greg is still somewhere only Kapit knew about. We've searched and searched. Nobody seems to know anything. Can you help me, Jass? Maybe you have an idea where he is.' I waited. It was like talking to myself. There was no response at all. The pale hand lay inert between my warm palms.

'Please, Jass. Help me. I need your help. Our Reg needs your help.' Something inspired me to say the next few words, despite my scientific scepticism. 'Maybe where you are you can see things, hear things, know things that we don't know about. Maybe you can help me from where you are with a bigger picture.'

I stayed holding Jacinta's hand, feeling hopeless and wretched. There was nothing more I could do. I don't know how long I sat there, listening to the sounds of the other small wards around me, the footsteps going backwards and forwards past Jacinta's half-closed door, the smells and occasional sounds of laughter coming from the nurses' station at the end of the corridor. Outside, sparrows chirruped in their ordinary way and the world went by as it does. I'd been looking past my daughter towards the windows but something drew my attention back to her face.

I exhaled sharply with excitement. Something was happening. Jacinta's lips moved, stilled, then moved again, but it might have been just a nerve twitching unconsciously. She exhaled and this time, I was sure there was movement that wasn't just a spasm. I waited, tense with excitement. I seized her hand tighter. 'Jass! Jass, I'm here, darling. Talk to me. Help me.'

Her long exhalation seemed to be shaping a word. Her eyelids flickered, and opened and her large blue eyes moved slowly around, unfocused. I seized her other hand. 'I'm here, Jass. It's me, Dad.' Her focus moved up as if to settle on me but she passed me by, slowly scanning the room. Then my daughter smiled straight past me at someone near the door. I swung around to see who it was coming into the room, concerned about confronting my estranged wife. But it wasn't Genevieve. In fact, it wasn't anyone. There was no one there at all, just the empty corridor beyond the door. I turned back to my daughter who was now moving her lips, trying to say something. 'Jass!' I said. 'Jass!' I was so shocked and startled at this development that I nearly tripped over the chair leg as I jumped to my feet. Jass was saying something, very soft, just one long whispered word—a long soft monosyllable, topped and tailed by her dry lips. I put my ear down to be closer and I heard what she was saying. Then her eyes closed again. I jumped to my feet and ran to find a nurse. A pretty dark-haired woman in a polka dot blouse looked up as I skidded to a halt.

'My daughter,' I said, 'in room 407. She just spoke to me.' Together we ran back to the room and I stepped aside to let the sister through. But Jacinta was lying as still and silent as she'd ever been and the nurse looked at me doubtfully. I was stung. 'As true as I'm standing here,' I said. 'She opened her eyes, smiled at something and whispered a name.'

'Whose name?' the nurse asked, picking up Jacinta's wrist, checking her pulse against her watch.

'A woman's name,' I said. The nurse looked expectantly at me but I shook my head. 'No one I know.'

The nurse put the hand down gently. 'She might be coming out of it. Or it might have just been some sort of reflex action. It's not for me to say. I'll tell Doctor what you told me.' She had soft, kind eyes. 'Don't give up hope. She's young. She can do it.' Tears sprang to my eyes as the young woman left the room.

I sat down again, but nothing more happened. To look at my daughter now, I'd never believe it either. But she *had* opened her eyes, she had smiled and she had breathed a name I didn't know.

I rang Bob from the hospital to see if there was any more news. He told me no, and to calm down and go home. 'We're throwing everything we've got at this,' said Bob. 'We're talking to everyone, searching everywhere. Get some sleep.'

'You're joking,' I said.

FIFTEEN

'Pam,' was the word my daughter had whispered. And my mind had finally made the jump to remember who and where I'd heard the name from. 'She's the woman who comes for the rents,' Renee had told me, way back then when life seemed relatively simple and I was just helping Bob out with an investigation. I'd taken the name to Surry Hills police to find that a Pamela Nyree Dobronski, who operated several leaseholds in the area, all used as brothels or parlours, was a person 'known to the police'. She'd retired from the game herself, the young detective explained, but still had a lot of active interests in different establishments. She wasn't what you might call sweetness and light, he added, especially since they'd locked her youngest up for armed robbery last year.

Now I was driving to an address in Albion Street. I was hanging on the hope that Jass, wherever she was, had heard my desperate request about her brother, and had brought something relevant to our search from the unknown place she drifted in. I had to hang on to this hope, because it was the only thing I had.

The Albion Street address turned out to be one of a pair of terraces given over to the oldest profession and I knocked on the door until it was opened by a vision in leopardskin and high-heeled black sandals.

'Pam Dobronski,' I said. 'I'm looking for her.' I was aware of a large woman coming down the hall behind the leopardskin girl, filling the narrow hallway.

'Who wants me, Brenda?'

'Some bloke,' said the girl, turning away, her retreat blocked by Pam's bulk.

'I'm expecting the technician from Energy Australia,' she said, 'about that fucking excuse the language fuse in the kitchen.'

I mumbled something and stepped inside, closing the door behind me.

'The same fuse your people fixed last month and now it's blown again,' Pam was saying, jerking a thumb that revealed too much gold on her fingers, eyes frowning under too much aqua eye-shadow.

'I'm not from Energy Australia,' I told her, 'and I'm not looking for a girl. I want to talk to you, Mrs Dobronski.' I was about to pull out my warrant card from sheer force of habit, but stopped. 'My son, Gregory McCain, has been kidnapped and your name came up as someone who might help me.'

'You're a cop,' she said. 'I can smell you buggers a mile off. Get out of here.' She pushed past me and opened the door. 'Piss off.'

'My son is only seventeen. A man called John Kapit took him and now Kapit's dead and no one knows where my son is. Please. If you have any idea of where he might be, please tell me.' Here I was again, talking to people like Pam Dobronski about a missing child. My child. My children.

'Out,' she said. 'I don't owe you any favours.'

'If it's a question of paying you for your time—' I said, but she interrupted me.

'Don't insult me. You couldn't pay for my time. You don't have enough.'

'Renee,' I said, 'who worked at the House of Bondage. She's dead. I'm scared the same thing will happen to my son.'

But the bulky body remained motionless, indicating the door, adamantly set against me.

'I've got a couple of fellows living next door,' she said. 'It only takes a coo-ee and they're both here like a shot. They'll throw you down the street. Just leave now if you don't want broken bones.'

I remained standing there. 'Please,' I said, 'if you know anything.'

Pam Dobronski put her fingers to her lips and came out with a whistle that nearly broke my eardrums. I heard thudding footsteps from next door and within seconds, just as she'd said, the doorway was blocked by two huge Tongans. I raised my hands in surrender and walked out, defeated again.

Back at my place, I couldn't sit still after Charlie had left. The only lead I'd got had been futile and now the grief and fear I'd been holding at bay surfaced. Unable to be still, I walked outside, and cried like a baby, standing near my ruined painting, lying on the ground from the day before. I walked back inside, blinded by tears, groping around for something to wipe my nose with. For fifteen years I'd practised letting go of problems that were worrying me, and with good effect, but now I realised I'd never really had a problem worth the name until this moment. I groped around for a tea towel because someone was knocking on the half opened door. I turned to see a very embarrassed tradesman, and remembered that after the break-in I'd rung a Mr Camilleri to come and measure up wrought-iron grilles for the windows and door. He stood there, looking away, trying not to notice my emotional state.

I got myself organised while he taped and measured and finally left, assuring me of a quick job.

My agitation and concern over my missing son kept me prowling. I walked down to the back fence, causing a pair of noisy miners to fill the air with their high-pitched alarm calls—*'Help! Help! Help!'* I paused because I could hear the metallic sound that had teased me before, coming from the little park over the fence. Then I heard my name being called in a low voice. 'Mr McCain, please come over here. *Please.*'

The urgent tone made me wary as I peered through the grevilleas and hakeas that grew against the back fence. That odd metallic squeak came from the little green-painted swing, sticky on its rigid supports, swinging back and forth. Every time it moved to its zenith, the bolts made the sound that had teased me earlier when I'd heard it, late at night.

'It's me, Mr McCain. Come over. I don't dare be seen going into your place.'

A woman with platinum hair and far too much make-up sat on the swing. I swear I'd never seen her before. Thoughts of the twenty-six-year-old night club dancer who lured men to a horrible death came to mind, but the Colt was a steady companion of late so I climbed over and pushed my way through the spiky brush to emerge on the other side. I was ready for anything. I stood still, scrutinising the woman, Elizabeth Taylor on a very bad day, yet I felt she was familiar. Then I nearly fell over in shock. It was Staro, dragged out to the nines.

'Mr McCain, you've gotta help me,' Staro said, awkwardly getting off the swing, high heels digging into the bare soil.

'Get inside,' I hissed, making a way for him through the bushes like I would for a woman, helping his narrow backside over my fence, watching his wobbling big feet in the silly heels scrambling through the overgrown backyard. Together we hurried up to the house.

Staro dived inside the door and huddled in a corner in my kitchen, pulling out a cigarette.

'Christ, Staro,' I said, 'the entire police service is out looking for you. What's going on?'

'You've got to help me,' he said. 'I want to turn myself in, but you've got to help me.'

He looked around wildly. 'Have you got a proper drink round here?' I looked around and found an inch or so of the brandy Charlie hadn't drunk. I poured it over some ice blocks and handed it to him.

'I know I shouldn't,' he said coyly, and I got angry.

'Don't go queeny on me, Staro. I don't care if you bust or not. Just tell me what happened at Centennial Park.'

'There was a three-quarter moon that night. I saw her face, clear as anything. And I'm nearly sure she saw me.'

'*She?*' I said.

Staro nodded. 'Real tall and strong. Scared the shit out of me.' He gulped his drink. 'I took off. I was too scared. I couldn't wait for you.' He put the drink down and took the platinum wig off. 'Drag is so *hot*,' he said. Now he looked more like my poor informer, with his hair sticking up all over his head and a bad case of eye make-up.

'We got your prints from Dr Jeremy Guildthorpe's place,' I said, 'and too many people think you did all of them.'

He sat down suddenly and I remained standing, wary. 'I didn't know,' he said, 'what it would be like. Coming off the 'done. Not drinking either. No pills. There was nothing I could take.' He looked at the glass of brandy and shook his head. 'All these terrible things started happening in my brain. Like I had some crazy committee up there. All these worms squirming around. Sometimes I wanted to cut my head open and let them out.'

I nodded. I remembered only too well.

'Voices screaming at me, telling me I was hopeless, useless, reminding me of all the times people had used me like shit.' He covered his face with his big hands, false nails curved like talons. 'All I could think of was that bastard, Guildthorpe.' He took his hands away from his face. 'When I was a kid I met him in a café up at Darlo. The lady there used to give me a feed. He was the first person in the world who took an interest in me.' Sooty tears ran down his face, and he pushed them away with impatient fingers. 'I didn't have a family in Sydney. My stepfather kicked me out. Mum had a drinking problem.' I waited till he continued. 'I thought Dr Guildthorpe liked me. He was a teacher and he said he liked kids. I believed him. I thought he cared about me. He taught me some things. He helped me to read a bit. He gave me books. He took me out sailing a couple of times.' Staro finished the last of the brandy and looked around.

'There's no more, Staro. I'll go and get you something from the bottle shop.'

Staro shook his head. 'No,' he said, 'I've got to get used to it. Where I'm going there's not going to be any brandy.'

'But there'll be heroin,' I said.

He looked at the empty glass. 'I want you to take me in. I won't be so scared if you come with me. Do all the stuff, you know. Booking me.'

I sat down opposite him. 'Tell me the rest,' I said.

Staro ran his false nails through his hair, pressing it down. 'You're the only person in the world who doesn't use me,' he said. 'You're my only friend.'

I stood up, uncomfortable with his pathos. You poor bastard, I thought, if that's the case.

'I thought Dr Guildthorpe was a friend. Then, one night at his place... He's got this ritzy place—Roman swimming pool, marble floors, arty stuff.'

'I know,' I said. 'I've been there.'

Staro took that in. 'Right. Well, one night years ago at his place, we got real drunk. We'd been smoking a lot of dope, too. I didn't use heroin in those days. He raped me. There was nothing I could do.' Staro looked up at me and his face under the make-up was that of a lost child. 'That was the end of me,' he said. 'I didn't care what happened to me after that. I started working the Wall.

Anything anyone wanted. I just didn't care. Heroin helped a bit. In the beginning.'

'Staro,' I said, remembering the other times I'd heard the swing creaking at night. 'Have you sat in that swing other times? At night?'

He shook his head. 'No,' he said, 'never been here before today. I wanted to contact you often, but I was too scared.'

He collapsed over the table and I could see that he was doing everything in his power to stop himself from sobbing out loud. I walked around behind him, putting my arm on his heaving shoulders. In that moment, I was just another fellow addict, albeit with many years' recovery, sharing my experience, strength and hope with a fellow sufferer.

'I've been running all my life,' sobbed Staro. 'I'm so tired of being scared all the time.'

I nodded, remembering.

'I went back to his place,' he continued. 'I don't know why. I wanted him to see what had become of me. But he didn't want to know me now. Not all these years later. He only likes them young and pretty. He was telling me to get out and I saw that CD cover, *The Last Castrato*, and that was the last straw. I knew that's what he'd done to me.' Staro shuddered, remembering what he'd done to Guildthorpe. 'Look at me now,' Staro was saying. 'I thought I'd hit rock bottom when I started on the streets. But I went even lower. Now I'm a murderer. I've killed a man.'

'Even that, Staro,' I said. 'You can come back from even that.'

He looked up at me as if I were mad. 'This'll finish me,' he said.

'Others have done it worse and harder than you and come back. You'll have to face the consequences of your actions—we all do, eventually. But it's up to you how you do your time. You can go further down in hell, or you can make the decision to turn your life around. There are programs available in prison. It's up to you.'

Staro looked at me, and I could see in his face that he almost believed me, because he knew I'd been there and back.

I looked directly into his eyes. 'You can become the person you were supposed to be before all the shit happened to you.'

He covered his face in his hands.

I rang Bob. 'Is there any news on Greg?' I asked and I was aware that Staro was listening intently to me.

'The lead we got about Greg,' Bob said, and I waited, willing him to give me good news, 'it's fizzled out. Now we're acting on a report from Campbelltown.'

'Campbelltown?'

'Kapit has... had... a small property there. The local boys are searching it at the moment.' I turned back to Staro, my mind miles away, searching a hobby farm. Then I told him about my visitor and rang off. 'Bob's sending a car for you, Staro. He's a decent man.'

'Come with me,' Staro pleaded.

'I can't,' I told him. 'I have to wait here in case my son Greg turns up.'

I saw Staro pay some attention, dimly aware that there was other pain in the world apart from his own.

'What's happened?'

And I brought him up to date with my situation.

When the squad car arrived, Staro made a pathetic figure. I'd lent him a shirt and some trousers but they were far too big, and with his not quite washed off make-up and bare feet he looked like a walk-on from *The Pirates of Penzance*. As they led him away, I felt like Judas Iscariot.

Inside, I went through the motions of tidying up, my mind full of my son, wondering what he might be doing, how frightened he'd be feeling. I'm thinking of you, Reggie, I told him. I'm praying for you in my way, willing that you be safe from harm.

I noticed a fax lying in the tray and I picked it up, frowning, wondering how long it had been there, not realising for a moment what it was all about. *Jack, I'll give you the full report when I see you,* I read. *But briefly, the metallic traces on the anonymous letters you gave me to test come from a cosmetic made by Pretty Woman, a subsidiary of Colgate Palmolive. They make all sorts of glitter gels and sprays. Didn't know you were into such things!* It was from Nigel, the other particle man.

I put the fax down and walked into Greg's bedroom, staring sightlessly at a plastic gilt swimming award that lay crookedly on his bedside table. Now I knew who'd written those nasty letters and where those traces had come from. I was stunned. Nothing was the way I'd thought it was, and despite my scientific understanding of how things work, I seemed to have very little understanding of human beings. Especially women.

I walked outside again, feeling sick. I stood near my ruined painting and thought that probably it hadn't been John Kapit who'd trodden it into the ground. I walked down to the back fence again and the sad little playground where Staro had sat on the swing. And so had someone else, I thought. Someone who's lost her job and wants to punish me. The swing fitting was making its eerie sound again, but now that I knew what it was, it didn't sound eerie at all. She used to wear that glitter gel all over her breasts and belly in the late afternoon so that when the sun shone through the horizontal slats of the blinds in her bedroom, she sparkled and shone like a treasure. I tried to see it from her point of view. Had I treated her badly? Given her reason to hope for something more? I'd rarely made mention of my personal life to her. In fact, it was difficult for me to remember ever saying anything of a personal nature to her. She'd been as eager—I'd have to say, more eager—than I. How had I given her cause for such spite against me? I'd never made promises, I'd never even implied I'd see her again. Each of our times together could have been the last time, until either I or she rang again and made another date. It had been such a casual affair. It was she, in fact, who'd referred to herself as the 'convenient association', and I'd continued the joke. Except she hadn't been joking. Another woman, another witch. My first sponsor had been right: I should have turned around and walked the other way.

I poked a clearing through the grevillea bushes, disturbing some noisy miners who briefly cried their alarm before resettling. I could see that someone had just vacated the swing, which even now was making smaller and smaller arcs towards finding the still point. I thought of Florence and how I'd never noticed her interest in me until it was too late to do anything except flounder and make everything worse. And now I was drawn to Iona Seymour. Before it's too late, a voice in my mind said, turn and walk the other way.

Suddenly, I could hear Charlie's voice. He was knocking on the back door and calling me. 'Where are you, Jack?' he was saying. 'I've got Dad with me. He wants to talk to you. Can I bring him in?'

So now my father sat in the place Staro had just vacated.

'I'm very sorry,' he said, fiddling with his packet of tobacco, 'about Greg. Charlie rang and told me. I wanted to let you know that…' He stopped. 'I wanted to let you know… I wanted to help somehow.' He'd got dressed up for his trip south, with an old deerstalker hat I hadn't seen since I was a boy, and his sports coat and the knitted tie made by a loyal P & C member years ago in his teaching days. He looked around the table and then the room. 'I need an ashtray,' he announced.

I found him a saucer. Charlie had brought some take-away Chinese food along with them. Here we are, I was thinking, the men of our family, together for the first time in years, but without my son. There was something of the feeling of a wake about it and I shivered at the notion. I distributed plates and spoons around, serving myself a small pile of rice I knew I wouldn't be able to touch. I was thinking of my children, of how precious they were to me, how little I knew them.

'You got that photograph with you?' my father was asking.

I passed him the picture of Rosie smiling into the sunlit November of long ago. He pushed it away impatiently. 'No, no,' he said, 'not that one. The photo of the young fellow.' I told him I hadn't seen it since the day of Kapit's murder. I hadn't told him about that earlier and obviously Charlie hadn't either. I hated to acknowledge how close that man had come to me, even though he'd died because of it. 'I've remembered who it is,' my father was saying. I was jolted back to the present.

'Who?' I said, more harshly than I'd intended.

But my father was off on a tangent of his own. 'I dreamed about the bathroom at Springbrook, in the old house,' he said.

'Who is it in the photograph?' I said, anger rising up in me.

'You know how the ferns outside the window used to press up against the bathroom window?' our father was saying, as if he hadn't heard me.

My anger mounted until it was a fury. '*Who was it in the photograph?*' I yelled at him. 'For chrissakes just listen to me and answer my questions and if you can't be helpful, you miserable old bastard, *piss off out of here!*'

My father flinched as if I'd struck him in the face. Charlie looked taken aback. My heart was pounding at breakneck speed in my chest, filling my head with its sound. A warning came from somewhere that this is how men have sudden heart attacks, so I tried to calm myself, breathing deeply, practising some sort of detachment from the powerful anger.

'I've done without you all my life,' I said to him, 'so don't come here thinking you can do me any favours. It's too little and it's too late.' I took a deep breath and controlled myself. But I wasn't sorry for what I'd said. It had needed saying.

'I remembered I caught a boy once, hiding in the ferns, perving on Rosie,' my father was saying in a low voice, looking away from me. 'And that's when I remembered who it was. In the photograph.'

I turned to face him, too stunned to speak for a moment. 'Snotty Kirkwood?' I whispered.

'No,' said my father. 'Julian Bower.'

Charlie was looking at me, then at our father, who sat desperately rolling a cigarette. 'Why didn't you ever tell anyone this before?' I finally managed to say.

My father kept rolling the cigarette as if his life depended on it. He shook his head. 'I couldn't,' he said. 'I only remembered today.' He looked up at me a second, then looked away again, attention back on the cigarette paper which he licked along one side, pressed together, then put in his mouth. Charlie picked up the matches and lit it for him. He inhaled deeply. 'It's the sort of thing adolescent boys do all the time,' he said. 'Trying to spot girls in a state of undress.'

'Except that this time, the girl went missing,' Charlie said.

'Why didn't you tell the police this,' I said 'after Rosie went missing?'

'I'm sure I did,' he said.

My head was spinning as if the clouds of nicotine smoke were in my lungs, not my father's. The fax machine started humming again and I walked over to it to give myself something to do. I glanced at the cover sheet and saw it was from Jane. I picked up the second page and stared at it. 'Here he is,' Jane had written underneath and I saw the twin peaks at the amelogenin marker of the DNA profile from the trace on the knife handle. Whoever killed Frank Carmody was male. I handed the graph to Charlie who took it without a word. 'It's him,' I said, and Charlie knew exactly which him I meant. He looked at the graph, looked at me. 'The mutilator murderer is a male after all,' he said, and I nodded.

I completely forgot my father's presence or that moments before

I'd been homicidally enraged with him. Some huge burden of fear that I'd been carrying for weeks fell away and Iona was cleared to shine briefly in my memory. But not for long. My son's absence brooded over everything else in my mind. I put the faxed profile in a large manila envelope and propped it up against the wall on the top of the sideboard. Then I rang Iona's number but there was no answer.

As the number rang out, I noticed that our father was looking around, awkward and ill at ease. 'Take him home, Charlie,' I said, putting down the phone and together with Charlie, I helped him out of the chair he was sitting in.

'Don't forget your tobacco,' I said, picking it up and shoving it in his pocket. He turned to me as if he were about to say something and I could see there were tears in his eyes. We stood in silence together for a moment and then I patted his arm. I noticed the little folder of paper matches lying near the ash-filled saucer. I picked them up, too.

'Don't forget your matches,' I said to him.

When they had gone, I tidied away a few of the last things left out on the sideboard and there it was, the small, folded square of paper. Iona's prayer. I picked it up and read it. As I read it my mood changed I became angrier and angrier. Although she wasn't the murderer she was guilty as hell. Complicity is horrible. I slipped the prayer into my wallet and was putting it back into my pocket when my mobile rang and it was Bob. I prayed that it was about Greg, and that he'd been found safe and sound.

'No,' he said gently, 'it's not about your son.'

My heart rate went down and I listened to what he was saying. 'We've turned up something. A bloodstained Tyvek suit.' I pulled my mind away from my son and tried to make sense of what Bob was telling me.

'Where does that fit in?' I asked.

'In a bin at Centennial Park actually,' said Bob. 'It's on its way to Jane right now.'

The disposable Tyvek spacesuits that we wear in the labs are used for lots of different purposes. A light polyester one-piece overall, designed to fit all shapes and sizes, the spacesuits are often worn by crime scene examiners these days, where they serve to protect the investigator against contamination from his surroundings. I remembered the tall figure with the long blonde hair who had stepped out of the car as I waited near the Coogee fishermen's club.

'Do you remember when "Rosie" stepped out of the car at Coogee?' I said to Bob. 'Wearing the trademark red jacket and what had looked like floppy white trousers?'

'Of course,' he said. 'A spacesuit. Then it can be dumped. Most of the blood would fall on the killer's lower body. This one will have Carmody all over it.'

'And maybe some of "Rosie", too,' I said.

•

On the drive to Annandale, a few things started falling into place. The shopping I'd seen Iona doing, the weird mix of vegetarian and meat, health foods and sugary biscuits. My unconscious mind had tried to present this observation to me on a couple of occasions, and I now understood why the eggs in the frypan had stirred something in my mind. Eggs implied bacon, and bacon was one of the things I'd noticed in her shopping trolley the day I contrived our chance encounter. Iona had been shopping for two people. Ring me, Michael had written on the post-it note and stuck it to the front door of her house. What could I conjecture from that? That she already knew his phone number indicated intimacy. But he didn't have a key to her place. Or maybe he did, and had left the note on the way out after realising she wasn't around. Was the library, which at first I'd thought to be the secret flesh-eating retreat of a spurious vegetarian, really the larder of another person altogether? Michael the meat-eater. The phrase kept playing through my mind.

Why does someone do the shopping for another person, I was asking myself as I slammed the car door shut and started to walk up the overgrown driveway, lifting rose canes out of my way. Usually, because they're married to them, I told myself, but in this case, Iona's ex-husband was in West Africa. A person is shopped for because they can't do it themselves, because of illness, incompetence or some other problem.

But then I recalled the strong sense I'd had of decay when I'd first stood in front of the house. Though I hadn't grasped the connection at the time, Poe's 'Fall of the House of Usher' had come into my head—a tale of madness, involving a brother and sister and their decrepit mansion. With my understandable oversensitivity concerning relationships between brothers and sisters, I'd been right on the money with this one. I knew I'd have to tell Charlie that, and maybe he'd make a footnote somewhere on his next journal publication, but I'd been distracted away from the truth I'd unconsciously picked up on day one. Iona had a brother, Julian, the young man in the photograph.

As I stepped onto the chequerboard tiles of the veranda, I found that the front door was exactly as I'd left it the previous day, closed but not locked. I opened it cautiously and stepped inside. I tried to sense whether there was anyone else here, but the dimness was ambiguous and the slight sounds I could hear might have been the house cooling at the end of a hot day. I crept up the hallway, pulling a pair of disposable gloves out of my pocket, putting them on, treading carefully with silent footfall, creeping through the deserted rooms, heavy with the scent of cedar and smell of damp. In the front parlour, where I'd eaten cucumber sandwiches, I saw that the newspaper with my startled face was still lying on the table, next to a take-away food container. And there was something else. I walked to the table and picked up an envelope which was addressed to Iona and underlined with a flourish. I didn't have to send this one to Sarah. Even I could see it was the same expensive linen-based paper, the same French sepia ink and the same hand that had written the 'Rosie letters'. The investigator in me wanted to seal it up immediately; the man wanted to rip it open. I stood there a moment until the professional won the day: I couldn't afford any more complications. I slipped the stiff envelope into my pocket. Then I tiptoed up the staircase, step by step, hardly looking at the blue monkey painting, straining my attention ahead, trying to pick up the slightest movement in the air that would convey another presence. At the top of the landing I paused, before creeping to Iona's bedroom and softly pushing the door open.

It was exactly as I'd remembered it, the long curtains, now dark as evening closed in, the portrait in the oval frame, the bed where we'd made love. I withdrew and made my way down the hallway, past the other two bedrooms until I came to the door with the crystal knob. I couldn't help thinking of Bluebeard's castle and I prayed that Bluebeard wasn't home and armed with a knife, waiting for me. Slowly and cautiously, I opened it and stood a second, waiting. I saw the grille door behind was also slightly ajar. It made a sound as I pushed it, and I froze, waiting, too scared to move until I was certain I was quite alone. When I felt sure there was no one else in the place, I crept forward, into the library.

The big old texts seemed darker and heavier now, crammed into their shelves, thickening the atmosphere of the library. The long table that ran down the centre was covered in dust, except for one large hand print at the far end. I walked over to it and without touching it, placed my own hand over it. It revealed a hand a good deal bigger than mine. Iona Seymour was a strong tall woman. Julian could be of considerable size now. Suddenly spooked, I swung around, but there was nothing behind me, just the two doors opening out onto the dark corridor and the aged books lining the walls on each side of me. I went over to the small cave-like annexe that housed the narrow bed and the fridge, noticing the toiletries on top, a toothbrush and paste, some soap in a container. With the toe of my shoe hooked under the bottom of the door, I opened the fridge. The packets were undisturbed, sitting together as before, frosty red meat under stretched plastic wrap. I squatted and opened the horizontal door of the small freezer compartment.

It was almost filled up by four plastic take-away food trays. I juggled one out. It bore a label with the date 14.11.99 on its lid. There it was again, the sickening, impossible connection to my sister Rosie's birthday and the day Warren Gumley had died. A shiver went right through me, despite the warm summer night. I pulled out the one next to it, dated 17.11.99. Nesbitt's death day. I pulled out the other two containers. Only one of them was dated, and it was the date of the Centennial Park murder. I realised that there they all were, Gumley, Nesbitt, and Carmody, yet Kapit's relics had no date on them. I lay the containers on the floor in front of me. My blood ran cold and it wasn't because of the slight chill falling from the small fridge. That fourth container was supposed to be me and I shuddered as I picked it up. I couldn't readily discern what was inside it, because of the frosted nature of the plastic, but I didn't have to open it to know what it contained.

I rang Bob and told him where I was.

'I was just about to ring you,' Bob said. And what he went on to tell me momentarily distracted me from the plastic containers. 'A woman called Pam Dobronski phoned someone she knows here, and there's a message for you to call her.'

Pam, I thought, as I pulled out my notepad. Maybe she *does* know something about Greg. A thrill of hope quickened inside me and I remembered the way Jass had opened her eyes to look straight past me and smile, and how the soft name had wafted from her mouth like the barest breeze.

'I'll call her straightaway,' I told him. Greg, I told my son, I'm right on after you, I promise.

I came back to the matter in hand. 'Bob,' I said, 'send some people to search and secure 293 Reiby Street, Annandale. Julian Bower, brother of Iona Seymour, née Bower, and son of the Reverend Bower, past incumbent of the Anglican rectory at Springbrook, is someone you must pull in if you can find him. Julian Bower would be a couple of years older than me,' I told Bob. 'His year of birth should be around the late 'fifties.' And I told him how I was thinking. 'I have a letter here in the "Rosie" handwriting addressed to his sister.'

'And Jane's got a DNA result.'

'She faxed me a copy, too.'

'So we know now that the mutilator murderer is a male,' said Bob.

I stared at the four plastic containers lying on the floor in front of the fridge with Bob's words in my ear. Though they'd frosted up even more since being removed from their freezing environment, I could just discern the darker shapes within. I switched the phone to my left hand and prised the lid of the first one open with my right. A slight sound from somewhere startled me and I turned round again, looking out and down the corridor behind me. 'Hold on, Bob,' I said. I walked to the grille door and gently closed it, looking down the hall. There was nothing there. The closed grille gate, even without the key, offered some sort of delaying device between me and anyone who might suddenly arrive. I replaced the lid, but not before I'd noted the shrivelled worm of dried meat and two round organs that lay frozen to the bottom of the container. 'Yes,' I agreed, 'he's male. And I've just found his trophy room.'

SIXTEEN

I replaced the containers exactly as I'd found them and closed the door of the freezer. I palmed the toothbrush into my pocket and left the library. Despite the late sunlight lying on the floors, it was hard not to get spooked as I made my way down the stairs, past the monkey painting and into the hallway outside the parlour. It didn't give me a comfortable feeling to see the empty plastic takeaway container sitting right next to my photograph on the table and I felt very glad that soon this place would be bustling with police activity. I hurried back to my car, aware that my fingertips were icy cold. Even the killer's hideous handiwork couldn't eclipse the fear in my mind for the safety of my son.

I couriered the toothbrush to Jane, asking her to fax the result to Florence at the Institute in Canberra. She said she would rush it through for me. A little while later found me at the brothel in Albion Street and after I'd convinced the lass in leopardskin that there was really nothing she could do for me, Pam Dobronski came into the room. 'You're a helluva lucky fellow,' she said, as she plonked herself down in a chair opposite me. 'I hate cops. But I got thinking after you left. If my Brettie hadn't got in with the wrong lot, he might've had a chance and not be serving seven years now. But his mongrel bastard of a father dragged him down.' She turned and yelled out the door. 'Vicky? Bring in a couple of stubbies, will ya, darl?'

I shook my head. 'Not for me.'

Mrs Dobronski looked at me as if I had a disease as the leopardskin stepped in with two small bottles of beer. 'Can't trust a man who doesn't drink,' she said.

I remembered a time when I'd thought exactly the same.

'So,' I said, 'what can you tell me, Pam?'

'Seeing as how he's dead now,' she said, 'he can't do anything about it.'

'About what?'

'Terrible way to die, but,' she leered. 'Wouldn't do much for your sex life.' Pam found her remark very funny. 'So there's no damage done if I tell you that John Kapit was the bloke I collected the rent for, for that unlicensed place—the House of Bondage.'

Bob met me in a squad car and we drove to the House of Bondage, 42 Marian Street, speeding through the evening traffic. I was glad he was driving because my mouth was dry with fear of what I might find, or what I mightn't find, and my hands were trembling even though I had them gripped together.

As I walked in a woman, naked except for garter belt and boots and armed with a huge green dildo, screamed at me, but Bob pushed past with his warrant and we were inside without further opposition. We raced past the bathroom and the memory of little Renee haunted me so that I almost saw her jumping up off the toilet with her black lace pants around her ankles. Now she was dead, and I feared for my son. 'There's a real dungeon here,' she'd said, 'the original cellar... I could chain you up down there and do what I liked with you. No one would hear you.' I repeated her words to Bob and we found the staircase and pounded down to the lower level. We kicked open another bathroom, a bedroom and at the end of the small hallway, behind the stairs, we came up against a locked door. I bashed at it with everything I had. Bob joined me and together we kicked and kicked until the hinges gave with a wrench.

'Greg?' I called into the darkness. The slice of light from Bob's torch cut through the musty air to the sandstone wall where manacles and chains lay in a heap on the earthen ground to reveal my son crouched blinking in a corner. Near him was the black and yellow gym bag containing two hundred and thirty-three thousand dollars that I'd left on a dusty table in a derelict house in Newtown.

'Dad?' His voice was croaky and I ran to him, trying to pull the manacles off with my bare fingers. I vowed to myself I would never scold him about his crop circles again. I could hear Bob upstairs roaring for keys as I took my shivering son in my arms.

'It's okay,' I whispered as he sobbed against me. 'It's okay. It's all over. I'm here.'

I took Greg to Genevieve's and left them together. Then I gave Bob a lift back to work on my way to the hospital. I don't know what mother and son were talking about, but I wouldn't have liked to be Genevieve, I was thinking. Kapit had tricked Greg into his car by saying that his mother was in hospital and he would drive him straight to her. In my pocket was the sealed envelope I'd taken from the table at Iona's place and in the boot was the accounts book and the gym bag stacked with money.

'I almost feel sorry for Genevieve,' I said to Bob. The traffic was horrendous and every light seemed to be waiting to turn red at our approach but I felt incredibly light. I couldn't imagine ever having a problem again. I wanted to laugh, except when I thought about Jass, there was nothing to laugh about.

'You're going to have to start what the Americans call "dating" again,' said Bob, glancing at me. To shut him up, I reminded him of his own experience with a singles advertisement, where the only woman who'd sounded half-interesting had turned out to be his ex-wife, Sheila. As we waited at another red light my friend turned to me again.

'Jack, what the hell are you going to do about the money?'

I considered as I took off. 'I don't know,' I said. 'Do what you suggested. Put it away. Sit tight. Think it over.'

I was aware of Bob staring at me and glanced over at him. He was grinning like an idiot.

'I don't think you realise what a lucky bastard you are,' he said.

Now I was grinning as well, so hard I could barely talk. 'I do, I do,' I said. 'Two hundred grand plus, four frozen dicks and the return of my son. All in one day. That's what I call good policing.'

I didn't think it could get any better until the hospital called.

•

After I'd dropped Bob off, I drove to St Vincent's. I didn't know how I was feeling. Confused, joyful, anxious, apprehensive. I found it hard to wait for the lift and instead raced up the stairs. When I got to the room, I saw that a young doctor and the nurse I'd spoken with before were both with my daughter. Jacinta's face was lit by the brilliance of her eyes as she turned to smile at me.

'Dad?' she whispered, and I was there, half-sitting, half-kneeling on the bed beside her, her hand in mine.

'Jass,' I said, 'you've come back.'

'Yes,' she whispered, still with the same slight smile, 'I've come back.'

'Where were you?'

'Some other place. Places.' She closed her eyes and shivered. The doctor went to the chart at the foot of the bed, made her annotation and said goodnight. 'Some of them weren't good places,' Jacinta whispered. I grabbed her and hugged her, feeling the bones of her ribs and shoulders. She was painfully thin but there was colour in her face and life in her eyes and I thought I'd start crying. I wasn't sure whether I could trust myself to speak for a moment.

'You're safe now,' I said finally. 'You got yourself home.'

At this my daughter's eyes flew open. She shook her head on the pillow. 'Uh-uh,' she muttered, 'something did.'

I tightened my hold on her hand. 'I was so lost,' said my daughter and a tear rolled from her eye and sank into the linen of the pillowcase. She tried to get out of bed but sank back. 'How long have I been here?'

'Eleven days,' I said. 'I found you at Renee's place, passed out.'

'Dad,' she whispered, as I held her and looked into her eyes, 'there was something in my bag at the flat...' Her face was severe with concern.

'It's safe,' I said. 'You get well. We can sort that out later.'

'But he'll come after me—' she started to say.

'No he won't,' I said to her. 'He can't come after anybody any more.'

Her whole body softened with relief and I realised then how much fear she'd been carrying in that thin little body.

'I'm glad,' she said. 'What happened?'

'He ran into someone and had an accident,' I said. 'He's dead.' It was almost true. Time enough later to tell her that Kapit had died at my place. I wondered if Charlie would make something of that: the man who'd taken my place in my wife's bed now taking my place in the bed from which there is no awakening.

'He offered me a place to stay,' Jass was saying, 'and then he gave me heroin. Then he started working on me.'

I lowered my head. This was one aspect of my daughter's life that I didn't want to think about.

'Jass,' I said, 'you don't have to tell me these sorts of things—'

'What sorts of things?' she demanded, and I remembered her old, sharp, difficult ways and how hard it had been for me to get on with her and how much easier it had been to drive to Canberra every week. I saw her face drop as she comprehended my implication. 'You don't think I had sex with bloody John Kapit?' Jass was saying. 'How *could* you? He's an *old man!*'

I laughed with relief and because Kapit was younger than me.

'I'm an old man, too, Jass,' I said. 'And they say you can't teach old dogs new tricks. But I want to be a good father. I want you to tell me what you need from me.'

Jass threw her arms around me and I was surprised at the strength in her skinny arms.

'How's Reg?' she asked. 'Still trying to flatten his curls?' I nodded. There'd be time enough to tell her what had happened to her brother. Jacinta smiled then, her old smile, and her thin face softened.

'I've been such a fuckwit,' she said, looking at the healing tracks on her arm. 'I feel I've been given another chance to really do something with my life. I don't want to muck everything up again. I was booked into a rehab in Queensland. I took that money to help with my recovery. I was going to give some of it to the rehab house. It seemed the right thing to do with dirty dealer's money.' There was a long pause. 'How's Mum?'

I'd been waiting for this. 'Your mother and I—,' I started to say and then looked up because Genevieve appeared as if conjured by her name. She hurried over to Jacinta and threw her arms around her.

'Darling, it's wonderful that you're with us again.' She straightened up and gave me a curt nod. 'I've been here every day,' she said, 'waiting for you to wake up. Waiting to take you home with me where you belong.'

'Home?' said Jacinta and I could hear the alarm in her voice. 'I don't think so. I don't think I could live at home again.'

My mobile rang and I went to the window with it. The voice on the other end of the line still had the power to make my chest tingle. 'Jack?' she said. 'It's me, Iona.'

'Yes,' I said. 'I've been waiting to hear from you.'

'I'm staying with a friend,' she said. Again I felt the absurd jealousy surge up in me. In all that had happened over the last couple of days, I'd forgotten Iona's wretched friend.

'At Glebe. He says I must talk to you.'

'*He* says?' Now jealousy mixed with confusion. I wanted to know who this damned friend of hers was.

'He's very wise,' she was saying. 'I have a feeling you'd like him.' I was about to say, what on earth makes you say that, when she continued. 'Michael's a Franciscan priest. He's been very good to me.' I wrote down the address she gave me. I still didn't know what to make of all this.

'I have something for you,' I said. 'I'll bring it with me.'

'Maybe I could live with Dad, then,' said my daughter and from that I understood that Genevieve had filled her in on the changes that had occurred in Jacinta's absence. I glanced at my estranged wife, automatically bracing myself. Genevieve looked as if she'd been struck in the face. However, she didn't go into one of her more creative displays as I would have expected. Instead, she rose slowly from the chair she'd been sitting in, leaned over Jacinta, kissed her and came over to me. I could see she was shaking all over.

'Jack,' she whispered 'I'm sorry. I'm so sorry.' I could see the sobs she was trying to suppress and I felt for her. 'I didn't know about him. I don't know what to do. No one told me about him. How was I to know?' I put my hand on her arm.

'Take it easy, Gen,' I said. 'I'm in the same boat.' If I'd been a bigger man than I am, I'd have taken her in my arms and comforted her, but some things are just not possible, so I took my leave of our daughter and my wife, and drove to the address in Glebe.

•

It was a wide street some blocks away from Glebe Point Road, where the roots of old fig trees wove like snakes under and through the tar of the footpath and parts of the road while their canopies made a green roof overhead. Fig birds pinged to each other, and figgy debris littered the roofs of parked cars. I walked up the neat stone path to the little terrace house and rang the bell. I could see a figure through the ruby and blue glass front door panel and it was hers. She stepped back to allow me inside and I followed her down the hall to an open area where sunlight streamed in and a man stood up with his hand outstretched to greet me.

Michael was about my age, with soft pale hair and a guarded smile. We shook hands and I sat down opposite Iona, while Michael disappeared to make coffee.

'I owe you some explanation,' she said in that throbbing voice, pushing her hair behind her ears. 'I've told Michael everything so we can speak quite frankly.' Her deep-set eyes flickered a smile. I noticed she'd put fresh lipstick on.

'This was the man you were referring to?' I asked. 'The person who'd suggested you go to the meetings?'

Iona nodded. 'My situation was very like that of an addict's partner or mother,' she said. 'Michael recognised the similarities. The meetings were very helpful even though I always found it painful to talk.' Her face darkened and the frown on her forehead made her haggard and plain.

'Tell me what you might have said,' I asked her, still angry and hurt, yet at the same time touched by her suffering. Michael came back with the coffee and a pale rose herbal tea in a glass for Iona.

'Some of this you will have guessed already,' she said, 'and some of it will have only come to you because of your involvement in the investigation of those terrible murders.' I remembered the prayer in my pocket and wondered if I'd ever have the courage to confess how I had followed her and purloined it.

'My brother Julian is... was, I suppose you could say, my responsibility. He was always different from other kids and we all knew that. But I loved him nevertheless. In fact, I probably loved him more because of his disabilities.'

'The scar,' I said. 'That scar you have?'

She lowered her eyes. 'Years ago,' she began, 'when he thought I'd done something to hurt him, he attacked me.' She looked up at me and over at Father Michael, who seemed bewildered by this part of the conversation.

I said nothing, letting the silence exert its own pressure and Father Michael sat back in his chair, eyes closed, either meditating or dozing.

'You think I've been irresponsible. But it only happened once and it was such a long time ago. Then he got help.'

'Help?' I said. 'What kind of help?'

'Medication,' she said.

That kind of help, I thought. Some sort of sedation to slow everything down, deaden the acuteness. A holding operation.

'By the time we'd left Springbrook,' Iona was saying, 'he'd had a complete nervous breakdown. By that, I mean he hadn't been able to cope with day to day living at all. He wouldn't come out of his room, he wouldn't speak to us. He wouldn't let anyone near him except me. I tried to ask him what it was, if we could help him in some way, but he'd just push me away. We moved to Sydney and he spent some time in a psychiatric institution. He came out of that place a great deal worse, in my opinion, than when he went in. Various experiments had been tried on him, different drugs. Eventually, after a series of hospitalisations, he decided no one could help him. By that stage, my marriage was over and Julian came to live with me, in the house our parents had bought after my father retired from active ministry. My father died, my mother'—she paused and nodded to me— 'as you know now, went into a nursing home where she's been for a long time. They're good to her. I visit when I can bring myself to it. We were never close. She was...' Again, Iona stopped. 'That is quite another story,' she said, leaning forward to pick up her tea. She took a sip, put it down again and covered her face with her hands. 'I don't know where he is. I don't know what he's done. I suspect the worst.' Yes, I thought to myself, you are right to do so. She took her hands away from her face and found a little lace hanky in a pocket, blew her nose and pushed her hair back again.

'He lives with me but at the same time,' she said, 'he is a total recluse. He goes nowhere. He sees no one. He is terrified of the outside world. He even had a grille door installed inside the house, to lock himself away where no one could find him. He lives in what had been our father's library. There's a sort of alcove there. I'd hear him come out and use the bathroom. Sometimes he'd have a shower.' She pulled out a photograph and handed it to me. I looked at it. I could recognise him as the same boy in the photograph I'd found in the box of postcards at Jeffrey Saunders' place. He was younger in this, a slight smile on the lopsided face, a beautiful boy of about thirteen. I passed it back to her. 'I love him,' she said. 'He's my brother. I know what he suffered.' Her eyes flashed the fire that I knew so well as she addressed the Fransiscan. 'You people don't know what you do to children's souls and hearts with your hideous ideologies. The more sensitive and intelligent the child, the more the damage.'

Michael nodded, and I had the feeling he wasn't just humouring her, but knew what she meant.

'In our house,' she continued, 'God was a fascist dictator whose secret police were everywhere.' She stood up and walked to the windows, pulling the curtain across because the sun was heating the room and falling on the lounge chairs. 'So that's how it was,' she said, standing near the window, looking out. 'While Julian's been living with me, he's read and studied in the library and written huge essays. He showed me one once and I told him it was wonderful. It was, if you like reading about the darkest Dionysian mysteries.'

I thought later I'd certainly pick her up on that one.

'I taught music,' she was saying, 'I did my radio programs. Peter had been very generous when we divorced. I was able to manage quite well on my own. But I could never do any of the normal things women do. I could never invite a man friend back to the house.'

I interrupted. 'But you asked me there,' I said, 'with him just up the corridor.'

Her eyes widened. 'How did you know that?'

'I didn't have to be Sherlock Holmes to work that one out,' I said, more snappishily than I'd intended. I knew I'd have to tell her about what I'd found in the grilled library.

'I liked you,' she said, 'And Michael said it was time I started to have a life of my own.'

Again I waited. 'I began to get worried when I found he'd been into my room'—she looked away—'and had been wearing my clothes. Even a wig I'd had for years and never used. I tried to talk to him about it, but he wouldn't talk. I started keeping an eye on him because he was starting to do bizarre things. One day, I found him wearing our father's clerical garb.' Father Dumaresque, I thought to myself. 'And,' Iona was saying, 'he was starting to go out at night. He'd never done that before.' The way she said the last few words sent a shiver down my spine. 'I'm not ashamed to say that I started following him,' she said. I hoped she would take such a liberal view when and if I confessed my own actions in this area. 'I bought him a mobile phone, so he could contact me, I told him, if he had an anxiety attack away from the house. But it was really for my sake, so that I could ring and check up on his whereabouts.' I remembered the stake-out at Coogee Beach and the mobile ringing from a parked car. I brought my attention back to Iona.

'I was horrified to find him going to the sort of brothel that caters to sadism,' she said. 'I checked up on it. I found out what sort of a clientele it attracted.' She came away from the window and sat down at the edge of the chair, looking as if she were poised for instant flight. 'It's hardly surprising,' she said, shrugging, 'when God is a fascist, and caretakers become his gaolers and enforcers, pain and pleasure become hopelessly confused.' Then she looked at me and her voice was tender. 'That was when I saw your daughter going there one night. I knew her face so well. I'd been very touched by newspaper accounts. But at that stage, and even when we met later, I had no idea that you were Jacinta McCain's father. When I rang the police with my information all I knew from the newspaper was that the girl's father had been a police officer at one stage.' There was no reason to disbelieve her. 'By the time I'd found out who you were, Jack...' she stopped.

'Go on,' I prompted.

But she wouldn't be drawn. She drank more of her tea. 'I wondered if my brother might be capable of killing men like those...' Her voice faltered. 'He had a violent hatred of any crime against children or young people.' Although Julian Bower could not acknowledge his own destruction at the hands of the adults who had charge of him, he could see it quite plainly in other cases. 'And yet,' Iona was saying, 'it was only a suspicion. He was out late on the nights of the killings. But he'd taken to being out late more frequently on other occasions, too. This suspicion kept tearing me apart. I started following him, seeing where he went. He just seemed to walk the streets like a ghost. Or he'd sit in a coffee shop till all hours. I'd go home exhausted. Doing that brought home to me all the life I'd wasted living as my brother's keeper, to use a biblical phrase. I think I nearly had whatever a breakdown is myself. I had to take time off work, and my radio program suffered. I talked to a priest—Michael here.' She indicated him with a slight nod in his direction. 'He helped me understand I needed to be free. That I had to let go of my brother and make a life for myself. Last year I'd suggested to Julian that we should sell the house and go our separate ways.'

Michael leaned forward. 'Iona was in a terrible bind,' he said. 'I advised her to tell the police of her suspicions, but to do it anonymously. That way, her mind would be at rest. If her suspicions were true, she was prepared to deal with the consequences of that. If not, it would mean great emotional relief for her.'

'But then Jack started to suspect that *I* might be the killer,' she said in that rich, trembling voice. 'That was terrible. Because it brought him right up close to my brother. I was so afraid that I'd betray the poor soul. I was terrified when Jack told me he'd found a knife in the laundry. I remembered my father kept his fishing things in a box down there. But I feared that the knife blade might show more than bits of scales and fish skin. Somehow, I didn't mind if the police came at him through an anonymous tip-off. But if I'd betrayed him directly, led them straight to him, I don't think I could have lived with it.' She shrugged. 'I know that's inconsistent and illogical.' She looked over at me. 'You probably despise me for that. It makes no sense. But that's the truth. Michael has let me stay here while I sorted out what I was going to do next.'

Michael gathered up the coffee cups and I realised I hadn't touched mine.

'That's it, Jack,' she said. 'Now you know everything.'

'I don't think so,' I said. 'What about the afternoon you left the bedroom and vanished?'

Iona looked at her hands and clasped them. 'I heard the sound of the grille door. It makes a very small, distinct sound. And I was frightened he'd find you. I didn't know what might happen if he did.'

I shuddered to think of him passing the room in which I'd been so vulnerable. Iona must have seen my thoughts. 'He would never have gone into my room,' she said.

'That's not true,' I found myself saying. 'Your clothes, your wig. Your writing things. He helped himself to all of those.'

She was shaking her head vehemently. 'Not ever while I was there,' she said. 'You were never really in danger that afternoon, but I couldn't take the risk. I needed to know what he was up to.'

I pulled out the envelope addressed to her from my pocket and handed it to her. She glanced at it, frowned and looked up at me.

'Where did you get this?' she asked, slowly taking it.

'I was at your house in a professional capacity. I found this and some other items.'

Iona paled. She shrank back into the chair, clutching the unopened letter. 'What did you find?' she whispered.

I looked at Michael who was watching me intently. I took a deep breath. 'I found evidence of murder,' I said. 'Evidence of four murders, to be exact.'

Iona stared at me. Her face was like stone. Slowly, she handed me back the stiff white envelope. Her voice was barely audible; I had to lean forward to catch her words.

'Open it,' she was saying. 'You open it. I can't bear to.'

Reluctantly, I took the envelope from her hand and prised it apart. It was quite brief. The handwriting was 'indistinguishable', as Sarah would say, from that of the 'Rosie' letters and it was brief.

'*Goodbye*,' I read aloud, '*I should have done this years ago. I'm going to drop from a great height. And that will be the end of it.*'

'I'm sorry,' I said to Iona.

Michael stood and went to her, taking both her hands and for a moment I thought there was something else between them other than pastoral care. But he gently raised her. 'Come on, Iona,' he said. 'Let's walk. Let's go out into the sun and walk down to the water and we can say a prayer for Julian.'

I took my cue and Michael showed me out. I was walking down the stone path when I heard her running down the hall, sobbing. 'He was so beautiful,' she was crying, 'when he was a little boy. He shone like a star. They destroyed him. *He was so beautiful!*'

I didn't turn round but I heard Michael's voice and the door closing again and all was quiet in the leafy street as I went to my car. The investigation into the mutilator murders was over as far as I was concerned. Now it was time for the law to move in and weigh up the evidence. I doubted if there'd be a trial. Not after that note and what I now knew about Julian Bower.

•

All I had to do now was make one last trip to Canberra. A decision had been simmering somewhere in me for a long time. I was going to take six months more leave if I could get it, and take Greg along if Genevieve agreed. We'd do a journey during the long school holidays. Maybe to the centre. Maybe to the top end. It would give me the chance to really start painting again. If Jass was serious about rehabilitation, we could perhaps visit her on the way. Maybe take her along for part of the journey if that seemed advisable. Somehow, the kids needed to learn how to live with each other. And I had to learn from them. And I wanted to revise a few things about living with myself as well. I had to come to terms with the fact that I'd never know what happened to Rosie.

'So Julian would have known about Rosie's disappearance,' I said to Charlie, as we fitted the pieces together a few days after Iona's revelations. He'd been feeling miserable alone at his place missing Siya.

'I'm worried that I'm going to end up a lonely old man,' he said.

'Bring over some fish and chips,' I suggested, 'and eat with us.'

He did, arriving some time later.

'It was the talk of the town for years and he only lived down the road,' Charlie said. 'Then the pressure builds as Iona tells him she wants to live her own life and sell the old house and he can't handle it. The self-hatred becomes more externalised. He becomes homicidal. He starts looking for victims to revenge himself on. He uses the name of the girl who was abducted from his street and she becomes a symbol for him of the innocent victims of men like Gumley and Nesbitt and Carmody. It gives him the sort of self-righteous gloss he needs to excuse his savagery.'

'Then there was Kapit,' said Charlie, 'who was supposed to be you. I'm glad you've ordered security grilles for your place now. Until they drag Julian Bower's body out from somewhere, he could still be out there.'

Greg was almost back to his old self again. He'd been given a week off school if he wanted it, but he said he'd rather get straight back. 'It's good,' he said pragmatically, 'that Kapit's kaput.' He looked to me to see if I was going to react to his flippant pun but I said nothing. 'That way, I don't have to hang round wasting time in the witness box.'

I could see he was remembering all the times I'd had to do just that, the endless days in court, being sent home unheard, my cases being adjourned to a later date. The whole ponderous, cumbersome mess and muddle of the rule of law to which there is simply no alternative.

'He's made it much easier all round,' said Charlie.

Outside, I heard the noisy miners alarming again. Something was disturbing them. I walked into the garden. They were fussing around in the cypress trees, darting from the dark green recesses over my roof and back, and I stood listening. But I could see nothing untoward and I heard nothing apart from the swing of the sea and the hum of the distant airport.

Later, I was to wish that I'd taken more notice of their warning.

We watched the news bulletin and looked at each other as the newsreader mentioned Julian Bower whom the police were seeking 'to assist them in their inquiries' into the mutilator murders. The reporter was standing outside the Police Centre and I briefly saw Iona behind him, flanked by two detectives, being hurried inside. I hoped they wouldn't be too hard on her. I was now convinced of her innocence in any complicity. As a brother myself, I could understand her unwillingness to believe the worst about a sibling. There was nothing in fact to lock her into being an accessory before, during or after the killings.

'Do you think they'll find him?' Greg asked me.

'I think they will but he'll be a corpse. Iona told me he used to talk about jumping off Govett's Leap. I told Bob and the Springbrook cops are going to have a look around the valley floor.'

I dished out the meal and Greg and Charlie set the table. It was good to have my brother and my son eating at my table. I invited Charlie to join us the next night as well. I could feel a cooking session coming on.

'Was there really a masseur who used scented oil?' Greg asked me later over dessert. 'Or did you have a liaison with some woman?'

I was aware of my brother's raised eyebrow.

'Greg,' I said, 'there are some answers I don't have to give you. But this time, I'll tell you that both your questions have part of the truth in them. I have nothing further to say except that I might be seeing someone from time to time.' It seemed best to mention it as the subject had been brought up, although I wasn't feeling very confident at all that Iona and I had much going for us at the moment.

Greg shrugged. 'I suppose you have to. But I don't have to like the idea. It feels weird to think of you with anyone else except Mum.'

My brother put his arm around my son.

Later, I packed my briefcase, taking the last couple of outstanding reports. The DNA profile from the knife handle was still propped up in its envelope against the wall and I packed that away too. I didn't want even this trace of the mutilator killer left in my home.

•

Next morning, with Charlie staying over to keep an eye on things at Maison La Perouse, I drove down to Forensic Services in Canberra and spent the rest of the morning finishing the reports, faxing them to the relevant investigators and putting in my application for six months' leave. Karen, the department's secretary, looked up at me from over the tops of her gold-rimmed glasses as I put it in her tray to go to the boss.

'You look like you could do with a break,' she said. 'I heard about your son.'

I thanked her and took the profile that Jane had developed from the knife handle trace out of its envelope. I hoped by now that the reference sample from Julian Bower's toothbrush which Florence would have received from Jane would give us the perfect match we needed to lock him inexorably into the murder.

I walked down the corridor with the profile in my hand, not looking forward to the upcoming encounter with Florence.

I knocked at her office door but she wasn't home, so I took my white coat from the rack and gloved up in the lab annexe. When I entered the lab, I stopped in shock at the sight of the last person I ever imagined encountering in here. 'She's lost her job,' I remembered her flatmate saying. 'She's moved in with someone.' It had never occurred to me that Florence might have been the someone.

Both women looked up as I came in and stopped in my tracks. Alix's jaw dropped and Florence looked equally stunned. This gave me the advantage and I grabbed it.

'Good morning, ladies,' I said. 'Alix, a word.' I beckoned and she came like a lamb to the doorway, gorgeous in a hot pink dress and earrings. 'Down here,' I said, backing out of the laboratory and down the hall a little way. 'I don't want everyone listening to this.' She followed but I could see the anger in her eyes. She'd only ever shown me the sweetness and light before.

'Don't say anything,' I ordered her. 'I could have you charged. I have inside information about those threatening letters you sent me,' I bluffed, 'and physical evidence that locks you to them. I don't know what you're doing here, but I never want to see you or hear from you again. If there's any more malice from you in any form whatsoever, I'll have you charged and convicted so fast you won't know what's hit you.'

Her eyes narrowed and her pretty mouth turned into a thin white line. 'You bastard!' she hissed. 'Men like you disgust me. All you can do is use people.'

I remembered how she was often in Sydney for her work as a corporate trainer.

'It was you, wasn't it, sitting on the swing in the park behind my place, spying on me, late at night?' I felt a twinge of guilt as I thought of a man who followed a woman into a church, and who knifed a bag of oranges in a supermarket. 'Don't you have a life?' I thundered.

She looked so shocked at that I knew I'd got it in one. 'You used me just as much. You flirted with me, you made the moves, you invited me to your place, you phoned when you hadn't heard from me in a while. You did everything to keep the association going. It suited you and you know it. You knew I was a family man. So don't go judging me from some superior, victimised position. Whatever we did was mutual. We're even. Okay?'

I walked back to the lab door where Florence was standing, pretending to fix a notice that had fallen off a board near the doorway.

'Don't you dare walk away when I'm talking to you!' Alix yelled up the hallway.

'I'll walk away from you whenever I see you!' I said. 'I have nothing more to say to you and I don't want to listen to you.'

I turned my attention to Florence. 'Are you going out or coming in this door, because I'm about to close it.' Florence stepped inside, still without a word, and I slammed the door shut. My heart was beating, but it was done and I was pleased that I'd had the chance to file that one away.

Florence busied herself at her work station. 'I got a match for you,' she said, still not looking at me.

'Great,' I said, barely listening. 'But I cannot tolerate this childish behaviour any more, Florence.' I could feel the hot flush of anger renew itself across my back. 'I'm sorry I was insensitive towards you. I'm sorry I hurt your feelings.' I saw something soften in her face as I spoke. 'We are professional people,' I continued in a reasonable manner, 'and we have to work together.' Her earlier words started to sink in and the anger subsided. 'Right,' I said, 'you've got a match. What match?'

She turned to face me this time, and her face was impassive. 'Bevan Treweeke. From the tissue Bradley Strachan sent from the morgue.' She passed me a printed profile. As I looked, my heart started racing again. I read the name at the top of the page. 'Bevan Treweeke,' I repeated. 'This is from the morgue tissue sample?'

She nodded, passing me another one. 'And this one?' I said, glancing down at the name on the second profile, noting that it also carried Bevan Treweeke's name.

'That came from one of the other beer bottles in the Holden,' Florence said. In the following silence, I stared at the two profile printouts in my hands. Identical peaks and troughs, identical colours. Identical tabulated numbers. Bevan Treweeke *had* been in the car when Rosie was taken. The chrome star from the Holden, like the star in the east of the Christmas legend, had led me to my sister's killer. I could do nothing for a few seconds except stare.

'Here's the profile from the other beer bottle,' she said. We put them together and studied them briefly, but apart from having identical twin peaks at the amelogenin locus, indicating another male, the second individual's profile was quite different.

'Two men were involved,' said Florence, looking over my shoulder and voicing my thoughts. 'Two men drinking beer. Two different results from the beer bottles.'

The odds were I'd never find out who the second man was. But that didn't matter. I felt I had the story now. Bevan Treweeke had grabbed Rosie from outside our house. How or where she'd been killed I'd never know, but at least I knew now who was responsible. I thought of him hanging himself using the engine block as a counterweight and I was glad. It was a great pity, I thought, that Bevan Treweeke had ever been born.

I put the three printouts down on the desk, side by side, the two profiles of Bevan Treweeke and the other, unknown male result. I felt I'd never forget the shape of their graphical profiles as long as I lived. I felt I could close the case on Rosie now, knowing that Bevan Treweeke and another unknown male had taken her. I could live with that.

Then I pulled out the profile from the knife handle that Jane had faxed me from its manila envelope. I straightened the paper with the unknown beer-drinker's profile on it and in doing so, brushed Florence's computer mouse accidentally. On her colour monitor, the screen saver vanished. A profile she'd been working on filled up the screen. I glanced at the peaks and troughs, the tabulated numbers underneath and then looked more closely. This profile was familiar. My puzzlement didn't last long because I almost immediately saw that its perfect match was lying on the desk beside the two Bevan Treweeke profiles. I looked again at the profile from the trace on the knife. On impulse, I held it up next to the profile showing on the screen. My eyes flickered between them. I'd done this thousands of times. Troughs and peaks, colours, tabulated numbers all identical. The DNA profile from Julian Bower's toothbrush must have already been emailed to Florence by hard-working Jane. I felt elated. Sometime in the future, if Julian Bower ever came to trial, Florence would be called to testify about what she'd found when she compared the profile taken from the knife that killed Frank Carmody with the sample Jane had developed from his toothbrush. I felt pleased that two such disparate investigations were both well on the way to being beautifully wrapped up. Now, all that remained for us to do was attach the relevant certification to the profiles and send them to Bob. I looked again at the profile drawn on the screen and its identical twin in my hand. This was the sort of visual evidence that a jury could immediately evaluate as identical. No complex scientific explanations were required. Perfect match. Snap.

'Come and have a look at this, Florence,' I called, keeping my voice neutral. 'Jane must have worked overtime last night to get this through to us.' Florence came over frowning and I noticed she had new glasses with dark frames and that her eyes looked bigger behind them.

'What are you talking about?' she snapped, peering at the

graphical profile on the screen. 'What's Jane got to do with it?' My heart sank. I knew things were going to be awkward between us for some time but this bridling hostility wasn't what I needed right now. But when I looked at Florence, I realised that she was genuinely bewildered rather than hostile.

'I gave her a sample from the suspect's toothbrush yesterday,' I explained, remembering the hideous contents of the fridge underneath Julian's toiletries, 'and here it is already.'

Florence studied her screen, looked at me and shook her head. 'I don't know what you're talking about.'

I pointed to the screen. 'Jane's profile here,' I said, pointing from it to the printed out version in my hand, showing her the perfect match.

'That's not Jane's,' said Florence, pointing to the graph on her screen. 'That's mine. I ran it on the CE yesterday.' The Capillary Electrophoresis machine runs the DNA molecules through an electric field, separating them by size, lining them up with a camera that detects the blue, green and yellow dyes that have been added during the Polymerase Chain Reaction, the replicating process that allows the analyst to amplify even the tiniest fragment of DNA into testable quantities. 'And then I ran it through Genotyper,' Florence continued, referring to the software. 'Jane's had nothing to do with it at any stage.'

Now it was my turn to be bewildered. 'What is it then?' I asked. 'Where *did* it come from?'

'It's the trace I got from the top of one of the beer bottles. From the Holden.'

Now I was completely confused. 'The beer bottles?' I said. 'But you told me that's where you found Bevan Treweeke.'

'And I found this one as well,' she said, pointing to Julian Bower's profile on the screen. I still didn't understand. 'Hasn't Jane sent you anything?' I asked.

Florence shook her head. 'Not for weeks,' she said.

We stood there and I suddenly felt sick at heart. 'Don't tell me we've got a contamination.'

It had never happened before, but I hadn't been involved in an investigation like this one either. Things were already complicated enough without more reruns, re-amps and possibly having to recut original samples again. 'That's all I bloody need,' I said. 'You'll have to run the whole thing again. Julian Bower's sample has somehow got itself mixed up with Bevan Treweeke's from the Holden.'

Florence stared up at me through her new glasses, her face white. 'That has *never* happened in my laboratory,' she said, as if she had personally forbidden it.

'Yet somehow,' I persisted, 'there's been contamination.'

Florence shook her head slowly, and I could almost see the analytical mind ticking over. 'That's not possible, Dr McCain,' she said, her voice so polite that I hardly noticed the distant formality. 'There hasn't been the chance for contamination to take place,' she said. 'I personally did the whole process that resulted in the Bevan Treweeke result. From cutting the samples right through to the final profile. I ran the results through Genotyper myself late yesterday. You've just arrived here with your own Julian Bower result and Jane's reference sample is still in another state. There's been no chance of interference with the tubes. In this case, contamination is a logical impossibility.'

I stared back at her, my mind coming to an amazing realisation as Florence spoke the words. 'What you're looking at are two clear and distinct individuals, both present in the Holden.'

Stunned, I looked at the screen, then again at the suspect's graphical profile in my hand. Florence was right.

'It's the same person,' said Florence, looking at the profile from the knife handle, 'as the other person in the Holden.' I watched while her fingers traced the peaks and troughs, pointing to the identical tabulation. 'Identical result at every locus.'

We looked at each other. My mind was already unpacking the implications and I barely noticed that the fax on the bench near the fridge door had come to life and was churning out paper. Florence went to it, standing a moment to see what it was.

'Here's Jane's result just coming through now,' she said, 'from the toothbrush.'

She tore the fax off and brought it back to me, glancing down at it herself. She frowned at the tabulated numerical sequences on the profile in her hand.

'What is it?' I said, alerted by her straining concentration. Florence held it up to me, speechless. The same peaks and troughs, the exact sequence of numbers as the profile shimmering on her screen and the same as the faxed result in my hand from the hilt of the knife.

There have been a few moments in my life when the ground beneath my feet seemed to shift and slip as if the fabric of the planet was dissolving under me. We had three perfectly identical samples from three totally different sources, the murder weapon, the toothbrush and one of the beer bottles from the Holden. Julian Bower had been at all three locations. For a second, the laboratory seemed to sway. I put out my hand to steady myself and Florence took it, holding me for a second. I now understood why Mrs Bower had lied to the police. I remembered 'Julie B.' in Bevan Treweeke's list of 'birdwatchers'. And the Bowers' phone number in Treweeke's book, which didn't refer to the Reverend as Debbie Hale had thought, but to Julian.

'It's the same person,' I said. 'The murders. And Rosie.'

'Yes.' Florence nodded, forgetting her animosity in this moment of truth. 'Julian Bower was in the car that took your little sister.'

SEVENTEEN

I walked outside into the afternoon. Gangs of lorikeets shrieked overhead and the sun shone into my face, blinding me. Knowing part of what had happened was no comfort and I found myself standing stupidly in the yard with tears running down my face. Suddenly I was a quarter of a century away with my sister Rosie running up the backyard, away from our mother's hateful words, out through the house and onto the footpath at the front where the Holden was about to snatch her up and take her out of our lives. But now, I knew who was in that car. When the car drove away with Rosie in it, the pedophile Bevan Treweeke had a younger companion, Julian Bower, with him, an adolescent boy whose mother, cleaning the windows in the tall rectory building at the corner, saw her son's new car, the one he'd just acquired, collide with the white rails, and later, discovered that the same car was wanted in connection with the abduction of Rosie McCain.

I drove back to Sydney and it wasn't until I drove past the stone walls of Long Bay Gaol that I realised I'd done almost the whole trip from Canberra on automatic pilot.

When I came in at the kitchen door, Charlie took one look at me, sat me down and made coffee while I told him and Greg about the DNA result. The man who stalked and killed men in Sydney, who wrote letters signed with our missing sister's name, was the same man who'd taken Rosie. Now the reason why Julian Bower had signed the letters that lured sex offenders to their deaths with her name made sense.

'Charlie,' I said, 'he was doing it to atone.'

Charlie nodded. 'You've got it,' he said. 'He projected his guilt onto them and killed them. Because he'd done something similar and *he'd got away with it.*'

I stood up. 'Talk about projection,' I said. 'This is a classic case.'

Charlie agreed. 'Julian Bower seeks out men like him, who look as if they've "got away with it" too, because they all had relatively light sentences for very serious offences. By punishing them, killing them, he somehow punishes himself, feels less guilty about his crime, about "getting away with it" and at the same time he feels self-righteous about it. Even superior. He's doing the right thing, as he sees it.'

I frowned. 'But, Charlie, I don't fit his profile.'

'He'd have to get you,' said Charlie, 'eventually. You're an aggrieved person. It's as if you stand pointing a finger at him throughout the years. The injured brother, then the frustrated investigator.'

Greg looked to the vacant spot on the wall where the photograph of the anonymous youth had been. 'He must have freaked when he saw the old picture of himself on the wall,' he said. 'He must have thought you were right onto him and it was only a matter of time.'

'But I didn't know that,' I said. 'I didn't know that at all.'

'He would have thought you did,' said my brother. 'More projection.'

I thought of what Rosie's ghost had said when she came to me in the night: 'Apply the new knowledge to the old.' She hadn't been talking about scientific breakthroughs at all—she was talking about our new understanding of the workings of the human mind. I suddenly remembered the old saying that for every finger you point at another, three fingers are pointing back at yourself.

I went to the shoebox of old postcards and photographs and took out the one of Rosie. 'I'm going to get this enlarged and copied for each of you.'

Greg came over and gave me a hug, then he stepped back and looked at me. 'You look tired, Dad. Look after yourself,' he said. 'We need you.'

The phone was ringing and I picked it up. It was Iona. I could hear the noisy miners alarming outside. *'Help! Help! Help!'* they piped.

'My mother's died,' she said.

'I'm sorry to hear that.'

'I didn't ring for sympathy,' she said, 'but to tell you that she kept saying your name.'

'I understand,' I said. 'I know what she wanted.'

'Can you tell me?'

'I will,' I said. 'But you could tell me something. Do you remember any old postcards or photographs from your family that might have ended up in a secondhand shop?'

There was a slight pause before she answered. 'After Dad died I did a lot of clearing out. Furniture, ornaments. Things like that. There were boxes and boxes of all the postcards he'd collected from his travels. There could have been old photographs mixed up in them. A fellow came up from the antique shop at Blackheath and gave me a cheque for the lot.'

I didn't know what else to say to her. Sometime I had to tell her the awful truth about her brother. My heart had to get around the fact that she was the sister of the man who'd taken my sister.

'I'll call you,' I said, ringing off.

Greg and Charlie decided to go to the pictures in town and Greg said he'd stay over at Charlie's.

When they'd left I went to the carton my brother had foisted on me and stared at it. This was the moment I'd been putting off; I needed to get stuck into this now and clear it out of my life. For a long moment, I stood there, undecided. Reluctantly, I opened the top flap and peered in at the sight of my mother's paraphernalia. My heart sank. The carton was filled with exercise books. I opened one and flipped through it. It was hard to read the writing, especially towards the end of the various entries, because I could quite easily see where the incomprehensibility of drunkenness was reflected in the indecipherable handwriting. Some bits she must have written in the darkness, because page after page was over-written in a tangle of scribble. Or blind drunk, I thought bitterly. The readable sections were the usual laments of the alcoholic: feelings of alienation, isolation, of being on the outside looking in, the general sense of betrayal by everyone and everything. I pulled out a few more of the books and skimmed through. More of the same. Give or take a few negative attitudes, it was something I myself could have written fifteen years ago. Lamentation, darkness and victimisation. I put the books back and closed the box. I knew now exactly what I had to do. I carried the box out to the recycle bin in the cypress-lined side passage, lifted the lid, and upended it, shaking it. Books poured into the bin except for one that escaped, falling open at my feet. I bent to pick it up, my eyes catching sight of something she'd put quotation marks around. The writing was execrable. But gradually I made it out.

After I'd read it, my eyes filled with tears and I leaned against the recycle bin for a moment. Then I tore out one page, folded it carefully, and put it in my pocket. Goodbye Mother, I said to her. I'm sorry things went the way they did in your life. I'm sorry things were never resolved for you and I'm sorry you died the way you did, unable to choose another way of living.

I was about to go back to the house, when I became aware of another presence signalled by four plaintive notes in the air. I looked around but couldn't spot him. The kingfisher can sit motionless for as long as it takes to notice a slight movement in the grass or in the water. I waited for him to move but if he did, I didn't see him. After a while, I went inside.

•

'You can take her home,' said the consultant, Andrew Somersby, when I visited the hospital the following day. 'I mean that metaphorically,' he said over his shoulder. 'She's adamant about not going back to her mother's place, but she's ready to leave.'

Jacinta was up, dressed and sorting through clothes and toiletries when I knocked on her door. She gave me a kiss and patted a chair for me to sit on.

'I've just had a terrible fight with Mum'—she sighed, hands on hips '—again.' Then she zipped up her washbag and handed it and a little overnight bag to me. 'I wish I could get on with her.'

I was about to say that no one could, and not to worry, but I knew I was biased.

'There's no way I can go back and live with her again.'

'What are you going to do?'

'I've talked with Greg,' she said, 'and I know he's got reservations about me staying at your place.'

I looked at my daughter with renewed respect, pleased that she and her brother were starting to negotiate with each other in an adult way.

'You're always welcome to live with me,' I said. 'You two kids could have the bedrooms and I could get a daybed set up for the lounge area for myself.' I went over to her and clasped her hands. 'I'm seriously thinking of moving, anyway, because I want to take some long service leave and a few other things. This time next year, we might be living in a big house again.'

Jacinta shook her head. 'I've been talking to some friends in NA,' she said. 'I'm going to the Sallies' rehab place near Brisbane. I'll need some money, though.'

Amazing to think that with everything going on, I'd almost forgotten the matter of over two hundred thousand dollars. 'I don't know what to do about that money,' I said. Jacinta laughed. 'I do,' she said. 'Just give it back to me.' She scooped old flowers, bits of paper, sweet wrappers into a bin. 'No,' she said, 'you'd better decide. Just give me what I need for the next six months and bank the rest. I'll be able to make a better decision when I come home again.'

I sat on the chair and she sat on the bed. Her colour was back and there was a light in her eyes that I hadn't seen before and although the arms that poked out of the pink tank top were pale and thin, there was no mistaking the strength of the spirit in front of me. Outside, I could hear white cockatoos shriek.

'Being here,' she said, 'and being so out of it like I was—' she looked around the small room '—was like a rapid de-tox. But I have to look at why I got into such a mess in the first place. If I don't do that, I'll end up using again.'

I nodded. I knew exactly what she meant.

'I had to do the same,' I said. 'I'm still doing it.'

Jacinta laughed. 'Yeah. You had a lot of stuff, too.'

I raised my eyebrows.

'Your mother,' she reminded me. 'And your father.' She hopped off the bed and went to the window. Outside it was a beautiful afternoon and noisy miners sang and swooped despite the traffic and filth of the city outside. 'One day,' she said, 'I'd like to hear some of your story. Maybe do a meeting or two with you.'

I wanted to give her a hug, tell her that I didn't blame her in the slightest for how she'd been living the last year and a half. I wanted to tell her that children learn addictions and neuroses from their parents, just as they learn language and other things. But now wasn't the time.

She leaned forward out the window on her thin arms and squinted up at the sky. 'The world,' she said, 'is such an amazing, horrific, astonishing place.'

All I could do was nod my agreement and pat her hand. 'I'm staying at Charlie's until I go to Brisbane,' she said. 'I'm flying up next week.'

'How long will you be away?'

My daughter looked down at the street. 'It's a six month suggested stay,' she said. 'One month intensive and if people want to, they can stay up to a year. I'll have to work on the place. It's a farm.'

Like imagining Staro, I had difficulty picturing Jacinta carrying out the eggs and milking routine.

'Would it help if I flew up with you? Helped you settle in?'

She smiled. 'I think it would,' she said. 'I'll think about that.'

'It's not going to be easy,' I said cautiously. 'Do you think you'll be able to fit into that sort of environment?'

My daughter turned around to me and her face was suddenly old and tired. 'I managed the environment of being a street addict,' she said. 'That wasn't very easy either.'

I came over to her and put my arms around her then. My street addict was home and I kissed the top of her head. 'What time do you want me to pick you up?' I asked.

'Don't worry,' she replied. 'Charlie's organised all that. He said come over and have tea with us tomorrow night. Be sure and bring Greg.'

•

I bustled around with salads and table-setting like a housewife, wearing an apron left in the kitchen by one of Charlie's ex-girlfriends, while Charlie dealt with a baked lamb shoulder and rosemary potatoes. The two kids sat out on the timber deck and we brothers decided to leave them as much time alone as possible.

'Here we are,' said Charlie, piling the potatoes onto a plate and putting them back into a low oven. 'Two crusty old bachelors again. Doing it hard.'

I smiled at that and heard Greg's laugh from outside. He was standing against the railing looking down at his sister stretched out on the cane lounge chair, and she was looking up at him. They were talking together, laughing together.

I pulled out the piece of paper with our mother's scrawled writing on it and passed it to him. 'Here's something for you,' I said.

'*If Claire hadn't died,*' Charlie read out loud, '*my life would have been very different. Forgive us our trespasses as we forgive those who trespass against us.*' Charlie raised his eyes to mine. 'Claire,' he said. 'There was a sister in our mother's family who died. It could be her.'

I nodded. 'It won't be hard to check,' I said. 'And it's not hard to guess what age Claire was when she died,' I added.

We were silent together, each lost in thought. On and on it goes, I thought, generation after generation. Until somebody notices it.

Charlie came over to me and put his hands on my shoulders. 'You've done a wonderful thing,' he said. 'Stopping the buck being passed.'

'Shucks,' I said. But I stopped my jokey awkwardness. 'I can only hope it holds,' I said to him. I changed the subject. 'I've got all this money. Even if I go halves with Pigrooter, I'll still have over a hundred grand.'

'Why should you go halves with someone called Pigrooter?' said Charlie. I told him the story. 'I've thought about it,' I said, 'and I think it'd be fair to give you twenty-five, each of the kids twenty-five and put the rest away for a while and think about it.' Charlie gave a funny little grin and cocked his head. 'That'd be nice,' he said. Then he started serving up the meal.

'Come and get it!' he yelled out the door.

Later, the four of us sat around finishing up the *rizogalou*, the rice and milk pudding that Siya had taught Charlie to cook. Greg and my brother shared some beers; my addict daughter and I sat with our mineral water and coffees. Jacinta looked more comfortable than I'd ever seen her. She'd always been an itchy, worrisome sort of child.

'What's it like?' Greg asked his sister, 'being in a coma?'

'It's like I was asleep,' she said. 'But sometimes I had really vivid dreams. I didn't even realise I'd been in a coma until I woke up and they told me. Then I saw how wasted my body was. And I was pretty shocked. It was as if I saw what I was doing to myself for the first time.' She looked around at all of us. 'And because I'd been out of it in a different way for so long, I feel I've been away for a long, long time.'

'You have,' said my honest son. 'It was hard when you were there, it was hard when you went. I suppose it'll be hard for a while now, too, having you back with us.'

The awkward silence that followed his words was finally broken by Jacinta. She looked over at me and her eyes were luminous with tears.

'Some time before I woke up,' she said, 'I could feel you there, wanting something from me.'

'I asked you if you could help me from wherever you were,' I said, feeling a little foolish at the admission. 'I was desperate because Greg was missing. I needed some direction about where Kapit might have taken him.'

'A lot of the time was just a black blankness,' Jacinta said. 'But I had nightmares, too, dreams and nightmares. I was in a nightmare just before I woke up. Some terrible dark world like an undersea place with these long cold tendrils and they were coiling around me. I was trying to prise them off, but for every one I pulled away, another two or three fastened onto me. They were revolting, like huge leeches. And then I thought I heard your voice, Dad. I tried so hard to get to you but I couldn't. The leeches had me. I knew if I didn't get away in that moment, I'd never get away, and I'd have to stay in that world. Your voice gave me some extra strength. I think I opened my eyes, but I'm not sure.'

'You did,' I said, excited that she remembered the moment. 'I was sitting beside you. You opened your eyes and you smiled. But not at me.' Jacinta looked puzzled. 'You seemed to be looking straight past me,' I said, 'to someone else.'

Jacinta's face lit up. 'I remember now. I saw this beautiful girl, standing near the door. I felt so happy to see her. She encouraged me. Just by being there. I remember trying to say something, someone's name.' I remembered the whispered monosyllable and how it had finally led to Greg's return to us. A shiver ran through me, but not of fear. Had Rosie been there too, helping me?

'She wore a yellow sundress and a blue and yellow enamel necklace,' I said.

My daughter's eyes widened in surprise. 'You *have* seen her!' she said. 'Who is she?'

I pulled out the photograph in my pocket and passed it over to Jacinta. Rosie smiled out at us again, the photographic image created out of the November sun and shadow of twenty-five years. 'My sister Rosie,' I said. 'Your little aunt.'

Jacinta took the picture with her to the window again and studied it. Then she turned to me. 'But how could I have seen her?'

There was nothing I could say. I looked over at Charlie. He shrugged. Greg put out his hand and Jacinta passed him the photograph. He frowned over it a few moments and then handed it back to her. She was about to give it back to me when she stopped. 'This is so precious,' she said. 'Can I keep her?'

I nodded. 'I'm having copies made,' I said.

'I'll take her with me to Queensland,' said my daughter. 'She's sort of a guardian angel.'

'Can I stay here tonight, Dad?' Greg asked. 'I'd like to spend a bit of time with my sister seeing as she's going away.'

I looked at Charlie. His shrug said 'why not?' and so it was that I drove home alone, feeling that many things were falling into place.

I couldn't sleep for a long time thinking about Claire and Rosie and Jacinta so that when I did finally nod off, I went to a very deep place. From the depths of sleep I thought I remembered a crashing sound, as if someone had smashed a window. I sat up in my bed and gathered myself. I knew I was alone in the place, with Greg and Jacinta at Charlie's and that no one could get in. The security grilles had been fitted while I was in Canberra. Every pane of glass in the place could be shattered and still no one would be able to get in through the grilles.

I stood up, breathing hard, shocked by this awakening, gathering my wits. A roll of thunder in the distance filled my hearing. Was that what had woken me? I strained to hear. Now I could hear nothing, except my own pounding heart and breathing. The house was quiet as the grave, and as dark. There was no ghostly apparition standing near the door. Navigating by touch and memory, and the very few visual clues, I walked out to the main room. I didn't want to switch on a light just yet, wanting the cover of darkness. I could just make out the outlines of the table where I worked and boxes and cartons nearby. As I looked further, I saw that there was something wrong. My table and the cartons seemed to be covered in something that lay, in jagged shapes, like stiff paper cut-outs. I stepped further in to see what it was, reaching for the light switch. It didn't work. I didn't like this one bit. Some instinct made me pick up the bronze statuette of Kuan Ti from his position on the sideboard, and I gripped him hard as I went over to the table. As I came closer, I could make out shards of smashed fibreglass and for a moment I was completely bewildered.

I looked up towards the skylight over the table and thought I saw rolling storm clouds through the jagged gap. As comprehension hit me, something flew out of the darkness, crashing me to the ground. I felt the sturdy weight of Kuan Ti jolted out of my grasp and skid somewhere along the floor. I struggled and yelled but almost instantly my mouth was stifled. Whoever had crashed through the skylight in a hooded Tyvek spacesuit had me pinned to the ground, towering over me like some demented monk. I felt my windpipe closing in a choking cough. I couldn't breathe. I heaved and struggled, fighting not only the hooded man, but my own system. Silhouetted by the jagged square of starry night that filled the ruined skylight, I could see his arm swing back and the outline of the raised knife in his gloved hand. I remembered the empty take-away container next to my startled photograph in the newspaper left lying on the dining table at Iona's house. The mutilator had come to complete his collection.

As a coughing fit exploded through me, I was not the only one shocked by its force. He hesitated a moment in his deadly downswipe and, with all my desperation, knowing that another few seconds without breathing would leave me without any strength, I blocked the descending weapon arm as I'd been trained to do a thousand years ago, resisting the slashing arc with all that remained of my strength. The choking eased a little, enough for a sobbing breath and I started yelling, wordless noises, grunts and shrieks, as I fought my murderous assailant with everything I had. Terror speared up my spine, galvanising me: he was not going to get my balls without a fight. My supine position on the floor gave me little leverage and I knew my life depended on getting up. I was still weak and the strength of my right arm was failing as the killer pressed on it with all his strength and body weight. I managed another in-breath. If I didn't make a successful move now,

I'd be hacked to death just like the men whose deaths I'd investigated.

Rosie came into my mind and almost without thinking I yelled at him. 'Rosie's here! She's come to get you! She's by the door, you murdering bastard!' His grip and pressure lessened by a fraction and in that split second, I made my left hand into a fist and lashed as hard and fast as I could into his body, somewhere near the upper right quadrant of his abdomen, punching him in the liver as hard as I could, following through the punch with a sideways roll of my body. It seemed to take forever. He doubled over around the assault and I kept rolling, out from under his weight, fighting to regain my feet. I was halfway up, but suddenly he was onto me again. His gloved hand smothered my face again, gouging for my eyes, the other at my neck and I realised he must have lost the knife.

This gave me renewed hope and I tried to push his hands away, but lost my balance again and tripped, jerking my head back, painfully colliding with Kuan Ti's long pole-knife. I felt the rush of blood from the back of my head and the smell terrified me further. As I twisted around, I heard him scrabble on the floor and he'd grabbed the knife again and was slashing the floor where I'd been, but my body had jerked away involuntarily, from the pain of my injured head. Next swipe and the killer's knife whistled past my nose and twanged deep in my polished floorboards. He dived onto it with both hands, pulling it out. I scrabbled behind my head, fingers closing around Kuan Ti. Julian Bower looked up momentarily to improve his positioning and I used that moment to smash the god of detectives, prostitutes and triads into his upturned face. I felt an initial resistance, then Kuan Ti's pole-knife slid sideways into Julian Bower's right eye, deep through the cortex of his tortured brain. He slipped backwards, screaming, a hand clapped over his face.

'Where is she?' I screamed at him, straddling him, beating his head with my bare hands, not caring that blood poured all over me. 'What did you do with her?'

His screams had stopped. His one good eye opened and stared straight at me and it was like looking into the face of a demon from Hieronymous Bosch.

'You'll never find her,' he choked. 'She's out of time.' I wasn't going to let him get away with that.

'You killed her! You took her from us!' I yelled at him, pulling his head up, banging it back on the floor, frenzied with rage and frustration. *'Tell me where she is!'* I screamed.

But the dying man under me was past speech. Some last shred of decency forbade me from kicking him into eternity, so I crouched there, watching him die. Another person might have found some pity, maybe whispered some home-made prayer for him. Not this one.

•

After all the questions had been asked and answered, I sat with Bob while he brought the records up to date. The trail of violence that had started with the abduction of my little sister had ended now with me sitting in this office, writing my statement about the events of Julian Bower's death. Now the case could be closed. It had been a long time coming. Bob and I talked, conjecturing what might have happened as we always had in the old days. The old pedophile and the young Bower boy had taken my sister. That was all I knew. Maybe one of them had killed her. Maybe the two of them. We had no way of knowing what had happened.

I went to an AA meeting because I needed to restore my equilibrium. After the formal proceedings, I was chatting to an old acquaintance, dunking a biscuit into a cup of tea, when a young tear-away who used to ring me when he first got sober and life's events seemed more than usually difficult, skidded over. He was an inspector now at a suburban police station. We shook hands and chatted about the things that recovered addicts—along with the rest of the human race—find important: women, kids, work, loss, life, fun. He was just about to take his leave when he turned back.

'You knew Marty Cash, didn't you?' he said.

I nodded, remembering the money now safely back under the floorboards in my bedroom.

'I haven't seen you around for a few months,' he said, 'so maybe you haven't heard.'

'Haven't heard what?' I asked, forgetting to undunk my biscuit.

'He's a vegetable now,' the young bloke said and bounced away again. I was about to go after him and ask him for more details, but I was pretty sure I knew what had happened to Pigrooter. Feral pig hunting is a dangerous sport.

I abandoned my ruined cup of tea. One of the promises of AA is that providing we practise its principles in all our affairs, problems that once baffled us will fall away, and I felt a great deal better knowing that old Pigrooter had been removed as a threat.

I drove home with the plan for an extended trip around Australia becoming clearer in my mind. After Jacinta detoxed we could even fly from Darwin up north to parts of Asia, I was thinking. It would give me a break and time to write postcards to Iona. I had more than enough money now to do a few things I'd always wanted.

•

A week later, Jacinta, Charlie, Greg and I knocked on the door of the rectory at Springbrook and the vicar's wife came to the door. I'd rung the day before, asking permission for what we wanted to do.

Mrs Bailey showed us around to the back again, past the low stone wall with the clematis that Charlie and I had encountered on our first visit here. Tall mountain eucalypts stood straight and slim at the end of the garden. Even the butcherbird remembered us, and his dying fall of rich notes pierced the air.

I'd bought a Peace rose and even though November wasn't the ideal time to plant it, I wanted to do this for Rosie. I couldn't bring myself to do it anywhere near our old home, because that was the place she'd had to flee. Just as my own daughter had done years later and Claire a generation before.

I didn't want to plant it at La Perouse, because I knew that was only a transit home for me. I wanted to bring Rosie back from the men who'd killed her, and also celebrate my Jacinta's homecoming, and planting this rose where Rosie had smiled in the photograph in the rectory's peaceful garden, golden with sunshine and bees, seemed a good way to do it.

'I want to put it there,' I said, pointing to the wrought-iron grille just visible in the stonework some metres behind the sundial. 'Just near where she's standing in the photograph.'

Greg was standing up close to the dial, muttering his calculations of the seasonal corrections, trying to work out the time told by the pointer in the centre. 'It's reasonably accurate,' he said, comparing the shadow on the dial to his wristwatch, 'give or take quarter of an hour.'

Jacinta joined her brother, walking round the stone pedestal, following the inscription written around the sundial's face.

'*I will keep account of time until you are out of time,*' Jacinta read out.

'About here?' Charlie asked, putting the rose down near the grille and looking back at me.

'Maybe a little closer to the wall,' I said. 'That way it's protected from the wind.' Roses are pretty tough but they give more if they're happy about their position and wind is always a problem for growing things. A whirlwind of the Lord, I thought briefly, reminded again. Then the words my daughter had just read out from the sundial floated into my consciousness. 'Read that again, Jass,' I asked as Charlie repositioned the rose bush. 'Read out those words again?'

Jacinta reread the words, more emphatically. '*I will keep account of time until you are out of time,*' she quoted, looking up at me. 'Why,' she asked. 'What's so great about that?'

I suddenly knew where my sister was. 'She's out of time,' Julian Bower had said to me as he died. She must have been killed elsewhere and somehow, Treweeke and Julian had got her body here, maybe by night, driven it in the car, buried her in the soil under the sundial. I recalled the date 1975 stamped on the metal disk. Maybe the excavations at the end of the garden, awaiting the construction of the sundial's footings, had suggested a grave site. I looked at the pedestal again, at where it was sunk into the soil with a circle of snowy alyssum surrounding its base.

'She's here,' I said, suddenly knowing it. 'Rosie's buried here. They put her under the sundial.'

EIGHTEEN

It didn't take long to locate her. Almost as soon as the backhoe operator had lifted the first lot of soil, we could see that the earth had been disturbed there once, the lighter sandstone of the subsoil mixed up with the darker loam of the top. And far deeper than was necessary to support a sundial. Colin Swartz from Springbrook police drove Greg and Jacinta home to Charlie's place, while my brother stayed with me.

'I'll ring Mum,' Greg had said before they left, 'and tell her what's happened.'

I nodded and thanked him and he knew he had my blessing.

Now, blue and white Crime Scene tape secured the back garden and Mrs Bailey kept up the supplies of tea and sandwiches for the small group. Two young Crime Scene detectives from Parramatta waited with us while the digger moved the topsoil and the pedestal of the sundial. The operator took it very gently, just scraping down through the layers but once he'd got a metre or so down, I took off my coat and so did Charlie and, without a word, the two Parramatta detectives who'd been gently scraping the dug-out earth gave us their shovels and we jumped down into the trough we'd made.

I could feel tears running down my face as I dug, but it wasn't grief, it was some sort of old release. So that when my shovel scraped on the thin brownish sticks, so much a part of the earth now that they were barely recognisable as anything else, I knew it was my sister's rib cage and I got down on my knees and started pushing the dirt away with my hands. I could feel Charlie's hand on my shoulder and I worked like an archaeologist, smoothing around the bones as they revealed themselves. Soon, I had one side of her skeleton in high relief and the domed vault of the back of her skull. She was lying curled up like a baby in the sandy subsoil, turned into the earth with the bones of her hands gracefully folded near her head. Something shone in the dirt near the delicate bones of the cervical vertebrae and I knew what it was even as I tugged it free. I passed it up to Charlie and he took it wordlessly from me: the blue and yellow enamelled silver necklace I'd given her only days before her death.

I heard a voice I knew and climbed up to see Bradley Strachan striding over, carrying his boots and overalls. He'd come up from Sydney, I was later told, because he thought it would be easier on me if the examination in situ was done by someone I knew rather than a stranger. I hadn't realised people I only knew professionally would be so kind.

Later, when Bradley lifted Rosie's skull out of the soil and turned it round, I could see the fracture lines over her left eye socket. His gloved finger gently touched the ruined post-orbital ridge. 'Blunt instrument,' he said to me. 'Severe blow to the frontal area.' He looked up at me from my sister's bones. 'Do you want to stay for the rest?'

I did. It was the least I could do for my sister.

We didn't bury her near our mother in the local graveyard after all. Charlie, the kids and myself, with our father silent and chain-smoking, took her ashes and threw them together with some yellow and blue irises over the cliff near Springbrook Falls where the dark tree-covered ridges fall sharply away to gold and purple sandstone walls and the valley floor gathers the shimmering water into a winding river a kilometre below. As I shook the container, the small cloud of dark dust became invisible almost immediately. We walked back to the car in a silence my father maintained until we dropped him back at his shed. Charlie put out a hand to help him up the step into his one-roomed home but the old man ignored it and walked inside.

'Doesn't amount to much, does it?' he said, just before closing the door. 'A life.'

We four looked at each other and it was Greg who banged on the door in anger.

'Yours mightn't,' he yelled. 'Speak for yourself.'

Then he ran away ahead of us, his long body heading off up the driveway, out onto the road, away from the sad, rented house.

Charlie, Jacinta and I jumped in the car and caught up with him right down the end at the corner where Mrs Bower had seen the Holden and lied about it. A large brown pool had collected in the elbow of the corner from recent rain and a butterfly flirted dangerously low across its surface.

Jacinta swung the back door open as Charlie slowed the car. 'Come on, Reg!' she yelled after the running figure and he stopped and turned round. 'Hop in, ya dag!'

A sun shower had come from nowhere, and slanted rain fell diagonally through the sunlight. The sudden shower stimulated every bird in the area and the butcherbird's chimings were drowned by the sort of bird chorus I'd only heard once or twice in my life, and then only at sunrise. Currawongs, magpies, noisy miners, kookaburras and, overhead, the ringing calls of a blazing flock of rosellas. We got out of the car and looked around and up as the volume increased. Jacinta looked like a delighted little kid again as she listened, head cocked to one side. My brother stood with his eyes closed, taking it all in and Greg stood grinning at the puddle, watching its surface wrinkle under the sparkling sun shower.

I glanced up and there he was, sitting on the lowest bough of the huge eucalypt, with his sharp, angular head and beak, the soft gold shining from his breast contrasting with the brilliant blue of wings and head—a sacred kingfisher, taking no notice of me. I held my breath and waited, signalling the others with a whisper and a slow hand movement. Everyone froze, staring at him. And now, in this magical moment of the birds' chorus with the rain falling like a shower of gold through a summer afternoon, my sacred kingfisher swooped over the reflecting surface of the puddle, a streak of gold and cerulean blue.

Gabrielle Lord is widely acknowledged as one of Australia's foremost writers. Her psychological thrillers are informed by a detailed knowledge of forensic procedures, combined with an unrivalled gift for story-telling.

Her first novel, *Fortress,* was published in 1980 and has been translated into six languages, as well as being made into a successful film starring Rachel Ward. Since *Fortress*, Gabrielle has published many other best-selling novels, including *The Sharp End, Feeding the Demons* and *Whipping Boy.* Her stories and articles have appeared widely in the national press and been published in anthologies. She has written for the film and TV and is currently working on a new novel.